Tash Aw was born in Taipei and brought up in Malay[illegible] He moved to England in his teens and now lives in Lo[illegible] *[illegible]nony Silk Factory* is his first novel.

For au[illegible]
harperperennia[illegible]

From the revi[illegible] *[illegible]ilk Factory*:

'Beguiling . . . The vice-like grip of the dead, the paper-thin ties of the living: many compelling themes are braided into this original, haunting novel. Aw picks at the knots in relationships, and in Malaysia's history, to unravel strands of illumination. Yet there are several loose ends from which readers must spin their own stories. It is these frayed seams, these broken ties – the constant clutching after, yet eluding of connection – that exert the most powerful emotional pull' *Independent*

'Absorbing . . . a rich, intense novel . . . The strength of Tash Aw's writing can be seen in the three narratives. Each voice is distinct and each offers a subtly different viewpoint, remaking the material afresh . . . The beauty and danger of nature are everywhere in this delicately drawn novel' *TLS*

'Bewitchingly written and gracefully assured . . . The story Aw tells is mercilessly gripping and his prose is lucid, uncluttered, beautiful . . . Aw orchestrates a graceful ballet of dissonances and congruences, of echoes and discords' NEEL MUKHERJEE, *The Times*

'This is a serious, gripping, ambitious first novel . . . Aw knows the route to a reader's mind – first, through the ear – through whispered disclosures of the heart . . . The messy menage of jealousies and fatalistic fears is superbly accrued . . . Here, in this novel where so much is told, but at an angle, and more is concealed, the truth is a chimera, a character in itself. In less gifted hands it would all have imploded. But Tash Aw sings it like a chorus, in perfect pitch, in a book to be prized' TOM ADAIR, *Scotsman*

'This book begins with such brio that Tash Aw's second outing will be eagerly awaited' MAGGIE GEE, *Sunday Times*

'Tash Aw's striking debut is as elusive as it is exotic. Beginning in playful and indeed almost picaresque mood, *The Harmony Silk Factory* evolves into a novel of quiet regret and long suppressed pain. Its three narrators speak with distinctive and compelling voices. Aw is a skilled and sensitive writer' *Daily Mail*

'A suspense-laden colonial saga set in Thirties and Forties Malaysia, full of *English Patient*-style riffs' *Tatler*

'He writes with what seems like effortless fluidity'
ALFRED HICKLING, *Guardian*

'A novel that metamorphoses seamlessly from quest to confession'
HEPHZIBAH ANDERSON, *Observer*

'This beautifully constructed debut novel melds different narratives as it looks back through time . . . Author Tash Aw writes with an assurance that belies his 29 years. His prose is clear and descriptive, yet it changes deftly in character as the narrative view changes'
Sunday Business Post

TASH AW

The Harmony Silk Factory

HARPER PERENNIAL
London, New York, Toronto and Sydney

This edition produced for The Book People Ltd.,
Hall Wood Avenue, Haydock, St. Helens, WA11 9UL

Harper Perennial
An imprint of HarperCollins*Publishers*
77–85 Fulham Palace Road,
Hammersmith
London W6 8JB

www.harperperennial.co.uk

This edition published by Harper Perennial 2005

First published in Great Britain by Fourth Estate 2005

A catalogue record for this book
is available from the British Library

ISBN 0-00-7762410

Typeset in Bembo by
Palimpsest Book Production Limited, Polmont, Stirlingshire

Printed and bound in Great Britain by Clays Ltd, St Ives plc

For my parents

PART ONE

Johnny

1. *Introduction*

The Harmony Silk Factory is the name of the shophouse my father bought in 1942 as a front for his illegal businesses. To look at, the building is unremarkable. Built in the early thirties by itinerant Chinese coolies (of the type from whom I am most probably descended), it is the largest structure on the main street which runs through town. Behind its plain whitewashed front lies a vast, cave-dark room originally intended to accommodate light machinery and a few nameless sweatshop workers. The room is still lined with the teak cabinets my father installed when he first acquired the factory. These were designed to store and display bales of cloth, but as far as I can remember, they were never used for this purpose, and were instead stacked with boxes of ladies' underwear from England which my father had stolen with the help of his contacts down at the docks. Much later, when he was a very famous and very rich man – the Elder Brother of this whole valley – the cabinets were used to house his collection of antique weapons. The central piece in this display was a large kris, whose especially wavy blade announced its provenance: according to my father, it belonged to Hang Jebat, the legendary warrior who, as we all know, fought against the Portuguese colonisers in the sixteenth century. Whenever Father related this story to visitors, his usually monotonous voice would assume a gravelly, almost theatrical seriousness, impressing them with the similarity between himself and Jebat, two great men battling against foreign oppressors. There were also Gurkha kukris with curved blades for speedy disembowelment, Japanese samurai swords and jewel-handled daggers from Rajasthan. These were admired by all his guests.

For nearly forty years the Harmony Silk Factory was the most notorious establishment in the country, but now it stands empty and silent and dusty. Death erases all traces, all memories of lives that once existed, completely and for ever. That is what Father sometimes told me. I think it was the only true thing he ever said.

We lived in a house separated from the factory by a small mossy courtyard which never got enough sunlight. Over time, as my father received more visitors, the house too became known as the Harmony Silk Factory, partly for convenience – the only people who came to the house were those who came on business – and partly because my father's varied interests had extended into leisure and entertainment of a particular kind. Therefore it was more convenient for visitors to say, 'I have to attend to some business at the Harmony Silk Factory,' or even, 'I am visiting the Harmony Silk Factory.'

Our house was not the kind of place just anyone could visit. Indeed, entry was strictly by invitation, and only a privileged few passed through its doors. To be invited, you had to be like my father, that is to say, you had to be a liar, a cheat, a traitor and a skirt-chaser. Of the very highest order.

From my upstairs window, I saw everything unfold. Without Father ever saying anything to me, I knew, more or less, what he was up to and who he was with. It wasn't difficult to tell. Mainly, he smuggled opium and heroin and Hennessy XO. These he sold on the black market down in KL for many, many times what he had paid over the border to the Thai soldiers whom he also bribed with American cigarettes and low-grade gemstones. Once, a Thai general came to our house. He wore a cheap grey shirt and his teeth were gold, real solid gold. He didn't look much like a soldier, but he had a Mercedes-Benz with a woman in the back seat. She had fair skin, almost pure white, the colour of salt fields on the coast. She was smoking a Kretek and in her hair she wore a white chrysanthemum.

Father told me to go upstairs. He said, 'My friend the General is here.'

They locked themselves in Father's Safe Room, and even though I lifted the lino and pressed my ear to the floorboards I could hear nothing except the faint clinking of glasses and the low, muffled rumble which by then I knew to be the tipping of uncut diamonds on to the green baize table.

I waved at the woman in the car. She was young and beautiful, and when she smiled I saw that her teeth were small and brown. She was still smiling at me as the car pulled away, raising a cloud of dust and beeping at bicycles as it sped up the main street. It was rare in those early days to see expensive cars and big-town women in these parts, but if ever you saw them, they would be hanging around our house. None of our visitors ever noticed me, though, none but that woman with the fair skin and bad teeth.

I told Father about this woman and how she had smiled at me. His response was as I expected. He reached slowly for my ear and twisted it hard, squeezing the blood from it. He said, 'Don't tell stories,' and then slapped my face twice.

To tell the truth, I had become used to this kind of punishment.

Even when I was young, I was aware of what my father did. I wasn't exactly proud, but I didn't really care. Now, I would give everything to be the son of a mere liar and cheat because, as I have said, that wasn't all he was. Of all the bad things he ever did, the worst happened long before the big cars, pretty women and the Harmony Silk Factory.

Now is a good time to tell his story. At long last, I have put my crime-funded education to good use, and have read every single article in every book, newspaper and magazine that mentions my father, in order to understand the real story of what happened. For more than a few years of my useless life, I have devoted myself to this enterprise, sitting in libraries and government offices even. My diligence has been surprising. I will admit that I have never been a scholar, but recent times have shown that I am capable of rational, organised study, in spite of my father's belief that I would always be a dreamer and a wastrel.

There is another reason why I now feel particularly well placed to relate the truth of my father's life. An observant reader may sense forthwith that it is because the revelation of this truth has, in some strange way, brought me a measure of calm. I am not ashamed to admit that I have searched for this all my life. Now, at last, I know the truth and I am no longer angry. In fact, I am at peace.

As far as it is possible, I have constructed a clear and complete picture of the events surrounding my father's terrible past. I say 'as far as it is possible' because we all know that the retelling of history can never be perfect, especially when the piecing together of the story has been done by a person with as modest an intellect as myself. So now I am ready to give you this, The True Story of the Infamous Chinaman Called Johnny.

2. The True Story of the Infamous Chinaman Called Johnny (Early Years)

Some say Johnny was born in 1920, the year of the riots in Taiping following a dispute between Hakkas and Hokkiens over the right to mine a newly discovered tin deposit near Slim River.

We do not know who Johnny's parents were. Most likely, they were labourers of southern Chinese origin who had been transported to Malaya by the British in the late nineteenth century to work on the mines in the valley. Such people were known to the British as 'coolies', which is generally believed to be a bastardisation of the word *kulhi*, the name of a tribe native to Gujarat in India.

Fleeing floods, famine and crushing poverty, these illiterate people made the hazardous journey across the South China Sea to the rich equatorial lands they had heard about. It was mainly the men who came, often all the young men from one village. They arrived with nothing but the simple aim of making enough money to send for their families to join them. Traditionally viewed as semi-civilised peasants by the cultured overlords of the imperial north of China, these southern Chinese had, over the course of centuries, become expert at surviving in the most difficult of conditions. Their new lives were no less harsh, but here they found a place which offered hope, a place which could, in some small way, belong to them.

They called it, simply, *Nanyang*, the South Seas.

The southern Chinese look markedly different from their northern brethren. Whereas Northerners have candle-wax skin and icy, angular features betraying their mixed, part-Mongol ancestry, Southerners appear more hardy, with a durable complexion that easily turns brown in the sun. They have fuller, warmer features and compact frames which, in the case of over-indulgent men like my father, become squat with the passing of time.

Of course this is a generalisation, meant as a rough guide for those unfamiliar with basic racial fault lines. For evidence of the unreliability of this rule of thumb, witness my own features, which are more northern than southern, if they are at all Chinese (in fact, I have even been told that I have the look of a Japanese prince).

I have explained that my ancestors probably came from the south of China, specifically from Guangdong and Fujian provinces, but there is one further thing to say, which is that even in those two big provinces, people spoke different languages. This is important because your language determined your friends and enemies. People in our town speak mainly Hokkien, but there are a number of Hakka speakers too, like my Uncle Tony who married Auntie Baby. The literal translation of 'Hakka' is 'guest-people', descendants of tribes defeated in ancient battles and forced to live outside city walls. These Hakkas are considered by the Hokkiens and other Chinese here to be really very low class, with distinct criminal tendencies. No doubt they were responsible for the historical tension and bad feeling with the Hokkiens in these parts. Their one advantage, often used by them in exercises of subterfuge and cunning, is the similarity of their language to Mandarin, the noble and stately language of the Imperial Court, which makes it easy for them to disguise their dubious lineage. This is largely how Uncle Tony, who has become a hotel tycoon ('a *hôtelier*' he says), managed to convince bank managers and the public at large that he is a man of education (Penang Free School and the London School of Economics), when really he is like my father – unschooled and really very uncultured. He has, to his credit, managed to overcome that most telltale sign of Hakka backwardness, which is the lack of the 'h' sound in their language and the resulting (and quite frankly, ridiculous) 'f' which comes out in its place, whether speaking Mandarin, Malay or even English. For example:

Me (when I was young, deliberately): 'I paid money to touch a girl down by the river today.'

Uncle Tony (in pre-tycoon days): 'May God in Fevven felp you.'

He converted to Christianity too, I forgot to say.

Johnny Lim was obviously not my father's real name. At the start of his life he was known by his real name, Lim Seng Chin, a common and truly nondescript Hokkien name. He chose the name Johnny in late 1940, just as he was turning twenty. He named himself after Tarzan. I know this because among the few papers he left when he died were some old pictures, spotty and dog-eared, cut carefully from magazines and held together by a rusty paper clip. In each one, the same man appears, dressed in a badly fitting loincloth, often holding a pretty woman whose heavy American breasts strain at her brassière. In one picture, they stand on a fake log, clutching jungle vines; his brow is furrowed, eyes scanning the horizon for unknown danger while she gazes up at him. Behind them is a painted backdrop of forested hills, smooth in texture. Another picture, this time a portrait of the same barrel-chested man with beads of sweat on his shoulders, bears the caption, 'JOHNNY WEISSMULLER, OLYMPIC CHAMPION'.

I'm not certain why Johnny Weissmuller appealed to my father. The similarities between the two are non-existent. In fact, the comparison is amusing, if you think about it. Johnny Weissmuller: American, muscular, attractive to women. Johnny Lim: short, squat, uncommunicative, a hopelessly bald loner with poor social skills. In fact, it might well be said that I have more in common with Johnny Weissmuller, for I at least am tall and have a full head of thick hair. My features, as I have already mentioned, are angular, my nose strangely large and sharp. On a good day some people even consider me handsome.

It was not unusual for men of my father's generation to adopt the unfeasible names of matinée idols. Among my father's friends, there have been: Rudolph Chen, Valentino Wong, Cary Gopal and his business partner Randolph Muttusamy, Rock Hudson Ho, Montgomery Hashim, at least three Garys (Gary Goh, 'Crazy' Gary and one other I can't remember – the one-legged Gary) and too many Jameses to mention. While there is no doubt that the Garys in question were named after Gary Cooper, it wasn't so clear with the Jameses: Dean or Stewart? I watched these men when they visited the factory. I watched the way they walked, the way they smoked their cigarettes and the way they wore their clothes. Did James Dean wear his collar up or down in *East of Eden?* I could never tell for sure. I did know that Uncle Tony took his name from Tony Curtis. He admitted this to me, more or less, by taking me to see *Some Like It Hot* six times.

So you see, I was lucky, all things considered.

My father chose my name. He called me Jasper.

At school I learned that this is also the name of a stone, a kind of mineral. But this is irrelevant.

Returning to the Story of Johnny, we know that he assumed his new name around the age of twenty or twenty-one. Occasional (minor) newspaper articles dating from 1940, reporting on the activities of the Malayan Communist Party, describe lectures and pamphlets prepared by a young activist called 'Johnny' Lim. By 1941, the inverted commas have disappeared, and Johnny Lim is Johnny Lim for good.

Much of Johnny's life before this point in time is hazy. This is because it is typical of the life of a small-village peasant, and therefore of little interest to anyone. Accordingly, there is not much recorded information relating specifically to my father. What exists exists only as local hearsay and is to be treated with some caution. In order to give you an idea of what his life might have been like, however, I am able to provide you with a few of the salient points from the main textbook on this subject, R. St J. Unwin's masterly study of 1954, *Rural Villages of Lowland Malaya*, which is available for public perusal in the General Library in Ipoh. Mr Unwin was a civil servant in upstate Johore for some years, and his observations have come to be widely accepted as the most detailed and accurate available. I have paraphrased his words, of course, in order to avoid accusations of plagiarism, but the source is gratefully acknowledged:

- The life of rural communities is simple and spartan – rudimentary compared to Western standards of living, it would be fair to say.
- In the 1920s there was no electricity beyond a two- or three-mile radius of the administrative capitals of most states in Malaya.
- This of course meant: bad lighting, resulting in bad eyesight; no night-time entertainment; in fact, no entertainment at all; reliance on candlelight and kerosene lamps; houses burning down.
- Children therefore did not 'play.'
- They were expected to help in the manual labour in which their parents were engaged. As rural Malaya was an exclusively agricultural society, this nearly always meant working in one of the following: rice paddies, rubber-tapping, palm-oil estates. The latter two were better, as they meant employment by British or French plantation owners. Also, on a smaller scale, fruit orchards and other sundry activities, such as casting rubber sheets for export to Europe, making gunny sacks from jute and brewing illegal toddy. All relating to agriculture in some form or another. Not like nowadays when there are semiconductor and air-conditioner plants all over the countryside, in Batu Gajah even.
- In the cool wet hills that run along the spine of the country there are tea plantations. Sometimes I wonder if Johnny ever worked picking tea in Cameron Highlands. Johnny loved tea. He used to brew weak orange pekoe, so delicate and pale that you could see through it to the tiny crackles at the bottom of the small green-glazed porcelain teapot he used. He took time making tea, and even longer drinking it, an eternity

between sips. He would always do this when he thought I was not around, as though he wanted to be alone with his tea. Afterwards, when he was done, I would examine the cups, the pot, the leaves, hoping to find some clue (to what I don't know). I never did.

- So rural children became hardened early on. They had no proper toilets, indoor or outdoor.
- A toilet for them was a wooden platform under which there was a large chamber pot. Animals got under the platform, especially rats, but also monitor lizards, which ate the rats, and the faeces too. A favourite pastime among these simple rural children involved trapping monitor lizards. This was done by hanging a noose above the pot, so that when the lizard put its head into the steaming bowl of excrement, it would become ensnared. Then it was either tethered to a post as a pet, or (more commonly) taken to the market to be sold for its meat and skin. This practice was still quite common when I was a young boy. As we drove through villages in our car, I would see these lizards, four feet long, scratching pathetically in the dirt as they pulled at the string around their necks. Mostly they were rock grey in colour, but some of the smaller ones had skins of tiny diamonds, thousands and thousands of pearl-and-black jewels covering every inch of their bodies. Often the rope would have cut into their necks, and they would wear necklaces of blood.
- Poor villagers would eat any kind of meat. Protein was scarce.
- Most children were malnourished. That is why my father had skinny legs and arms all his life, even though his belly was heavy from later-life over-indulgence. Malnutrition is also the reason so many people of my father's generation are dwarfs. Especially compared to me – I am nearly a whole foot taller than my father.
- Scurvy, rickets, polio – all very common in children. Of course typhoid, malaria, dengue fever and cholera too.

- Schools do not exist in these rural areas.
- I tell a lie. There are a few schools, but they are reserved for the children of royalty and rich people like civil servants. These were founded by the British. '*Commanding the best views of the countryside, these schools are handsome examples of the colonial experiment with architecture, marrying Edwardian and Malay architectural styles.*' (I quote directly from Mr Unwin in this instance.) When you come across one of these schools you will see that they dominate the surrounding landscape. Their flat lawns and playing fields stretch before the white colonnaded verandas like bright green oceans in the middle of the grey olive of the jungle around them. These bastions of education were built especially for ruling-class Malays. Only the sons of very rich Chinese can go there. Like Johnny's son – he will go to one of these, to Clifford College in Kuala Lipis.
- There the pupils are taught to speak English, proper, I mean.
- They also read Dickens.
- For these boys, life is good, but not always. They have the best of times, they have the worst of times.
- Going back to the subject of toilets: actually, the platform lavatory continued to be used way into the 1960s. But not for me. In 1947, my father installed the first flush cistern and septic tank north of Kuala Lumpur at the Harmony Silk Factory. Before that, we had enamel chamber pots. My favourite one was hand-painted with red-and-black goldfish.
- So imagine a child like Johnny, growing up on the edge of a village on the fringes of a rubber plantation (say), tapping rubber and trapping animals for a few cents' pocket money. Probably, he would have no idea of the world around him. He only knows the children of other rubber-tappers. They are the only people he would ever mix with. Sometimes he sees the plantation owner's black motor car drive through the village on the way to the Planter's Club in town. The noise of the

engine, a metallic rattle-roar, fills Johnny's ears, and maybe he sees the Sir's pink face and white jacket as the car speeds past. There is no way the two would ever speak. Johnny would never even speak to rich Chinese – the kind of people who live in big houses with their own servants and tablecloths and electricity generators.

- When a child like Johnny ends up being a textile merchant, it is an incredible story. Truly, it is. He is a freak of nature.
- Unsurprisingly, many of the poor Chinese become communists. Not all, but many. And their children too.

Mr Unwin's excellent book paints a vivid picture indeed. However, it is a general study of all villages across the country and does not take into account specific regions or communities. This is not a criticism – I am in no position to criticise such scholarship – but there is one thing of some relevance to Johnny's story which is missing from the aforementioned treatise: the shining, silvery tin buried deep in the rich soil of the Kinta Valley.

3. The Kinta Valley

The Kinta Valley is a narrow strip of land which isn't really a valley at all. Seventy-five miles long and twenty miles wide at its widest, it runs from Maxwell Hill in the north to Slim River in the south. To the east are jungle-shrouded limestone massifs which you can see everywhere in the valley: low mountains pock-marked with caves which appear to the eye as black teardrop scars on a roughened face. There are trails through the jungle leading up to these caves. They have been formed over many years by the careful tread of animals – sambar and fallow deer, the wild buffalo and boar, the giant seledang – which come down from the hills to forage where the forest meets the rich fruit plantations.

As a boy, I used to walk these trails. The jungle was wet and cool and sunless, but by then I had learned where to put my feet, how to avoid the tree roots and burrows which could easily twist an ankle. The first time I discovered a cave I wandered so deep into it that I could no longer see any light from the outside. I felt with my hands for somewhere to sit. The ground and the walls were damp and flaky with guano. The air was rich with an old smoky smell, like the embers of some strange sugar-sweet charcoal fire. There were no noises other than the gentle drip-drip of water. The darkness swallowed up my movements. I couldn't see my hands or my legs, I couldn't hear myself breathing. It was as if I had ceased to exist. I sat there for many hours – I don't know how long exactly. Nor do I know how I found my way out of the cave or what made me want to leave. Night had fallen by the time I emerged, but it did not seem dark to me. Even the light from the pale half-moon annoyed my eyes as I made my way home.

As long as a hundred years ago, the first Chinese coolies discovered these caves and built Buddhist temples in them. For them too these caves were a place of comfort and solace and refuge. A few of the larger temples survive today. My favourite is the Kek Loong, which contains an enormous Laughing Buddha. People say his expression conveys infinite love and wisdom, but to me he has always looked like a young boy, naughtily chuckling because he has done something wrong.

You would expect that a valley would be bounded by two mountain ranges, but that is not so with the Kinta Valley. To the west, as soon as you cross the Perak River, the mangrove swamps begin to unfold before you. The land is flat and muddy, criss-crossed by slow-running streams. The journey to the coast takes you past coconut plantations and fishing villages. Everywhere there are flimsy wooden racks of fish, slowly drying and salting in the sun and the sea breeze. In most places along the coast it is difficult to know where the land ends and the sea begins. There are a thousand tiny inlets which break the coastline, an intricate tapestry of coves. This is where the notorious nineteenth-century pirate Mat Hitam used to hide, deep among the mangrove trees. From here he would launch raids on the hundreds of trading ships following the trade winds down into the Straits of Malacca, for three centuries the most lucrative shipping lane in the world. The straits were, and still are, sheltered and calm – the ideal route for a ship laden with tea, cotton, silk, porcelain or opium, travelling between India and China. Here, the men of such ships rested their weary, wary souls. Shielded from the open, treacherous waters of the Indian Ocean, they gathered their spirits before striking out for the South China Sea. It was said by fishermen and merchant seamen that the straits were the most beautiful place in the world. The water was smooth enough for a child's boat to sail peacefully – the gentle waves caught the amber light of the setting sun and the breeze, steady and warm, propelled you at a speed so constant that seamen were said to have become mesmerised. Some insisted that they felt in the presence of God.

It is here, in this idyll, that Mat Hitam and his men struck. For nearly twenty years, his small fast boats terrorised the stately ships filled with valuable cargo. Mat Hitam himself became a godlike figure, feared for his ruthlessness. It is an established fact that he was the rarest of all people: a black Chinese. No one was certain where he came from. Some theories say that he was from Yunnan Province in southern China, but it is more commonly believed that he was not an exotic foreigner, and was instead born within these shores. Whatever the case, I have no doubt that his mysterious appearance aided his exploits. He died in 1830 (or thereabouts), in the early days of British rule in Malaya. His last victim was Juan Fernández de Martin, a Jesuit missionary who, as his throat was cut, placed a curse on Mat Hitam so powerful that two weeks later, the Black Pirate died of a twisted stomach. He was bleeding from his eyes as he died, and the expression on his face was 'empty as hell and full of fury'.

His spirit lives on in the hidden coves and apparently sleepy fishing villages which dot the coastline. They are impossible to police, and it is here that Johnny smuggled 20,000 tons of rice from Sumatra during the drought of 1958. I am told that small boats carrying illegal Indonesian immigrants land here every day. I'm sure that if Johnny were alive today he would find some way of making money out of this.

At one or two points along this coast, the sea does appear cleanly and without interruption. One such place is Remis, where my father once took me to swim. It was the first time I had swum in the sea. As I walked on to the beach the dry needles of the casuarina trees, scattered across the sand, prickled underfoot. It was a very hot day and even though the afternoon sun was weakening, the sand was still white to my eyes and warm to the touch. When I was waist-deep in the water, I turned to look at Father. He was standing in the pools of shade cast by the trees, watching me with his arms folded and eyes squinting slightly. I walked until I could barely touch the bottom with my toes, then I started swimming, kicking off with uncertain froglike strokes. At some point, I stopped and began treading water, my arms flailing gently in front of me. The sea was deep green, the colour of old, dark jade. That was the first time I ever noticed my skin, the colour of it. Not brown, not yellow, not white, not anything against the rich and mysterious green of the water around me. I turned to look at Father. I could barely make him out in the shade, but he was still there, one hand on his hip, the other shading his eyes from the sun.

On the way home I asked him if I could go swimming again. I was twelve, I think, and I wanted to go to the islands around

Pangkor where I had heard the sun made the sand look like tiny crystals. I longed to see for myself the Seven Maidens, those islands that legend held disappeared with the setting sun; I yearned for their hot waters. But Father said he wouldn't take me.

'Those places no longer exist,' he said. 'They are part of a story, a useless old story.'

'Why can't we go just for a day?' I ventured. 'Have you ever seen them, Father?'

'I told you, I hate islands.'

'Why?'

'Actually, I don't like the sea much,' he said simply.

I knew better than to test him when he was in one of these moods. I noticed, however, that even though I had just spent the afternoon in the sun, my skin was white compared to his. It refused to turn dark, remaining pale and unblemished, a clean sheet beside his dirty sun-mottled arms.

No one ever stops to visit the valley. Buses hurry past on their journey north to Penang, pausing briefly for refreshments in Parit or Taiping. Their passengers sit for ten minutes at zinc-covered roadside truck stops, sipping at bottles of Fanta and nibbling on savoury chicken-flavoured biscuits; and then they are away again, eager to leave the dull central plains of the valley for the neon lights and seaside promenades of Georgetown. When I was young it was possible to spend a week in Ipoh without hearing a single word of English. No one had a TV in those days (apart from us, of course). Then, as now, Western visitors were rare. The only white people I ever saw were the ones who *had* to be in the valley – alcoholic planters and unhappy civil servants. Only once do I remember seeing a tourist, and even then I was not certain he had come to the valley by design. I was indulging in a favourite childhood pastime, climbing into the lower reaches of the giant banyan tree that dominated the river bank near the factory. I reached for the thick hanging vines and swung in a broad arc, rising high until I faced the giddying sky; and then I let myself go, tilting and falling into the warm water. When I surfaced I saw an Englishman sitting on the bank, his folded arms resting on his raised knees. A canvas satchel hung limply across his shoulders. The other children who were with me ceased to play; they splashed quietly in the shallows, nervously hiding their nakedness in the opaque water. I wanted to climb the tree and dive into the river again, but the Englishman was sitting at the base of the trunk, perched uncomfortably on the lumpy roots. It did not occur to me to be afraid; I simply walked up the slippery bank towards the tree, passing very close to him. I noticed that he was not looking at me, but staring blankly into the distance. He was not an old man, but his face was just like my father's, scarred by a weariness I had rarely seen in other men. He looked lost; I am sure he had wandered into the valley by mistake. I climbed swiftly up into the branches, crawled out to the end of a large bough, and as I fell forward into the water I caught a glimpse of the man's thick silvered hair. When I emerged from the water he had gone, and the other children were singing and shouting again. The white man was a spy, we agreed, laughing, or a madman. Or perhaps, said Orson Lai, he was a ghost who had returned to haunt the scene of some terrible crime. Yes, we decided, our voices hushed with childish fear, he had to be a ghost. No one ever visits the valley.

Nowadays, there is even less traffic through the small towns of the Kinta. The new North–South Highway allows a traveller to speed past the valley in less than three hours. The journey is soothing, untroubled. You fall asleep in air-conditioned comfort and, in truth, you do not miss very much. Between the hills and the invisible sea, the landscape is flat and unremarkable. Nothing catches your eye except for the many disused tin mines, now filled with rainwater. You see them everywhere in the valley, quiet, gloomy pools of black water. I used to search for the largest ones, the ones so big I could pretend they were the ocean itself. But this pretence rarely worked. Once I stepped off the tepid, muddy shelf which ringed the pool, I was in water of untold depth, water which now covered the work of my ancestors. The temperature plunged. Every year boys from my town drowned in such pools. The shock of the cold made their muscles seize up. This was how my friend Ruby Wong died. He was my only friend from my childhood and he was a good swimmer, one of the best. Although not nearly as strong as me and slight in build, he had a smooth, easy stroke which barely broke the water yet propelled him steadily at considerable speeds. He could swim without coming to shore for an hour at a time. Once, we swam across the swirling brown waters of the Perak, Ruby leading the way. We were not even out of breath when we reached the other bank.

This time we had chosen the old mine near Kellie's Castle. It was known that only the bravest could swim the biggest pools, and there were few larger than this. We were only fourteen but we did not think twice about swimming it. Night had begun to fall when we got to the pool. I undressed quickly, eager to feel the water. Swimming in the dark felt different, special: the absence of light made my skin look less pale. The sky was blank and black with cloud. There was no moon; nothing was illuminated. Even the ripples of the water as we slid into the pool did not show.

On this swim, as on every other, there was no purpose, no silly races, no 'first to the other side wins'. We just swam. A few feet from the edge, where the shelf fell away, I prepared myself for the cold. It gripped my whole body, squeezing the air from my chest. I breathed sharply, chokingly, but I had known that feeling before and so I continued to strike out. Pull. Kick. Pull. Kick. I heard Ruby's choking breaths echoing my own, but I kept on swimming into the blackness, my eyes closed.

'Jas,' came the first call. Ruby's voice breathed the word, it did not speak it. '*Jas.*'

I opened my eyes and searched for him in the infinite darkness. 'Ruby?' I said, still swimming forward.

By the time I realised, several seconds later, that he was no longer there, it was too late. I swam furiously in different directions, not knowing where to look, where to turn next. In the moonless night I thought of the chickens we kept in the yard behind the factory. I don't know why they came into my thoughts. When you entered the coop to select one of them for slaughter they would run away in zigzags, never knowing where they were going or who they were escaping from. The victim always had a vacant expression on its face, not terrified or even sad, just lost.

Of course it was fate that the first car I met, after walking an hour on the deserted road, was Father's. It had to be Father who found me, naked and wild-eyed. I shouted out what had happened to Ruby. Whether I made sense or not I don't know.

'He's not playing tricks on you,' Father said. That was just how he spoke. Never asked questions, always statements.

'No, I'm sure!' I screamed.

'You're not telling stories.'

There was no need for me to answer.

'Then he's dead already,' he said, opening the door for me to get in. 'We'll go back for your clothes tomorrow.'

I was afraid he was angry with me for making him go all the way home before doubling back to Kampar for his evening playing cards. I was afraid, so I said no more.

And that is how my friend Ruby Wong died, more or less.

This, then, is where the Kinta Valley lies, trapped between hills and swamps. This is the valley which became Johnny's little empire, where he was man and boy, where he started a family, where he was once respected by his people, where he destroyed everything.

4. How the Infamous Johnny Became a Communist – and Other Things

In 1933, two things happened. The price of rubber fell to four cents per pound and Johnny killed a man. It was the first man he killed, and although rumour had it that he did it in self-defence, I believe that the terrible deed was just as likely to have been carried out coldly, with malice aforethought (which I have learned amounts to murder). In any case, the exact events are unclear, and the records from the Taiping Magistrates' Court are somewhat muddled.

At this point in his life, Johnny was working in the Three Horses tin mine just off the Siput–Taiping road. Many young men (and women too) had begun to work in the mines. The price of rubber was now so low that many plantation owners – even English and French ones – were forced out of business. The plantations ceased to operate and were soon overwhelmed by the jungles which surrounded them. The morning bells which roused the workers ceased to toll, and the kerosene lamps which illuminated the scarred bark of the trees were no longer lit. There was no more work to be found in the plantations. So the young people began to drift further and further away from their villages in search of work, and most of them ended up in the mines.

By all accounts, Johnny was a well-regarded boy. He was quietly spoken, diligent and unimaginative, and was therefore perfect for working in the mines. Although barely in his teens, Johnny was no longer a manual labourer. He had risen above that. His work did not involve digging into the wet, heavy soil for twelve hours each day, nor carrying basketfuls of ore from the bottom of the open-cast pits to be stored, ready for melting. He did not have to do this because, in spite of his lack of intellect, Johnny had one other attribute: a gift for understanding machinery.

There is a story about how Johnny first discovered his in-built ability to assemble and operate machines. There are many different versions of this story, but the essence of it is as follows. Johnny was thirteen years old. He had been drinking palm-flower toddy with some other delinquents, and he had enjoyed it. The sensations were new to him, as fresh in his body as the morning sun that follows a monsoon night. He went to see an old Indian man who lived on the edge of a rubber plantation, who brewed toddy the old way – the only way they ever did (and many still do), illicitly, hushed-up in the half-dark of the jungle. The man collected the young flowers himself; he soaked them and bought the yeast from Cold Storage in Georgetown. He fermented the toddy just as he might have nurtured children. He remembered when each barrel was filled – *born* – down to the day, the hour even. He knew what the weather had been like at the time of each filling, and he knew how this would affect the taste of each vat of toddy. He knew which ones would be sweet or sour or just strong and tasteless. Whenever he produced something memorable, a toddy of remarkable clarity or distinctive taste, he would give it a special name – White Lakshmi, perhaps, or Nearly As Good As Mother's Milk.

Johnny was fascinated by this. He visited the old man often, and drank often too. But all this time he was disturbed by the way the toddy was brewed. He didn't like the old kerosene drums the old man used to ferment the toddy in. Some of them were rusty, and on others the lids didn't fit properly. The old man said that this was *the way things were done*, that toddy had to be varied and different. Every sip had to provide you with the sensation of stepping off a cliff without knowing what lay beneath. Mad fool, Johnny thought; he did not accept this. He wanted every mouthful of toddy to be as good as the best toddy he had ever tasted. He didn't enjoy discovering a bitter toddy, or a new and unusual one. He knew, too, that people sometimes fell sick after drinking toddy; they became blind, they died. On top of all this, one day when they had been filling bottles, they found a rat at the bottom of one of the barrels. It lay bobbing amid the sediment, curled up and peacefully preserved in the alcohol. Not even the cat touched it when they threw it out into the long grass.

So Johnny went away and thought for a long time. He drew pictures in the sand, idle mid-afternoon sketches of simple machines. He didn't know what he would do, but he knew, instinctively, that he would do something.

People still talk about Johnny's invention in the valley; they say nothing as magical has been seen since. Not even the revolving dining room at the Harmony Silk Factory, built when I was in my teens, could rival Johnny's first, instinctive creation. This is high praise indeed, for the revolving dining room was itself a much-admired feature of our house. The entire floor would split in half and a partition wall would emerge from a vault beneath the floor, separating the one large room into two smaller ones. Hidden in the ceiling, behind the walls and under the floor was a simple but highly effective clockwork mechanism. Polished mahogany panelling adorned the room, drawing the attention of a visitor (more specifically, a policeman or a rival 'businessman') to the décor rather than the construction of the room. Fake European masterpieces, painted by artists in Penang, hung in gilded frames on the walls. (I looked them up in books when I was at school, and discovered that my two favourites were *The Fall of Icarus* by Bruegel and *The Death of Actaeon* by Titian.) One of the two rooms – the second, smaller one – was built into the thick rear wall of the factory, making it soundproof and totally secure. The purpose of this was originally to provide a hiding place in case of an emergency. It was conceived of at a time when we had a new police superintendent who arrived in the district determined to put an end to all crime, from the most petty thefts to the largest organised rackets. The new Sir was often seen striding down the main street of our little town, his bushy flame-red moustache always immaculate, his waxen English skin still strangely unblemished by the sun. He never spoke to anyone, and people began to fear him. This was when our revolving dining room was built. Endless sketches were made, parts were ordered from Singapore, carpenters all over the country were put on notice, timber was felled in north Borneo. By the time the necessary machinery had been installed, however, the superintendent – Malcolm – was firmly in Johnny's pocket. He came to the factory and drank Napoleon brandy late into the night, and he acquired a Chinese mistress called Wendy. When he visited our house, I noticed he had a gold wristwatch with an ebony face. It looked brand new.

But it was Johnny's first creation, the Amazing Toddy Machine, which was the most famous and enduring. Although very few people actually saw it, its reputation was widespread, and its products enjoyed even farther afield. At the heart of this new invention was a large glass tank in which the various raw components were mixed. Everything could be seen clearly in this tank – the initial chemical reaction, the colour, the consistency – and regulating the process was made easier. Nothing was left to chance. The transparency of the machine allowed the brewer to intervene if he thought something was going wrong. The tank was sealed, so any impurities (not to mention animals) could not find their way in. As the system grew, Johnny found a way of increasing the output dramatically – more glass tubes were attached, linking more tanks to each other, all bubbling away at various stages of ferment. At some point a distillation mechanism was added, ensuring the final product was as clear and smooth as spring water. For a while, purely as a novelty, the toddy was filtered through layers of mangrove-wood charcoal, drip by slow drip. People were puzzled by the taste of this, but fascinated too, and soon even more glass tubes and tanks were added. At its height, the machine was said to have resembled a tiny crystal mountain, sparkling with a life of its own.

Johnny's gift for machines has always been evident to me. Even as a young child, I knew that while other people could perhaps take apart a car engine and then reassemble it, not everyone could do it as Johnny could. It wasn't so much what he did but how he did it – steadily and gently, with a rhythm all his own. The parts of the engine fell away into his hands like pieces of silk; he held greasy steel bolts the way you or I might hold a newborn chick. I used to watch him fixing things. Whenever he repaired a clock – that was my favourite – his short peasant's fingers, clumsy in every other way, would suddenly move with all the delicacy of a silk-weaver's. Where other men might have used tweezers or screwdrivers or other tools, Johnny seemed only to use his fingers, touching each part of the clockwork. I always pretended to be doing something else – passing through the room or reading a book. He never knew I was watching.

The Toddy Machine was the beginning of a particular episode in Johnny's life that goes something like this:

Armed with this gift, this knowledge of machines, Johnny becomes well known. People all over the valley hear about the toddy, they hear about the young man who made it. The mines need people to work in them, but these are hard times for the Chinese mines. They have been in the valley for fifty, sixty years, long before the railway was built between Port Weld and Butterworth. They are big, open-cast mines with old-fashioned gravel pumps. But it is not good for them now because new mines have opened all over the valley. British mines.

What makes these British mines different is that they do not need many hundreds of coolies to work in them. This is because they have, at the heart of the mine, a mechanised colossus never seen before in these parts. It is called a Dredging Machine, and it does the work of a thousand coolies. It sits astride the mine as the goddess Guan Yin herself sat on a vast lake, floating for all eternity. The Chinese fear this machine for they do not possess one. The British do not need many men, they simply need a few good ones. Of all the Chinamen in the valley, only one will be able to understand the Dredging Machine, and it does not take long for the British to learn of his existence.

The first time Johnny sees the dredger he does not see the monstrous, angry machine everyone else sees. Instead, he sees a living creature. He understands it at once. He sees limbs – huge mechanical limbs – and a body; he senses organs buried deep within it, and a heart too. It is as if he has always known this thing. When he is shown the machine, the words of explanation are as familiar to his ears as the rising and falling of the damp November winds. He has heard them a thousand times before. Even on that first day, he wants to start working with the machine. The British man who is in charge stands behind him, watching as he works the levers which turn the cogs which run the pump which fires the pistons which bring the ore up to the surface from the depths of the mine. The five minutes – the test of Johnny's understanding of the machine – turn quickly into ten, twenty, forty minutes, an hour. Johnny and the machine cannot be separated. The machine wants to be worked by Johnny. 'Quite remarkable,' the man in charge says. 'The dredger loves this boy.' They are like a mother and her child who, after a lengthy separation, fall into each other's arms with relief. Johnny is then taken to the longhouse where the special workers are given lodgings. It is made of rough, unplaned wood, full of splinters which embed themselves in Johnny's feet and hands. The rain drums loudly on the zinc roof, but the house is dry and secure. Johnny sleeps on a thin mattress laid out on the floor. At night he can hear the scratching of small animals, but they are outside and he is inside. He is also given a piece of paper saying that he is now an employee of the Darby Tin Mine. Everyone is smiling. They do not yet know of the bad things Johnny will do.

About two months after Johnny first begins working at the Darby mine, the dredger breaks down for the first time. At first no one knows what to do. In case of emergencies, the workers have been told that one of them is to run to the foghorn and sound it three times, long and hard. The meaning of an 'emergency' is unclear, though. Only twice before has the foghorn been sounded: once when the monsoon rains, heavier than usual, washed away an entire face of the mine; and another time when the Chief Engineer's wife, the only Englishwoman in the area, appeared suddenly and without reason, in the middle of the afternoon. On other occasions, even when someone was badly hurt or even killed in an accident, no alarm was raised and work went on as usual.

For a long time, there is nothing but a huge, empty silence. The roar of the dredger, which usually drowns out every other sound, is not to be heard. The workers do not know what to do. When at last the foghorn blows, pathetically, three times in the mid-morning air, it barely carries to the cream-painted hut where the British Sirs sit, leafing through papers which no one else can understand. One by one the Sirs come out of the hut, each fixing his hat to his head. Their shirts are damp and stick to their skins. Their faces, the workers can see, are heavy with heat, fatigue and disgust.

'Call for that Chinaman Johnny,' No. 1 Sir barks as the Sirs stand assembled before the broken behemoth. Johnny is brought to them. His hands and forearms are covered with grease. His face is dirty and grey with dust and lack of sleep.

'What's the matter with this bloody machine?' No. 1 Sir says.

'I'm not sure. Sir.'

'You're *not sure*? What do you think we pay your wages for?' No. 1 Sir screams.

'Calm down. Wretched thing probably doesn't understand you,' Sirs Nos 2 and 3 say. 'Look at him.'

Johnny stands there with black hands hanging loosely at his side.

'All right. Do you know where the problem is?' No. 1 Sir says, slowly this time.

Johnny nods.

'Well then, take me to it, don't just stand there like an imbecile.'

They go deep into the machine. On a clean blue canvas sheet laid on the floor, Johnny's tools are neatly spread out, ready for use. Dozens and dozens of tools, all shiny and clean.

'Here,' Johnny says, pointing.

The Sirs walk around the part of the machine which Johnny has pointed at. No. 1 Sir has his hands in his pockets. No. 2 Sir checks his fingernails as he paces back and forth. No. 3 Sir rubs his brow. Sirs Nos 4 and 5 say and do nothing – they are young, and do not yet know anything.

'It's the belt,' says No. 1 Sir.

'It's the rotator,' says No. 2.

'It's the oil supply. The wiring, I mean,' says No. 3.

Johnny says, 'The parts in the gearbox are broken, I think. They are not moving.'

'Well, *fix it*,' No. 3 says.

'The machine – it requires new parts,' Johnny says. 'Maybe.'

'You bloody well fix it now,' No. 3 Sir says. His face is red and shining with sweat.

They watch as Johnny goes back to the machine. He does not know what he is going to do, how he is going to fix this unfixable problem, but he knows that he will find a way. Somehow, he will.

Piece by piece, Johnny takes the gearbox apart. He brushes each piece with a wire brush, washes it in water, then wipes it with grease. He gives it new life. He feels no fear: his hands are calm and strong and his eyes are cool and level. Turning to pick up another tool, he catches the eye of No. 1 Sir, who is blinking to keep out the heat and dust of the afternoon. At last, Johnny turns to the Sirs and says, 'It is ready.'

The Sirs look at each other. 'About bloody time,' No. 1 says.

Johnny walks to the control box and rests his hands on it. He trusts the machine, he trusts himself. The whirr of the dredger is uncertain at first, but soon it becomes a steady growl, and then the familiar roar fills the entire space, drifting out into the valley, singing in Johnny's ears.

One by one the Sirs walk back to their cream-coloured hut. 'Imagine – millions of tons of ore under our feet,' No. 1 says, putting his wide-brimmed hat on. 'That damned Chinaman will be the ruin of us all.'

'Nearly twenty past four,' says No. 2.

'Just in time for tea,' says No. 3.

Johnny packs up his tools, one by one, making sure he cleans the grime and grease from each one. He wraps them up in his blue canvas cloth and listens to the song of the machine.

Four days later, the machine breaks down again. Once more, Johnny is summoned to repair it, and again he succeeds. The next day it breaks down again. And the next day too. By now Johnny has taken to sleeping next to the faulty part of the machine. He can hear its heartbeat, feel its pulse. It is weak and failing.

By now the workers have become used to the great silence that has fallen over the mine. They know there will be no work for them. Without the machine, the tin remains buried deep under their feet. There is nothing to wash, nothing to grade, nothing to store or melt. So the workers sit around, placidly chewing tobacco or betel leaves, their lips and tongues becoming stained with the juice of this stupor-inducing nut. As the days go by, the dry earth around the longhouse becomes pock-marked with patches of red spittle.

At the start of the second week without the machine, the Sirs come to where Johnny is working. His tools are laid out on the mattress beside him. Some of his tools have had more rest than he has.

'What on earth is this monkey doing?' says No. 1.

'I told you not to let a Chinaman loose on the dredger,' says No. 2.

Johnny looks at them with young eyes made old by work.

'So,' says No. 1, 'what do you have to say for yourself?'

Johnny blinks. Their suits are white and blinding in the sunlight. 'I need new parts,' he says, turning back to the machine.

'How dare you answer back!' No. 3 shouts.

'Parts indeed.'

'It's his fault anyway.'

'When,' No. 1 says slowly. 'Will. It. Be. Fixed?'

Johnny's chest rises and falls heavily. He doesn't know how to answer. 'Soon,' he says. But he knows it is useless. The machine is dying in his hands, like a sick child on its mother's breast.

'Soon?!' No. 1 explodes.

'Soon??!' echoes No. 2.

'What does that mean?' say Nos 3, 4 and 5.

Later that morning the Sirs make an announcement at a specially arranged workers' meeting outside the cream-painted hut. The workers are told that they will not be paid to sit around doing nothing. The mine cannot afford to pay their wages if no tin is being processed.

'It is simply uneconomical for the Darby mine to continue like this,' says No. 1, his voice rising above the angry murmur. 'As long as the Dredging Machine is not working –'

'But that is not our fault!' someone shouts.

'– as long as the Dredging Machine remains –'

'That is none of our business! Get the damn machine working!'

'Until the machine is fixed,' says No. 1 with all the authority he can muster, 'THERE WILL BE NO PAY. So go home, all of you.'

'That's the problem with coolies,' says No. 2 as the Sirs back into their hut, locking the door.

'Where's that lazy dog-boy?!' the men outside shout. 'Where's Johnny? It's all that bastard's fault!'

'Let's teach him a lesson!'

'My children will go to sleep hungry!'

'Damned son-of-a-whore!'

'He's doing this to kill us all!'

When they find him they are swift and brutal. They hit him with their bare fists and kick him with shoeless feet, again and again. Johnny closes his eyes as the first blow strikes him on the side of his face. He crashes on to the machine and feels it press against his body, cold and lifeless. Soon he can no longer feel pain. He does not see or hear the men set fire to his mattress. 'That will teach him to sleep all the time, lazy animal. Now maybe he will work to fix this machine.'

By the time they leave him they are no longer angry. They walk slowly off the mine and go home, heads bowed, arms hanging limply by their sides.

When Johnny opens his eyes again it is night. He sees, through swollen eyelids, the grey bulk of the machine. Slowly, he moves his head so that his ear touches the dredger. He can hear nothing, and suddenly his arms and legs and head and chest start to hurt, and he collapses again.

'You had it coming, I must say,' No. 2's voice says. 'You're not as clever as I thought.'

In the dark, Johnny can barely make out No. 2's figure standing over him.

‘I told him,’ No. 2 says, pacing slowly before Johnny, ‘I told him not to do it, not to take on a dirty Chinaman like you. I told him a Chinaman’s place is IN the mines, loading and carrying, but no – he had to put you in charge of the machine. A Chinaman operating the biggest dredger in the valley? Well, that’s plainly ridiculous. And he fed you and clothed you and housed you. What foolishness.’

‘I need new parts,’ Johnny whispers.

‘Over my dead body,’ No. 2 says. ‘*You* are responsible for what’s happened, you cretin.’ He kicks Johnny’s tools into a pile. Many of them have been burned with the mattress, their shiny faces now blackened with soot.

‘Pack up,’ No. 2 says. ‘I never want to see you here again.’

Feebly, Johnny begins to gather his tools. They are still hot from the fire.

‘Don’t forget,’ No. 2 says, ‘that you are responsible for this machine. It’s your fault.’

Johnny raises his gaze to meet No. 2’s.

‘Don’t you dare look at me like that,’ No. 2 says. He kicks Johnny away with the tip of his shoe.

Johnny’s hand lands on his pile of tools. He finds that his hand has come to rest on a screwdriver. Its handle is smooth and fire-warm. Johnny grasps it and thrusts it deep into No. 2’s thigh.

The court case was short but complicated; there were many difficulties. First of all, no one was certain of Johnny’s age, not even Johnny himself. It was not unusual for children of lowly rural backgrounds to have no birth certificate – why was there need for one? – and as a result, the precise date and location of Johnny’s birth remained a mystery. Advocates acting for the Darby mine insisted that Johnny should stand trial for the most serious charge: attempted murder. His physical appearance alone, they argued, suggested that he was at least eighteen. But Charlie Gopalan, a local barrister who specialised in such criminal cases, convinced the magistrate that Johnny was merely fourteen, and should not, under the circumstances, go to prison, where he would surely fall under the influence of communist guerrillas. Mr Gopalan was a man who had earned the trust of the British. He had studied at the Inner Temple and his clothes were nicely tailored in Singapore. His round-rimmed glasses added to his serious, scholarly manner. In pictures from the newspaper archive in the Public Library, he appears a small, neat-looking man, often holding a briefcase and a hat. He is even said to have begun translating Homer's *Odyssey* into Malay. His word, in any event, carried much influence.

There was also the matter of No. 2's condition. Johnny had managed to stab him in the fleshy part of the thigh, in exactly the place where the artery is at its thickest. The blood loss was immense. It was reported in court that the two men were found nearly lifeless, writhing feebly as if swimming in a shallow pool of blood. For a month after the stabbing, No. 2 remained in the General Hospital in Ipoh. Though he was for some days on the brink of death, he improved steadily. Doctors praised his bravery and admired his 'buffalo-like' constitution, and his progress was such that by the time of the hearing, he was able to walk, albeit gingerly. The familiar rosy-pinkness of his complexion was by now fully restored to his cheeks.

Thus the case against Johnny was half-hearted, the lawyers becoming increasingly bored as the days wore on. In the face of Mr Gopalan's persuasiveness, the magistrate decided that it was sufficient that Johnny received ten lashes of the rotan, 'to teach boys like you to know and respect your position in society'. He was cleared of all charges.

What no one knew at the time was that gangrene or septicaemia or some other mysterious infection had worked its way into No. 2's blood, unnoticed by the doctors who had tended to him. He collapsed, was rushed to hospital, but again made a near-miraculous recovery. Once more, doctors marvelled at his God-given strength, and when he collapsed a second time they knew he would pull through – and he did. Month after month this continued, until finally No. 2 died, exactly a year and a week after first being stabbed by Johnny.

The coroner had no choice but to record a 'death by natural causes' verdict.

I do not believe that Johnny would have been saddened by the news of No. 2's death. I believe, in fact, that it was this first killing which hardened in him a certain resolve. Now he was a killer but he did not feel bad. He knew, for the first time in his life, the sensation which was to become familiar to him later in his life, that powerful feeling of committing a crime and then escaping its consequences. It was this incident which set him on the path to becoming the monster he ultimately turned into.

It was many years before he could find work easily. Ordinary people were fearful of a person such as Johnny. He might not have been a criminal in the eyes of the law, but the law didn't understand human nature. The law couldn't always tell good from evil, people said. For a long time Johnny moved from town to town, village to village, plantation to plantation, never knowing how long he would stay or what he would do next. Without the kindness of strangers he would surely have perished. It was during this period of his life that he experienced his first real contact with communists. It was inevitable. The valley was, at the time, teeming with them – guerrillas, sympathisers, political activists. An ill-humoured youth full of hatred (for the British, for the police, for life), Johnny was perfect communist material. Of the many journeyman jobs he was given during these years, I'm certain that all but a handful were communist-inspired in some form or another. This wasn't surprising, given that every other shopkeeper, farmer or rubber-tapper was a communist. These people offered Johnny more than an ideology; they offered a safe place to sleep, simple food and a little money. That was all he cared for at that point in time.

5. Johnny and the Tiger

I like to think of those years which Johnny spent wandering from job to lousy job as his 'lost' years, the years which became erased from his life, the years during which he vanished into the countryside. I see him disappearing into the forest as a boy and emerging as a man. That is certainly what seems, extraordinarily, to have happened. Who knows? Perhaps something terrible happened to him during those years in the wilderness, something which turned him into a monster. Or maybe it was the irresistible force of fate which led him down this path; maybe he was simply destined, from the day he was born, to jump off the back of a lorry on to the dusty, treeless main street in Kampar, in front of the biggest textile trading company in the valley. No one knows about the small odyssey which led Johnny to Kampar. All anyone can be sure of is that one day he turned up and got a job, his first regular employment since the Darby mine incident, at the famous shop run by 'Tiger' Tan.

The reasons behind Tiger's name were a mystery. By all accounts, he was a gentle, softly mannered, home-loving man who, on account of his devout Buddhism, never ate meat, even though he was one of the few people in the valley who could afford to eat it every day. He had plump arms which hung loosely by his side when he walked. His movements were slow and unhurried, as if he had all the time in the world. He looked every bit the prosperous merchant that he was.

You would never have guessed that in his spare time he was also the commander of the Communist Army for the whole of the valley.

By the time Johnny came under his employ at the Tiger Brand Trading Company, Tiger Tan's life seemed, in every respect, a settled state of affairs. After many years, he appeared to have laid to rest the unfortunate events relating to his short, sad marriage. His wife had left him very soon after they had married. She took their baby daughter with her and converted to Islam in order to become the third wife of the fourth son of the Prince Regent of Perak. She went to live in the teak palace on the gentle slopes of Maxwell Hill, and it was there that the child was raised, amid the splendour only royalty can provide. The child was given an Arabic name, Zahara, meaning 'shining flower,' though neither her name nor her hardy peasant-Chinese blood could save her from dying of typhoid when she was seven years old. After her death, her mother was sometimes glimpsed at the great shuttered windows of the palace singing old Chinese love songs at the top of her voice. She sang with perfect pitch, her tongue capturing the words and releasing them across the valley like grass seeds in the wind. If you strolled along the path which ran along the grounds of the palace, you could sometimes hear these songs:

A traveller came from far away,
He brought me a letter.
At the top it says 'I'll always love you,'
At the bottom it says 'Long must we part.'

I put the letter in my bosom sleeve.
Three years no word has faded.
My single heart that keeps true to itself
I fear you'll never know.

It took Tiger a full twenty years, perhaps more, to forget the pain of his wife's desertion. At first, he spent every waking hour trying to convince himself that both his wife and child had died; he told himself over and over again that they had travelled to distant lands and perished in their journey. As the months went by he began to believe it. All his friends, all the people who came to his shop – none of them mentioned the fate of his young family. They could see his suffering and did not wish to add to it. They understood that the human mind is a strange creature. Unless it is reminded of something regularly, it gradually forgets about that thing. In that way we may forget about the most terrible things that happen in our world. Little by little, Tiger's memory began to lose its imprint of his wife and baby daughter until, truly, they ceased to exist in his world.

All that had happened a long time before Johnny showed up at his shop. Tiger's life had long since become settled. His business had been flourishing for many years and now he began to sink more and more into the comfort of his home, a modestly sized but comparatively luxurious stone-and-teak house on the outskirts of the little town. He filled it with exotic furniture – Portuguese chairs from Melaka, English pine tables treated with wax to protect against the humidity, painted chests of drawers from 'Northern Europe'. He had a formidable collection of books too. Marxist texts in Chinese, mainly, but also a number of English-language books, including a small collection of Dornford Yates novels.

In his spacious garden there was a small orchard. He tended to his fruit trees with great care. He especially loved the mango trees for their dark tongue-shaped leaves, which kept a thick shade all year round. Of all the fruits, however, he loved the rambutan best, and the ones he grew were considered particularly fine: deep red in colour and not too hairy. He took these down to the market where he sold them wholesale. The few cents he made from this gave him as much pleasure as the hundreds of dollars he made each month from trading textiles and clothing, and so he began to devote more time to his garden. He pruned the trees so that their shapes would become more attractive and their new branches more sturdy; he agonised over which trees to use for grafting new stock; he tied paper bags over the best fruit to protect them from flying foxes and insects.

For Tiger, it turned out to be perfect timing that, just then, a strong, hungry-looking young man came asking for work at the Tiger Brand Trading Company.

When Johnny first arrived in town, he did what he always did. He drifted into the nearest coffee shop and had a glass of iced coffee and a slice of bread with condensed milk. He asked the shopkeeper for work – there wasn't any. Coffee shops were usually poor sources of work, for they were almost always small enough to be run by the members of a single family. Out on the street, he stopped a few people and asked them where they thought he might find work. All of them echoed what the coffee shopkeeper had told him: 'Tiger Tan's well-known shop,' they said, pointing at a large shophouse in the middle of a terrace on the main street. It was a busy-looking place which seemed to be full of expensive, high-quality merchandise. He realised, as he approached the shop, that fine red dust had settled all over his clothes during his three-hour journey from Tanjung Malim.

'I'm looking for work,' he said to a girl unloading fat bales of cotton from a lorry. The girl jerked her chin in the direction of the shop. 'Ask boss,' she said.

Johnny hesitated before going in. The shop smelled clean and dustless. There were many customers inside, and there was laughter and a rich hum of voices, punctuated with the click-clack of an abacus.

'Yellow shirt, over there,' the girl said as she pushed past Johnny.

Johnny looked over to a darkened corner. A neatly dressed

man sat quietly in front of a pile of papers and a small money box. He had kicked off his shoes and was sitting with one ankle resting on the knee of another. Every few seconds he lifted his chin and fanned himself with a sheaf of papers. His hair was combed and brilliantined.

'I want work,' Johnny said simply. 'I am a labourer.'

Tiger looked at him hard, assessing him quickly. After all these years he had become a sharp judge of character. It was well known that Tiger could see things in you that you might not have realised yourself.

'What's your name?' he asked Johnny.

'Lim.'

'Where are you from?'

'Nowhere.'

'What do you mean, nowhere? Everyone comes from somewhere.'

'I mean, I don't know.'

'OK – where have you just arrived from?'

'Tanjung Malim.'

'Before that?'

'Grik – and before that Kampung Koh, Teluk Anson, Batu Gajah, Taiping.'

'That's a lot of places for a kid like you,' Tiger said. This boy looked perfectly ordinary to him – no distinguishing physical features, nothing unusual in his behaviour. He could have been any one of the young drifters who turned up at the shop from time to time. And yet there was something curious about this particular one, something which, unusually, Tiger could not put his finger on. 'Tea?' he said, offering Johnny a chair.

Johnny sat down, his baggy shorts pulling back slightly to reveal hard gnarled knees criss-crossed with scars.

'Of all the jobs you did,' continued Tiger, 'which one did you work at the longest?'

'Yeo's plantation.'

'Near Taiping?'

'Yes.'

'Yeo's pineapple plantation, right? The boss is Big-Eye Chew – that one?'

Johnny nodded.

A small smile wrinkled Tiger's eyes. 'Why did you like it?'

'I liked the other workers,' Johnny said, looking at his reddened, dust-covered canvas shoes. 'I liked the way they lived. Together. The bosses too.'

'I know that camp well.'

'The workers there were like me. But I couldn't stay. I had to go.'

'Why?'

'I had done bad things, people said.'

'Sometimes that happens.'

Johnny cleared his throat. Tiger poured more tea.

'What are you good at?'

'Everything,' Johnny said, 'except machines.'

Johnny proved to be one of the most diligent employees ever to have worked at the Tiger Brand Trading Company. He began by doing what the other casual workers did – packing, loading, storing, sorting. Back-breaking work. But Johnny was not like the other illiterate workers. He observed and he learned. Soon, he knew the names of all the different textiles he handled, and how they were made. He learned to tell the difference between chintz and cretonne, Chinese silk and Thai silk, serge and gabardine. He especially liked the printed patterns of milkmaids and cowsheds on the imitation French cotton made in Singapore. But more than anything, he loved the batik and the gold-woven *songket* which were delivered to the shop by the old cataract-eyed Malay women who had made them, here in the valley.

'Put them on the last shelf, over there,' Tiger snorted, pointing to a recess in the farthest corner of the shop, every time a new supply was delivered. 'Low-grade rubbish.' Compared to the imported foreign material, it was true that the batik was rough. The dyes were uneven and the patterns, traced out by hand, were never consistent. The colours faded quickly even on the best ones, leaving only a ghostly impression of the original shades. But Johnny liked the irregular patterns. He must have, because later in his life, when he could afford to wear anything he wanted, he would always wear batik for special occasions such as Chinese New Year or Ching Ming. They were his lucky shirts too. He would wear them if one of his horses was running in a big race in Ipoh, and sometimes, if he had to put on a jacket and tie, he would wear a lucky batik shirt *under* his starched white shirt, even though it made him hot and sweaty. He had red ones, blue ones and green ones. The blues were my favourite. From far away, when he wasn't looking, I used to trace the outlines of the patterns with my eyes. Brown dappled shapes stretched like sinews, swimming in the deep pools of the blue background. On his back these shadows danced and shifted quietly – hiding, folding over, tumbling across one another.

In Tiger's shop, however, batik was considered second-rate, hardly worth selling. You didn't go to Tiger Tan if you wanted to buy ordinary material made in broken-down sheds in Machang.

'Remember,' Tiger said to his employees, 'this is a place where little dreams are sold.'

Before long, Johnny was given more important tasks, such as counting stock and then, finally, serving customers. Tiger gave him two new white shirts to wear when serving in the shop, and Johnny kept them clean and neatly pressed at all times. It turned out he was a natural salesman with an easy style all his own. Like Tiger, Johnny was never loud nor overly persuasive. He pushed hard yet never too far. He cajoled but rarely flattered. Although he always tried to sell the most expensive things in the shop, he knew it was better to sell something cheap than nothing at all. He had a sense for what each customer wanted, and he always made a sale.

The incident with the White Woman, for example, became legendary. Like so many other things in Johnny's life, this incident seemed to happen without the faintest warning or explanation. Why she should have picked him instead of any other person in the shop no one will ever know. Perhaps there was no reason at all, just one small step on the curious path of fate.

The White Woman was a mixed-race widow of great and strange beauty. She stood a full six feet tall and although all who saw her agreed that her features were striking, none could agree on exactly what her features were. Everyone said different things of her face. Was she moon-faced or gaunt? Doe-eyed or cruel? Butter-skinned or powdery-white? She was the mistress of a rubber planter in the valley, a Frenchman named Clouet ('Kloot' was how people pronounced it) who drank too much *samsu* and did not care for his plantation. He had suffered badly in the great crash at the start of the thirties and now all he had left were a few hundred acres of dry rubber trees and a wife who hated the mosquitoes and skin rot of the tropics. He had a woman he loved, but their lives were a forked path. He could not live with her nor be seen in public with her for fear of losing his job. He wasn't even allowed to take her with him into the Planter's Club. Every so often, her washing lady would come into town and spread gossip about Clouet taking the White Woman away to France. But everyone knew it would never happen.

A hush crept across the shop when she entered. She stood for a second, casting her gaze from shelf to shelf, inspecting the bales of cloth and the neat piles of folded-up clothing. Three times a year, she came into Tiger's shop to buy the best of the new merchandise. Usually, she would send a note in advance of her visit to let Tiger know when she would be arriving and what she needed to buy. In addition to all the usual items on a wealthy woman's list, such as French tablecloths and plain unbleached Indian cotton for the servants' clothing, she would also include camisoles or nightdresses because she knew that Tiger would prepare discreet little parcels for her, protected from the gaze of the other customers. Tiger would make sure that he was personally on hand to receive her, but on this occasion, no note preceded the visit. The White Woman had unexpectedly passed through Kampar. The recently built bridge at Teluk Anson had been swept away by floods the month before and work on a new one had not yet started. Her diverted journey took her too close to Tiger's shop for her to resist temptation. Tiger, however, was not there that day, and all who were present in the shop noticed her displeasure. She kept her hat on and picked at the beads on her purse while she looked around the shop, casting her gaze upon the assistants until finally, her scowl came to rest on Johnny.

'I will assist you if you wish,' Johnny said. He was the only one of the people in the shop who dared to speak.

'Where is Mr Tan?' the White Woman said.

'He is away today – on business,' Johnny said. 'I am in charge today.'

The White Woman approached the counter and laid her purse on the glass cabinets displaying lace handkerchiefs. Johnny noticed the soft black satin of the purse. Across the black surface, little beads were stitched meticulously into the shape of a dragon chasing a flaming pearl across a stormy sea.

'What would you like, madam?'

'Show me something beautiful,' the White Woman said, looking at Johnny. 'Do you think you can do that?'

Johnny looked her in the eye. 'I think so,' he said.

He moved slowly from one end of the shop to the other, touching bales of cloth, feeling their texture before deciding whether to take them or leave them. Sometimes he unfurled a length of fabric against the light and narrowed his eyes. No one in the shop knew exactly what he was looking for – he seemed to be searching for something hidden All this time the White Woman watched him with increasing fascination, her initial irritation beginning to fade. She could not figure out what this curious young man was doing. There seemed to be a mysterious logic to this actions – but what?

'Here,' he said at last, 'these will make you happy.'

'What's this one?' she said, feeling some cloth between her fingers. It was thin and silky with a single cream-coloured flower printed across it.

'It's French.'

'It doesn't look French to me. The pattern isn't very rich.'

'But it is French, madam, the very latest, I am told. You can wear it next to your body, even in the hot months. See how it touches your skin,' Johnny said, gently sweeping it over her hand.

'I'd use it for tablecloths.'

'This,' said Johnny draping another length of cloth over his shoulder, 'is very special.'

'It has no pattern at all.'

'That is true. But see how the light shines on it, and through it?'

'Am I to wear that?'

'Of course not. But your windows – are they big? I thought so. Use this to make curtains.'

'Curtains? Without a pattern?'

'I have seen them in the latest American magazines,' Johnny said, holding up the cloth in front of his face. 'I can see you but can you see me?'

'No.'

'Next, my favourite, something so beautiful it will take your breath away,' Johnny said, undoing a brown parcel.

'It's batik,' the White Woman said, plainly and somewhat quizzically.

He pushed a plate of pink lotus cakes towards her and refilled her teacup.

'We are exporting this,' Johnny said, dropping his voice to a whisper, 'to Europe. No one knows about this yet. This is specially made for us –'

'But it looks like ordinary batik.'

'A batch of the very same material with exactly the same pattern has just been sent to Port Wellesley for shipment to London, Paris, America.'

'I see.'

The people in the shop were intrigued. This was the first they had ever heard of batik being shipped to Europe. Their minds raced. Was it possible that the same sarongs used by their grandmothers would be used in London? How did Tiger keep this secret?

The order was placed, the notes counted out and the goods dispatched that same day to the White Woman's home.

'You sold her batik,' Tiger said over and over again, reaching for the whisky when he learned what had happened. 'She will never come back to the shop again.' His mood lightened, however, when he realised that Johnny had sold the entire stock of unsellable batik which had languished for many months at the back of the stock cupboards. He had also got rid of a large quantity of cheap Chinese gauze at a highly inflated price. The peony-printed satin, an expensive lapse in Tiger's judgement (he had over-ordered from the new mill in Singapore before he had even seen a sample), was sold without a single cent's discount.

After a few days a note arrived from the White Woman, thanking the Tiger Brand Trading Company for always keeping beautiful yet practical textiles in stock. The note singled out Johnny for special praise, and Tiger proudly showed it to all his customers. He also began to regard Johnny in a new light.

During the time he worked in the shop, Johnny lived in Tiger's house along with several other young men and women, all of whom (so Johnny understood) worked in one way or another for the party. Although they were all employed at Tiger's shop, their paths did not otherwise cross. In the evenings they went their separate ways, disappearing into the night and reappearing before daybreak for their communal breakfasts, always taken at 5.15. Johnny wondered what kind of things they did after they slipped out of the house at night. Attending passionate lectures, plotting attacks on administrative buildings across the valley, spying on VIPs in Ipoh, cleaning machine guns, setting booby traps deep in the jungle. Maybe they were even killing people. The thought made him shiver with excitement. He wanted to be with them.

Johnny himself had not yet experienced life as a true communist. Up to that point he had, of course, worked in many places run by people with communist leanings, but he had never yet been approached to *do* anything. Someone had given him a leaflet once. The words seemed cold on the thin paper, and did not arouse in him any feelings of duty. He tried reading some of the books on Tiger's shelves. He reached, first of all, for Karl Marx, though he did not know why. Perhaps he had heard that name before, or perhaps the simple, strong sound of the words as he read them slowly to himself compelled him to take it into his room. *Das. Ka-pi-tal.* He said it several times in the privacy of his room. His lips felt strange when they spoke, and he felt curiously exhilarated. But he had not understood anything in the book. Even the Chinese version was beyond his comprehension. What the words said was plain enough, but the meaning behind them remained hidden from him. He grew to prefer the English version. Every night he would look at the book, reading a few lines in his poor English, hoping he would suddenly find a trapdoor into that vast world he knew lay beyond the page. Somehow it made him feel more important, more grown-up, as if he was part of a bigger place.

One Friday afternoon when all the shops were closed and the muezzin's call drifted thinly across town, Johnny came across one of the other men in the garden. He was resting in the shade of a *chiku* tree, legs apart, sharpening a parang with smooth, strong strokes. His legs and bare torso were flecked with cut grass and his hands rough with dirt.

'I need to light a bonfire,' Johnny said, 'to burn grass and old leaves. When will you be finished?'

'I'm finished,' the man (Gun was his name) said.

Johnny started for the far end of the garden beyond the fruit trees where he kept the tools. The steady metallic ring of the sharpening blade cut the hot afternoon air.

'Hey,' Gun said, 'I heard about you.'

'What about me?' Johnny said, barely turning around.

'The Darby mine. Everybody knows.'

'So what? I can't even remember that.'

Gun began to laugh – a high-pitched wail, like a wounded animal's call in the middle of the jungle. 'Hey, brother, don't have that hard look on your face. You're a real big-time hero, don't you know that? Everyone talks about the guy who chopped that English bastard's leg off.'

'I didn't chop his leg off.'

'Sure, of course not,' Gun continued, eyes squeezed shut with laughter. 'Come, sit down.'

'Who told you – Tiger?' Johnny said, watching Gun carefully. The parang was balanced between Gun's knees, glistening and hot.

'No, everyone knows. Like I said, you're famous, brother. Why do you think you're still alive and healthy? Why do you think you're always able to find work? Have you thought about that? It's because we – our people – take care of each other here in the valley. In the whole damn bastard country, in fact. The whole bloody wide world. Do you agree?'

'I suppose.'

'OK, look. I'll explain something to you. Come, sit down I said. You're still new, fresh, as far as I can tell – even though you're one goddam murderer already!' Gun broke into laughter once more, baring his cigarette-stained teeth. 'You have backsides for brains, you have no idea about the work we do.'

'I know everything about the shop.'

Gun looked at him with narrowed eyes. 'Not the shop, you goddam idiot, the army. The communist army. M – C – P,' he said in a slow, under-the-breath voice. 'Know what that stands for? Malayan Communist Party. That's who we work for.'

'I knew that, sure,' Johnny said, kicking a clump of grass. 'Where do you work?'

'You think I'm going to tell you, you bloody dogshit? You're not one of us. Not yet anyway. Trouble is, Tiger wants you in the shop, not out there doing what the rest of us do.'

'What do you do?'

Gun lifted the parang and held its blade erect before Johnny's face. He looked at it with cold black eyes and smiled with his yellow-brown teeth. With a single fluid swipe of his arm he brought the blade down on to the ground before them. It sliced sharply into the earth, clinking against the tiny pebbles in the soil. He smiled at Johnny, the corners of his upper lip curling back hard. 'That's what we do.'

Johnny's face coloured, his blood ran hot. He had felt the rush of air against his cheek as the parang swept past him. He had seen the sun glinting off the blade. At last, he knew he was truly and irreversibly a communist.

'What I think,' Gun said, as he prised the parang from the soil and wiped it clean with his fingers, 'is that anybody who can cut up and kill an English big shot, well, that person might be very useful to us.'

'Will I fight for the liberation of man's soul from the chains of bourgeoisie?' Johnny said.

Gun stared at him blankly.

'What do you want me to do?' Johnny said.

Gun laughed. Johnny could not tell if it was in contempt or in friendship. 'That's up to Tiger,' he said.

The only problem with being a communist – for Johnny and for Tiger – was that it interfered with business. It interfered with running the shop and serving customers and deciding which clothes to display in the glass cabinets. For Tiger, the problem was one he had faced for many years now. He had become accustomed to it all – the rotten, ever-present fear of exposure and arrest, the risk of betrayal. Sure, he was among his people; and yes, he knew he had their trust. All the same, he was careful not to make enemies. He never took advantage of suppliers or customers. People are people, he told himself. A single vengeful word whispered in the ear of the District Police Inspector would be sufficient for Tiger to be locked up in Tambun Prison for the rest of his life. For more than a decade, this fine gentleman had coordinated the activities of the Perak guerrillas from the genteel surroundings of his shop. Now, as the 1930s drew to a close, the strain of this duplicity weighed heavily on him. The knowledge that he was sending young men to be shot, maimed or imprisoned for life began to disturb his sleep. He wanted to close his doors to the world, to shut himself in his home with his books and furniture and fruit trees, but no: the call from China was becoming more urgent, more violent. The Japanese were in Manchuria now and Chinese all over the world were being called to arms. These were times for action, the party said, for the enemy was at the gate; but all Tiger longed for was to grow the perfect guava. He felt age in his bones and reluctance in his heart. In his sleepless nights he had the same thought over and over again: he had to stop, he could not go on.

He was glad he had Johnny.

Early one evening when the sun had calmed to a deep amber,

an idea came into Tiger's head which made him shiver gently with happiness. He had spent the day planting papaya seedlings he had grown from the seeds of his own fruit. Though the work was not heavy, it was enough to make a man of his age feel as if he had earned a rest. After dousing himself with cold water he sat in the cane armchair in his library with his supper of cold noodles. When he finished those he poured himself a small glass of cognac. He had not been to the shop at all that day. He thought of Johnny, he thought of the customers; he tried to fill his ears with the noise of the shop, the smooth-sharp sound of heavy scissors cutting through cloth, Johnny's low mumbling voice, the clink of coins on the glass counter. He wondered how the shop looked without him in it, and the image of the Tigerless place did not trouble him. He knew then that the Tiger Brand Trading Company would survive his death and, more than that, would flourish. His whole world – which he had created – would grow unendingly. The thought was cemented when, at that moment, he saw Johnny running up the stairs at the front of the house, leaping two steps at a time. Elation mixed with relief, that is what Tiger felt. Now he knew there was no more reason for him to continue the struggle.

'Johnny,' he called, no longer able to keep his thoughts to himself.

'What's the matter, Tiger? Are you all right?' Johnny's brow creased with uncertainty.

'I want you to sit down with me,' Tiger said.

Johnny sat perched on the edge of a chair facing Tiger. He could feel the frame of the chair pushing through the thin upholstery, cutting into his buttocks.

'Courvosier?' Tiger said, holding up the bottle of cognac.

'No, thank you.'

'It is said,' Tiger said, his face glowing and puce-coloured, 'that tending to your garden is good for your soul. I can certainly testify to that. After a day's work I feel cleansed. Funny, isn't it?' He chuckled gently.

Johnny looked mystified.

'I don't know how to explain this feeling to you. It is as if the work I put into looking after my plants makes me a better man. It makes me feel that I am a good person –'

'You are a good person –'

'– and for those few hours that I am in the garden, none of the bad things I have done in my life matter very much; they do not exist in my garden.'

'You have never done any bad things.'

Tiger smiled. 'Don't speak. Listen. You know I have worried about the shop. You know I am an old man now. That does not mean I do not care about the future of the shop, the future of everyone who works there, everyone who depends on the shop. I care. But I am old and tired, and soon I will die. I have spent much time in my garden lately, I know, but I feel no harm can come from this. Why? Because I have you, and you are ready for greater things.'

'Greater things,' Johnny repeated in his blank monotone.

'Yes, greater things! Tell me – what would happen to the shop if I was dead?'

'Do not say that.'

'But what if? What if? What would you do then?'

'Nothing. I don't know.' Johnny's face was stubborn and dull.

'Do you think the shop would survive?'

'Yes.' Johnny's reply was instinctive.

'Why do you think it will survive?'

Johnny did not answer.

'Because of you. All that is mine will be yours upon my death.'

Johnny did not protest, but remained expressionless as before.

The following weeks saw a small revolution in the textile business in the valley. Following the example set by the larger companies in KL and Penang, Johnny introduced village-to-village selling. It had always occurred to him that there were many people who might have wanted to visit the shop but, for one reason or another, were not able to. In many parts of the valley, the roads were little more than dirt tracks twisting through the jungle. When the rains came they washed mud on to the roads, and in the hot season the dust was so heavy and the sun so strong that a traveller could barely open his eyes. If these people could not come to the shop, Johnny thought, the shop would go to them.

Every Tuesday Johnny would cycle out into the jungle, taking with him a selection of cloths, heading for small villages beyond the reaches of the single tarred road running between Kampar and Ipoh. Each journey would last two full days and nights, and on the morning of the third day Johnny would reappear at the shop with no merchandise left on his bicycle. He built a little wooden platform on the back of his bicycle, fashioned from an old piece of teak which had once been the seat of a chair, worn smooth through years of use. Johnny lashed this tightly to his bicycle, and then tied the bales of cloth to it so that they stuck out at right angles. He soon became a familiar sight in the smaller villages of the valley – a stern-faced man riding a funny contraption which seemed less like a bicycle than a moving pile of textiles. The children looked forward to hearing the ring of his bell every few weeks, for he always brought with him a large bag of boiled sweets which he would distribute generously.

But sweets were not all Johnny brought. In each of the villages, he would seek out the people known to have communist sympathies. He brought news, from Tiger, of what the party was doing in the rest of the valley. He told them about secret lectures and campaigns to raise funds for the movement in China. He gathered information too, and soon he knew which farmers had sons who wanted to join the party, which villages were not sympathetic to the Cause, which people could be relied upon to provide donations. He knew the villages as he knew people – some were friends, some reluctant allies, others plain enemies. There were beautiful ones, ugly ones, dull ones, naughty ones. Soon he knew everything. More than Tiger himself.

On these trips Johnny began to feel a swelling sense of duty. Not only was he working to cement the future of the shop, he was imparting the word of the party. True, this wasn't quite the same as hand-to-hand combat in the jungle, but representing the party in his way was surely more noble and demanding. His way required cunning beyond that of a simple soldier. It required charisma and intelligence and, above all, the ability to read and write. In this respect Johnny had became superior to the other men, for he was now armed with literacy. On each journey to the outlying villages he took with him the Communist Manifesto in English, together with a pocket dictionary he had found in Tiger's library. He also took an exercise book in which he wrote out all the words he did not understand. Fraternity. Absolutism. Antagonistic. Jurisprudence. He wrote these down on one side of the page and on the other he wrote out the meanings of the words in Chinese, simplifying and paraphrasing them to facilitate the memorising process (Proletariat | Me). Then he simply looked at the lists of words, learning them by heart. As he cycled along the uneven tracks, veering to avoid the rocks and the potholes and craters carved out by the floods and the droughts, he spoke the English words aloud, letting the Chinese translations echo silently in his head. At first they seemed strange and fascinating. Sometimes his voice seemed not to belong to him – he did not recognise the person who made these wonderful sounds. But soon he grew to love these noises. He loved feeling the words form at the base of his throat and then well up in his mouth before dancing in the quiet jungle air.

When at home, he began to creep more frequently into Tiger's library. For a long time, this was a place which had intimidated and mystified him, but now it began to feel warmer. Its allure became stronger yet less forbidding. But which ones should he read? They were still indistinguishable from each other. He could by now read most of the words on the spines, but the names – they were names, weren't they? – remained shadowy and foreign. Once, he ran his fingers along the spines of a row of guava-coloured books, feeling the indented gold letters with his fingertips. Perhaps the touch of his flesh against the printed letters would suddenly reveal all kinds of hidden secrets. He came away, breathlessly, with *A Choice of Shelley's Verse* and something by Dornford Yates. Those two books kept him busy for many weeks. He filled three whole exercise books with lists of new words which would stay with him for the rest of his life. As an old man he would often quote Shelley, muttering under his breath if he thought no one was listening. The fitful alternations of the rain this, the Deep's untrampled floor that. I don't think he ever fully understood the meaning of it all.

From time to time, though, he still felt a shiver of excitement when he thought about the dark, rough life of a soldier like Gun. He had once visited the home of a small-village communist lieutenant and spied, through a half-open door, a rifle propped up against the wall. It leaned brazenly on the wooden slats like a household implement to be picked up and used casually at any time. That night Johnny slept in the next room, not ten feet from the gun. He dreamed he was walking barefoot through the night-clad jungle holding that same rifle. He walked into a clearing lit by a fire. It smelled of meat and mud. The men were laughing, their heads thrown back, their throats open wide. The gun was light in his hands as he shot each one of them in the head. When he woke he looked at his hands. They were strong and calm, but his pulse was throbbing heavily.

6. *Three Stars*

Some people are born with a streak of malice running through them. It poisons their blood for ever, swimming in their veins like a mysterious virus. It may lurk unnoticed for many years, surfacing only occasionally. Good times may temporarily suppress these instincts, and the person may even appear well intentioned and honest. Sooner or later, however, the cold hatred wins over. It is an incurable condition.

I can pinpoint the exact moment when I knew for certain that my father was afflicted with this terrible disease. I had just left school and announced my intention never to return to the valley. I was eighteen. I did not want to see the Harmony Silk Factory again. Father did not flinch at my words; he merely nodded and said, 'I will take you to your destination.' It was raining heavily as we drove through Taiping, where he was to drop me off at the bus station. We drove through the Lake Gardens, along avenues lined with umbrellas of dropping jacaranda. Raindrops found their way through the gaps in the barely opened windows and fell lightly on my arms. Without warning, Father slowed to a halt and got out of the car. He walked on to the grass and stood in the rain, gazing out at the silvery lakes. I had no desire to get wet, so I remained resolutely in the car; I had no idea what he was doing. At last I could bear it no longer and, holding a spare shirt over my head, ran towards him. I stood at his side for a while and suggested that we move on. He had a curious expression on his face, as if concentrating on something in the distance. 'Do you know,' he said quietly as if speaking to himself, 'the word "paradise" comes from the ancient Persian word for "garden".' I did not reply; I tried to remember if there had been an article on this subject in the latest *Reader's Digest*. 'The Persians had beautiful gardens. They filled them with lakes, fountains, flowers. They wanted to recreate heaven on earth.' His eyes blinked as the wind blew fine raindrops into his eyes. I looked into the distance, trying to locate what he was looking at. I thought, perhaps my father was capable of appreciating beauty; perhaps he was not completely black-hearted and mean after all. In the midst of the downpour I began to feel guilty that I had judged him harshly all these years. I was scared, too – scared of discovering someone I had never known, a different father from the one I had grown up with. But then I heard a sharp slap, and saw that he had swatted a mosquito on his neck. A small black-and-red smudge appeared below his jowl where he had caught the insect. 'Bastard,' he spat as he walked back to the car. His voice was as hard and cold as it always had been, and his eyes were set in anger. As we drove away I knew that I had been mistaken. That tender moment had been a mere aberration; it changed nothing. My father was born with an illness, something that had eaten to the core of him; it had infected him for ever, erasing all that was good inside him.

Why I did not inherit his sickness I do not know. Someone told me at Father's funeral that sons never resemble their fathers. What passes from elder to younger lies far beneath the surface, never to be seen or even felt. Perhaps this is true, but if the inheritance remains undiscovered, how are we to know it exists at all? I am merely thankful that I have never known any of my father's traits in myself. I could not, in a thousand years, comprehend the crimes he committed.

It did not take Johnny long to become known across the valley. As Tiger's right-hand man he automatically gained the respect of the people he met, and as Tiger became more withdrawn, Johnny's presence was felt more keenly than ever. People even began to seek Johnny before Tiger if they had any information to share or money to give. It was during this flowering of confidence that Johnny went to Tiger with a proposal.

'I want to give a lecture,' Johnny said. 'The kind you used to give, open to all. I have been reading, you see. Books.'

Tiger's eyes shone with pride. This boy was now truly a man.

'Nothing too big,' Johnny continued. 'I want to tell them about the books I have read. About *idealogy*.'

'Yes, i-de-*o*-logy. Good. Tell me, son, what has made you want to do this?'

'I want to help people – just as you have helped me.'

'How are our people these days? You have stopped bringing me news. I guess everything must be fine.'

'Everything is fine. One or two small things. Nothing bothersome. I don't want to trouble you with anything but the most serious.'

'I see . . . thank you. Is there anything on your mind?'

'No.'

'If there is something, you must tell me. You are a fine, capable man but you are not yet ready for the whole world.'

'Am I not?'

Over the next few weeks Johnny spread the word that he would, under Tiger's auspices, be holding a lecture in Jeram. Things were not going well in the party, he said. He had discovered this during his travels. There was a worm eating its way to the heart of the party and its awful progress had to be halted.

'A lecture? What kind of thing is that?' some people said.

'A big meeting,' said Johnny, 'with free beer for all.'

The lecture was held in a large wooden shack on the western fringes of the Lee Rubber Plantation near Kuah. The unruly shrubs of the jungle had crept in among the rows of rubber trees and it was difficult to see the paths leading to the shack. It was not a comfortable place. Many years ago it had been used to store processed rubber sheets, but it was too far from the administrative heart of the plantation and, long abandoned by the owners of the estate, it was now used as a not-so-secret place for local young men to meet and drink toddy and *samsu*.

The shack was nearly full, with people squatting or sitting cross-legged on the dirt-covered floor. A few kerosene lamps hung from rusty nails on the walls, casting a poor, dull light on the small assembly. When moths fluttered too close to the lamps, the light would flicker and pulse, and huge shadows would flash around the room.

'Strong leadership is key to survival,' Johnny said as he walked round the room. He was wearing a coarse green canvas shirt. On its breast the three stars of the MCP were stitched roughly into the fabric. With one hand he brandished a copy of the Communist Manifesto (in English, for added effect) and with the other he handed out bottles of warm Anchor. Most of the people there were too poor to buy beer and many had never even tasted it before. 'Without a strong leader we are doomed.' He spoke with the loud, authoritative voice he had been practising for some weeks. 'A weak leader, one who does not live with his men, is damaging to the Cause.' He grasped the three stars on his breast.

'Yes, damaging to the Cause!' several people roared, raising their bottles aloft.

'The Cause!' others echoed.

'This is no time to be soft. We cannot sit back and shake our legs. Resting On My Laurels, Westerners say. Look what's happening in China.'

'Look what's happening in China!'

'Look what's happening in China!'

Johnny suppressed a smile as he noticed the rapidly emptying beer bottles and reddening faces in the audience. 'If the Japanese Army invaded the valley next month,' he continued, 'would we be able to fight them? No! Why? Because we are not prepared. Why? Because our leaders are not strong.'

'Curse our leaders! Damn them!'

'If we are not properly led, then the Japanese, the British – anyone can destroy us,' Johnny said, opening a crate of whisky.

'No, no one can destroy us!'

'Not if our leaders are strong. But our leaders are not strong.'

Bottles of whisky were passed among the men and women in the room. They drank straight from the bottle, taking one sharp gulp before passing it on.

'What's that coward Tiger Tan doing, huh?' someone cried. 'Where is he?'

'Tiger? Who is that person? He is invisible nowadays.'

'He has done a lot of good in the past,' Johnny said.

'The past? Shit! What about tomorrow?'

'I was OK in the past but in the future I might be six feet under – because of Tiger!'

'Tiger is a good man,' Johnny said.

'But a weak leader!'

'A weak leader!'

'Johnny should be our leader!' someone said, and soon there was a chorus of similar voices. Over and over they chanted his name.

Johnny smiled. 'Tiger is a good man,' he said simply.

I have often wondered how Johnny must have felt when he cycled back from his triumphant lecture, tasting real power for the first time. I imagine his eyes black and hard, his mind calculating, always calculating. I have travelled along many of those same tracks, both as a child and as an adult. The roads are surfaced now, mile after mile of broken grey bitumen. There are still many potholes; not even tar can withstand the force of a flash flood. Recently, I decided I would cycle the route from Jeram to Kampar, from the site of the long-destroyed shack to where the Tiger Brand Trading Company once stood. I did not know where to begin this journey. The jungle had long ago swallowed up the old rubber plantation, so I made a rough guess and skirted along the notional western border of the vanished estate. The hut and the rows of rubber trees were no longer there, of course. They were only phantoms of the mind now.

I struck out for Kampar in the weakening five o'clock sun. The road was deserted. There was – is – little reason for anyone to visit Jeram, and in many places the surface of the road was hidden under layers of pale mud. The rain had carved shallow gullies in this mud, and I decided to follow these scars, travelling in broad arcs along the road. I imagined they were Johnny's tracks, made just after his lecture. They were not straight because he had been intoxicated with power. Like Johnny, I cycled like this for many miles, my sweat-soaked shirt stuck to my back and my eyes blinded by the sun.

Still I could not feel Johnny's wild excitement; I could not understand.

His thoughts did not become mine, and so I cannot tell you why he would go on to do the things he did.

A month after the lecture, Tiger Tan was found dead in a clearing in the jungle not far from his home. He had been shot twice, in the face and in the heart, though the post-mortem could not determine which shot had killed him. Either way, it seems certain he knew his killer. The shots were clean and accurate, fired from very close range, suggesting that he had been in the company of his murderer. Of his face, all that remained was his mouth. In the numerous newspaper reports following his killing, his mouth was described simply as being 'open'. It was obvious to all, however, that the wide-open mouth was an expression of shock and terror, his last stifled cries ringing hollow in the endless jungle. Maybe he did not even cry out. Maybe he opened his mouth one last time to ask 'Why?' It was a terrible way to die, for sure. Many years later, a young boy who did not believe in the Legend of Tiger Tan went fishing in the area where Tiger was killed. Perhaps he even walked over the exact spot where Tiger's body lay. As he waded through the cold shallow water, he became aware of a man strolling aimlessly through the trees. The man kept appearing and then disappearing in the dense foliage. He was wearing old simple clothes and he seemed to be talking to himself. 'Must be a madman,' the boy chuckled to himself as he continued fishing. As he was leaving the jungle, the boy heard that the man was repeating the word 'Why' over and over again. 'Why what, old man?' the boy called out as he approached him. It was only when the figure turned round that the boy saw his face, a seething, boiling mass of shapeless flesh.

Nothing had been stolen from Tiger's pockets. Neither his gold wristwatch nor his jade ring had been taken. Later, the police gave these items to Johnny. They folded them up in a white brocade cloth the Chief Inspector had bought from Tiger's shop some time before, and placed the delicate parcel in a black lacquer box. They brought it to the shop, where Johnny was making preparations for the funeral. They bowed low and gave Johnny the box. Witnesses to this scene say that the great Johnny, who was never known to cry, had 'blood-red' eyes, 'glasslike' with tears. He accepted the box graciously and said quietly, 'This is the beginning of a new time.' All who were present felt the truth of these words.

The box remained with Johnny for the rest of his life – a symbol of triumph, perhaps, or at least the start of a new life.

The funeral lasted three days, during which the shop remained closed as a mark of respect. On the third day, once the minor ceremonies were over, the final offerings to Tiger's spirit were made in the middle of Kampar. Anyone who had ever known Tiger was free to attend. A crowd began to gather before the morning became hot. Many people had travelled overnight to attend the occasion, and now stood waiting patiently for their turn before the great, dead man. Even small children queued up to pay their respects. When they approached the coffin they peered nervously at the body. '*Pai!*' their parents commanded, and so they did, bowing their heads and lowering their burning joss sticks three times.

Little bundles of paper money marked with silver and gold were handed out to all those who came. Each person took this paper money and dropped it into a huge tin drum which held within it a fierce fire, a bonfire of heavenly money for Tiger's afterlife.

During the days of the funeral Johnny was the focus of attention. He was seen everywhere, organising everything, talking to everyone. Many people remarked how difficult it must have been for him and how well he was coping, but then again they didn't expect any less. Here was a great man, they said, a pupil in the mould of the teacher, a son in the image of the father.

In the middle of the afternoon, while people waited for the priest (who was late) to arrive, a cloth supplier was seen to approach Johnny. No one heard his exact words, but it became widely known that he asked to speak about business arrangements with Johnny now that Tiger was dead. Perhaps he wanted payment up front; perhaps he wanted to withdraw the shop's credit for the time being; maybe he even threatened to expose the shop's communist links in order to extort larger payments from Johnny. Perhaps he had simply misjudged Johnny's character, believing that the young man would not be as firm as old Tiger had been. He was wrong. Johnny turned on him with cauldron-black eyes and struck him with a single smooth blow administered with the back of the fist. The man's entire body spun from the force of the blow and collapsed on the floor. Johnny had his men drag the man out on to the dusty road, where he was left to recover in dazed silence, in full view of the scores of mourners. None of them had any sympathy for him, and a few even rounded on him, telling him he should be ashamed at his lack of courtesy. No one was deeply sad when they heard, some months later, of reports from Penang of this man's death by stabbing in a bar fight in Georgetown.

Johnny had arranged for an altar to be built in the shop. White marble framed with carved jade – nothing too showy. A photograph of Tiger was set into the smooth marble face. It was a picture from his younger days, hair waxed and neatly combed, his gentle smile revealing only one gold tooth. An offering to Tiger was laid out before this altar, chrysanthemums and boiled eggs and a poached chicken. An earthenware jar was placed here too, full of burning joss sticks lit by the processing mourners who came to bow to Tiger's image.

Not a word was said when Johnny took over the Tiger Brand Trading Company, running and controlling every aspect of its business as Tiger had before him. It seemed perfectly natural that this should be the case. In fact, it might be said that the people of the valley would have been shocked if Johnny had not taken over. There was a new sense of urgency at the shop. Business was as brisk as it ever had been, but both the workers and the customers noticed that there was more energy in the shop now. No one could explain this – it came from Johnny, was their simple explanation. Small things changed too. New light bulbs were fitted, making the shop less gloomy, so it could stay open later, well after dark. People would call in for a chat on their way to dinner. They would share jokes with Johnny and with each other as he counted up the day's takings. The light in the shop made everything look golden.

Very soon, people began to forget about Tiger. For a time, however, there was talk about who might have killed him. The police? Unlikely. They didn't have enough evidence about Tiger's 'other' activities. A rival businessman? Never. Tiger had no rivals, and besides, without Tiger there would be no business. A rogue bandit? No – remember he still had his valuables with him. Most likely it was a traitor, a police informant whom Tiger had taken aside to reprimand. The man (or woman) had panicked and shot Tiger. But some people – generally when drunk – began to say things about Tiger, things no one would have dared to say before. They said maybe he deserved it. He had got fat and lazy and he enjoyed his money just a little bit too much. Sure, he'd done a lot for the party, but he'd become a danger. He wasn't the one cycling from village to village keeping the Cause alive in the valley. He wasn't the one making money for the shop, money that could buy food and clothes for our boys in the jungle. All Tiger did was to tend to his goddam fruit trees. Sometimes he was even seen picking weeds from the grass in his garden, for God's sake. What a stupid thing for a man like Tiger to do. They weren't saying that they were happy he was dead, but they weren't saying they were sad either.

Johnny still found time to visit the odd village as he had done before, but his old contacts knew that their boy was now a man, and now they would have to travel to him. A few times a year he organised lectures which grew less clandestine and more well attended. At these events there was generous hospitality, free food and drink for everyone. There was less lecturing, more laughing. The people loved him. Like us all, they wanted someone to worship and adore, and so they poured their hopes and fears into this young man who they did not, and never would, truly know.

It was at this point in his life, when he was just becoming a famous man, that Johnny met my mother.

7. *Snow*

My mother, Snow Soong, was the most beautiful woman in the valley. Indeed, she was one of the most widely admired women in the country, capable of outshining any in Singapore or Penang or Kuala Lumpur. When she was born the midwives were astonished by the quality of her skin, the clarity and delicate translucence of it. They said that she reminded them of the finest Chinese porcelain. This remark was to be repeated many times throughout her too-brief life. People who met her – peasants and dignitaries alike – were struck by what they saw as a luminescent complexion. A visiting Chinese statesman once famously compared her appearance to a wine cup made for the Emperor Chenghua: flawless, unblemished and capable both of capturing and radiating the very essence of light. As if to accentuate the qualities of her skin, her hair was a deep and fathomless black, always brushed carefully and, unusually for her time, allowed to grow long and lustrous.

In company she was said to be at once aloof and engaging. Some people felt she was magisterial and cold, others said that to be bathed in the warm wash of her attention was like being reborn into a new world.

She was magical, compelling and full of love, and I have no memory of her.

She died on the day I was born, her body exhausted by the effort of giving me life. Her death certificate shows that she breathed her last breath a few hours after I breathed my first.

Johnny was not there to witness either of these events.

Her death was recorded simply, with little detail. 'Internal Haemorrhaging' is given as the official cause. Hospitals then were not run as they are today. Although many newspapers reported the passing of Snow Soong, wife of Businessman Johnny Lim and daughter of Scholar and Tin Magnate TK Soong, the reports are brief and unaccompanied by fanfare. They state only her age and place of death ('22, Ipoh General Hospital') and the birth of an as yet unnamed son. For someone as prominent as she was, this lack of detail is surprising. The only notable story concerning my birth (or Snow's death) was that a nurse was dismissed on that day merely for not knowing who my father was. As Father was absent at the time, the poor nurse responsible for filling in my birth certificate had the misfortune to ask (quite reasonably, in my opinion) who the child's father was. The doctor roared with shock and disgust, amazed at the nurse's ignorance and rudeness. He could not believe that she did not know the story of Johnny Lim and Snow Soong.

Snow's family was descended, on her father's side, from a long line of scholars in the Imperial Chinese Court. Her grandfather came to these warm southern lands in the 1880s, not as one of the many would-be coolies but as a traveller, a historian and observer of foreign cultures. He wanted to see for himself the building of these new lands, the establishment of great communities of Chinese peoples away from the Motherland. He wanted to record this phenomenon in his own words. But like his poorer compatriots, he too began to feel drawn to the sultry, fruit-scented heat of the Malayan countryside, and so he stayed, acquiring a house and – more importantly – a wife who was the daughter of one of the richest of the new merchant class of Straits Chinese. This proved to be an inspired move. His new wife was thrilled to be married to a true Chinese gentleman, the only one in the Federated Malay States, it was said. He in turn was fascinated by her, this young *nonya*. To him she was a delicate and mysterious toy; she wore beautifully coloured clothes, red and pink and black, and adorned her hair with beads and long pins. She spoke with a strange accent, the same words yet a different language altogether. This alliance between ancient scholarship and uneducated money was a great success from the start, especially for Grandfather Soong (as he came to be known), who was rapidly running out of funds.

His talent for finding an appropriate partnership appears to have passed on to his son TK, who proved to be even more astute. While managing to cling on to his father's scholarly heritage, TK also managed to learn the ways of the new Chinese – the ways of commerce and industry. He did so through his wife, Patti, who was the daughter of no less a person than the *kapitan* of Melaka's right-hand man. TK and Patti were a formidable pairing indeed.

TK had always shown exceptional promise, even as a young boy. He passed his examinations in law at the University of Malaya with the highest honours and for a brief spell studied at Harvard before impatience, boredom and cold weather brought him home. For a while, he considered pursuing a career in banking in Singapore, but opted instead to return to the valley, where there were none of the distractions that abounded in Singapore – nightlife, foreign money, women. He was a notable calligrapher and painter, and his home was decorated with many scrolls of Tang poems, written in his own flowing hand. Many of them have been rehung in that old house, the same house which was Snow's home and, briefly, Johnny's too. The house is now inhabited by Patti's relatives – my cousins, I suppose, though I do not know them.

Like me, TK was the only son of a wealthy family in an area where wealthy families were uncommon. People would have known and talked about him simply because of who he was, even before he had done anything of note. It is a difficult thing to live with. When you know that everyone talks about you behind your back, while looking at you with silent eyes, it can sometimes have an effect on you. For although people may admire your standing in life, they may also boil with jealousy and hatred. It makes you think differently from other people, and eventually it distorts your personality. That was the case with TK. A young man like him wearing smart Western clothing and spending his time painting would have aroused much comment. In the end, it was the burden of what other people said that made TK settle down and build a life and a family for himself, just as his father had before him.

First, he changed his appearance. He swapped his Western suits for the traditional Chinese clothes his father once wore, the attire of a Manchu civil servant – long shirts made of the richest brocade, trousers of plain, good silk. This kind of dress was no less conspicuous in rural Malaya, and many people thought it was merely a phase which he would soon leave behind. But he persisted with it to the end of his days; it is how he is dressed in the stiffly posed photographs that survive. He continued reading classical Chinese texts; he wrote and he painted. But his demeanour changed. Whereas before he had been flamboyant and easily excitable, now he was serious and calmly spoken. At last, sighed his parents, he took an interest in business. He benefited from family connections and became involved in large-scale enterprises such as commercial loan-making and the import and export of tin and rubber to Europe. He got married too.

Patti was said to have been a woman of notable beauty, although to my eyes hers must have been a beauty of that particular age. Certainly, the worn sepia-tinted portraits do not do any of their subjects justice, but even so, she appears sullen and withdrawn. If you look closely, you can see where Snow inherited the cold streak that she was said to have possessed. Patti's mouth is drawn tight and thin, her eyes hard and dark. Her looks are not dissimilar to her daughter's but her beauty (if it is beauty) is of a harsher variety.

Though I close my eyes and search my memory I cannot recall ever having seen TK and Patti Soong, my grandparents. They exist only as ghosts, shapeless shadowy imprints on my consciousness. Sometimes I wonder if there is any chance that I might have liked them, loved them. Even ghosts and shadows are capable of being loved, after all. But always, the answer is 'No'. I would not have loved them even if I had known them, because when the debits and the credits have been weighed, TK and Patti fall on the wrong side of the line between good and evil. It was their desire for Snow, my mother, to marry a rich man that pushed her into the arms of Johnny. Nothing can ever atone for that.

By the time Snow was of marriageable age, Johnny was already well known across the valley. He was the sole owner of the most profitable trading concern in the valley and was widely admired in all circles. As with all beautiful young women of a certain background, Snow had already had a good deal of experience of suitors and tentative matchmaking. All of these possibilities had been created and choreographed by her parents. They took her to Penang, KL and Singapore, where she was displayed like a diamond in a glass box. Yet it was closer to home, at the races in Ipoh, that they found the first serious contender. He was a beautiful-looking boy with a powder-pale complexion to match Snow's. He had large, clear eyes and stood tall and erect with all the dignity you would expect from a son of the Chief Superintendent of Police. When he was introduced to Snow he kissed her hand – *kissed* it – a gesture he had learned during his days travelling in Europe. He complimented Patti on her sumptuous brocade dress and quietly whispered a tip for the next race in TK's ear.

It wasn't long before Snow and the Superintendent's son were allowed to take tea together. They sat exchanging polite conversation. She talked about books – novels she had read – while he nodded in agreement. Although TK and Patti were pleased with his dignified manner and solid background, it was his family's home which brought greater excitement to them, for the Superintendent had recently built a modern, Western-style house in which many of the rooms had wall-to-wall carpets. The main dining room had one wall of pure glass so that it served as an enormous window. Such daring was indicative of considerable wealth, an impression which was confirmed by the quality of the jade jewellery worn by the boy's mother: dark in colour with a barely marbled texture. To top it all, Snow and the boy looked such a pretty pair and would surely attract all the right comments when the time came for them to venture into the public eye.

Thankfully, before such an understanding was reached between the parents, TK and Patti discovered that the boy's parents were not quite as wealthy as they seemed. The Superintendent's lavishness at the races had taken its toll on the family's finances, and it was thought that much of his wife's fabulous jewellery was borrowed from sympathetic relatives. It was clear that the dowry which TK and Patti expected in return for the hand of their daughter could never be fulfilled.

Scarred by this experience, TK and Patti became cautious and especially thorough in their appraisal of potential suitors. They asked many questions, they made enquiries. They did not want to make the same mistake twice. In letting the match with the Superintendent's son progress to the extent it did, TK and Patti had been careless. One such mistake was forgivable; two mistakes would not be. Not only would it reflect badly on them, it would also diminish the value of Snow's attractiveness. The size of the dowry would almost certainly be smaller. Yet their diligent investigations made the prospect of a match more and more remote. Every search turned up some unpleasant detail about the family in question, ranging from full-blown scandals to questionable associations: lunatic grandfathers, homosexual uncles, bastard children, gambling debts, hushed-up divorces.

The plain truth of it was that it was 1940, and there was little money in the valley, certainly nothing that could match the wealth of the Soong family. Snow was not yet twenty. There was still time, but a suitable match *had* to be made soon.

For all their meticulous planning, TK and Patti's first proper meeting with Johnny was precipitated by events beyond their control. It so happened that a new man was appointed as head of the British mining concern in the valley, a fine young gentleman called Frederick Honey. He arrived with impeccable credentials, having gained a rugger Blue at Oxford and a keen grasp of tropical hygiene and colonial law from the School of Oriental Studies. His reign over the British tin-mining enterprise was, ultimately, short-lived, for he was lost to a boating accident in 1941, when he drowned in the waters off Pangkor island in a treacherous monsoon storm; his body was never found. It is clear, however, that during his short tenure in the valley, he was much admired. TK Soong was, as you can imagine, quick to see the value of having Mr Honey as an ally, and eager to make an impression on this formidable new *tuan besar* as soon as possible. It was decided in the Soong household that a gift should be sent to Mr Honey, something instantly suggestive of the Soongs' status and influence in the valley; something unusual and beyond the reach of an Englishman newly arrived in the country. But what? A whole roast pig, perhaps? No – too ostentatious. A scroll of the finest Chinese calligraphic paintings? No – not grand enough.

'How about some textiles,' Patti said in desperation to her husband. 'From that man, what's his name – Johnny Lim?'

TK paused. He was inclined to dismiss the idea at once, but the paucity of previous suggestions persuaded him to consider for a moment. He paused for quite some time. 'It'll be fruitless,' he said, but nonetheless decided to summon Johnny to the house.

Johnny had long since ceased to tour the countryside by bicycle, but the call of TK Soong was one he could not resist. He arrived at the house and found himself seated in the enormous room in which the Soongs received their visitors. Its vastness amazed him; his eyes could barely take in the details of its space: the rattan ceiling fans rotating slowly, arrogantly, barely stirring the air; the softness of the light through the louvred shutters; above all, the books, which lined an entire wall, row after perfect row.

'We have heard many good things about you,' TK said as

Johnny began to unpack his bags on the table which had been specially set up for him. 'Thank you,' he said, still marvelling at the books.

Behind his back Patti tugged at TK's sleeve. 'How old is he?' she whispered. She had heard that Johnny Lim was a young man, and in her mind's eye had pictured a wild-haired, loud-mouthed tearaway with dirty fingernails. Yet before her stood someone neat and compact, who seemed almost middle-aged, whose movements were laborious and heavy with experience. A fleeting image tickled her imagination: Johnny and Snow seated on bridal thrones of the type that perished with the death of nineteenth-century China. 'I must say, Mr Lim,' she said as she fingered a piece of English chintz, 'now that I see your wares, I can understand why people are so complimentary about you. About your shop, I mean.'

Johnny lowered his head and did not answer. He unfolded a length of *songket*, its gold threads shining and stiff and stitched into an intricate pattern.

'This piece of cloth, for example,' Patti continued, running her hand over a piece of brocade, 'is very beautiful. Very fitting for a woman, wouldn't you say?'

Johnny nodded.

'Not for an old woman like me, of course, but for a younger woman. Do you agree, Mr Lim? It must be very popular with fashionable ladies.'

'No, not really,' he said truthfully. 'It's too expensive.'

'Ohh, Mr Lim,' Patti laughed. 'Truthfully, do you think it would suit a young woman? No one very special or very beautiful, of course.'

Johnny half shrugged, half nodded.

'Would you mind if I asked my daughter to see this? I'm sure you're too busy to spend much time with her, but if you could spare a few moments –'

'I would be pleased to meet your daughter,' Johnny said. His pulse quickened. Even though he had heard about the Soongs' famous daughter he had not for a second thought that he would be introduced to her.

'I'm sure you're just saying that to be polite, Mr Lim,' Patti said with a laugh as she got up to leave the room. 'After all, my daughter is hardly worth meeting. I'm sure you will be disappointed.'

'I'm certain I will not.'

'If you insist,' Patti said, disappearing out of view.

A minute elapsed, and then another, before she reappeared. 'My daughter, Snow,' she said.

It took Johnny several moments to gather himself. She was a disappointment, a shock. He had expected a tiny, exquisite jewel, but instead he found himself looking up at a woman who seemed to tower endlessly above him. He breathed in, trying to swell his chest and lift his shoulders to make himself taller. When he looked at her face he found her staring intently into his eyes, and he quickly lowered his gaze. He felt embarrassed, cheated – though he did not know of what.

Poor Snow. She had grown used to being courted by lively, attentive men, but now she was confronted by a suitor who seemed more interested in his fingernails. At one stage she noticed he was gazing at a spot just above her collarbone, and for a brief moment she thought that he was staring at her neck. Then she realised he was looking at the books on the shelf behind her. She tried to engage him in conversation, but it was no use. This curious man sat like a deaf-dumb little orphan child before her. He was small and dark with an impenetrable moon-face. She searched for some clue as to what his character might be and concluded that there was none: no character whatsoever. She began to feel sorry for him. Later, her parents told her that he was a textile merchant, very rich and well known. Snow had not heard of him. As she watched him leave the house, she knew, from the glow of contentment on her parents' face, that all parties had reached an understanding. The negotiations – the courtship – would soon begin, but the business had already been concluded. That afternoon, TK and Patti had bought from Johnny a few lengths of *songket* and some hand-blocked European cotton, which would in turn buy them favour with the British. And as for Johnny, he had gained himself entry into a world he had always dreamed of.

Johnny and Snow's first organised meeting was, unusually, in public and unsupervised. TK and Patti felt that given Johnny's impeccable and restrained manners, it would not be imprudent to allow the pair to meet in such a way. They were not afraid of the gossip which would inevitably follow. This was, after all, an alliance they wanted people to talk about. All their instincts told them that this was a match they should be proud of.

When Johnny and Snow appeared at the new picture house in Ipoh, a gentle commotion broke out in the crowd. Every head turned to see if the whispers were true. Was that really Johnny Lim – at the pictures? And was he here with TK Soong's famous daughter? What did she look like? Where was she? For most people it was too much to bear, and throughout the film, a constant murmur of voices filled the auditorium. It was the first time many there had ever seen Snow. Men leaned forward in their seats, peering down the aisle just to catch a glimpse of the back of her head; women touched their own faces, noticing all of a sudden how plain they looked compared to her. And when the lights came up there was pandemonium. Johnny and Snow were nowhere to be seen.

Afterwards, the couple dined at the famous Hakka Inn. For Johnny, it was the realisation of many childhood fantasies. They were presented with roast suckling pig and jellyfish, black mushrooms and abalone, steamed grouper and a large dish of noodles.

These were things he had never eaten before. He felt ill at ease going to smart restaurants. They were too bright for him, too full of movement and voices, and he always felt as if he was being watched as he ate. He had only ever been to restaurants to celebrate the conclusions of particularly large business transactions. This time, he tried to think of the experience as the biggest business venture of his life. Because to him, it was.

Once Johnny had overcome his initial awkwardness, however, he began to notice how rich and sweet the food tasted. He ate quickly, sinking deliciously into this new-found land of honeyed aromas and silken textures. He was like the rat in the childhood proverb, dropped on to a mountain of fragrant rice grain.

'The food is good,' he said. She did not know if it was a question or a statement, so she simply nodded, and he returned to his solitary feast.

Snow watched him feed. She wondered, as she always did when she was sent to meet a new suitor, whether she would be happy with the man before her. She always took it for granted that she would end up as the man's wife. The choice was not hers, and accepting her fate early would make it less of a shock. So far she had not met anyone with whom she thought she could be happy. Even the Superintendent's son, beautiful though he was, would have been unsuitable as a husband. He was far too inward-looking and concerned with the neatness of his clothes to notice her. Living with him would have been like gazing at the stars. A marriage could not be happy if the husband was prettier than the wife, that much she knew.

This new man did not bring her much hope either. As she saw it, the problem was not that she considered herself beyond his reach (beautiful wives and ugly husbands often made good matches), but that he did not seem to appreciate that she was at all attractive. For a while she entertained the idea that he had been tragically hurt by the death of a lover. He had a reason for being withdrawn, a sad and compelling story. She looked closely at his face for signs of a life or a love lost. She found him attempting to force an entire black mushroom into his mouth. This particular one was larger than the others, and he was having difficulties. He stretched his mouth sideways like a smiling fish in order to accomodate it; his lips quivered in an attempt to accept the sumptuous gift from the chopsticks. Eventually he succeeded, but then, after a few uncomfortable chews, was forced to spit the mushroom on to his plate. It landed softly on the gravy-soaked rice, and he repeated the whole exercise, this time succeeding easily. His chopsticks immediately reached for another mushroom, and he noticed Snow looking at him. His lips were thick and slicked with grease.

'The food is good,' he said, raising his eyebrows slightly.

She nodded, eyes fixed on his lips. No, she thought, there is no love story here. He was not capable of love. It was better that she prepared herself for this now.

He walked her to the bottom of the steps leading up to her house. All the lights were out, which usually meant that Patti was listening at the darkened window.

'The evening was enjoyable,' Johnny said. Again, Snow was not sure if this was a question, but all the same she could not bring herself to agree.

'I am sure I will see you again,' she said, and went into the house, walking swiftly to her bedroom to avoid her mother's interrogation. Strangely, she did not hear Patti's footsteps nor the opening or closing of doors. The house was full of a confident, approving silence.

Six months later they were married, after a courtship which, as TK would say, was 'full of propriety and politeness'. Johnny moved into the Soongs' house while he searched for a new home for himself and his wife. During this time he revelled in the Soongs' hospitality, becoming so accustomed to it that he almost believed it was *he* who was being generous and welcoming: the lavish parties were thrown by *him*; the elaborate dinners were prepared by *his* cooks; the people who came to the house were *his* guests. To these guests, it seemed obvious that the sumptuous events were paid for by this rich new tycoon, and Johnny did nothing to dispel this presumption. Instead, he adopted a demeanour of excessive modesty to fuel the belief that he was indeed the magnanimous, yet somewhat reticent, host.

Guests: Thank you, Mr Lim, for such a splendid dinner.

Johnny (as self-effacingly as possible): Oh, please, no – thank Mr and Mrs Soong. This is, after all, their house. They have enjoyed having you here this evening, I know.

Guests (to themselves): What a noble, honourable man is Johnny Lim, too gracious even to accept thanks. How respectful to his elders, how civilised, etc., etc.

For the Autumn Festival in the year they were married, for example, the festivities at the Soong house were referred to as Johnny Lim's Party, even though he had nothing to do with it. That he played no part in its organisation is clear from the extravagant yet tasteful nature of the evening's revelry and the type of people who were in attendance. It was the first significant function at the Soong household since the marriage of Snow to Johnny, and it was an event that was talked about years afterwards. Many of the guests were English – and not just the District Education Officer either, but luminaries such as Frederick Honey and all the other *tuan besar* of the British trading companies. It is said that even Western musicians from Singapore were engaged to perform for the evening. A striking operatic troubadour, six and a half feet tall, sang whimsical songs in French and Italian. His face was daubed with theatrical paint which obscured his fine features, but even so, everyone present commented on the delicacy of his looks and the flamboyance of his costume – a flowing cape of Ottoman silk lined with iridescent scarlet. He sang so angelically and played the piano with such lightness of touch that no one could believe that he had not come directly from the great concert halls of Europe. 'What *is* someone like him doing here in the FMS?' people wondered aloud as he improvised familiar songs, teasing his audience. The noble Mr Honey sportingly lent himself to all the women as a dancing partner; he skipped to a traditional Celtic tune, linking arms with his companions as their feet clicked lightly on the teak floor-boards. Johnny stood awkwardly in a corner, surveying the scene, trying his best to seem proprietorial and calm. He smiled and tried to tap his foot to the music, but couldn't keep in time. A scuffle broke out among the servants in the yard outside, and it was up to the magisterial Mr Honey to restore peace. All night there was a constant stream of music to match the flow of alcohol. 'It's at times like these,' the guests said, watching Mr Honey regaling a group of men with stories of adventure, 'one almost feels glad to be in Malaya.' At the end of the evening, when the air was cool and the tired guests began reluctantly to drift home, they realised that the music was no longer playing; the lid of the piano was firmly shut. As the guests departed from the darkening house rubbing their aching temples, they struggled to remember what had happened throughout the course of that evening: it had been too wonderful to be true. Had he really existed, that painted troubadour? He had simply vanished, phantom-like, into the tropical night. What a marvellous party Johnny Lim had given, they thought; what a marvellous man he was. They certainly made a lovely couple, Johnny and Snow.

Only one photograph survives of my mother. In it, she is wearing a light-coloured *samfu* decorated with butterflies. The dress clings delicately to her figure, slim and strong like the trunk of a frangipani tree. Her hair is adorned with tiny jewels too small for me to identify. When I hold a magnifying glass to the picture the poor quality of the old paper makes the image blurred and soupy. Her face is young and soft. Sometimes, I stick the photo into the frame of a mirror so that I can see my own face next to hers. My eyes are her eyes, I think. The photo is too old to give me any more clues. I found it when I was fifteen, in an old tin box in Father's closet, together with the pictures of Tarzan. It was in a cracked leather frame far too big for it, and when I looked carefully I could see that it was because the photo had been carefully torn in half. Two, maybe three other people would have been in it, but only my mother and father remain, sitting close to each other but clearly not touching. They sit at a table at the end of a meal; before them the remains of their feast appear as dark patches on the white tablecloth. Behind them, merely trees. Beyond those, a part of a building – a ruin, perhaps, somewhere I do not recognise. I am certain it is not in the valley. Throughout the years I have looked at hundreds of books on ruins: houses, palaces, temples; in this country and abroad. Not one resembled the place in the photo. I do not know where it is. Perhaps it does not even exist.

On one side of this incomplete portrait, a hand rests on my mother's shoulder. It is a man's hand, of that I am certain. His skin is fair – that too is obvious. On his little finger he wears a ring, probably made of gold. It looks substantial, heavy. Time and time again I looked at the ring through my magnifying glass, but it gave me no clues. It was just a ring.

I took the picture and hid it in my bedroom. Father never mentioned it, and neither did I. I wanted to ask him whether there were any other photographs of my mother, but I never did, because then he would have known that I had stolen the picture. I never dared ask him about my mother; I never knew what questions to ask. Besides, I know he would not have told me about her even if I had. All I have to go on is that single photograph.

Whenever I look at it I fold it in half so that Johnny is hidden and I can only see my mother.

A few years ago, I did something I thought I would never do. I succeeded in visiting the old Soong home, the house which my mother and father lived in. I had always known where it was, tucked away a mile or so off the old coast road, west of the River Perak, yet I had never seen it. Partly this is because it is difficult to get to. There are no bridges here, and to get across the river you have to drive a long way south and then double back, travelling slowly northwards along the narrow roads that wind their way through the marshy flatlands. During the latter half of the occupation, the house was used by the Japanese secret police as their local headquarters. They brought suspected communists and sympathisers there to be tortured in the same rooms where TK and Patti and Snow and Johnny once slept. The cries of those tortured souls cut deep into the walls of the house, and when I was a boy I knew – as all children did – that the place was haunted. In those days I did not know that the house had been Snow and Johnny's. Back then it was merely one of those things which children feared in the same way they feared Kellie's Castle or the Pontianak who fed on the blood and souls of lone travellers on the old coast road. We were taught to fear these things and so we did, never once questioning them. We believed in those things as we believed in life itself. When, several years ago, I finally learned of the significance of the house, I simply smiled, as if someone had played a joke on me.

How funny it is that the history of your life can for so long pass unnoticed under your nose.

When I say I 'visited' the Soongs' old home, I am exaggerating slightly. My first attempt to visit the place was not entirely successful. I had planned everything meticulously, but in the end my efforts proved to be fruitless.

I decided to go as a Tupperware salesman. This was the first thought that came into my head and it seemed a sensible one, as Tupperware was all the rage in the valley at the time. I purchased a large selection of Tupperware in different colours and sizes and loaded it into my car. I stole a brochure from my dentist's waiting room and bought a new briefcase into which I packed several 'order forms' which I had typed myself. I put on a tie, of course, and combed my hair differently. I had allowed my hair to grow longer than usual, as I thought this would help me to feel like a different person. I gave myself one last look in the rear-view mirror of my car before I set off, and I was pleased with what I saw. My own mother would not have recognised me.

The door was answered by a pubescent child – a girl, I think, though she was dressed as a boy. I searched her face for a resemblance to me but found none. She stared at me with fierce eyes.

'What are you selling?' she snapped. She sounded much older than she looked.

'Tupperware,' I said, suddenly feeling confident at the sound of the word. I stepped aside and pointed at my car. Large piles of Tupperware rose into view through the windows.

'We don't need . . .'

'Tupp-er-ware,' I said slowly. 'Would you kindly ask your mother?'

'She's not here.'

'Anyone else here?'

She closed the door and bolted it. 'There's a tall man selling things,' I heard her call out to someone inside. When the door opened again a young woman stood at the entrance. She looked at me coldly but did not speak.

'I'm selling Tupperware,' I said. 'It's from America. It's very useful.'

She remained silent. I felt my nerve begin to weaken. I had to make a final attempt. 'May I come in and show you?' I smiled.

She held my gaze for several seconds. I held my breath to hide my nervousness and tried not to blink.

'OK,' she said and let me in.

I stood in the middle of the large sitting room and looked around me. The room led out to a verandah which ran along the entire length of the back of the house. Through the half-open shutters I could see that the land fell away to the jungle, which appeared as a soft green carpet. The walls of the room were decorated with long scrolls bearing Chinese calligraphy. They were executed in a flowing and flamboyant hand, the characters swirling and greatly exaggerated. One scroll caught my eye. It was the famous Tang poem by Li Po:

Moonlight shines brightly before my bed,
like hoar frost on the floor.
I lift my head and gaze at the moon,
I drop my head and dream of home.

'What are you looking at?' the woman said. She had a slim face and clear skin. She too looked nothing like me.

'I was just admiring your calligraphy,' I said. 'It's very beautiful. Did you do it?'

'No,' she said, suppressing a smile. Her shoulders dropped and her voice became softer. 'No, that was done by my great-uncle.'

'Really?' I said. 'He must be a famous artist.'

She giggled. 'No, he wasn't. He's dead now. He died during the war. My family saved all his paintings from the Japanese, and we put them back on the walls just like they were when Great-Uncle TK was alive.'

'That's interesting. He died during the occupation, did he? What was his name? Maybe I've heard of him.'

'TK Soong,' she said. 'Say, you're asking a lot of questions, aren't you?'

'Oh, I apologise. It's not every day a poor salesman like me sees calligraphy of this standard, you see.'

She smiled again.

'And like I said, I may have known him.' I looked at the scrolls once more, keeping my back to her so she could not see my eyes. Though my head remained tilted upwards my gaze scanned the sideboards and cupboards for signs of photographs or mementoes – anything.

'I don't think you could have known him,' she said. 'How old are you, exactly?'

'Look who's asking questions now,' I laughed. 'How old do you think?'

'Let me see . . .' she said. I turned round and presented my face to her, smiling. 'I'm usually good at guessing people's ages, but you're difficult.'

Behind her I caught sight of myself in an old mirror. The glass was scratched and blurred and dusty, silver strips peeling away behind it.

'Why are you touching your cheek?' she said. 'Are you all right?'

'Yes,' I smiled. 'So how old am I?'

'I'd say in your forties. Late forties maybe.'

I opened my eyes in mock horror. 'Not too far wrong.'

'Then you definitely wouldn't have known Great-Uncle TK. Or if you did you must have been a tiny baby. He died in 1943.'

'How did he die?'

'Well . . .' she said, looking at her fingers, 'you know . . .'

'I'm sorry I asked. I'm just a stranger after all.'

'It's OK, really. I'll tell you – the Japanese. That's what everyone says. I don't know the details.'

'Did he have any children?'

'Just one. My mother's cousin. No, second cousin – I'm not sure.'

'Did she live here too? Your great-uncle's daughter, I mean.'

'Of course. Don't all children live with their parents? In fact, she lived here even after she was married.'

'That's nice.'

'She was married to Johnny Lim, you know – the notorious Johnny Lim.'

'Oh yes, I think I've heard of him – I'm not from around here, you see.'

'Oh. Where are you from, then, Mr Tall Man?'

'KL.'

'Wow, long drive.'

'It's not bad. I stay in Ipoh for a week at a time.'

'Sounds like you miss home.'

'Not really. So, your mother's cousin who was married to Johnny . . .'

'Lim.'

'Johnny Lim, yes. I guess that must have been her room,' I said, pointing to a door which seemed to open into a larger room.

'No, that was my great-uncle and great-aunt's room. That one was Johnny and Snow's,' she said, pointing to a closed door. She paused and looked me in the eye, as if remembering something. 'Hey,' she said, taking a step towards me, 'how did you know my great-uncle's child was a girl? I didn't tell you it was a girl.'

'Supernatural powers.' I tried to laugh but my face suddenly felt hot.

Just then an old man's voice called out from behind the closed door. 'Who is it, Yun?'

'No one, Grandfather. Go back to your nap.'

The door opened and a bald, bent-over man emerged. He had sparkling clear eyes which widened when they saw me.

'Good afternoon,' I said, trying to sound cheery. 'I'm selling Tupperware.' It sounded like a lie.

I did not recognise him. I was certain I had never seen him before, and what's more, I was sure that he had never seen me. And yet the way he looked at me made me nervous.

'I know you,' he said.

'Oh really?' the young women giggled. 'You know this guy, Grandpa?'

'Your face,' he said. 'I know your face.'

'Who is he, Grandpa? Tell me,' the young woman said. 'I'm dying to know.'

'Excuse me,' I said suddenly, 'excuse me for interrupting your afternoon.' I walked towards the door, opening it in one swift motion, and when I reached the top of the stairs I began to run, leaping three steps at a time.

'Hey, Mr Tall Man, what about the Tupperware?' the woman shouted as she came after me.

I didn't look back as I drove away on the dry, dusty road that wound its way through the plantation. The car jolted over rocks and potholes but I didn't ease off until I reached the main road. My face was hot with embarrassment and anger. I had still not seen the room my mother had slept in.

By the time I reached home I had resolved to go back to the Soong house as soon as I could.

And so a few months ago I went there again. I had left a gap of about six months – plenty of time for me to regain my composure and for the people at the house to forget the strange travelling salesman who had fled before selling anything. I drove through the swampland with the sea-salty air swirling through the open windows. I left the car and walked the final mile to the plantation, my stride measured and calm. It was a night of perfect clarity, you must believe me. The moon was bulbous in a velvet sky and made my clothes shine. I stopped and looked at my hands and saw that my skin, too, had become pale and phosphorescent.

The house was dark. It looked exactly like the house from my childhood nightmares. It was waiting, ready to take me. I walked up the steps and tried the front door. I put my ear to it and listened for movement. Nothing. I walked along the verandah to the shuttered teak doors and put my hand on the rain-washed panels, pushing gently. They fell open at once, making no noise. The room burned with moonlight; where it fell on the floor the boards turned a startling white before me. I saw my reflection in the mirror. When I reached out to touch it, it shattered into a thousand pieces. In the broken pieces I could see parts of my face and they were hot to the touch. I stepped over the shards of glass and walked towards Snow's room and stopped at the threshold before entering. I came into a small windowless anteroom. I could make out two chairs and a coffee table. At the far end of the room I noticed another door and made my way towards it. I know this door, I thought, I know this place. I have been here a thousand times before. I have carried it inside me since I was born and I know all that it held within it. A bed. An old man asleep on it. Next to him, a beautiful woman: Snow. The walls are hung with waterfalls of hot red silks. Snow opens her eyes and rises to sit up. Her hair is sleep-tangled but I can see her eyes have not shut. They have not rested for many years now. She turns to me and smiles. Come, she says and I walk slowly to her. She holds her arms wide open and I kneel before her slowly slowly lowering my head into her breast. Her arms close around me, her hands stroke my hair. Don't cry she says don't cry my child my son. Her fingers smooth my face my cheek my brow my dry cracked lips. With her long white fingers she pulls her white blouse aside and gives her white breast to my mouth. Drink my child my son she says and I drink. When I finish I can smell my breath and it is sweet and soft. Are you happy my son she says and I nod. I feel something cold and hard on my cheek and when I turn my face I see it is a pistol, Johnny's pistol. She turns her body and lets me see the old man on the bed. I do not see his face but I know it is Johnny, I know it is. She puts the pistol in my hand and her lips to my ear. Her breath is cool and powdery and flutters like a moth. Shoot him she says shoot him for all the things he has done. Once more I bury my face in her breast but she is laughing pushing the pistol into my hand. Shoot him. Her skin is wet with my tears. Mother I say. The gun is cold and hard, her skin is soft and wet. Don't cry my son she says don't cry. I cling to her with all my life and she kisses me on my forehead.

8. How Johnny Became a God – In the Eyes of Some

In 1957, on the day the country achieved independence after 450 years of foreign rule, my father was shot by an unknown gunman. The assassin fired twice from close range but did not succeed in killing him. This was not the first attempt on Father's life – he had survived one previous assassination attempt during the war, in 1944 – but it had a marked effect on his appearance. Whereas the first attack had merely left him with a scar (a pale puckered star on his left calf), this one shattered the bones and muscles in his right shoulder. Even the best doctors in the valley were not able to prevent that shoulder from hanging awkwardly at a downward-sloping angle for the rest of his life.

The shooting happened as the nation gathered around television sets to watch the independence parade in KL. Those scenes which have become fixed and stale in our memories were fresh and startling then, newborn images in our newborn world. The Stadium was a boiling sea of banners and bodies. We had never seen people dancing in public before. Not like this. Men with men, women with women, men with women even. They did the *joget*, swaying and step-stepping in little circles, lifting and dropping their shoulders to a strange, shared rhythm. They held their new flag above their heads, letting it catch the wind: thirteen stripes, a sickle-moon and a star. There, too, was the Tunku, the Father of the Nation, raising his hand and repeating the word 'Merdeka' three times, the people on the Padang echoing back, the chant coming through the television sets as clear and sharp in our ears as breaking glass. Independence. Freedom. New Life. That is what the word meant to us. And although the innocent dreams we had for our country have died in the years since then, suffocated by our own poisoned ambition, nothing will ever diminish what we felt. Nothing will rob us of those stuttering sepia-washed images of Merdeka Day.

It was at this moment, after the third cry of 'Merdeka', that Father's would-be killer struck. We had driven into Ipoh for the afternoon. Father attended to some business at CY Foo's and left me to wander the streets on my own. I sat, as I always did, on the steps of the Hong Kong and Shanghai Bank. I enjoyed doing this because from here I could see all the streets spreading out before me. Everywhere was silent, deserted. I sat still and looked for movement; I saw only a stray dog trotting aimlessly round the block. It kept appearing in different places, half-heartedly sniffing the ground, before wandering out of view again. I could not work out what it was searching for. Occasionally someone would emerge from a doorway, break into a run and then vanish into another building. The whole town had, it seemed, shut itself away for that day, never venturing far from their television sets.

Father and I arranged to meet in our usual place, the nameless Hainanese coffee shop on Sweetenham Street. Frankie, the old man who ran it, used to embrace Father whenever we walked into the shop. Father would raise his arms stiffly, bringing them round to touch Frankie's back. After all these years, I remember Frankie because he was the only person I ever saw Father embrace.

On the way to Frankie's place I heard the crackle of wireless sets and caught a glimpse of the odd television screen. The parade had started; I realised I was late and quickened my stride. By the time I got there I could see, over the heads of the many people gathered there, that the great celebrations were drawing to a climax. The Tunku was just leaving his seat and approaching the microphone; the Union Jack had already been lowered. The cheers rang out from the television, each louder than the previous one. A few of the men in the room raised their fists in unison with the people on the television. I looked for Father and found him peering intently at the screen. He was leaning forward, his chin resting on his upturned palms. From the back of the room I could see that many of those present were mouthing 'Merdeka' slowly, as if unsure how to pronounce this unfamiliar new word.

It was all part of this scene for me, part of these new and unreal images. A man stood up in the middle of the room with his arm outstretched. No one else looked at him; only I saw the gun in his hand. He stood there poised like a temple statue, calm and utterly still. As the third shout rang out from the TV, the man cocked the pistol and Father suddenly turned round. Perhaps it was to search for me, to make sure that I too was witnessing this occasion; or perhaps it was his instinct for survival, so deeply and mysteriously a part of him, which alerted him to the quiver of danger.

The gunman fired at virtually point-blank range, but Father had already begun to drop his body, pushing, diving, scrambling head first into the mass of bodies around him. The bullet ripped off his epaulette before smashing into the TV set, exploding it in a colourful shower of blue lights and silver sparks. As he fell,

Father pulled at the legs of a table next to him, obscuring the assassin's view for a split second. All around me, men began to run for cover. I watched them but I could not hear their screams. I watched in silence as the gunman cocked the pistol again. This time I saw it clearly: a matt-black .38, old and well worn. I also saw the man. He was Chinese, aged anywhere from eighteen to forty, dressed in khaki trousers and a white cotton shirt. His hair was cut short back and sides and combed with a centre parting. He was dressed like every other man in the room: I would not be able to recognise him if I saw him again.

He fired once more. I do not know how it happened, how the bullet found its way to Frankie's stomach. I saw the old man collapse, doubling over and sinking to his knees before falling to the ground. The side of his head hit the concrete hard; the sound it made cracked loudly in my ears. The third shot was aimless and desperate. It shattered a glass cabinet full of coffee beans, filling the air with the smoky-sweet smell of rough Javanese coffee.

The gunman pushed past me as he fled. His arms were slick with sweat. His clothes smelled of ripe fruit and mud. I felt his hot, heavy breath on my face and heard the thin wheeze in his chest. In a second, the shop emptied. I watched as people disappeared into the bright dusty street, melting into the quiet afternoon.

I went to Father. His mouth rose in a half-smile.

'Did you see the Merdeka?' he said.

I nodded. Through the black blood and angry flesh on his shoulder I caught a glimpse of bone. It was pure, glowing white. I moved to the other side of him, trying to hold him and drag him to the front of the shop. He was heavy, immovable. His eyes closed slowly and he chuckled so faintly that if my face had not been next to his I may never have heard it.

I don't know quite how I managed it, but finally I got him into the back seat of the Mercedes. I had just turned sixteen and

I had never driven before. Somehow, though, I made it, stuttering through the white empty streets to the General Hospital. The nurses there put their arms around my shoulders and told me not to worry. They brought me warm bottles of Green Spot and stale curry puffs.

'Can you believe it, all by himself, you know. He got his father here all by himself,' I heard one of the nurses say in the next room.

'He's not his father's son for nothing,' whispered another.

Later that evening, as I sat waiting for news of Father's condition, a nurse brought me the blue batik shirt Father had been wearing. It had been badly damaged in the shooting: only one sleeve remained and a few of its buttons were missing. But the people in the hospital had washed it and pressed it and folded it neatly. It was only when you held it up to the light that you could see the faint outlines of the washed-out bloodstains.

There were no witnesses other than me. No one else admitted to being there. People were afraid to get mixed up in police business. They did not want to become targets themselves for the dwindling but by now hardline group of communist guerrillas who roamed the darkest reaches of the jungle, where even the British Army could not get to.

In failing to kill my father, these communists only succeeded in strengthening his aura of invincibility. People began to say that Johnny could not be killed, that the bullet passed straight through his heart but still he lived to rule the valley. That is because he did not *have* a heart, other people said. He was other-worldly, not flesh and blood at all but a phantom. His son was half-man, half-ghost. Soon, I noticed that every time we walked into a shop or any other public place, a hush would descend and men would lower their gaze. Father began to be more casual in his behaviour – he stopped carrying a gun himself and, while many of his accomplices had armed bodyguards, he strolled freely down the main streets of all the towns in the valley.

His right shoulder hung in an odd way now, stiff and unmoving, jerking from time to time with an occasional spasm, which made it look as though the shoulder was trying to bring itself level with the good one. You might have thought that this incident changed Johnny. Perhaps the spirit of independence infected him with notions of human pride and sympathy; but it did not. He grew even more withdrawn, more inside himself.

To understand why he was hated so much by the communists – those people who, after all, were once his own – you have to go back to the war. You have to remind yourself, as I have many times, that he was a communist but also the second richest man in the valley. You must also remember that the richest man was his father-in-law, TK Soong.

But even the undisputed Number One Tycoon would have to defer to a god. Johnny knew that much.

When, in mid-1941, the Japanese began to make landings in Thailand, Johnny seemed to be the only man in the valley who thought that they might, some day very soon, invade Malaya. One or two of the people who came into the shop muttered quietly about 'what the bastards were doing in China', but otherwise people went about their business as usual. Even the English planters whom Johnny met while with TK were unconcerned. Over *stengahs* of whisky they joked about what would happen if, God forbid, the Japs did invade.

'I'd mow them down with my Bren gun. Every bloody one of those slit-eyed animals.'

'I'd feed them to my dogs.'

'I'd invite them to tea with my mother-in-law and *murder* them with hospitality.'

TK's response was similarly placid. With the unshakeable

assurance possessed only by the very wealthy, he behaved as if life would go on as usual for him and his circle of friends, even if war did eventually come to Malaya. 'British, Japanese, Dutch, Russian – all the same,' he said with a shrug. This attitude surprised Johnny but did not alarm him. On the contrary, it made him feel cleverer than even the wisest old men. Only he knew that the Japanese would reach the valley – the question was how long it would take. So Johnny began to listen to the crackling World Service broadcasts on his wireless set. He did not blame TK and the other old fools for believing that Malaya would never fall, for the reports sounded calm and full of confidence in the might of the British Army. But Johnny knew better than this. He drew a line on a piece of paper, dividing it in two. He headed one column 'Date' and the other 'Place', and then he made notes from the wireless reports. He made entries which simply read: 24 July | Camranh Bay. When the piece of paper was merely half full, Johnny knew for certain that he had been right all along. The Japanese were moving swiftly and inexorably southwards, unimpeded, it seemed, by mountains or jungles or oceans. A quick mental calculation told Johnny that they would be in Malaya before the end of the year. As a communist, he was especially at risk. He had heard rumours of Japanese torture methods and he did not want to find out if the rumours were true. He had to act quickly.

At dinner that evening, he looked at TK, who was wearing a silk shirt with a perfectly cut mandarin collar. With his silvery hair and thin nose, TK radiated silent authority. Johnny remembered the time Humphrey Yap, another of the rich old tin-mining men, came to visit, together with Tuan Frederick Honey. The four of them had withdrawn after dinner to talk about various matters such as the future of the mines, the new district officer – all the usual inconsequential things. For a time Johnny felt honoured to be in such company; he could not have envisaged this several years previously. He tried to contribute to the conversation, but found it nearly impossible to do so. Everything he said was ignored, passed over without comment. Not once did the other men address him directly, and Johnny felt invisible, as if he had dissolved into thin air. Without looking at him, Tuan Honey called out to him to ask for some tea; and then a glass of cognac; and then a refill. All this time they had been laughing and joking, even breaking into song – but never with Johnny. TK was who the important people wanted to see, not Johnny. Johnny imagined a Japanese general standing astride an armoured tank, riding into the conquered lands for the very first time. 'Bring me the most important and powerful man in the valley,' the general would say, and there would be no hesitation: everyone would point to TK Soong, not Johnny Lim.

Johnny thought of the shop. How long would it take, selling textiles, for him to become as respected as TK? Perhaps never. The shop itself was still named after Tiger, for God's sake. He thought of the rows and rows of textiles, rolled up in tight bales stacked against the old wooden shelves. He had never truly been interested in them anyway. How demeaning it was to sell these dull limp rags that people wore next to their crotches, next to their sweaty skin. His shop, the most famous in the valley, was just a shop, a goddam useless shop. He was admired, even loved, but not by the people who mattered. When the Japanese came to Kampar they would only see a shit-worthless shop and a shit-worthless shopkeeper.

Unless, of course, something was done.

Sitting there at dinner looking at TK, Johnny knew at once what he had to do.

It took several days for Johnny to lay the foundations for his plan. He collected all the equipment he needed, travelling as far afield as Tanjung Malim. He called in on many of his old contacts who were pleased to see him after such a long time. Everyone remarked that he was in particularly good cheer, and he affected half-hearted demurrals. He invited them all to come to the shop and promised them special discounts. 'Great things always happen when there are many people around,' he said. At home he tried to behave as usual, but his excitement was not easily contained, especially as he grew closer to putting his plan into action.

'How's the shop?' TK asked at dinner one evening. 'You seem to be working very hard, always at the shop late.'

'So-so,' Johnny replied. After a short pause, 'A few small problems. Nothing much.'

'Problems?' TK looked up, resting his chopsticks on the table. He did not like problems.

'It's nothing, really.'

'Tell me – what are these problems?'

'Really, they're very small things. I should not have mentioned them even.'

'If there is a problem,' TK said, 'perhaps it will help you to speak to me about it. I have an interest in my son-in-law's business, after all.'

'As I said, it's nothing,' Johnny smiled, 'but I would prefer not to discuss these matters here, at home.' He glanced at Patti and Snow.

'Of course, of course,' TK said, 'it's not polite to talk about these things in front of women.'

'Maybe you'd like to come to the shop instead?'

'Yes. That way you will be able to explain any problems – if there are any – fully.'

'What a good idea.'

'Tomorrow?'

'No – the day after would be better.'

'Fine. Let's say eleven o'clock.'

That evening Johnny lay on his side of the bed, cocooned in his world of hot hazy dreams.

'What's the matter?' Snow asked.

'Nothing,' he said, and turned on his side. He could not fall asleep.

The day TK came to the shop, it rained heavily and unexpectedly. It was mid-August and the dry season was at its peak, shrinking the rivers into cracked brown beds and rotting the overripe mangoes and jackfruit which lay blackening on the ground. At this time of year the people of the valley shut themselves indoors in the afternoons. They fan themselves with rolled-up newspapers and wait for the odd breeze to stir the heavy air. Occasionally, even at the driest times of the year, there may be a brief rain shower, sweeping swiftly across the valley, gently moistening the parched leaves of the trees. Barely an hour after it passes the earth is dry again and does not smell of water.

But the rains which came on the day TK travelled to the shop were not like these short showers. On that day the valley woke up to an unfamiliar smell: the flower-sweet breath of overnight rain. The sky was a brooding grey. From early in the morning, people went out into the streets, walking in the warm rain. They left their umbrellas at home and splashed childlike through the puddles, their feet clad only in flimsy rubber slippers. They shopped for food at the market, where water streamed off the tarpaulins and made the ground soft and slippery. Sometimes raindrops would hiss on the charcoal fires upon which sardines and cuttlefish grilled; the smell it made filled the air with the scent of the sea.

Johnny wondered if the weather would affect his plans. He worried that all the little fuses and wires he had prepared might have become damp during the night. Who could have thought of rain at this time of the year? He felt a sudden shiver of doubt. It was too late now. All was set in motion. If he was to become the most famous man in the valley he had to carry on regardless. He would not fail.

The intricate system of wires, fuses and timers ran all over the shop, hidden from sight behind panels, skirting boards, door hinges and floorboards. Johnny went to the main control box in his money room as soon as he arrived at the shop. All seemed fine. A sleepy-eyed boy had arrived early, his thin singlet drenched in rain.

'Go make some tea,' Johnny said, 'and fetch yourself a new shirt from the shop.'

Once he was alone Johnny ran through the entire circuit, testing connections and switches to make sure nothing had been affected by the damp. Only one isolated part of the system, which lay behind some earthenware pots in a roofless corridor, had to be hastily replaced. As he fixed the small defect, Johnny resisted the temptation to smile. It would be his finest day yet.

When TK arrived at the shop, business was brisk. People sat patiently on high stools, waiting to be served. They drank complimentary cups of coral-red pu-erh tea which were the hallmark of the shop's legendary hospitality. Johnny himself was serving behind the counters that morning. Customers remarked that he seemed to be exceptionally vigorous and enthusiastic. Everyone was pleased to see him serving in the shop again; they shared jokes with him and teased him about his good health. It must be marriage, they said, winking and roaring with laughter.

'Ah, here is the man who had made it all possible,' Johnny proclaimed loudly when TK came into the shop. All heads turned. A chorus of greetings bubbled across the shop. 'Soong Sir, good morning,' people said, making little bows.

TK's long white eyebrows lifted in bemused pleasure.

'Please, everyone, excuse us. It's not every day that Mr Soong visits the shop, and when he does, we all know that something important is happening,' Johnny said. 'We have some private business to attend to.'

'What is it? Maybe buying the whole of the Kinta Valley from the British?' someone said, and everyone in the room laughed politely.

'TK Soong does not need my help to do that,' Johnny said, smiling, as he led TK away to the money room.

A new pot of tea was ordered and brought to the room. Oolong was TK's favourite and Johnny laid out the cups while the tea steeped gently in the pot. Two minutes. Then Johnny poured the water away, filling the pot again with just-boiled water.

'I see you've learned how to make tea – properly,' TK said.

'Yes. You taught me that, of course,' Johnny said. Before he sat down he shut the heavy door and bolted it twice.

'I see you are well liked in the shop,' TK said. 'True to your reputation as a man of the people.'

'I try my best.' Johnny looked at TK's long wispy beard.

'So, before you tell me what your problems are, tell me how you find my daughter,' TK said. 'Is she satisfactory?'

'Of course,' Johnny lied. He did not know whether she was or not, or even in what way she was meant to be 'satisfactory'. The truth was, he wasn't interested.

'Now tell me what are all these problems you have created for yourself,' said TK.

'Problems?' said Johnny, hating TK even more now. 'Like I said, they are not really –'

'Just tell me.'

Johnny looked at him with flashing eyes. 'Three small things,' he said as calmly as possible. 'The first concerns a new shipment of sackcloth which I was proposing to sell on to Gim's warehouse in KL. The second is a new venture – rice – which I am thinking of importing from Thailand. And finally, just a small question concerning your tin-mining businesses when you die.'

'Pardon? I am still very much alive.'

'Of course, of course. But I am merely planning for the future.'

'I do not know what you mean,' TK said. 'Tin mining has been a family business for a very long time.'

'Best to keep it in the family, then.'

'Yes, I suppose. But I have not devoted much thought to it.'

Johnny cleared his throat. 'Father,' he said. 'Did I tell you that Snow and I, well, we are planning to have a baby. It will be a son, of course.'

TK's eyes widened.

'Yes,' Johnny continued. Lies, he found, came easily to him now. 'I hope Snow has not mentioned anything. It is the kind of thing best kept between father and son-in-law, I think.'

'I see now, I see,' TK said, mouth pulling into a wide smile. 'I see why you have been so mysterious about your so-called problems. Problems, indeed! You have no problems, you merely wanted to make an old man happy.'

'So you are agreed the tin mines are to stay in the family?'

'Of course! There is no question of anything else. The rubber business too, and the tea plantation – everything will go to you to hold on trust for my grandson. What else can I do? I have no sons of my own, after all. What a happy man I am! Thank you.'

'So you are certain it will all pass to me?'

'Who better? I may have had my doubts about you but now I see that you are an able man indeed!'

Johnny smiled and bowed his head. He checked the time on TK's watch.

'One more cup of tea?' Johnny said.

'Why not,' said TK as Johnny poured the tea. 'What's more, I propose a toast.'

They lifted their cups, holding them level with their chins.

'To Johnny Lim, and to my grandson,' TK said.

They moved the translucent cups slowly, touching them together with the faintest clink.

The first explosion was loud, clean and sharp. The second,

which followed exactly six seconds later, was louder still but blurred by the sound of shattering masonry and splintering wood. The initial blast, which happened just as the two men concluded their toast, spilt tea over TK's shirt. As he dabbed at it with a handkerchief, Johnny leapt to his feet and ran to the door. *Fire, Fire*, people were shouting in the kitchen.

'Don't move an inch,' Johnny said to TK. 'You'll be safe here. The walls are solid stone and the door is thick.' TK looked at him with puzzled eyes and continued dabbing at his shirt. As Johnny went out he pulled the door to and locked it from the outside.

The money room was midway between the shop and the kitchen. From where he was standing, Johnny could see flames engulfing the kitchen and a mass of fleeing customers.

'Hurry, hurry! Get out!' he screamed at the workers still in the shop. 'Get everyone out before the whole place goes.'

Another small explosion, this time in the shop, shattered the glass cabinets and sent bales of cloth tumbling from the shelves. Sharp screams. People looked around. The blast seemed to come from the ceiling, but the rafters looked intact. Noise seemed to come from all around them. They did not know where danger would come from next.

The fire was spreading in the kitchen now, encouraged by more small explosions which belched and spurted amid the flaming mass. The old wooden rafters began to crash down on to the blackened stoves and the sacks of rice. There was no means of escape through the rear of the building now. Johnny heard screams. Someone, maybe more than one person – he couldn't see – trapped in the fiery tomb. He saw a figure stumbling blindly in the flames; it passed like a shadow across his field of vision, howling in terror. He turned his back and went to the front of the shop where the air was clear.

'Everybody, run!' he screamed as loudly as he could. 'Stand far away!'

The crowd now assembled outside moved slowly backwards. They saw Johnny's face contorted with anguish. His eyes could barely open in the heat of the fire and his face was black with soot; his mouth grimaced, turning upwards, smile-like, at the corners. Behind him they could see the first of the flames from the kitchen begin to leap and lick at the main room at the front of the shop. Smoke was now smothering Johnny, but still he stood at the doorway with his arms stretched out on either side of his body to prevent anyone from going back into the fire.

'Come out here with us!' people shouted.

Instead, Johnny turned round and dived into the smoky, fiery sea.

There were small gasps and cries of confusion followed by a prolonged silence. Everyone knew that Johnny had gone back in to save those who were still trapped inside. He was going to save his father-in-law. He was risking his life for people who were in all likelihood already dead. But if anyone could save those poor souls, it was Johnny.

No one was certain how long he remained in that fire-filled hell. Some said as little as ten minutes, others said a whole hour. All, however, agreed that it felt like a lifetime. The morning's heavy rain continued to fall, but it did not seem to lessen the ferocity of the blaze. Where each raindrop fell on the inferno, a thin column of mist hissed into the air, and as the fire grew stronger the whole shop became transformed into a giant spitting monster, shrouded in haze. It was later said that this hellish creature could be seen fifty miles away from the slopes of Maxwell Hill.

The crowd backed away even further, for the heat was too intense now even for their rain-soothed faces to bear. They could feel the glow of the fire throbbing on their cheeks, even as they covered their noses and mouths to protect against the choking smoke. Several of them exchanged glances now and then. No man on earth could withstand that fire; only a god could survive that long in a fire like that, their eyes said. Another small explosion caused half the shopfront to collapse across the entrance. Many people thought: surely this is the end of Johnny now.

What happened next is not disputed by any of the surviving eyewitness accounts. Old or young, man or woman, Chinese, Indian, Malay – all say the same thing. They were not crazy from the heat or the shock, they did not imagine it. It actually happened.

The flames, they say, parted.

The dancing fire opened up, separating in two as if commanded by Allah, Guan Yin, Moses, Shiva – whoever.

And out of the parted flames emerged Johnny. All around him the great fire burned strong and bright, but it did not touch him. He walked steadily and firmly, his magnificent head held proudly. On his shoulder he supported the limp soot-blackened body of his father-in-law. Next to TK, Johnny appeared fresh and unspoiled. Though his face was dirty, his eyes shone brightly. He carried TK out to the crowd of people and laid him gently on the ground. Slowly, Johnny took off his own shirt and held it aloft to catch the rain. He touched it to TK's face, cleaning away the soot; he put his ear to TK's mouth, listening for the faint breaths; and then, slowly, he looked up at the anxious faces around him. He smiled a gentle smile and his eyes said: I have saved this man.

Everyone remained still and silent. There was no need to speak. As they looked at Johnny the same thought ran through their minds: this man was no mere human, he was something more.

TK lay on the wet dirt gasping thin breaths. His smoke-burned lungs would never serve him properly again. He would spend the remainder of his days frail and infirm and in gratitude to Johnny, to the man who had saved his life when it seemed lost for certain. With his head resting on Johnny's knee, TK opened his eyes to the soft rain. In the distance the famous Tiger Brand

Trading Company lay smouldering, lost for ever. Like everyone else present, TK knew that it was the end of his time as a great and powerful man. He knew it was the beginning of a new time in history.

9. The End

Not long after the shop burned down and Johnny saved TK's life, the Japanese invaded Malaya. They marched unimpeded through the northern states and in just two months took control of the entire country. Penang, Pearl of the Orient, and Singapore, the great Lion City – both surrendered in a matter of days. Between these two treasures the valley fell swiftly, almost unnoticed, into the hands of the Japanese. They ran through the towns and villages, barely pausing to plant flags of the Rising Sun before moving on. The red dust kicked up by the soldiers' boots hung in the air, turning it crimson before settling on the leaves of the trees; all along the roads the trees turned red, and in some parts of the valley it was said that the streams ran deep scarlet. A hush fell across the land. At night people closed their eyes and covered their ears. They did not want to hear the sound of locked doors being broken down nor the distant crackle of a village set on fire.

It was here, in the early months of this strange new land, that Johnny's most terrible deed was committed. Nothing in his later life can ever be compared to what my father did on 1 September 1942, the day my mother died and I was born.

By the end of January 1942 a Japanese administrative office had been firmly established in the valley and was beginning to put things in order. The head of the Kempeitai, the Japanese secret police, was a man called Mamoru Kunichika. After the war he published a book about his memories of wartime Malaya called *Memories of Wartime Malaya*. The photograph of him on the dust jacket shows a genial-looking man, thin and angular, with smiling eyes. The book presents a picture of the valley so calm that you wonder if war was actually taking place at the time. It tells the story of a young man plucked from the relative obscurity of Kyoto University and thrust into the secret service solely because of his academic brilliance and fluency in South-East Asian languages. He finds himself in Malaya, where the local people are welcoming and cooperative. They are glad to be rid of the British and thankful for Japanese rule. Of course there are disturbances now and again, for communist guerrillas are active in the jungles, but by and large the occupation runs smoothly, without incident. The book is full of anecdotal incidents of Japanese and local people sharing cigarettes and whisky and other such wartime luxuries; minor altercations with deceitful servants; 'amusing' misunderstandings of local customs, etc.

We are told how he acquired his nickname, 'The Marquis'. Not long after he arrived in Malaya, he was visiting the regional administrative office in Tapah when he was introduced to an (unnamed) 'eminent and influential leader of the Chinese community'. This Chinese gentleman seemed young but very enlightened, unlike most of the sullen-faced and devious Chinese Kunichika had come across. Although, through his education, Kunichika had managed to overcome the traditional Japanese prejudices against the Chinese, he nonetheless felt the need to be cautious when dealing with them. Mistrust runs deep between the two peoples, he says. However, this Chinese gentleman made him feel perfectly at ease because of his dignity of bearing and propriety of etiquette, and Kunichika felt no need to be wary. The gentleman thought that Kunichika himself must be a man of good breeding and considerable education; he asked Kunichika if he was of samurai descent, for he had read about the histories of the great samurai families and recognised Kunichika's surname. Bashfully, Kunichika answered: yes, he was. It was a relief to have one's background appreciated, writes Kunichika, especially by such an unlikely person. This gentleman went on to say that it was an honour to meet such a distinguished person, and that if Kunichika did not mind, he would address Kunichika by his proper title, the Marquis. Kunichika felt inclined to tell him that this was technically not his correct title, but refrained, so as not to cause any offence. That was how he got his nickname. As for the Chinese gentleman, well, Kunichika and he became good friends during the occupation, spending much time together despite comment from Kunichika's colleagues and the man's Chinese friends. After the Japanese surrender in 1945, Kunichika took his leave from his friend and parted with tears in his eyes.

The war was a happy experience for Kunichika, so his story goes.

Yet it is not difficult, if you bother to read old newspaper reports and books on the occupation, to piece together what Kunichika did when he got to the valley. It is not difficult to know why his other nickname, the one given to him by the ordinary people of the valley, was the Demon of Kampar.

Kunichika did not think like a soldier. He had other ways to fight a war, ways more dangerous than bayonets and bullets. The very first thing he did was to send his agents across the valley with bundles of cash. They used it to pay for information: who was a communist, who was in touch with British officers still in the jungle, who was planning a movement against the Japanese. Above all, Kunichika wanted to find out who was the most influential man in the valley. He knew such a man could be of immense help to him. It took just two days for his men to return with an answer.

Johnny had been waiting for this moment for many months.

He wanted to be found; he wanted to be taken to the head of the dreaded Kempeitai. Just as Kunichika had decided, long before he reached these new shores, what he would do if ever he was in this position, Johnny knew too what his own course of action would be. The two men were destined to find each other. Their first meeting had already taken place in their minds, many times over. When Johnny walked into the room and saw Kunichika he felt comfortable, as if he had known the other man for many years. Kunichika smiled and Johnny bowed slightly. Kunichika knew that he had found the man who could help him achieve everything he wanted. An offer was made and accepted. There was never any doubt as to this outcome. There was no bargaining, no hesitation, no need even to shake hands. For Johnny the price had never been so right.

Johnny called a meeting of the most important men in the valley. He told them that they had a duty to protect the interests of the people, and that it was up to them to ensure that the valley survived the occupation with minimum damage. He had thought about it long and hard, and had come to a difficult conclusion. There were no easy options in war. They had to get on the right side of the Japanese. They had to flatter, placate and please in order to deceive and survive. They had to accept that the British were gone and the Japanese were their new masters.

The room fell silent.

It is not easy to explain the turmoil that must have ravaged these men's minds; it is not easy to explain the history of the Chinese and the Japanese. Even I, a man who, as a child, sat on the laps of Japanese generals who fed me boiled rice porridge spoonful by spoonful – even I am aware of the centuries of enmity. Most of these men never thought the day would come when they would have to make such decisions. Some of them refused to believe the state their country was in. The British, they thought, would be back in a few weeks and order restored. But the British did not come back. With every passing day the memory of the country they once knew receded further into the past, and they began to doubt whether they would ever see it again. In this whirlpool of despair and confusion they had no choice but to acquiesce, to defer to the one man who seemed to know exactly what to do.

Johnny instructed these men to collect taxes from the people in their respective parts of the valley. They were to tax whatever they could: tin, rubber, palm oil, rice, barley, whisky, salt fish, chilli sauce, fermented anchovies – anything. Authority to do so came directly from the Imperial Japanese Army. In the first year of the occupation alone, the people of the valley paid $70,000,000 in taxes. This was used by the Japanese to build new fighter planes. If I were a better mathematician I could tell you how much this would be worth today, or how many jumbo jets it would buy. Very many, I am sure.

Every month the money was handed over to the Japanese by Johnny and Chan Toh Kwan, a banker. The Marquis accepted the money graciously, with a touch of embarrassment, leaving the cheque on the table for the duration of the half-hour meeting. Tea was drunk and pleasantries exchanged. Chan's sons, who were at school with me, would tell people how their father went 'mad in the head' during these meetings. He broke out in a heavy sweat and found his throat too dry to speak. He left the talking to Johnny, who had taken over all negotiations with the Japanese. Often, Chan felt so weak and strange that he would have to leave the meeting early, leaving Johnny to deal with the Kempeitai alone. No other man could have done this; no one had Johnny's conviction. Chan, for example, was terrified of being branded a collaborator. He survived the war and returned to the OCBC afterwards, though he kept a low profile, avoiding public places for fear of being assassinated. Years later, he became addicted to video games and locked himself away, becoming particularly adept at Pac-Man in his old age. He became convinced that people were watching him everywhere he went, that he was being spied upon while in bed and on the toilet. The war broke him, that's what his sons said. I remember them surrounded by groups of younger boys eager to hear their stories of the war. They were keen to tell as many people as possible about their father, to convince them that he was not a traitor. I don't think it worked. Once opinions are formed they are not easily changed. Curiously, they never spoke to me on the subject of war; they never discussed their father or mine. They didn't dare.

The people of the valley paid their taxes because Johnny said they had to. It was hard, but they trusted his wisdom. They were not siding with the Japanese, they were not funding the war against their brothers in China, he said; it was merely a matter of survival. In secret lectures he told them they were fooling the Japanese into believing the valley was friendly. They had to be patient while their boys in the jungle mounted a campaign to topple the Japs.

Trust me, he said. Believe me.

And to this day I think people still believe what he said.

In early August 1942 Johnny began to organise a top-secret top-level meeting of the senior commanders of the Communist Party. An underground movement had already established a guerrilla army called the Malayan Anti-Japanese People's Army. Johnny must have thought of the name. It was ridiculous and overly grand for a group of malnourished, badly equipped Chinese adolescents camped in the jungle. Few people could remember or pronounce the name, and even its acronym was often forgotten. Nonetheless, this band of guerrillas proved to be a hardened bunch. They attacked police stations and ambushed groups of Japanese soldiers returning from nights out at the army brothels. Once, they even succeeded in kidnapping and killing a mid-ranking Japanese captain. The valley was full of talk of British commandos who had stayed on behind enemy lines to train and organise these guerrillas. People whispered about a twenty-million-dollar reward for the head of any white man found in the jungle. Some villagers even claimed to have seen British soldiers alighting in twos and threes from small boats along the mangrove coastline.

Sixteen men formed the Supreme Central Committee of Communist Commanders. The majority of them lived and fought in the heart of the jungle but a number of them led double lives. Like Johnny, they were men of commerce and industry. It took many days for Johnny to spread word about the meeting to these men. With Japanese ears in every village, the old network of communication had become slower and more cautious. The news seeped slowly across the country, whispered by hidden mouths into invisible ears. The sense of anticipation grew with every whisper.

Johnny has summoned us to a meeting.

Johnny has been in touch with the British.

Johnny has weapons. He has plans.

A date was set: 1 September.

A place too: the massive catacomb of limestone caves lying just beyond the southernmost tip of the valley.

The caves are a million years old and their secret depths have always inspired extremes in the hearts and minds of those people who come here. That is why, for over a century, Hindus have worshipped here at the shrines of Subramaniam and Ganesh. Once a year, the most devout of them paint their faces and unclothed bodies and walk barefoot over glowing embers of coal; others pierce their noses, cheeks, necks and arms with immense skewers upon which fruit and other offerings are balanced.

It is just as well that worshippers come every year to this holy site. The layers and layers of devotion might some day erase the evil of that single day in 1942.

I felt the sadness of that day when I visited the caves myself. I went there on the day I found out what my father had done. I stood in a corner of the innermost cave, tucking myself in beside a small shrine, hiding behind the many-armed figures which guarded its entrance, just as Johnny's men must have done that dreadful day. My shoulder scraped flakes of peeling paint on to the damp floor. The smell of camphor soot filled my head and I closed my eyes. I stayed, as those men did, until the last of the visitors had gone and the afternoon swiftly became evening. The men had mingled for some hours among the other visitors to the caves. I saw them all around me, lurking in the shadows, barely perceptible in my mind's eye. They glanced at each other now and then, catching each other's eye for a brief moment before moving on, gazing emptily at the painted walls and ceilings. Slowly, they established who was present. Fifteen leaders, each with several lieutenants, forty-four men in all.

The most important of all, though, was not yet there.

In the hearts of each man, doubt began to creep. Where was he? Had he been caught and killed at last? Forty-four was a very bad number, very unlucky for all Chinese, even communists. It meant: death.

Night fell quickly, as it always did, but this time it felt blacker and deeper than ever before.

One man broke the silence, whispering out into the dark. 'Friends, comrades, who is here?'

I am, the whispers multiplied, coming together as they did. Brief silence, all men waiting for the voice they most wanted to hear.

Hands on pistols: a figure approaching from the mouth of the outer caves, barely outlined in the darkness. Is it him? Someone asked. I don't know. Can't tell. Listen. A steady heavy tread, confident, afraid of nothing. No man had a walk like that. No man except Johnny.

The men relaxed their grips on their weapons. None could see the smiles on the other's faces. They stood huddled together in the dark, lambs awaiting their shepherd.

A flash of light, blinding, colourful. Smoke. Gas! Quick, boys! They dropped to the floor, fumbling and clutching at their clothes, tearing off their shirts to cover their mouths and noses. Pistols drawn, they searched for the invisible danger through stinging eyes. The thundering whipping cutting crack of machine-gunfire.

Johnny, where's Johnny?

They fired into the smoke, slowly choking and suffocating. Some of them stood up and were instantly felled.

Fight on, fight on, they urged each other. They did not fear death.

Johnny will save us.

That is what they believed right to the end.

One by one they were cut down. A few ran screaming from the burning fog and were bayoneted by Japanese soldiers as they emerged from the mouth of the cave. When at last the smoke began to thin, the Japanese searched the caves with torches. The streams of light danced on the wet and bloody walls and shone in the eyes of the survivors, who were arrested and taken away. They spent many weeks in Kempeitai jails, where two of them committed suicide: one broke a spoon in two and cut his own throat with the jagged pieces, and the other threw himself into a dry well in the prison compound. The other survivors, for the sake of a few pathetic pieces of information, suffered torture of varying lengths of time and severity. And then all were executed, either beheaded with a sword or shot in the back of the head.

The Malayan Anti-Japanese People's Army would never be the same again. Twenty-nine of the most important communists in the country were killed at the caves and another fifteen arrested and executed. Of the sixteen commanders only one survived. One. The Famous Chinaman Called Johnny.

Rumours (no doubt perpetuated by Johnny) spread quickly. The most popular version of the story was that Johnny had miraculously escaped the Japanese ambush by fighting his way through a cordon of soldiers and scaled a sheer limestone crag a hundred feet high before disappearing into the forest. Others said that Johnny had been seen in the heart of the valley, fifty miles from the caves, late that afternoon; that he had found out about the Japanese plans to attack the caves and had tried to use his connections to prevent the massacre. And there were a few who insisted that they had seen Johnny late that evening, his clothes bloody and riddled with bullet holes; he had simply walked through a hail of bullets and emerged unscathed. There was nothing the Japanese or anyone could do to him. People reminded themselves what had happened when Tiger's shop burned down. Remembering the events of that day gave them comfort. Their trust was safe with Johnny.

Only I among all these people know the truth. I have had the help of books, official records, memoirs; I have history on my side. If the poor uneducated people of the valley knew what I knew, Johnny's life would have turned out very differently. I know, for example, that no one but the sixteen commanders – no one – knew the date and location of the meeting. I also know that during the occupation, when no one had any money and tens of millions of dollars in crippling taxes were being poured into the Japanese treasury, my father built the Japanese–Malayan Peace Monument on the site of the smoking ruins of Tiger Tan's old shop. It was made of carved sandstone and marble, paid for by my father's personal funds. He bought a new motor car and smoked cigars with Japanese generals. He searched the valley for the biggest, most expensive building and turned it into the most famous palace of sin in the country. He named it the Harmony

Silk Factory. It was the envy of every man, woman and child in the country.

10. Conclusion

The funeral of a traitor is a tricky thing, particularly if that traitor was someone close to you. You may be tempted, as I was, to avoid it altogether as a sign of protest at the crimes that person has committed. But if that person is your father and you are his only son, you have no choice. If no one else knows that he was a traitor, then your protest becomes meaningless. So I stood alone throughout the three-day ceremony, locked away with only my terrible, secret knowledge for company.

In truth there was little for me to do. By the time I returned to the factory from KL all the arrangements had been made. People were only too keen to help. Mrs Ginger Khoo and her five children looked after the catering, serving a thousand meals over the course of the three days. Gurnam Singh, one of Father's former chauffeurs who had had to give up work because of chronic syphilis (now cured, he told me), was on hand to organise the tables, chairs and electric fans. Father's closest friends, his old business partners, were in charge of the most important things: the priest, the undertaker and the paper offerings. Securing my arrival was another one of their tasks, and my appearance was greeted with some relief.

'I am glad you have decided to make peace with your father,' Mad Dog Kwang whispered in my ear.

'There was never anything broken that needed repair,' I replied.

'Oh,' he said.

Many hundreds came to pay their respects. All kinds of people turned up – princes, peasants, politicians, criminals, pensioners, toddlers. They travelled from far afield, from the remotest reaches of the country, and some even came from abroad. There were mourners from Hong Kong and Indonesia and Thailand, together with the odd Filipino. A few white men were there too, though where they were from was anyone's guess. One of them was an Englishman, I think, though he was so old it was difficult to tell. He sat folded over in a wheelchair, barely able to move amid the crowd of bodies, looking lost and confused. He seemed not to be able to speak, though occasionally he coughed and wheezed a few curious sounds. 'Is he mute?' I asked Madam Veronica (as she now liked to be called – when I was a small boy I knew her as Auntie Siew Ching).

'Don't know. I heard that something happened to him in the war,' Madam Veronica said as she adjusted the gold bangles on her wrist.

'What's his name?'

'Can't remember. Peter Something. Or maybe Philip Something.'

I found myself standing next to this ancient Englishman on the first day. Trails of thick spittle hung from the roof of his gaping, trembling mouth, but no words emerged. Finally he repeated a few sounds; he clutched at my sleeve and stared at me with wild staring eyes.

'What the hell is he saying?' Mad Dog said as he walked past.

I listened carefully. 'He is asking me who I am. He is asking what my name is.'

The man's head jerked and nodded involuntarily as he spoke. I felt strangely sorry for him. 'I'm Johnny's son,' I said, wondering if he could understand me.

'Johnny's son,' he repeated blankly, 'Johnny's son.'

'People say I don't look like him,' I said patiently, 'I take after my mother, you see.'

When he looked at me I could see the fine red veins in his yellowed eyes. 'Sons never resemble their fathers,' he said before wheeling himself away slowly.

'Shit, you could understand that guy? No one even knows what language he's speaking,' Mad Dog remarked in an uninterested way.

'Crazy foreigners,' Mrs Khoo said as she swept past me carrying a plate of fluffy white buns in each hand.

Children played with yo-yos and plastic action heroes which Gurnam had handed out. 'Where did you get so many toys?' I asked him. 'I found them at the factory,' he said, 'many bags full of them. Just arrived from Taiwan.'

We burned the paper offerings on the second evening, once all the minor rituals had been dealt with. Father's friends had ordered the most elaborate and expensive offerings they could think of, the grandest luxuries fit for a man of Father's standing. First, there was a paper motor car, a Mercedes-Benz, bronze-coloured as Father's last car had been. It was five feet long and had a paper chauffeur sitting at its paper wheel. Then there was a paper aeroplane, a Boeing 747.

'Is he going to need that in the afterlife?' I asked Mad Dog.

'He never got a chance to fly in an airplane,' he replied, smiling, 'so we thought we would give him a treat.'

Finally there was a paper house, virtually life-size, a replica of the Harmony Silk Factory. It had galleried windows overlooking the courtyard, as the factory did, and an open-air kitchen at the rear. I wandered around this house, looking at the tiny details. Little potted ferns, carefully painted green, decorated the red-tiled courtyard. They were the only kind of plants which ever grew happily in the courtyard, and their dark leaves used to add to the coolness of that sun-shielded space. The shutters had been painted pale jade, and through the open windows I could see the black-and-white chequerboard floor of the upstairs sitting room. I saw the rosewood furniture that we never used, preferring instead to sit on rough wooden chairs. Father's safe room was there too, locked as usual. The shop was full of beautiful things, colourful cloths and sparkling glass cabinets and boxes of jewels. The revolving dining room no longer revolved, but it had its European Old Masters on its walls. My bedroom, which looked out on to both the courtyard and the back of the house, was kept as neatly as always. Through the window I could see the river, wide and brown and muddy. I could see the wooden pontoon underneath the ancient banyan tree. We used to swim there, my friends and I, diving from the bridge into the warm thick water. We used to climb the tree and swing from its trailing vines until we were twenty yards out and then let go, splashing from a great height into the river. Early in the evenings we would creep on to the pontoon and lower pieces of meat on fish-hooks into the water to catch catfish which emerged from murky recesses to feed at night. From my window I could see the herons and egrets and storks wade through the shallows in the morning. I used to wake up early – at dawn, when everything was pearl-coloured and soft – so that I could see them flying smoothly across the mist-covered water, their sleek heads tucked gently into their necks.

My books lined the teak shelves that Father built when I was ten and hungry to read. If I thought he was in a good mood I would read him stories from these books, singing and screeching as I imagined the voices of all the characters. Occasionally he would smile. I was pleased because I thought I had made him happy, and I would embellish my stories further, making them up as I went along. When he smiled he looked as if he remembered what life really was, and so I would tell even more stories. But sometimes he would realise I wasn't just reading from the book; he would get angry and scold me for making things up, for telling tales. His face would turn black with fury, as if he hated me more than anything in the world. Life would drain from his face, leaving it empty once more.

We set fire to the house, the car and the aeroplane just as it was turning dark. Hennessy XO was poured in a ring around the paper replicas to protect against thieving spirits; its heavy perfume laced the twilight air. As Johnny's son, it was my responsibility to set the offering alight, and I did so quickly, touching my burning roll of newspaper to the house in as many places as possible before the flames became unbearable. I ran back to stand with the other mourners. We stood under a purple sky and watched the house burn down.

Death, I remembered Father saying, erases all traces of the life that once existed, completely and for ever.

The next day I left as soon as I could. I slipped away from the throng of people returning from the cemetery and headed for my car, hoping to leave before I was missed. I did not want to say too many goodbyes.

The old Englishman in the wheelchair had parked himself in the kitchen where he sat nodding and mumbling to himself. He was holding a parcel wrapped in a piece of cloth. He held it up to me as I approached him.

'Thank you,' I said, resenting the number of gifts I had managed to acquire over the three days. People felt the need to provide me, the only son, with tokens of their respect for Father. And so I received an array of useless objects: small crystal swans, plaster of Paris Eskimos and mugs bearing the Prime Minister's portrait. I did not stop to open the box and hurried instead to the car. I threw the cloth-wrapped parcel into the boot together with all the other unwanted presents; its contents rattled as it landed on a cuckoo clock.

The Englishman followed me out, wheeling himself along the uneven road. 'Where are you going, my son?' he said.

'Swimming,' I said as I got into my car.

I didn't drive back to KL. I headed east instead, criss-crossing the winding river until I found myself in the swampy flatlands of the coast. I veered north, turning into ever narrowing roads until I could smell the salty winds coming in off the sea. Just south of Remis I caught the first glimpse of the foam-tipped waves through a thin forest of casuarinas. I had not been here for many years. I drove along until I found somewhere to leave my car. I undressed slowly under the trees, the dead needles tickling my feet. It was mid-afternoon and there was no one but me on the wide white beach. I walked across the hot sand into the water, watching the tiny crabs scurrying away from my path. Where the water was deeper, the waves folded over gently, catching the sun on their crests so that the light sparkled across the surface of the water. It was as if someone had cast tiny jewels all over the ocean. I swam far out from the shore, floating calmly in the blue-green water.

PART TWO

1941

24 September 1941

Accept your fate. Accept your fate. Mother's words invade my dreams. I pray I do not talk in my sleep. Johnny must not know. Not yet.

25 September 1941

Someone new came to visit us today. I was having my afternoon rest, dozing uneasily – my mind boils constantly, never capable of rest – when I heard voices in the yard at the front of the house. I became aware of one of the servants chattering rapidly. The second voice was unfamiliar. I lay in bed listening to it for a while, but could not recognise it. It was a man's voice, deep but not rough – a true baritone, I think Father would say. He was speaking flawless Malay, of the variety rarely heard in the valley nowadays, that is to say, old-fashioned courtly Malay. As I listened more carefully, however, I detected the slightest hint of an accent, though again it sounded unfamiliar to my ears. He asked to speak to Father. He said that he had recently arrived in Kampar – 'from abroad' – and had been advised to call in on the famous TK Soong. He apologised for the inconvenient timing of his visit but wondered if the servant would nonetheless announce his arrival to Mr Soong. He mentioned his name but I did not hear it.

Eventually I heard Father come out of his study.

'Professor? Welcome, welcome,' he said. 'Thank you for your letter. How good that you are here.'

'Please,' the visitor said courteously – in Mandarin, as if to make a point – 'you embarrass me with your kindness.'

Father laughed and replied in English, 'It is an honour to meet you.' There was a strange quality to Father's voice, one I had never heard before. He sounded nervous. He led the visitor into the large sitting room and I could no longer pick up their voices clearly. Across the corridor I could sense Mother pacing about in her room. Cupboard doors opened and closed. Her small jewellery box dropped and scattered its contents on to the floor.

After some minutes I decided it was no use trying to rest – the weather is so hot now that it is impossible to sleep at night, much less during the day – so I resumed my reading. I am revisiting *Persuasion*, which I am finding curiously annoying.

It was Mother who knocked on my door. 'Are you *decent*?' she asked, and broke into a laugh. I could tell immediately that she was with our visitor.

I opened the door to find her standing with a very tall man dressed in a light-coloured linen suit. I thought he was Chinese, but his features seemed wrong. I remained standing at the narrow doorway with my arms folded.

'This is our daughter, Professor,' Mother said. 'Nothing to look at, I told you, didn't I?'

'On the contrary,' the man said, bowing slightly. 'Kunichika Mamoru,' he said, extending his hand. On his little finger he wore a ring of muted gold, heavy and stately in the European style.

'The Professor has just arrived in the valley – all the way from Japan,' Mother said. She pronounced her words like a schoolgirl, stretching vowels interminably and emphasising special words. 'All' became 'aaaaaall' and 'Japan' 'Jap-AN.'

'Don't speak so loudly,' Father said, appearing behind Mother, 'you'll embarrass the Professor.'

'How can you embarrass someone so clev-ER?' said Mother, pushing past me into my room.

The man laughed.

I introduced myself, stressing my married surname.

'Your parents did not tell me you were married,' Kunichika said, smiling. I noticed his eyes move to take in the framed wedding photograph on my dressing table. 'But now that I have seen you I am glad that you have a husband to keep you safe from prying eyes – including mine!'

Mother laughed. 'Professor, you would not be interested in a *thing* like her!'

'Yes, Professor Kunichika, I am extremely fortunate to be married to my husband,' I said, looking him straight in his crystal-clear eyes. My neck felt hot and bare. I became aware that I had lifted my chin to look up at his face; suddenly that pose seemed stiff and awkward.

Mother snorted as she began, instinctively, to clear my books from my desk, tidying them into a pile in a corner of the room.

'Please, call me Mamoru. I insist,' he said.

He had very thick hair, black and glossy. His angular features – sharp nose and strong cheekbones – were accentuated by the colour of his skin, which was pale and spoke of northern climates. At certain moments he even looked slightly European. His body was lean and languid, but he seemed to be a man of considerable strength. Perhaps it was merely his height which created that impression.

'Isn't the Professor the handsomest man you have ever seen?' Mother said, linking her arm through his.

'The Professor comes from a famous samurai family,' Father said. 'He is a *marquis*.'

'Professor Kunichika is certainly a distinguished-looking man,'

I said. There was something elusive in his face, something that reminded me of the dark, delicate features of the foxes that emerge from the jungle to prey on our chickens. When disturbed, they simply stop and stare at you with cool eyes, their white faces shining in the night.

'Well, he is the handsomest man *I* have seen,' said Mother.

'What are you a professor of, Professor?' I asked.

'You seem disbelieving,' he said.

'You don't look much like a professor to me.'

Mother said, 'He's too handsome to be a professor, isn't that right?'

He shrugged and said, 'A little bit of everything.'

'Such as?' I said.

'Linguistics, Western literature – particularly Russian – philosophy . . .'

'*Philosophy*,' Mother breathed, nodding at me.

'Jack of all trades.' He laughed. 'Your father is a famous scholar, and I hear you take after him.'

'I don't aspire to any great heights,' I said.

Mother snorted again and mumbled something.

'I will certainly never be a professor,' I added.

'That is a shame,' he said with a sad smile. 'Tell me – if I don't look much like a professor, what do I look like?'

'I'd say you were a military man.'

He laughed out loud. His voice was rich and clear. 'Look at these hands – I can't even hold a shovel, much less a gun!'

Mother and Father both laughed loudly.

'It seems I am mistaken,' I said.

As they turned to leave, Kunichika said, 'I sincerely hope I will have the honour of meeting you again – and your husband too.'

Mother said, 'If that good-for-nothing fool is ever around, that is.'

'Please,' Father said, smiling.

I watched Kunichika leave and walk across the yard. I tried to hide behind the shutters but it was as if he sensed my presence, and he looked straight at my window; I had no choice but to acknowledge him. He took off his hat and waved at me, and then continued walking towards the path leading into the plantation. He did not have a motor car or even a bicycle. The walk through the plantation is a long one – very nearly a mile – particularly in this heat. How did he get here? I remained at the window for a while, watching him vanish into the shadows.

27 September 1941

In recent days I have not been able to stop thinking about my early times with Johnny. I suppose this is unsurprising, given what I have decided to do. When I remember the things we did I seem to be recalling events from a very distant past. I have to remind myself that all these things happened little more than a year ago. The details are still fresh in my mind, but I do not know how long they will last.

One of the things I think about most often is the very first time I saw him. It was in the middle of the monsoon season and it had been raining hard for two days. I had not set foot outside the house all day and was feeling somewhat restless. I stood at the window watching the storm turn the front yard into a paddy field. On such days all I can hear is the rain. Although we are surrounded by forest, I have noticed that birdsong and the call of cicadas cease, only resuming when the downpour eases. But on that particular day there was another sound, one I could not place at first. It began as a faint tinkling, like a small child cheerfully playing with three keys of a piano. As it got louder I realised it was a bicycle bell. I could not believe that anyone would be cycling in such weather.

And then he came into view, splashing through the puddles on the muddy track through the plantation. He came towards the house slowly, as if afraid of it. It wasn't until he was very close that I saw that, on the back of his bicycle, he was carrying something very large, covered with tarpaulin. I could not work out what it was that he was carrying, nor how the goods (if they were goods) were attached to the bicycle. His thin cotton shirt was soaked through; it stuck to his chest and stomach. I remember his baggy shorts too, heavy with water and bunched up around his thighs. There was something in the way he moved – with the freedom and uncertain strength of a young animal flexing its limbs – that imprinted itself in my memory. He peddled on unperturbed by the rain, as if he had spent his whole life exposed to the elements.

He disappeared from view, seeking shelter under the front verandah. I went out and stood at the top of the steps leading up to the house. I saw him sitting on the pedestal of one of the concrete stilts. He had a cigarette between his lips and was trying unsuccessfully to light a match.

'Are you all right?' I called out.

The sound of my voice made him leap to his feet. He seemed to be standing to attention, his hands by his side and neck held rigid.

'It is raining,' he said. Those were the very first words he said to me.

'Would you like a hot drink? You might catch cold,' I said, but he simply stood staring at me uncertainly.

'What do you have at the back of your bicycle? Are you selling something?' I asked as I came down the stairs.

'Textiles,' he said. When he spoke the word it sounded odd, as if he had been practising it but had not yet become accustomed to its sound.

I smiled. 'May I have a look?'

This seemed to take him by surprise, and he started towards

his bicycle, placing his hand on the tarpaulin as if to protect his goods from me. 'You would not be interested in this.'

'Why not?'

He shrugged his shoulders and frowned. I remember how worried he looked. He seemed a little confused, even sad.

'Are they secret things?' I said.

He shook his head. His hand was still firmly on the tarpaulin.

'Please,' I said. 'I would like to see them.'

He looked at me for a very long time, as if searching for something. I went to the tarpaulin and undid the string which secured it to the bicycle. When I lifted it up I found a dozen bales of cloth. They were simple, unadorned textiles. I ran my fingers over them and felt their texture – hard-wearing and strong. There were a few lengths of batik too, folded up into thick cubes.

'Cheap textiles,' he said, drawing the tarpaulin back over the cloths.

'I think they are very beautiful.'

He looked at me and for a second I thought he was going to break into a smile; but then his face collapsed into a frown again. 'I'm sorry to disturb you,' he said as he lashed the tarpaulin into place. 'I lost my way.'

I do not know why I wanted him to stay. I cannot explain that feeling. Standing there under the house with the rain falling around me, I wanted to implore him to stay, but I could not say the words.

Just then I heard Father coming down the stairs. 'What's happening down there?' he said. 'Who is there, Snow?'

'A cloth merchant,' I said as Father came to join us.

'So, what do you have to offer us?' Father said, not seeming to notice that the poor boy was standing with his head bowed. 'Come on, I haven't got all day.'

The rain-sodden creature began to undo the tarpaulin, all the time keeping his head bowed.

'Where did this rubbish come from?' Father said, barely having looked at the cloths. 'Who do you work for?'

'Tiger Tan.'

'I didn't know Tiger had started selling this nonsense. He used to be a good merchant,' Father said. 'What's your name?'

'Johnny. Lim.'

'Well, Johnny Lim, you tell Tiger not to send these rags around here again.'

Johnny nodded.

'Come on, Snow,' Father said as he left.

As we went up the stairs I saw Johnny cycling off into the rain. I kept looking to see if he would turn back, but he did not. He pedalled steadily until he had crossed the yard. As he reached the path through the plantation he stopped cycling and looked back at the house. Through the deluge I couldn't see his face clearly, but I convinced myself he was smiling. I turned away and lay on my bed, pulling a small pillow to my stomach. Even now, long after I misplaced that little beaded cushion somewhere in this house, I remember the gentle tickle of the embroidered flower patterns on my fingertips, just as I remember the smell of rain-wet earth blowing through the windows.

These are the things I have already lost, I know, but what will happen to the memories? Will they remain or will they slowly fade away as old photographs do, bleached to nothingness by sunlight? I feel as if I am about to throw open the shutters and let the light in. The burning, burning light.

28 September 1941

I am trying to remember when I arrived at my decision. I do not think I can point to a single moment in time and say, yes, that is when I decided I would leave my husband.

Leave my husband. The sound of those words thrills me and

frightens me. I am shocked by how the words appear on the pages of this diary, clear and indelible. Their sentiments will endure long after I am gone.

If I am being honest, it was only a few days after we got married that I first knew (or should have known) that I would not remain with Johnny for ever. Mother and Father invited a few friends to the house to be introduced to him. I insisted they did so – I did not wish for my husband to be treated as a leper, something awful to be ashamed of. About eight people came, friends of Father's whom I have known since I was very young. One of them had a daughter who was my age. Her name was Lemon and she was not yet married. She led me by the hand down the dim corridor leading to my bedroom; she padded quickly across the bare boards, the pale soles of her bare feet flashing against the dark teak floor. Giggling, she locked the door. She could not wait to speak about the experience of being married.

'What's it really like?' she asked, sitting elegantly on the mat with her legs folded under her (something my inflexible bones will not permit me to do).

'It's nice,' I replied, 'though really no different from being on your own. Life goes on just as it did before.'

'But surely it must be more exciting now, what with a man in your room!'

I laughed. 'Excitement? I'm not sure that is the object of marriage.'

'Snow, come on,' she said, lowering her voice in a conspiratorial manner. '*Your* marriage is all about excitement.'

I paused. 'What do you mean?'

She played with her jade pendant, rubbing it between her fingers. 'You know exactly what I mean, Snow. After all – Johnny Lim, well, isn't it exciting being with this type of man? Answer truthfully now.'

'What sort of a man is he?'

'Snow!' she exclaimed, throwing her head back in laughter. 'How you tease me! All right, if you want to hear me say it: he is a strong, healthy, labouring man, totally uneducated and wild. He's different from us. He's almost . . . *savage*. That's what you wanted, wasn't it? Admit it!'

'No,' I answered, 'it isn't what I want. He isn't savage.'

'Ooohhh,' she continued giggling, 'you've always made me laugh, dear Snow. Anyway, it's good that there are no secrets between us. I'm glad you tell me these things. After all, everyone in the valley has been talking about you and Johnny. Everyone knows you wanted a husband who is different from you, different from the rest of us. You've always been a naughty thing.'

I did not answer. I looked at her slim neck, encircled by the delicate gold chain around it. Next to her I felt tall and ungainly.

'Tell me,' she said, 'are your parents still very angry with you?'

I shrugged. 'Father gave his consent to the marriage in the end, so he has no reason to be angry.'

'My parents told me that your mother threatened to disown you if you married Johnny, but you insisted on doing so. Is that true? Oh, tell me it is, Snow – it's a wonderful story!'

I paused. 'No,' I said, 'that is not quite how it turned out.'

'Father said he would flog me if I followed your example – or sell me to the brothel in Kampar. That's where I'd belong, he said. Isn't that hilarious?'

'Yes,' I said, trying to raise a smile.

'So what do you and Johnny talk about?'

'Everything,' I said. 'Everything.'

'You do surprise me, Snow,' she said as she rose from her folded-flower position. She crossed the room and picked up my wedding photograph. She replaced it on my dressing table and looked around the room. 'You should furnish this place more luxuriously now that you are a married woman,' she said. 'Books alone are not very decorative, you know.'

We rejoined the others in the sitting room. Johnny was clearly uncomfortable. He looked very small in his large rosewood armchair and moved constantly, like a mouse caught in a box. The long calligraphy scrolls hung on the walls above him, unfurled like long tendrils trying to touch him on the shoulder.

'Your husband has been telling us how he has taken over Tiger Tan's shop,' Lemon's father said. 'He sounds as if he is doing very well – that is a good little shop he has there.'

'He is very proud of it,' I said, sitting next to Johnny. I looked at him and saw his eyes soften with my presence.

'He should be,' Chan Toh Kwan said, 'everyone needs towels now and then.'

'How fortunate he is to have married into this family,' Lemon's mother said.

'If you need to dress your servants,' said Mother, 'send them to Johnny. He knows exactly how servants dress.'

'Lemon,' I said, 'why don't you play the piano?'

She did not need persuading. She crossed the room and seated herself at the piano. Her reflection gleamed in its polished upright face. She said, 'What shall I play?'

'How about some Mozart?' Father said.

She began to play a most delicate piece, playful and bright, her fingers moving easily over the keyboard. When she finished she turned round and smiled. 'That's one I have learned recently. Can you guess what it is?'

Mother turned to Johnny. 'Do you know what that is?'

He frowned and looked down into his cup of tea.

I said, 'Well, I for one do not recognise it.'

Lemon pouted like a girl ten years younger and said, 'Oh Uncle TK, *you* know what it is, don't you?'

Father laughed. 'It's part of the allegro from a piano sonata. I can't remember which one, but I do know you've only played a small part of it, you naughty girl.'

She giggled. 'Sorry.'

'As you play so beautifully, we shall forgive you.'

'What next?' she asked.

Father said, 'Some Chopin?'

'TK,' Mother said, laughing, 'are you sure that's appropriate?'

'Mazurka or waltz?' asked Lemon.

'Johnny?' Father said. 'What is your preference.'

Johnny shrugged, head bowed.

'It appears Johnny has no opinion on the subject of music,' said Father.

'Nocturne,' I said. 'Johnny would like to hear a nocturne.'

'Oh,' said Lemon, frowning, 'I haven't practised any nocturnes.'

'Can't you remember anything?' I said.

She began to play something slowly. Her fingers were hesitant, but she produced a pleasant tune nonetheless, one I recognised from Father's gramophone. Then she stopped. 'I can't,' she said. 'I don't remember the rest.'

'Father,' I said, 'why don't you play? I'm sure you can play this one.'

'TK?' his friends chorused. 'We didn't know you played the piano. What a thing! And we thought only the women played musical instruments!'

Father stiffened. 'I don't. My playing days are long over. I never play nowadays.'

When the guests had left and the house was silent again I remember feeling a sense of strength. Johnny and I remained in the sitting room, alone, holding hands as we sat in the fading afternoon light. It was as if we had overcome some huge obstacle, crossed an invisible boundary. Now, replaying that day in my head, I can see that it was not strength I felt but something closer to blindness. I had overcome nothing; the obstacles were insurmountable. The boundaries, I have realised, are still there.

29 September 1941

The new bishop came to dinner tonight. He has recently arrived from Hong Kong, where he was dean. The detestable Frederick Honey is taking him on a 'driving tour' of the valley. This presumably means showing off to the bishop the extent of the British tin-mining empire which seems to have grown rapidly since Honey took over as head of the Darby concern. Honey has also acquired a new motor car, an enormous black creature whose roar can be heard a mile away.

'Climate, churchmanship, lack of spiritual discipline,' the bishop said, counting out his doubts about his new posting by holding up his stubby fingers one by one. He had drunk a considerable amount and his face had become redder and more rotund as the evening progressed. 'Responsibility and loneliness. Lack of friends – though I am hoping this will change.'

'Of course it will,' said Honey without looking up from his plate.

'And obviously,' the bishop continued, 'there is the whole question of the children's education.'

I saw Father stiffen. 'I agree, a child's education is of utmost importance,' Father said.

'A waste,' Mother whispered under her breath. I am certain no one heard it but me.

Father continued, 'But I am sure you will find the schools in Singapore more than adequate.'

'But,' the bishop said, as if no one else had spoken, 'there is the significance, yes, the *significance*, of being a bishop. Who knows, I might be offered something more congenial in the future.' He raised his glass and winked.

'So, thinking of leaving before you have even arrived,' Johnny said. Father glared at him, but he continued eating without once looking up, taking great care to hold his knife and fork as I have taught him to.

'I believe,' said Father, smiling kindly, 'that you will find Singapore very congenial indeed. I have heard it said that Singapore today is very nearly as entertaining as Hong Kong – though I cannot speak from personal experience.'

There was gentle laughter around the table, Mother's shrill notes rising above the rest.

Honey leaned sideways and nudged Johnny gently. 'Perhaps we should go to Singapore some time, without the wives, you know – have a bit of fun?' Everything Honey does seems stiff and calculated, as if he has read a book on How to Make Jokes, or How to Appear Friendly.

I said, 'Frederick, my existence does not depend on my husband. The two of you are free to go wherever you wish.'

'Please, not in front of the bishop,' Father said, smiling in his threatening way. It struck me that he has an extraordinary range of smiles.

Mother said, 'Anyone for a cognac?'

I got up and helped clear away some dishes. In the kitchen Mei Li was sitting on a low wooden stool, dipping little pink balls of sweet dough into a bowl of flour.

'Don't sit with your legs like that,' Mother hissed at her. 'Only whores behave like that.' She looked to see if I was listening. 'Only *whores* behave like that,' she said again.

We returned to the table and sat in silence for a while. A weak breeze rustled the tamarind tree outside. The bishop went to the window and stood before the open shutters with his hands on the ledge. His cheeks were red and clammy, and he must have been glad that the night was cooler than usual. When he turned round he looked very grave. He asked us about the Japanese.

'What about them?' Johnny said, looking into his glass. I thought he said it somewhat too sharply. I looked at Father and saw the little muscle in his jaw twitch.

'What do you think they will do next?' the bishop said, staring out of the window. 'They're marching straight through Indochina as if it weren't there.'

Johnny took a gulp at his whisky. 'We don't give a damn about them. There are things we can do to them, you know.'

Honey went through to the next room and lifted the cover of the gramophone. He visits Father so often nowadays that he has come to regard this house as his own. (Even Johnny remarked the other day that Honey seems more welcome here than he does.) We heard him humming away in his How to Be Cheerful manner.

Father cleared his throat. 'I hope you understand, Bishop, that Johnny merely speaks with the empty fury of youth. In fact, we are not at all worried about the Japanese. The monsoons will soon be upon us, and the Japanese will make little progress through Siam in such weather. I personally do not believe the Japanese are quite as bad as people make them out to be. Did you know that there has long been a small but very well assimilated Japanese community in Malaya? The local barber, for example, is Japanese. My view of them is that they are a very civilised race. I have met many fine Japanese – why, just a few days ago I made the acquaintance of an exceptionally cultured Japanese gentleman.'

'Yes,' Mother enthused, 'he is a marquis – we must introduce you to him.'

'Besides,' continued Father, 'with the British to protect us, what is there to worry about?'

'*If you were the only girl in the world . . .*' Honey sang, out of tune.

'Are you drunk?' I asked.

'No, Snow, I'm merely having a jolly old time,' he replied. '*There would be such wonderful things to do, there would be such wonderful dreams come true.*'

The bishop returned to the table and poured himself some cognac. He seemed jolly again, and launched into another story.

'Have I told you about my first visit to St John's? I thought I'd call in at what would soon be *my* cathedral. I was on holiday, so I dressed in lay clothing. Do you know what? The parish priest failed to include a prayer for me – because of attire! He told me later that he wasn't sure of the status of a bishop elect in collar and tie, so he decided to play it by the book. How ridiculous!' His laughter filled the room, competing with the music and the gentle, never-ending pounding of the mortar and pestle from the kitchen.

'You should have known,' said Johnny quite unexpectedly, 'that you were coming to a diocese with a High Church tradition. Conformity with clerical dress is always taken for granted there.' He got up and took his glass into the kitchen, where I could see him exchanging pleasantries with Mei Li.

The table fell silent with astonishment. The bishop looked blankly at Honey. Their expressions said it all: where did a person such as Johnny gain such information? Where did he learn to speak like that? From Father? No – for all his learning, Father knows little about Christians and barely converses with Johnny anyway.

I found myself smiling to hide my annoyance. Only I knew: it was another piece of trivia Johnny has picked up from Peter.

30 September 1941

The worst times are when we are together, alone, and I see in his face how thrilled he still is to be married to me. He wears the expression of a young boy who has found something precious in the fields and keeps it hidden in his room. He loves me as he would a lost diamond or an opalescent gemstone; he admires me and is fascinated by me. Yet he never touches me. He is afraid to.

No one else will understand this, and I have resolved to tell no one. It was my decision to marry him, I know. I remember

Mother's reaction when I attempted to speak to her about my situation a few weeks ago. 'You are his wife,' she said simply and laughed, as if there was no more to say. Later, as an afterthought, she came to my room and said, 'We could try and find you another man, but no one in the valley – in the whole country – will have you now. You must accept your fate.'

My fate. It seems I do not enjoy the luxury of limitless choice. Either I follow the course of *my fate* and remain with Johnny, unhappily, or I leave him, disgraced. The first option is full of dreadful clarity, the second cloudy and fathomless. I wish I lived in Europe: a nunnery would be the simplest solution, easy and face-saving. But I live here, and my decision is made. I plunge into the murky depths.

1 October 1941

This evening we took Professor Kunichika to the *wayang kulit* theatre on the outskirts of Kampar. He said he had read about the *wayang* and was curious to see if it really was as wonderful as he imagined. Father seemed very keen to organise an outing. 'Something to welcome our visitor to the valley,' as he put it.

We arrived just as the music was starting and the crowd settling down. Our little party had seats laid out specially for us – the rest of the audience sat on the dirt in front of the white canvas screen. Johnny had, predictably, asked Peter to come too, and I found myself in a chair next to him. 'How macabre,' he whispered, all gangling elbows and knees. I found him most irritating. The flat, discordant sounds of the wind instruments had a disquieting effect on me, and I tried my best not to show my discomfort. Kunichika had taken a seat on the other side of me, so now I was sandwiched between him and Peter.

The first of the puppet-shadows began to dance across the screen, huge and horrible against the pale, glowing light.

'What's happening now?' Peter kept asking.

I remained calm and did my best to explain, although I have never found the *wayang* particularly absorbing. 'It's a story from the Hindu epics – the *Ramayana*, I believe. The figure on the left is the hero, the one on the right is the villain who is about to steal the hero's beloved from him.' For some reason, I could not recall their names, even though I had heard them a thousand times before.

'I see,' Peter said, affecting boredom, 'the same old "good versus evil" chestnut.'

'In a manner of speaking,' I said, my patience wearing thin.

'The beauty of the Malay shadow theatre,' Kunichika said quietly in his deep, voice, 'lies in its ability to transform a great Indian text into something distinctively local. Look at the figures, delicately carved from buffalo hide. Their features are not Indian. The setting, the music – these are clearly Indo-Malay.'

'Thank you,' Peter said.

'The figure on the left is Bima, the other is Duryodana,' Kunichika added.

I shifted in my seat and caught the smell of Kunichika's clothes: cut grass and eau de toilette.

No one stirred. The shadows arched and fell across the yellowed screen, illuminated by a swollen, distorted light. I closed my eyes and envisaged the path I have chosen for myself. Johnny. How will I leave him? I thought about it again and again, as I have so often in recent weeks. The shadows seemed larger, more terrifying than I ever remembered. They swooped on each other, thrusting their misshapen heads and kicking their bony legs. The music – gongs, sharp drumming and shrill windpipes – rose to a crescendo.

'Snow, are you all right?' Peter asked, prodding me with a knobbly finger.

'Yes,' I said, pulling away. 'It's nearly finished now. The show's almost over.'

I excused myself the moment we arrived home. Johnny and Peter have gone out somewhere, as they frequently do nowadays. Kunichika is enjoying a drink with Father. I am alone writing this. It is a comforting thing for me to do. Silly, I know – as if by recording every detail my resolve will be strengthened. Nonetheless, writing may soon be the only thing I have left.

2 October 1941

It makes it worse for me, more painful, that Johnny seems not to have a clue about what I am about to do. He does not know what I am thinking – I am certain of that. To be fair, I have given him no clue whatsoever. I behave completely as normal. The pretence is exhausting; the effort of it occupies every second of my day and night. I hope the right moment presents itself soon. I do not know how much longer I can continue this subterfuge.

3 October 1941

When Father suggested the trip, no one responded. We simply did not know what to make of it.

'After all,' he said, 'there is a thing Westerners call "Honeymoon". It is a chance for newly-married couples to go away and enjoy being in each other's company.'

'But we have been married for more than a year,' I said.

'I suppose it will be a belated Honeymoon, if such a thing exists,' he said. 'Think of it merely as a vacation. Your mother and I think that it is a healthy and fitting thing for you to do.'

I still did not understand. 'You and Mother have never been on vacation,' I said.

'We are old people,' Father smiled, 'from a different era.'

The idea of being alone with Johnny unsettled me. 'This means you will not be accompanying us?'

'Of course not,' Father said, 'we would only get in your way.'

'Is it acceptable for us to travel alone?' I asked.

'That is something your mother and I have considered at length, and we have decided, for the sake of safety rather than decorum, that you should have a chaperone, someone who will ensure safe passage for you wherever you choose to go.'

'Who is it?'

He paused to finish his tea. 'Frederick Honey,' he said.

Instantly, Johnny said, 'Then Peter can come too?'

Mother left the table. There was silence. At last Father said, 'I don't see what harm can come of that.'

I thought about this for some time. The combination of Johnny, Peter and Honey was not one I wanted to be near. But then again, perhaps once we were away from my parents and this house, Johnny and I might converse more easily; the opportunity to tell him everything might arise.

'Where are we going?' I asked.

Father said, 'I thought perhaps you might like to see the Seven Maidens.'

4 October 1941

My powers of deception are being tested to their limit. Today Johnny came home and said, 'Peter has found a house for us. It is a house *and* a shop.' His voice was full of vigour and hope and longing. 'Soon we will be able to move out of this house, away from your parents – at last.'

I smiled to mask my unease.

'I will be able to run my own business, a shop with my own name. We will be able to build a new life without *them*,' he continued, dropping his voice and looking over his shoulder as if wary of some hidden danger. Since the Incident at the Shop, Johnny has been very restless; he speaks constantly about plans for a new shop. This enthusiasm seems to have escalated since Peter arrived in the valley last month.

I searched for something to say. 'What is this place like?'

'It is *magnificent*,' he said. I noticed that it was the first time he has ever used that word; he has learned it, no doubt, from Peter. 'It is by the river. I will take you there soon.'

'That would be nice,' I said. 'Have you thought of a name for it?'

'Yes,' he said, fetching a piece of paper. He reached for a calligraphy brush from my desk and wrote out its name in slow, uncertain strokes. He had obviously been practising this for some time. He showed it to me as if it were a secret, holding it close to his chest, just beneath his chin.

'The Harmony Silk Factory,' I said.

He gave me the piece of paper and brushed my hand with the lightest of fingertip-touches. That is the only way he has ever touched me.

5 October 1941

Honey called round again for tea today. He wore a white shirt and a cream-coloured suit made of linen that was crisp and flat as a sheet of paper. I have never seen him wear anything else. His tie, too, was the one he always wore – black with thin diagonal purple stripes.

'Frederick,' said Father without getting out of his chair, 'how nice to see you. How are the mines doing?'

'Reasonably well,' Honey replied, hovering at the threshold of Father's study. He looked at me uncertainly. 'Will you be joining us for a cup of tea, Snow?'

I looked at Father. He was sitting at his desk with a half-written poem on a scroll before him. Slowly, he placed his brush on its rest. 'Yes,' he said, 'why don't you join us briefly?'

'Let me see,' said Honey, inclining his head as he sat down. Father's gramophone was playing so softly that it was difficult to hear the music. 'Bach. The forty-eight. Prelude in, hmmm, F sharp major.' Though he is not fat his chin has a habit of wobbling when he speaks. I have always found his face perfectly ordinary and featureless. I decided once and for all that he looked like a schoolteacher.

'You have a very good ear indeed, Frederick,' said Father.

'Father always listens to music when he works,' I said.

'Always Bach?' Honey asked.

'Yes,' said Father. 'I feel there is a certain symmetry in Bach which mirrors the construction in Chinese poems. Chopin – whose works I am very fond of – I find too . . . what is the word . . .'

'Vulgar? Florid?' said Honey.

' . . . no . . .'

'Too poetic,' I ventured.

'Thank you, Snow,' Father said, looking me straight in the eye. 'Yes, too poetic in its sensibility. Too full of emotion, you might say. Inappropriate. It should only be listened to in times of turmoil.'

Honey laughed politely. 'Speaking of things vulgar and florid,' he said, 'what about this chap Peter Wormwood? I can only apologise for his performance at your Autumn Festival celebrations the other week. I'm terribly sorry. You must have a terrible impression of Englishmen. We're not all like that, you know.'

'Of course not,' Father said.

'What was he thinking?' Honey continued. His face became flushed and deep lines scarred his furrowed brow. 'What on earth was he thinking? I mean, that . . . *costume* . . . I'm so awfully sorry. It must have been dreadfully embarrassing for you – it certainly was for me. What sort of man behaves like that? He must be insane. Needless to say, we haven't welcomed him with open arms at the Club.'

'He hasn't been here for long,' I said. 'Perhaps he is uncomfortable in these surroundings.'

Honey regarded me with a strange expression. His voice quietened. 'There is one rule, one golden rule, which an Englishman observes when he comes to a new place: never ruffle any feathers. Follow local customs. Blend in. Be respectful. Even those of us who were never taught this, well, we just know. It's the key to our success here.'

'Yes,' I said, 'your success.'

Father began to cough violently. Ever since the Incident at the Shop, he has had these uncontrollable fits of rasping, wheezing coughs which suggest that, in spite of his protests, he has not quite recovered. I wonder if he simply does not want to acknowledge what Johnny did for him on that day. Even I do not know everything that happened between them.

'I know you were upset, Frederick,' Father said when he had regained his composure, 'you told me at the time. But frankly I still cannot understand what the fuss is all about. Call me an old fool, but I could not see what you saw. I thought his appearance somewhat unusual, of course, but only because I had never seen such dress in real life. In books, yes – it reminded me of the opera, of pictures of Venice and Vienna from the last century.'

Honey rolled his eyes. 'This is what I feared. You think we all dress and behave like that. Let me tell you, all that cheap Oscar Wilde nonsense is *not* an accurate representation of European attire.'

Father raised a laugh. 'The two of you will have plenty to talk about, that's for sure.'

'I'll be damned if I ever speak to that man.'

'It may be difficult to avoid him,' I said, resisting the urge to smile. 'He is coming on our trip to the Seven Maidens too.'

Honey looked at me with unblinking eyes. 'Dear God,' he whispered.

'Now, Snow, Mr Honey and I have some business to attend to,' said Father. 'Shut the door behind you, please.'

As I left I heard the lock on the door click quietly into place.

6 October 1941

When Johnny came to bed last night I pretended to be asleep. I have taken to doing this recently because I think it is easier for both of us. Bedtime is when I am at my most vulnerable; my body is tired and it is difficult to maintain my façade of innocence, and so I err on the side of caution.

Johnny undressed silently, adjusting the lamp so that only the faintest flicker of light invaded the room. I watched him through narrowed eyes, my head resting deep in a pillow. I am certain he did not know I was watching. In the dim light his skin looked taut and brown. His skin was one of the things I loved most when I first saw him. It spoke of a life exposed to the sun and the rain, as if it had been rendered smooth by the elements. The faint scars on his back were like the patterns on the hide of some strange, sinuous animal. My skin could never be like that, I thought; it is almost as if we were a different race.

He came to bed and for a while I remained motionless, inhaling his scent of earth and wet leaves. It was a long time since I had smelled that perfume. I felt the weight of his body next to me, depressing the mattress and pulling me closer to him. I allowed my body to fall slowly towards his until my cheek came to rest on his shoulder. His skin was warm and clammy. I put my hand on his chest, feeling his heavy heartbeat on my palm. At last I felt his fingers run lightly through my hair like a thin, prickly comb. It was as if he was afraid to touch me. My head began to itch; I wished his fingers would scratch me, claw at my scalp – anything except tickle in this manner. I could bear it no longer. I pulled away, withdrawing to the other side of the bed. I could not sleep.

7 October 1941

I know how I am going to do it. I have enacted it in my head, a thousand times over, every sleepless night. This is what will happen:

I choose my moment carefully, waiting until Johnny is in a particularly cheerful mood. Perhaps it will be at the end of a day when he has been with Peter and is filled with the blind, childish optimism that I see in his eyes every time they are together. I do not know what Peter has that inspires such exuberance, but I do know this: a child's optimism is less easily crushed than an adult's; or at least, once crushed, it is more quickly restored.

Finding Johnny in this buoyant state, I sit down with him and give him a drink. I have gone to great lengths to secure some wine. (A few days prior to this, I force myself to smile sweetly at Honey and tell him how pleasant it is to have him come to visit us; he is so taken aback he cannot resist my request for a bottle of French wine from his extensive collection.) This pleases Johnny because, thanks to Peter, he has recently become fascinated by the taste and exotic nature of wine.

Casually, I ask him about this new house he has seen. He needs little encouragement and begins to tell me about his plans, schemes that no one in the valley has ever imagined. Tiger would be proud, he says. He misses Tiger, I know. His voice barely rises above its usual gentle monotone, yet it is easy to sense how thrilled he is. His thoughts flow faster than he can speak; he pauses now and then, his brow furrowed as he tries to recall the words. Sometimes the force of his emotion is so great that he cannot find them; he looks at me with an expression that is at once imploring and resolute in its determination to continue unaided. The cloud that hangs heavily over me begins to lift: he does not need my help. He does not need me. That is why I want him to think of the shop. It is something – the only thing – that is truly his. People come and they go, fluttering at the edge of his world, never properly entering it. I, his wife; Peter, his fleeting foreign friend: even we merely hover outside. But long after we are gone, he will still have that shop. It belongs to him; it is utterly his: to mould, control, love and destroy. As he speaks he looks at me and it is as if we both know: I will never belong to him. Nothing needs to be said. A blank, inscrutable expression returns to his face. He realises, just as I do, that all the things that stood between us before we were married, well, they remain. We were wrong to believe that we could pull down the barriers. It was a mistake, a simple failure, that is all.

I begin to tell him that it's no one's fault, but I stop because I know, even if he does not, that the fault lies with me.

Thus, wordlessly, our world ends.

8 October 1941

I was sitting on the verandah reading when Johnny appeared. I was not surprised to see he had Peter with him.

'I heard you had dinner with the bishop,' Peter said. 'How was the Right Reverend? Fat as ever?'

'It was the first time I had met him,' I said, continuing to read, 'so I cannot say if he was as fat "as ever".'

'Well,' said Peter, 'one savage bout of dysentery is all it'll take to make his figure sylphlike.'

I did not answer. Johnny was holding a fine fishnet which he proceeded to add to the pile of things he has assembled for our trip. Peter stood with his scrawny arms folded across his chest. I knew he was watching me, but I kept my gaze firmly on my book. I heard Johnny packing and unpacking some boxes in the room. I wished he would hurry up and return, but he seemed to go on for ever, clanging metal plates, dropping tin cans, dusting off canvas sheets. All this time Peter and I remained motionless, unable to move. I read the same words over and over again.

Finally, I could bear it no longer. I snapped my book shut and looked straight into his face.

'How are you finding life in the valley?'

He looked startled. I noticed his milk-white skin had not reacted well to the sun – his cheeks and forearms bore hot, tender red burns.

'Fine,' he said, 'fine. In fact, more than that, it's a ball. With sequins and tiaras.'

'I'm pleased to hear that. Foreigners usually do not adapt well to the conditions here. They find us primitive.'

'Primitive? *Mais non, mais non*,' he said, looking at the house. 'If this is primitive then I am a savage.' He lifted both arms in a strange gesture I could not decipher. I think it was perhaps intended to be theatrical in its effect. I could not stifle a giggle. To my surprise, he laughed too, a whooping, singing laugh that seemed to come from the depths of his body.

Johnny returned and kissed me lightly on the forehead.

'Looking forward to our trip,' Peter called out as they got on their bicycles and pedalled away.

Another thing: this evening I noticed that the photographs of our ancestors which Father keeps in his study have already become hazy and indistinct in their frames. In a few more years we shall not even remember who those people were.

9 October 1941

Late this afternoon, as I was returning from a walk along the river, I heard Father conversing with someone in his study. The door was closed; the talking stopped abruptly when I entered the hall. I wondered if the visitor was Honey, but the tone of the voice seemed wrong. Curious to find out who the other person was, I hesitated for a moment before proceeding to my room. I closed my door firmly, making sure it made a noise as it shut.

After a considerable length of time I heard Father's study door open. I went to the window to see who the visitor was. It was Kunichika.

10 October 1941

We set off in the dark, dawn still an hour away. Five silent bodies in that huge black car: Honey at the wheel, Kunichika next to him in the front seat; and at the back, Johnny, Peter and me.

'What do you think of my new car?' Honey said in an attempt to spark conversation. No one answered. In the twilight I saw Peter trying to blink sleep from his eyes; he rubbed his face with both palms in the manner of a small child. Johnny remained quiet too, but I could see that his eyes were clear and lively.

'It feels like a tomb,' I said.

'Oh,' said Honey softly.

'I think it's frightfully grand, *splendidly* vulgar,' Peter said. 'There's nothing quite like a Rolls. I adore it, Honey.' He paused and coughed as he suppressed a giggle. 'You wouldn't mind if I called you by your Christian name, would you, Frederick?'

Honey merely grunted. He seemed determined not to exchange a single word with Peter.

From where I was sitting I had a perfect view of the nape of Kunichika's neck. His hair ended in a neat line halfway up the white stretch of skin. For most of today's drive that was all I could see, Kunichika's neck positioned right in front of me – rigid, smooth and perfectly straight. At times, if I had been staring at it for too long, it seemed not to be human.

In the brightening morning, we drove past oil-palm and rubber plantations. The dew-damp air was quickly burned away and a hot, gritty breeze blew through the windows, drying our lips and tongues. Johnny spent much time gazing back at the large clouds of dust rising up in swirls behind the car, chasing us as we sped along.

'We're being pursued by djinns!' Peter wailed before collapsing into his cackling laugh. 'Sandstorms, the Devil's red dust! God save us!' Johnny broke into a gentle laugh every time Peter made a comment; he stuck his head out of the window, his fine hair ruffled like the feathers of a small bird. He glanced at me, smiling broadly. He seemed a mere child. It hurt me to look at him because I knew that I would soon bring this fleeting happiness to an end, and all traces of the child in him would die, completely and for ever. I wished Peter would stop. I wanted to take hold of his wildly gesturing arms and bind them to his body.

'I say,' Honey called out, 'this is the right road, isn't it?'

We had come off the main road just south of Taiping. The car moved along slowly; the ground beneath us felt bumpy, full of rocks and potholes.

Kunichika said, 'We are heading due north.'

'Are we? Well then, I suppose we should still be all right,' Honey said.

I looked at Johnny. 'Stop the car, Frederick,' I said, 'Johnny will know.'

We got out of the car, shielding our eyes from the glare of the sun. Johnny looked around us. By some strange instinct, he seemed to know exactly where we were. 'Yes, this road is OK,' he said. His voice was clear and flat. No one questioned him. We climbed back into the car and continued to jolt along.

'You seem to know this part of the country intimately,' Kunichika said, turning round in his seat to look at Johnny.

'I have spent my whole life here,' Johnny said, looking out of the window.

'So have many people, but I am sure not all of them have the familiarity with the countryside that you do.'

'Johnny's a country boy at heart, isn't he?' Peter said. 'Just like me.'

Johnny shrugged.

'The jungle is a strange place,' Kunichika said. 'It changes all the time, shifting in shape and colour. It swallows whole villages in an instant. Once you move away from it you may never return, not truly. Only those who keep coming back to the trees and vines may sense their changing rhythms. I am sure Mr Lim will tell you that.'

'Nonsense,' Peter said, turning to Johnny.

Johnny hesitated. 'No, it is true.'

The car swayed like a boat as Honey carefully negotiated the potholes.

'It is not unreasonable for me to be curious about Mr Lim's familiarity with the countryside,' Kunichika continued, 'for it is exceptional that a shopkeeper should have such knowledge.'

'I disagree with you, Professor,' I said, raising my voice above the rough clatter of the engine. 'We never lose what we are born with. Even if we try – if we move away from our homes, as my husband has done – we are still part of the worlds of our birth. We can't ever escape.'

No one spoke. We continued to roll in and out of dips in the broken road.

Peter seemed to have shrunk into his seat, his head lolling pathetically to one side, gasping for air at the window. 'I feel seasick,' he said.

It felt as if many hours had passed before we rejoined the coast road and reached our destination for today, the Formosa Hotel. We arrived two hours ago. The others are downstairs having a drink before dinner. I am, of course, forbidden to enter the bar. I had heard from Father about the strictly observed etiquette in such grand British establishments; in one club in Kuala Lumpur, he says, there is a sign at the entrance to the smoking room that reads NO WOMEN OR DOGS. I looked out for these cold reminders, determined to be proud and unflinching, even humorous before them. In the end I could see no such notice, but the cold stare of the bartender spoke clearly of the well-entrenched customs of this place, and I decided not to test my bravado.

To tell the truth, I am grateful for this moment of solitude. After a day spent in the close company of those four, I find it strangely comforting to be alone. I enjoy the times I have to myself. Mother would be shocked to hear me confess this. It would be no use trying to explain. Women are not often on their own: they are constantly surrounded by men – fathers, husbands, sons. Those are the people we live for, whose lives press into ours at every moment. We obey, nurse, nurture and love. But in the end, we are and always have been, alone. That is why I am glad for moments such as these. They are, I have realised, the only times I am truly myself.

Later

When I arrived at dinner, I found Honey in the middle of telling a story. He was facing Kunichika as he spoke, but he had assumed his Public Speaking voice, so I deduced that his intention was to impress.

'. . . my men had to quell a veritable uprising. The whole thing was most unpleasant.'

'Not the "Murder at the Mine" story again, Frederick,' I said as I approached.

Peter got up from his chair, but as he did so he managed to nudge the table with his thigh. The small vase of drooping, nearly dead orchids toppled over, spilling its contents on to Honey's part of the table. The smell of stale flower water filled the air. 'Clumsy fool,' Honey muttered under his breath, not looking at Peter.

'Good evening,' Kunichika said, smiling as he pulled my chair back for me. 'This is the effect you have on men, you see.'

'Effect? Rubbish, the man's an idiot, that's all,' Honey grumbled.

'Sorry,' Peter said in a tone which suggested he was anything but.

'Continue with your story, Frederick,' I said, even though I had heard it several times before. The life of a tin miner, even one of Honey's grandeur, is hardly filled with excitement, and their few noteworthy stories tend to become repetitive.

'Thank you – I was nearly finished anyway. As you may have guessed,' he said, turning once more to Kunichika, 'our man died. A year and a week after he was stabbed by the Chinaman. Well, plainly, it was murder. However: English Law is a strange creature. I'm not sure if you can understand this, but . . .'

'. . . the accused could not be convicted of murder because the length of time between *actus reus* and death was greater than a year and a day,' said Kunichika.

'Well, yes,' said Honey, eyeing Kunichika with a faint frown. 'So they let him off. We have one dead manager on our hands and a homicidal Chinaman on the run.'

'It was such a long time ago, Frederick, long before your time. People aren't still talking about that, are they?' I said.

'When I took over as the head of Darby mine a year ago, I found that many people were still fascinated by this story. It had become a legend. What is it, now, eight years since it happened? Thing is, no one knew who this guy was. His name was probably an alias, he had no family, no home – nothing. And then he simply vanished into the jungle. He's still out there, this murderer.'

'Except he isn't a murderer in the eyes of the law,' Kunichika said.

'Hah!' said Honey, lighting a cigarette.

Johnny cleared his throat. He had remained silent throughout Honey's story – I must say I do not blame him, for these stories are not the most riveting. 'I have heard,' he said in an awkward and self-consciously bored manner (learned, no doubt, from Peter), 'that the so-called murderer was a mere boy.'

'Even children can be murderers, you know. Look at the Chinamen in the villages. Most of them are Commies by the time they're thirteen – nasty little buggers.'

'Are you sure this isn't some myth, like the ghosts that are meant to haunt Kellie's Castle or whatever that place is not far from here?' said Peter. 'Because it doesn't sound very plausible to me. Nameless man-child emerges from nowhere, chops leg off sixteen-stone Angus McHefty, gets freed by Lord Justice Snooty and then vanishes into the jungle, never to be seen again. Perhaps he's hiding in Shangri-La.'

I found myself smiling at Honey's bristling silence.

Kunichika said, 'It's always the case that details are lost in the retelling of stories. Sometimes things are forgotten, sometimes things are added. The tale of History is most unreliable. It is, after all, reconstructed by human beings.'

We found that hardly anything on the menu was available. 'What on earth can we have, then?' demanded Honey in his VIP's voice. The old Indian waiter seemed not to understand. In the end, we had mulligatawny soup, devilled chicken with boiled potatoes and cold English rice pudding.

'Ah, the taste of the Orient,' said Peter.

11 October 1941

A little more about last night. (It is raining heavily today so we are confined to our rooms for a while.) There was a string quartet playing while we had our dinner. As we were the only guests in the dining room, we wondered if the hotel had arranged the quartet specially for us.

'We're a long way from anywhere,' Peter said. 'Where on earth would they have found four viol-playing fossils at such short notice? Look at them . . .'

They were very old Chinese men with bent spines. Their dinner jackets had a greenish hue and were badly frayed.

'To think that the Formosa was, just a few years ago, the place everyone wanted to come to,' Honey said, lighting another cigarette. 'Look at it now.'

It was true, the hotel was decaying. In the dining room the chequerboard tiles on the floor were chipped in many places and a thick trail of dust ran along the window sills. The palms in their enormous pots were nearly dead. Up above the wide stone staircase leading to the rooms, the great crystal chandelier had long since ceased to work, and the hall was now dimly lit by a few old lamps.

I left the table to go back to my room. I tried to excuse myself with as little fuss as possible, choosing a moment when all four of the men were involved in a mildly heated discussion about the role of the Sultan in the affairs of state. I merely wanted to check that my diary was safe. The writing desk in my room (at which I sit writing this) is vast, but its leather surface is dry and scratched – more evidence of the Formosa's faded glory. More importantly, the lock on its drawer does not work, so I have been forced to hide this diary among the clothes in my travelling case. This is not ideal, but I have been careful to make sure that I am never far from it for too long.

All was in order. The diary was just as I had left it, tucked into the folds of a camisole, and I went back to the dining room. At the last minute I decided not to rejoin the men, and made my way instead to the colonnaded verandah at the rear of the hotel. The urge to be on my own was too great to resist. The Chinese lamps suspended from the ceiling no longer worked, of course, and darkness hung heavily over the place. Bats darted uncertainly over my head as I walked to the balustrade and placed my hands on the mossy stone. My eyes became accustomed to the night light and I could make out the outlines of a few objects: an old gazebo here, a small folly there; a small bridge over a dried-out pond, flower beds now reclaimed by the jungle. Things moved in the dark. Indistinct shapes snaking their way into the undergrowth, into the trees.

And then I heard footsteps approach from behind, the careful tread of feet that did not want to be heard. Two or three steps; pause; another three steps; pause. I remained facing the garden, my hands tightening slowly on the balustrade. Nothing to fear, I told myself, those footsteps are Kunichika's. Slowly, they came closer, until I swore I could feel his white breath on my hair. In a flash, I turned round.

'Oh, *hello*,' Peter called out brightly. 'What are you doing here? I was looking for the ah lavatory, but I seem to have got lost. Awfully dark out here, isn't it?'

'Peter,' I said, 'why are you creeping around in the dark?' I think I sounded cross, for he seemed taken aback.

'I'm most certainly not creeping around,' he said. 'Creeping isn't my *style*. One might ask the same of you, my dear. What on earth are you doing out here?'

'Nothing,' I said. 'Just looking at the garden.'

He stood next to me and peered out into the dark. 'Can't see anything. Are you sure there's a garden out there?'

'The remains of one, yes. Father says that in its heyday, this was the most famous garden in the country. The man who built it went on to run the botanical gardens in Penang.'

'How extraordinary. I didn't know you took an interest in matters horticultural.'

He leapt up to sit on the balustrade – a sudden explosion of arms, elbows and knees. I resisted the urge to comment on his lack of coordination. He pulled at his trousers, straightening their legs, and in doing so, managed to catch me with an elbow.

'Sorry,' he said.

'Goodnight, Peter,' I said, and walked back to my room, leaving him sitting on his own.

I checked on my diary again and went to bed. When Johnny eventually crawled in next to me I pretended to be asleep. He leaned over and kissed me on the forehead, and I sighed hazily. 'Sleep, sleep,' he said. His lips were thick and dry. He fell asleep quickly, mumbling and breathing heavily.

Above his gentle snoring I heard the scratching of rats out in the corridor.

12 October 1941

We were all glad to leave the Formosa, I think. Yesterday's confinement due to the rain had made us restless, and we waited anxiously to see if the sun would burn its way through the early-morning cloud.

'Rough night?' Honey said, with, I thought, the slightest hint of lasciviousness in his voice. 'You're looking tired.'

I ignored the remark and began to drag my case across the forecourt to the car.

'Let me help you,' Kunichika said, taking my things from me. He strode powerfully into the sun, descending a small flight of stone stairs in two quick steps.

The previous day's rain had washed thin rivers of mud on to many of the smaller roads, but we drove on regardless. This was the only way to Tanjong Acheh, the point on the coast where we will catch a boat to the Seven Maidens. That was Johnny's opinion. Even I was surprised at how certain he sounded. We are now a long way from Kampar – farther, surely, than any boy can cycle. Perhaps this was where he was born, where he grew up; perhaps he did not, as we all believe, spend his youth as a labourer in Tiger Tan's famous shop. His knowledge of this place seemed to come from some deep recess, something locked away so safely that even he may have forgotten its origin.

It was at that moment that I realised, with absolute clarity, that I did not know him at all. But then again I think I have always known that intimacy between us was impossible. That was why I wanted him: he would always be alien to me. And worse, it was I who pretended otherwise. I said things I now know were untrue. 'We are kindred spirits,' I told him as we held hands by the river, not a hundred yards from my parents' disapproving gaze. He looked at me with innocent eyes and believed every word I said. Then, as now, there lies an unfordable divide between us. Even Mother, in her own bizarre way, is at one with Father. She understands what he wants of her and vice versa. They each supply what the other needs. That is marriage.

At around midday, Honey stopped the car in the shade of a large mangosteen tree whose branches hung thinly over the road. We got out and leaned against the car while eating the tiffins we had brought with us from the hotel. There were boiled eggs, luncheon meat, fried bread and rice with *sambal belacan*. Peter let out a large yelp, as if something had startled him, and began rummaging in his rust-coloured satchel.

'I've just remembered something,' he said, and pulled out a camera. It was sleek and black and looked brand new. In his uneven, loping gallop, he ran a short distance away and turned to face us. He examined the top of the camera, uncertain of the buttons, while we continued to pick at our food.

'The fool doesn't know how to use the camera,' Honey said.

Johnny began to walk towards Peter to offer his help, but just then Peter raised the camera to his face and called out, 'Look *wonderful*, everyone.'

I tried to smile but the sun made me squint.

Peter beamed brightly and began to walk back to the car. Suddenly he stopped and raised his hand to his brow, shielding his eyes from the light. 'Hello,' he said, 'there's something further up the road. Some*one*, I think. A woman. Selling fruit, it seems to me. Come and have a look.'

We trudged out into the middle of the mud-streaked road. Sure enough, in the distance, we saw an old Malay woman with baskets of fruit set out on either side of her. She sat perfectly still, and looked as if she had been there for a very long time.

'How strange,' said Honey. 'We didn't spot her before, did we?'

None of us had.

'Where on earth do you think she's appeared from?' Peter said. 'And what is she doing here anyway? This road is hardly what you might call a highway.'

He was right. We had not seen another car since leaving the Formosa.

'She might have walked out of the jungle,' Johnny said, pointing vaguely at the thickly forested expanse around her. 'There are many hidden villages, even where you least expect to find them.'

Kunichika turned to Johnny and said, 'Are you sure?'

'I'm not convinced,' Honey said. 'Look at the undergrowth – no one could have walked through that carrying baskets of fruit.'

'Let's go and talk to her,' Peter said, like a child asking to be taken to the seaside.

She was several hundred yards away, and when we approached we saw that her baskets were filled with all kinds of fruit: jackfruit, rambutan, *chiku*, guava, mangosteen. We bought as much as we could and immediately began to eat. We had not realised how parched we were from the driving.

Peter whispered in my ear. 'Snow, is she *blind*?'

I had not noticed her eyes – pale and cloudy with cataracts. Speaking in Malay, I asked her where she had come from – had she walked far?

Her reply was in a dialect so strange, so *rural*, I could not understand it. I glanced at Johnny, but he shrugged his shoulders.

'What did she say?' Peter whispered with mounting excitement.

I paraphrased my questions in the hope of getting a more lucid response. Again, the same mumble. It did not even sound like Malay. I exchanged a quizzical look with Johnny. 'I can't understand either,' he said.

'I believe,' Kunichika said, 'that Johnny's hunch was right after all. She has come from a settlement a few miles from here. She says that her daughters helped her carry the baskets and will return later to help her home.'

'Well, tell her she'll be waiting a long time for her next customer,' Honey said.

I looked at Kunichika as he spoke, his thin lips widening into a smile. His voice sounded as if it belonged to a different person.

The old woman muttered something.

'What did she say?' Peter said as we began to walk back to the car.

Kunichika smiled and said, 'I'm not certain. Something beyond translation.'

I caught his eye as we climbed back into the car. He smiled and said, 'I did tell you I was a jack of all trades.'

We set off with renewed vigour, it seemed. Kunichika turned to Honey and said, 'We should not stay on this road for too long.'

I fell into a thin sleep with my head resting on Johnny's shoulder. In my sleep I felt the rolling and swaying of the car. I did not dream; my head was filled instead with the voices of the people around me, yet, curiously, I remained asleep. I did not wake until we reached the grounds of the rest house.

13 October 1941

This rest house is exceedingly comfortable, and I am reluctant to leave it – yet we must if we are to catch our boat this evening.

I have often glimpsed these rest houses, and have always wanted to stay in one, to be a foreign traveller, stopping en route at these simple inns that punctuate the journey to the far north. When we arrived late yesterday afternoon, I went immediately to my room to enjoy the view. The house is situated on a hill, nestled among ancient shade-giving trees. Beyond the flame-of-the-forest outside my window the land falls away and then undulates gently towards the coast. The Hainanese couple who run this place say that on a clear day the sea is easily visible; sometimes it appears so near that guests have attempted to walk to it. But there has been so much cloud in the sky that I have not glimpsed the ocean; rain seems close at hand.

Let me describe this room and why it appeals to me so much. It is large and airy with a smooth concrete floor painted the colour of clay. The furnishings are sparse – a bed, a dressing table and a small writing desk. The windows are so large that wherever I am in the room I am able to take in the view. After Johnny went down for breakfast this morning, I pulled the mosquito net aside and lay in bed gazing outside. The air was cool and the light soft. That was when it struck me: this is the first time I have been on a trip on my own, that is to say, unaccompanied by my parents. Even the most timid of my excursions have always been chaperoned. I do not know why I have not realised the significance of this trip before, or why I have been allowed to venture forth in this manner. Perhaps they believe – justifiably – that marriage makes a woman so undesirable that she will be safe from the murky dangers of men.

'You seem in high spirits today,' Kunichika said when I ran in to him on the landing.

'Do I?' I couldn't think of anything else to say. I had dressed hastily, eager to go outside, and the sleeves of my blouse had gathered uncomfortably at my shoulders. I pulled at them inelegantly.

'Would you care for a stroll?' he asked.

The others were nowhere to be seen; the breakfast room seemed empty. I nodded.

It was the most glorious morning I could recall. Everything was perfectly still, the air touched with the faint crispness of dawn. The light appeared to my eyes like syrup. I had never noticed such a thing before. I wanted to swim in it.

'The light is remarkable,' Kunichika said, 'it illuminates everything.' It was as if he had read my mind.

'One can see everything with utter clarity,' I said. 'There are no shadows, nothing is hidden.'

'Is it too sentimental a thing to say?' he said, and then paused.

'What?'

'Nothing,' he smiled, blushing a little.

I stopped walking and turned to him. His hesitant smile induced me to smile too. 'What were you going to say?'

'No, please – I am embarrassed to say it. I am embarrassed even to think it.' He walked a few paces ahead of me and paused under the boughs of a giant fig tree. On the perfectly clipped lawn, he looked like an ornamental statue.

I went to him and said, 'Now, Professor, you must tell me.'

He hesitated and frowned. 'Only if you call me by my name.'

I laughed and cleared my throat theatrically. 'Please tell me what you were going to say – Mamoru.'

He turned away and gazed at the valley before us. I could not see his face, but he seemed lost in contemplation. In a quiet voice, he said, 'On such mornings one feels as if life is – that life *begins* again. You feel – one feels – that whatever else one has previously done in one's life ceases to matter. All you have done wrong can be put right, all you have lost can be regained. Your slate is wiped clean. It's as if someone says to you, "Here is a new beginning."' He turned round and caught my eye. He shrugged and looked at his feet, laughing awkwardly. 'I'm sorry – it's silly sentimentalism, I know. Please, ignore what I said. Academics are prone to such emotional lapses!'

'It isn't silly at all,' I said. 'Not in the least.' For the briefest moment I was seized by an urge to speak endlessly – what of, I do not know. A sudden wave of unbounded optimism swelled in me, and for a second I thought I would reach out to touch him. But the moment passed, and I fell silent once more. Finally, I said, 'If only it could be so.'

'If only what could be so?'

'If only life could be like that – if only we *could* begin again. Wouldn't that be nice? If only mornings like these weren't just an illusion.'

He took my hand and pressed it firmly between his palms. 'Snow, it can happen. Life *is* a palimpsest. You must believe it.'

We continued our stroll and talked about the valley, about the trees, the rivers and people. I spoke about my childhood – I saw all these things from afar, but my parents never allowed me to venture close to them. I knew the names of all the trees, I knew what they looked like, yet I never knew the smell of their sap or how their leaves felt to the touch. Lying awake at night, I came to recognise the call of certain animals, and many times I saw wild boar and *rusa* bucks – but only dead ones tribal hunters brought to the house to sell for meat. I was familiar, of course, with the people of the valley – they spoke to me respectfully when they visited the house, and I replied with equal propriety. I never knew, of course, what they ate when they were at home, or what they said to their children at night, or how they loved their wives in the morning. I spent my whole life, it seems, observing the world from my window. And then Johnny appeared on that rain-sodden day.

'You must have been very in love with him,' Mamoru said.

I did not answer.

'Has he changed much since you married?' he continued. 'It is often said that nothing changes a man more than marriage.'

I laughed. 'On the contrary. He hasn't changed at all.'

'And is that . . . a bad thing?'

Again I did not answer.

'Your husband is an interesting man,' he said as we walked down a slope towards a cream-painted shelter.

'Johnny? In what way?'

'In many ways. He is a very successful man, considering his background.'

'I suppose so. But being a merchant is hardly an unusual occupation for a Chinese,' I laughed.

'He is an exceptionally influential one.'

'A shop and a bit of money doesn't amount to influence.'

'Do you believe that money is all that he has?'

'What do you mean?'

Mamoru shrugged his shoulders. 'I don't know. He seems somewhat mysterious. Not to you, of course, you're his wife!'

'He is inscrutable, that is for sure.'

'No one seems to know about his childhood, for example.'

I sat down on the wooden seat in the shelter, watching him lean languidly against the posts, his head nearly touching the eaves of the low roof. 'What about your childhood, Mamoru?'

'Unremarkable.'

'Liar.'

We laughed.

'Are you really a nobleman as everyone says you are?' I asked.

He looked sad. 'In a manner of speaking. My family are – well, let me just say that I understood everything you spoke of. You talked about growing up in a gilded cage, and it hurt me – because I know how it feels.'

'Tell me more.'

He seemed to be looking at something in the distance, his eyes narrowing slightly.

'What is it?' I asked.

'There's something in that thicket of trees over there,' he said, fixing his gaze on a dense patch of scrub and undergrowth about a hundred yards away.

'I don't see anything.'

'I think we should go back now,' he said. His voice had fallen and he seemed very determined. I knew it was no use arguing.

'What did you see in the trees?' I asked again.

'I don't know. Perhaps nothing.' Suddenly he did not seem open to conversation.

'Just as well we're heading back now,' I said, 'the sun's getting very hot. My skin is not used to being out in this heat.'

'Yes, you should go back inside.'

We walked in silence, the sun felt uncomfortable on my face and hands.

Honey was waiting for us when we got to the house. He had brought the car round and seemed very impatient to get going. 'You'd better hurry up and have some breakfast,' he said, looking at his watch.

'I do not think there is any need to hurry,' Mamoru said.

Honey seemed uncertain. 'We agreed to leave by ten. It's nearly quarter to nine.'

'We are on schedule.'

Honey frowned. 'If you insist.' In silent protest, however, he remained by the car, examining various parts of it (spuriously, it seemed to me) while we breakfasted and packed. I think he is still there now. I cannot understand why he is so keen to leave; I am perfectly content to stay at this little desk in this marvellous airy room. I shall not move until I hear Mamoru taking his things downstairs. Johnny and Peter are exploring the grounds, I presume. Just now I saw Johnny expertly scaling the boughs of a tree; and earlier I noticed Peter's shoes were thickly muddied. 'I've been tramping o'er hill and dale,' he cried.

16 October 1941

A difficult few days.

We left the rest house in reasonable cheer. Everyone had slept well and I was feeling particularly optimistic. 'This feels like a school expedition,' Peter said brightly, but before long, a row developed.

Honey had been taciturn and somewhat irritable from the start. We drove over a series of potholes in the road which seemed perfectly aligned: we went up and down, up and down – so evenly I could have counted the beats on a sheet of music to it. This of course caused great hilarity in the back seat. 'Just like riding a hobbled donkey,' Peter said.

'Bloody awful roads,' Honey snapped.

'Language,' Peter said with exaggerated severity.

'Bloody tinpot country,' said Honey.

'I shouldn't complain,' said Peter. 'We created it, after all.'

'Who's "we"?' Honey snapped. I wanted to point out that those were the first words he had addressed to Peter directly; but it was not the right moment, so I kept counsel.

'We – the British. Pax Britannica. You and I,' Peter said blithely, almost singing the words.

'I am not responsible for the well-being of these roads and nor is the British Government. I am not to blame for the weather, the floods, the wet rot, the dry rot, the bloody fungus that creeps into every damned thing here. I'm not accountable for the cheating, lying, untrustworthy natives who lurk in every corner, or for the fact that every Englishman, every civilised person in this place has to sleep with a pistol by his bed and a Bren gun in the sitting room. It isn't my fault that pet dogs get eaten by snakes the size of a train or that children get beriberi. It isn't my *fault*.'

'Of course not. It's no one's fault. It's just an awful mess and that's why we're all here, trying to get a piece of it for ourselves.'

'Look here, Wormwood, I've had enough of this Bolshevik nonsense. If you want to pick up a gun and fight with those Chinaman commies in the jungle then you just go ahead. It's hard enough to do our jobs without having to listen to your drivel.'

To my surprise, Peter did not back down. 'I'd sooner fight with the communists than with you –'

'This is treasonable insolence. It's people like you who are tearing the world apart.'

'Treason? Not against this country. What *jobs* do you have to do anyway? Deciding how much gin to order for the Club?'

'I run an enterprise that encompasses nearly two dozen mines across the country,' Honey said, as if that was the end of the discussion.

Peter did not respond immediately. After a while he said, 'How nice for you.'

Honey snorted. 'It's the sun, that's what it is. I've seen it before. Poor bugger comes out here and his head gets cooked by the sun. Goes crazy. Consorts with natives, thinks he's one of them.'

Beads of rain began to fill the sky, sparkling in the still-dazzling sunlight.

Johnny said, 'Look, a rainbow.' There it was, across an expanse of paddy fields, arched against a black backdrop of rain clouds. We drove through this curious drizzle for a while, the rainbow poised uncertainly in the distance. The heat waves rising from the road, the rain, the light – they all combined to make our eyes swim. Honey blinked hard and peered intently through the windscreen.

'There is a woman,' Johnny said, 'again.'

'Where?' I asked. I could see nothing from where I sat.

'Just there,' Mamoru said. 'The same one as before.'

We passed her slowly in silence. She sat impassively by the road, surrounded by her baskets of fruit. She watched us go by with glassy eyes.

After a while Honey said, 'I don't think that was the same woman.'

'We must be miles – *miles* – away from where we last saw her,' said Peter.

'Yes,' said Johnny as she receded into the distance.

I began to doze as the rain grew heavier and drummed on the roof of the car. I remembered the touch of Mamoru's hands on mine in the garden of the rest house. I imagined him as a young boy, alone with only himself for company. For a while, Johnny's peculiar odour (earth and perspiration) kept me from deep sleep, but soon I managed to shut myself off in my own universe.

I am not sure how much time had elapsed before I awoke with a sore neck, my head lolling uncomfortably to one side. The rain clouds had closed in on us and it was very dark. I could hardly make out the shapes of the foliage on the edge of the road. No one was speaking, and we were moving extremely slowly.

'Christ,' Honey said softly.

Peter leaned close to me and whispered in my ear, 'We're lost.'

Ahead of us, I could see that the rain had turned the road into a shallow stream of mud.

'Our road became completely impassable,' Peter explained, 'so we had to turn off on to another one. We haven't the foggiest idea where we are.' The way he said it, whispering breathlessly, made our situation seem an adventure. I could tell, though, that Honey was worried.

I turned to Johnny and asked if he knew where we were. He frowned and shook his head slowly.

'Keep going,' said Mamoru, 'we're doing fine.' He spoke clearly and firmly.

I wondered what would happen if we did have to spend the night in the car. Would I choose such a moment to speak to Johnny? If we perished here in the jungle I might never need to confront the subject, and he would die without ever knowing that I was prepared to leave him.

'Wait,' Johnny said, leaning forward. 'Up ahead. I think there is another road.'

'Are you sure? I can't see anything. We need a bigger road than this, not a smaller one.'

'Johnny?' said Mamoru.

'I don't know. I think there is one.'

'We'll keep going until we find it,' said Mamoru.

'There it is,' cried Peter. 'I can see it, just beyond that clump of palms!'

Honey hurried the car along, and we saw the curve of a road previously obscured by trees. This road seemed wider and firmer than the previous one, and we made better progress. We drove in silence – we were too relieved to speak, I think – with only Johnny's occasional directions puncturing the dark. In our retreat from the jungle, we had tacitly given up hope of catching the ferry that evening. I did not know where Johnny's directions would eventually take us, but I hoped that they would lead us back to the rest house from which we had set off. No one spoke as we unloaded our bags. We were all thankful for the return to this familiar place.

That night I experienced the strangest sensation, a feeling of deepest sleep and perfect lucidity. I did not dream, yet I knew – I saw – with complete clarity that I would soon walk out of Johnny's life.

The next morning I was the last to emerge. I found the others packed and ready to go. A map was spread out on the vast bonnet of the car. Mamoru was pointing at it; he drew his finger across it in a slow, smooth arc, tapping it now and then. Honey and Johnny stood with him, nodding and muttering in agreement; Peter was nearby throwing pebbles at a tree trunk.

'Isn't this exciting?' Peter said to me as he picked up a stone.

'It feels as if we're on a quest for Tutankhamun's tomb.' He did not smile. His brow remained locked in a frown.

The mood, it seemed to me, was different today. Honey was civil to Peter, who was almost monosyllabic by his standards. I looked at Peter to try to discern the possible onset of illness, but his eyes and complexion were clear. Apart from a strangely vacant expression, he seemed in decent health.

'You wear a troubled face,' I ventured quietly.

'How preposterous, my dear,' he protested, his face pulling into a broad smile. 'I expect it's the heat.' Immediately he fell silent again and looked out of the window.

We travelled swiftly. The roads had dried up a little and afforded us smoother passage than before. 'We have to keep up our momentum before the rains come again,' Mamoru said.

Very slowly, almost imperceptibly, I noticed the air beginning to change. It felt softer on my face and I tasted a faint tinge of salt. We were nearing the sea, I knew. I was not sure if anyone else sensed the change in the winds around us. I looked at each of the men in turn, but their faces showed only a stony blankness. What was this look that I had seen before so often on the faces of men? I do not know what emotions this façade protects, nor may I ever find out. I am locked away from that world.

Our conversation was polite, flitting from one insubstantial subject to another – I scarcely recall the things we touched on. Nor can I recall how this aimless chat turned so quickly into another row. This one again involved Honey, but this time – to my surprise – Johnny was his antagonist.

'It is simply ignorant,' Honey said, 'to believe that communism can solve the woes of China. The communists are no less beastly than anyone else who came before them.'

With speed of response that seemed surprising, Johnny said, 'The ordinary people of China would not agree with you.'

'Wouldn't they?' Honey seemed taken aback by this. 'You mean they'd surrender to a band of thugs who are trying to pull apart an ancient civilisation?'

'It is not the communists who have trampled on China and pulled it apart.' The end of his sentence created a huge, awful silence in the car. Honey did not reply. Immediately, I felt for Mamoru. Johnny's words felt strangely condemning of us all, but particularly of Mamoru. Everyone has heard stories of what the Japanese are doing in China at the moment. I wanted to say that it was not fair to include Mamoru in this, but I could not. 'Do not ever forget: Johnny is the one you chose, he is your husband,' Mother's admonishment rang in my head. Besides, how could I defend Mamoru when no accusation had been made? I waited for him to respond, and prayed a row would not ensue.

'Johnny is quite right,' Mamoru said. 'For the last century, many foreign powers have imposed their might on China. It is a sad thing to witness. The path of history is cruel and terrible. Historical texts contain tragedies greater than any written in ancient Greece or Elizabethan England. As an academic, I can tell you that history books do not make for pleasant entertainment.'

Johnny waited a while. 'The Chinese people believe communism is the only thing that will save them from oppression, and they are right.'

'Johnny,' I whispered.

'Well, I wish they wouldn't try and export it to jolly old places like Malaya,' said Honey.

I saw Johnny gathering himself to reply. He had an expression I had come to recognise, his broad face set in nearly cross-eyed determination. There was something else in his posture too, one which I had never noticed before. His shoulders straightened, making him look stouter. His neck had shortened, it seemed, and he looked *old*. I wondered why Peter remained so silent – I found his reticence frustrating and, in desperation, I nudged him with my right elbow. I hoped he would see the futility of this argument – he was the only one who could persuade Johnny to stop. I knew, even as I did it, however, that there was every possibility that Peter would encourage, rather than prevent an unpleasant scene. It was a risk I had to take.

'This is *so* booooring,' Peter said, stretching his arms sleepily. 'Please do stop, Johnny, you really are beginning to sound like my old housemaster. Besides, my pretty little head just can't keep up with all this.' He looked at Johnny and smiled, raising his eyes to the heavens.

Johnny settled back in his seat. Instantly, his demeanour changed. His face, neck and shoulders seemed to unlock, and he looked like a loose-limbed child once more. Nonetheless, he seemed sullen and withdrawn. I felt the need to provide him comfort, so I rested my hand lightly on his knee. Almost immediately he drew away, leaving my hand to fall limply. At first I thought that his leg had merely moved when the car went over a bumpy stretch of road; but he made no attempt to come back to me, and instead shifted his seating position so that he could rest against the door. All I could see was the back of his right shoulder.

The countryside melted and shimmered in the sun. Encased in our motorised black coffin, we wound our way steadily to the coast. The sound of the car's engine filled our world. I wished someone would speak. Mamoru and Honey remained absolutely still in the front, looking for all the world like two mechanised beings. Sometimes Mamoru would smooth the folds of the map; he would look down to check our progress and then wordlessly return his gaze to the road in front of him. On one occasion the light played tricks on my eyes: in the windscreen I saw his face smiling at me. I do not know how his image came to be reflected so strangely, and I looked away. I wanted him to speak to me, but he did not. No one was speaking – Johnny remained entrenched in his sulk, his body twisted away from me.

'Look,' I whispered to Peter. 'There it is.'

'What?' he said, rousing himself from his stupor. He kept his voice down, as if I had included him in some covert conspiracy.

'Kellie's Castle.' It was barely discernible, a few patches of red-coloured stone amid the dark green of the jungle.

'My goodness,' he breathed, leaning in close to me to catch a better view.

'Is it what you expected?'

'I had visions of something grander. Something bigger. It's difficult to see it clearly from here. Did *hundreds* of coolies really die building it?' He sounded thrilled at the possibility.

'So the story goes. There was an outbreak of malaria. The Scottish planter who built it lost his wife and child, and then he went mad.'

'How wonderful. Can you imagine being one of these madmen fifty years ago, arriving in the tropics with nothing but an untrammelled imagination and all of the jungle before them. They built the most bizarre monument and no one questioned their taste. It was as if everyone lost their sense of aesthetics. Look at that, isn't it beautifully revolting? I must say, though, that it doesn't seem very scary for a cursed castle. But at least it's there. It exists.'

I laughed. 'Did you think it was a myth?'

'Yes. Rather like those beautiful women who haunt these roads preying on lone male travellers.' His face shone with a certain liveliness, rosy and childlike, as he squinted at the castle. He spoke in a quick, breathless voice, never breaking out of a whisper.

'Pontianak, you mean,' I said. 'How do you know they are a myth?'

He covered his mouth to hush a giggle. 'What are they, anyway?'

'The ghosts of young women – girls – who commit suicide after having babies out of wedlock. They exact their revenge on men because, after all, it was men who made them become what they are.'

'Not just men – women too. All of society.'

'Yes, I suppose. But mainly men.'

He turned to me with mischievous, sparkly eyes. 'Do you think,' he said, 'that there will be violent objections if I put in a request for a detour? I want to get a closer look at the castle.'

Before I could say anything, he asked Honey and Mamoru if we could drive towards the castle.

'Don't be bloody stupid,' Honey said. 'We can't miss our boat again.'

'Isn't this trip meant to be a holiday?' Peter said.

'I'm sorry,' said Mamoru. 'I am myself interested to see Kellie's Castle, but we need to get to Tanjong Acheh quickly. There is only one boat a day to the islands. It makes the crossing at a specific time in the day.'

'Can't we just pay someone to take us there? We don't need to travel with the masses, do we?'

'That *is* what we are doing,' Honey said.

'A boat specially for us?' I said.

Honey nodded.

'I assumed we'd be on a ferry. Don't other people go to the Seven Maidens?' Peter asked. 'I thought it might be like Eastbourne in the summer.'

'The Seven Maidens are not well known,' said Mamoru. 'Their beauty is, however, legendary.' He turned round to face us, and, I thought, looked directly at me.

'Wonderful. Yet another myth,' said Peter. 'We haven't a clue what's in store for us.' He sank back into his seat.

'It was worth asking,' I said, reverting to a whisper.

He did not seem remotely perturbed by the rejection of his request. 'It's *always* worth asking,' he laughed.

We turned back to look at the castle but it had disappeared. 'Where is it?' Peter said. 'I could have sworn it was just there, in the dip below that hill.'

'No it wasn't, it was over there,' I said. I could not tell where anything was any more. The castle had vanished from our sight, and we continued to drive on.

The jungle gave way to tawny, parched grassland and coconut trees. Streams of murky brackish water cut across the road, and we went over wooden bridges that trembled under the weight of the car. We drew into Tanjong Acheh late in the afternoon. The collection of wooden huts and fishermen's shacks that formed the town stretched a few hundred yards along the coast. We slowed to walking pace, the car's engine rattling unhappily. On either side of the street, the shacks appeared empty. Their windows and doors were shut, giving the impression of a town long deserted. One house bore a painted sign on its façade. The words were faded, bleached by the sun and salt, but I could discern from the outline of a bottle and the remains of 'Fraser & Neave' that it must once have been the coffee shop where the local population congregated for cold drinks in the afternoon and coffee in the evenings. I listened for the sound of children's laughter, dogs barking or chickens squabbling, but I heard nothing.

'Do you think everyone's asleep?' Peter said, checking his watch. 'A bit late in the day for a siesta, isn't it?'

'It's a fishing village,' Honey said. 'They're probably out to sea.'

'Even the women?' I asked.

Johnny said, 'In places like these – poor rural areas – women have to work too. There are many female fisherman.'

'Yes, I have seen them,' Mamoru said. 'However, I thought that fishing boats went out to sea in the evening. They usually arrive home in the mornings, unload their catch and then rest during the day. One can see them dotting the coastline at dawn. In a small bay such as this their lights resemble fireflies in a jar.'

'You've been around a bit, haven't you?' Peter said. 'Very observant too, I must say.'

Mamoru laughed. 'I'm simply a tourist,' he said, 'with an academic's eye.'

'Yes,' said Peter, 'an academic's eye.'

'That is why I find it somewhat puzzling that the boats are not here at this time of the day,' Mamoru said. 'Perhaps fishermen's routines and practices vary from place to place. The tide may behave differently here.'

'I don't know why, but I've got the impression you've been here before,' Peter said.

'No,' Mamoru said, turning around to look at him. 'I have not.'

The road curved to a stop at a broken-down pier. A single boat bobbed gently by the jetty. It was a large boat, forty feet long, perhaps, with a cabin built on its deck. Its hull, once bright green, was clad in cracked, peeling paint; a dried-out tangle of netting stretched along one side of the deck.

'There she is,' Honey said.

'What, that wreck?' Peter said, his voice rising an octave.

'Well, there isn't another bloody boat around, is there?' Honey snapped.

We got out of the car and stood looking at the boat.

'Where's our ferryman?' Peter demanded. 'Please tell me we're not going to attempt this Stygian crossing ourselves.'

'For goodness' sake, be quiet. The owner of this boat is meant to be here,' Honey said. 'We've made arrangements for him to take us to the Seven Maidens. He's obviously been delayed. He'll be here sooner or later, I expect.'

'You made the arrangements, did you?' said Peter. 'Congratulations on a job well done. If you think we're willing to entrust our lives to a drunken maniac on a sinking tin like that, think again.'

'Peter,' I said quietly and touched his elbow. The last thing we needed was another row. Thankfully, he seemed to take the hint.

We looked around us. Nothing stirred.

‘I suggest we begin loading our things on to the boat,’ Mamoru said. ‘That way we will be ready to leave when the boatman arrives.’

The boat was deceptively spacious. As I descended the steep, narrow steps that led below deck, I was, in truth, slightly concerned about sleeping arrangements. If we were to spend any length of time on this boat, the lack of space meant that I would be sleeping (and dressing and washing) in the company of three men other than my husband. I was not sure I could do it. My fears were partly allayed when I saw that the area below deck was roomy and sensibly arranged, with a small partition which afforded some measure of privacy. There were three small beds, arranged at right angles to each other, a tiny cabinet and a table and chair. There were no portholes (as I imagined all boats had), nor any mirrors, but there was still enough light from the stair hatch to make the dimness acceptable. It smelled of camphor and damp, but was otherwise clean.

I was relieved, too, when Mamoru told me that only Johnny and I would be down below deck; the others would be sleeping above board.

‘This isn’t exactly *Le Normandie*, is it?’ said Peter, as he helped me carry my things to my bunk.

‘It’ll do,’ I laughed.

‘Are you sure you’ll be all right, Snow?’ he said.

‘What you mean to say is that a spoilt, delicate woman like me is not accustomed to surroundings such as these,’ I said.

‘Not at all,’ he said, stuttering a little. ‘Not at all. I just wanted to make sure you were comfortable.’ He seemed somewhat hurt.

‘I’m more durable than you think, Peter,’ I said. I must confess that I allowed my annoyance to show in my voice.

I began unpacking my things. My first thought was for this diary – now that we are on a boat, I am worried that it may get wet or become infected by damp rot. Johnny came into the cabin and dropped his bags on his bed. He left without speaking to me. A while later Mamoru appeared. He came halfway down the stairs but did not descend properly into the cabin.

'You must be tired from the drive today. I must admit to being somewhat fatigued myself,' he said.

I smiled. 'I'm fine, Mamoru. Glad for a rest, certainly, but I'm fine.'

'I'm sorry, this . . .' he waved a hand at the cabin, 'this is not luxurious, but we shall not be on this boat for long. If the boatman arrives soon, we will not even pass a single night here.'

'You sound as if you are apologising. Please don't – it's not your fault. You've had nothing to do with this.'

'Promise you'll tell me if you need anything?'

I nodded.

When he had gone I found a piece of waxcloth in Johnny's things. I placed it on the tiny table next to the bed and set my diary on it. I have been writing ever since. When I finish I shall wrap the diary in the waxcloth where it will be safe from the sea and all the things that lurk in its depths.

Later – by a kerosene lamp Mamoru brought for me

When I emerged on deck it was still light. The men were squabbling and there was no sign of the boatman.

'Yes! We have no bananas,' Peter sang in a child's taunting wail, 'we have no bananas or boatman today.'

'It isn't my fault,' Honey protested. He was standing at the side of the boat, squinting into the distance, searching for signs of life in the still-deserted town. 'What do you expect of the natives?'

'I expect them to be well trained and utterly compliant,' said Peter. 'Isn't that what I'm expected to expect?'

'What?'

'Look, it doesn't matter. The fact is, we have a boat but no boatman. How on earth do you expect us to get to the Seven Maidens by nightfall?'

'I don't know,' Honey said, seemingly defeated by Peter's logic.

'Well, you made the arrangements.'

'I did not. Besides, the Professor has a plan.'

Mamoru had been lifting up boards and shifting boxes to inspect various parts of the machinery. 'The Seven Maidens,' he said calmly, his voice full of quiet authority, 'are not far from the coast. The Straits of Malacca are some of the smoothest waters in the world. We will be able to navigate our way to the islands without the boatman. I am certain of it.'

'I didn't know you were good with boats, Mamoru,' I said. 'You seem very confident of getting us there.'

'Oh, I'm sure Professor Kunichika has plenty of little tricks up his sleeve,' said Peter. 'His sense of direction is *quite* extraordinary, isn't it? Especially for an academic.'

'Actually, I have brought with me some rudimentary nautical maps. I have nothing beyond these – and a foolhardy sense of confidence, of course.'

'No one knows where the Seven Maidens are. Only fishermen go there, only they know the way,' Honey said quietly. 'Still, I'm sure the Professor will get us there.' His voice faded even as he spoke, as if he had resigned himself to what lay ahead.

'There was an expedition two years ago,' said Mamoru. 'Well, actually it was more a field trip made by amateurs not unlike us. That is how these maps exist – they are less detailed than one might expect, but I have no reason to believe they are not accurate.'

'He's right. People bang on about the Seven Maidens all the time – I mean *our* people, Honey,' said Peter. 'Surely you've heard them at the Club. Botanists, entomologists, deranged lepidopterists, avian-minded planters from Norfolk, Oxford historians *manqué* – they all chatter endlessly about the Seven Maidens.'

'Yes, but I don't think that anyone believes they are real,' said Honey. 'Not truly. That's why all you ever hear is how two of the Maidens disappear at high tide, how they were formed from the bodies of murdered princesses. It's the stuff of local legends. Anyway, none of this matters. We've got to go now. We've no choice.'

'They exist, of that I am certain,' said Mamoru. 'The maps indicate that the journey should take no longer than five hours. These fishing boats are not equipped for long journeys. Look at this thing. Fifty nautical miles would be the standard range for such a vessel. A hundred would be far beyond its capabilities. Local fishermen do not travel great distances. Their fishing patterns are seasonal and easily affected by weather conditions. They would not venture far from home. If the Seven Maidens are within their fishing territory, then we should easily be able to reach them in time to strike camp tonight.'

'Of course the islands exist,' I added. 'Everyone who lives in the valley knows of them. They're famous.'

Peter shrugged. 'The Professor seems to have everything covered,' he said.

'Besides,' Mamoru continued, 'Johnny's knowledge of the coastline will stand us in good stead. We have already been witness to his excellent navigational skills.'

Johnny was sitting cross-legged against the little shack. 'I do not know the sea,' he said. 'I cannot swim.'

Nor can I, I thought to myself. I did not mention this, though, for fear of appearing timid and hesitant. I did not want Mamoru to think that I would shrink from adventure.

The boat undulated gently under our feet as we stood in silence. Mamoru looked at me to see if I was worried or upset by this proposed journey. I saw no trace of fear in his face, and I smiled my approval in return. The slow rocking movement of the waves induced a curious sensation in my head, and I felt as if I would swoon. I sat down on a wooden bench nearby and shut my eyes.

No one spoke, but all the sounds I heard indicated only one thing: no one opposed Mamoru. We were going to the Seven Maidens on our own.

17 October 1941

Our spirits lifted as soon as we set off. The light had started to fade, but we were not concerned. The steady rhythm of the boat as it cut through the water, rising and falling over the occasional wave, was thrilling to me. I could tell from the way Johnny and Peter sat – side by side, gazing quietly into the distance like a pair of hypnotised children – that they were happy too. I stood next to Mamoru as he steered, looking out at the open waters beyond the stern. Only Honey seemed unsettled. He examined the maps, frowning deeply.

'Don't worry, Frederick,' I called out over the noise of the wind and the motor, 'we'll be fine.' I was (and am) convinced that Mamoru would guide us safely to our destination.

'Look at the amber sky,' Mamoru said, turning to look at me.

'And the sea too,' I added. The deep colours of the fading sun spread in streaks across the waters on the horizon.

'Do you believe in God?' he asked.

I shook my head. 'I don't know. Do you?'

'No,' he said, 'although at a time like this, in a place such as this, I am not so sure. All my beliefs are ill-founded, all my convictions weak. Yet I feel strangely alive. Funny, isn't it?'

'Not at all,' I said. The wind continued to sweep through my hair. I made no attempt to smooth it away from my face as I had done earlier, but instead enjoyed the sensation of knowing that here, in the open seas, no one would comment on my appearance. I lifted my chin and allowed the breeze to cool my neck.

I felt whispers of wind on my collarbone, and I breathed deeply. Johnny and Peter remained silent and transfixed, staring at the setting sun. I put my hand on Mamoru's. His skin was taut and cool. He continued to look into the distance, charting our course with an unwavering gaze. The corners of his eyes creased into tiny lines and his lips began to draw into a smile.

It is astonishing how much light there is at sea, even when it is dark. Night does not seem like night. The moon illuminates everything; it creates a white midnight. We ate simply, sitting in a small circle around some hurricane lamps.

'This is a lavish little picnic, isn't it?' Peter said, reaching for another slice of tinned tongue. We opened tins of sardines, luncheon meat, dace and pineapple. A bottle of whisky had also appeared and was being passed around. We had also brought bags of rice, *ikan bilis* and groundnuts, and there were still some eggs from the guest house. We could not cook any of these things, however, because we could not find a stove.

'I'm sorry,' Mamoru said, 'but we will have to survive on tinned rations this evening. We shall reach the Seven Maidens before long, and we shall be able to prepare hot food over a fire there.'

'This is perfectly acceptable,' I said.

'I don't mind it out here, actually. It's rather wonderful,' Peter said. 'Johnny was just saying earlier how exciting it is to be in Neptune's realm.'

'I did not say that,' Johnny said, looking a little perplexed.

'Perhaps not in those words. But the sentiment was there, you must admit. You did say that it would be wonderful to die at sea, didn't you? "If I had to die somewhere, this is where I would choose," you said. And I agree! Wouldn't it be just splendid to fade into this vast expanse of water, to be nibbled by angelfish and sea nymphs. I should love to swim into the sun and simply dissolve into nothingness. How utterly ravishing that would be.'

I chuckled.

'How ridiculous,' Honey sneered. 'You couldn't possibly do that. What about your funeral? What about last rites? It's an abdication of responsibility.'

'Responsibility? Whom to?' Peter said, his mouth full of food.

'Everyone,' said Honey. 'God, for a start.'

Peter laughed heartily, making no attempt to stop little bits of food falling from his mouth.

'I knew it,' said Honey, 'not only are you a Bolshevik, you're a heathen too.'

'I'd like to say you were wrong on both counts,' Peter replied, 'but I can't bring myself to make the effort. It doesn't matter what you think of me.'

'*Do* you believe in God, Peter?' I asked.

He looked at me and seemed somewhat surprised by my question. It took him a moment or two to gather himself. 'In a place such as this – as perfect as this – who could not believe in God? Who can look upon this and say this is not God's Earth? Even if I didn't before I think I would now.'

I cast a surreptitious sideways glance at Mamoru.

'All this,' Peter said, waving his gangling arms around him, 'doesn't it feel new, innocent, eternal?' I had never heard his voice like this before. It sounded grown-up and sad. 'Gone is Babylon, Mother of Harlots and Abomination of the Earth. In its place is this, a place founded on something clear and pure. The new Jerusalem: "Its first foundation was Jasper."'

'What's Jasper?' Johnny asked.

'A kind of mineral, a precious stone,' Peter said. 'Didn't we bring some fresh fruit with us? I feel I'm about to succumb to scurvy. Now that's a real drawback to being at sea. I'd even be prepared to suck on a lime. Have we still got some of those delicious bananas from the guest house?'

'Yes, we have no bananas,' I said, 'but we do have some *chiku* and guava. I'll fetch them.'

Later, when I had retired below deck to write, Mamoru left Honey to steer the boat and brought me another lamp. 'It'll be better for your eyes,' he said, looking at my diary. 'What beautiful handwriting you have.'

I blushed.

'Maybe you'll write something for me one day.'

Up on deck, Peter was singing songs and attempting to teach Johnny the words and melodies. He sang in English, French and – I think – Italian. I did not recognise any of the songs, although one or two of them reminded me of ones I have heard Father play on his gramophone. Peter's voice assumed a surprising range, from self-conscious baritone to flighty falsetto, always in perfect pitch. Johnny – who I know for certain to be tone deaf – could not keep up, his flat, nervous voice stumbling after every few words. This did not seem to deter Peter from running through his seemingly inexhaustible repertoire, however, and they continued to sing the most unusual, awful duets, Peter's fluent notes floating above Johnny's irregular monotone.

Mamoru was deep in conversation with Honey. 'The waters are smooth and it is a very clear night,' I heard him say. 'We'll slow down a little but keep going through the night. We should encounter no problems.'

I did not sleep that night. In the next bed Johnny breathed heavily in his sleep, sighing often. I called his name to see if he was all right but got no response. I went to him and when I touched his forehead I found it cold and damp. I stroked his hair – which usually calms him down – but I could not seem to soothe his troubled sleep. I returned to my bed and continued to listen to his shallow breaths. The steady drone of the boat's motor and the constant rush of water in my ears eventually rose above Johnny's breathing, but still I could not sleep. I drew my dressing gown over me and walked barefoot on to the deck. Everywhere was painted a brilliant white, illuminated by moonlight. Honey had wrapped himself in a thin blanket and lay sleeping on a low bench, curled tightly with his knees drawn into his body. Peter was asleep too, spreadeagled on a rug laid out in the middle of the deck, his face turned up to the moonlight.

I went to Mamoru and stood by his side, very close to him. When he put his arm around my waist and drew me to him I was not surprised. I felt the coolness of his body through my clothes. We remained in this way for some time, both merely looking at the shining sea before us, neither speaking. When, finally, he moved away to light a lamp and look at a map, I returned to my cabin.

As I padded barefoot over the sea-smoothed boards I knew that the time was at hand. I would tell Johnny as soon as possible.

When I got into bed I became aware that Johnny was no longer breathing loudly. I could hear no sound from his bed.

'Are you awake, Johnny?' I whispered.

From the absence of a reply I knew that he was.

I paused, feeling the pronounced throb of my pulse in my temples and throat. My hands felt hot and curiously light. It was just as I had imagined. I felt no fear, no hesitation, but a clarity and certainty that seemed unshakeable. Even now, writing in the burning light of day, I can feel that unclouded conviction running through my entire body.

In the half-dark I felt my way to his bed and sat down next to him. He did not stir. I said calmly, 'There is something I have been meaning to tell you.' I waited for a response but there was none. I knew, though, that he was awake. I put my hand on his cheek and found it hot to the touch. I had to continue. 'Johnny,' I said, 'do you remember what you said to me not long after we first met? You said that if I ever died, or if I ever went away, you could not bear to live. You would let yourself die too, you said, rather than live without me. Do you remember how I laughed at that? Because it isn't true, you know that, don't you? If anything did happen to me you would survive. There are other things in your life now – the shop, for one. Many things. Everyone in the valley knows you now. If I died or disappeared into thin air, you would simply carry on, and eventually, you would forget me. It would be as if I had never existed. That is the way the human heart works. Death erases everything, you know. That's right: death erases all traces, all memories of lives that once existed. It's the same if someone goes away. After a while, they simply cease to exist in your memory.'

He did not move. I could not even hear him breathing. My voice filled that space completely, but I was determined to continue speaking. I could not stop now. 'I just wanted to tell you something, Johnny, because you are my husband. The first man I loved.'

I became aware that my voice was echoing louder than ever. There were no other sounds – I could hear neither the boat or the water. Nothing.

I stopped and listened. Footsteps on deck. Muffled voices: Mamoru, then Honey, then Peter. The orange glow of lamps flashing below deck for an instant before being moved away.

After a few minutes Peter's voice called out at the top of the steps. 'We've stopped,' he whispered urgently. 'The boat's broken down. We can't move. We're stuck.'

Johnny turned on to his side. 'You were going to tell me something, I think,' he said. His voice sounded small and hollow. I could not tell what emotions lay behind it.

'You'd better come up and have a word with Kunichika,' Peter said, 'both of you. He's threatening to climb overboard and swim under the boat to repair something – the propeller or the ruddy rudder or something like that. Meanwhile, Honey's falling to pieces. I think you two should talk some sense into them.'

By the time we got dressed and clambered on deck Mamoru

was already poised by the edge of the boat. He bent his knees a little and then fell forward, arms stretched out above his head. He arched his torso as he did so and disappeared into the water. He did not make even the smallest splash. He simply vanished from sight.

Some time later – a minute or two, I presume, though it certainly felt longer – he climbed back on board. I had prepared a blanket and draped it around his shoulders. His body shone in the pale half-light. My eyes played tricks on me: his skin appeared pure, glowing white.

'Well?' said Peter.

'The problem lies here,' Mamoru said, lifting a heavy board of wood towards the bow of the boat. He peered into the hull. 'The mechanical parts have failed. We will have to repair them. Somehow.' He sighed, and for the first time, seemed concerned. 'I am afraid it might take longer than expected to reach the Seven Maidens.'

'Christ almighty,' I heard Honey mumble under his breath.

Peter said, 'This shouldn't be too difficult to repair, should it? It's only a primitive little thing.' He spoke the words brightly but could not hide the slight tremble in his voice.

'I hope so,' Mamoru said.

'I hope you're equipped to deal with such vagaries of travel,' Peter said. 'Seeing as you are an academic.'

'I shall do my best.'

'Can't *you* do anything, Honey?' said Peter. 'You're in charge of tin mines, for heaven's sake. Who repairs all those monstrous dredging machines you have?'

'Not me,' Honey said. 'I look after other things. More important things.'

'Such as?' Peter said with exaggerated incredulity.

'Money. Relations with the locals,' Honey replied, snorting his derision. 'Things you wouldn't understand. Isn't this a case of stones in glasshouses, coming from a jobbing actor?'

'I told you before: I'm not an actor. Anyway, actors aren't renowned for their prowess with Malay fishing boats.'

'Why do you always look at me when things go wrong?' said Honey. 'What about your little friend there?'

'Johnny's a textile merchant, not a bloody mechanic. What do you expect him to do?' Peter said, raising his voice.

Mamoru raised his hand suddenly. 'Stop,' he said quietly.

We stood in silence for a moment. 'What's wrong?' I asked.

'The wind,' he said. True, a breeze had developed steadily, though none of us was aware of it until then. 'And the moon.'

As I lifted my head to look at the clouded-over night sky, Mamoru shouted, 'We must drop anchor now!'

'Mamoru, what's going on?' I said, but he was running across the deck, searching for the anchor.

It was Johnny who spoke. 'We have been drifting. The wind has pushed us off course. Without the motor we have nothing to resist it. Now that the light has gone it will be impossible to navigate.'

I looked again at the ink-black sky. It had darkened rapidly, soaking up the night like Father's watercolours on rice paper. Not a single star was visible.

Mamoru said that we had not been blown too far off course and assured everyone that we would reach the Seven Maidens as planned. I tried to tell him it was not his fault, but he paid no attention to what I said.

'I lost concentration, just for a moment,' he said as he rattled various parts of the machinery. 'I should never have let this happen.'

'Please, Mamoru, do not blame yourself,' I said. 'There's nothing you could have done.'

I watched him work. His strength surprised and scared me. He pulled at a metal shaft which seemed to break in his hands. The noise it made screamed in my ears. He said very little, in spite of my attempts to engage him in conversation. Obviously, he was still upset for falling short of his high standards.

'Mamoru, calm down, this is not your doing,' I said over the uncomfortable noise he was making with the machinery. He put his arms around a part of the machine as if constricting, suffocating it the way a python kills a pig. I thought he was making a noise, too, a low howl of pain that seemed to stay within his chest. Then he took a step back and kicked the machine. Small parts came loose and fell away. I did not know what he was doing. He seemed to be tearing it apart.

He stopped and glared at me. His face and forearms were dirty; the grease cut black streaks over his white skin. A fox peering from the dark. 'I think you should get some sleep,' he said.

I returned to my cabin immediately. The others appeared to be resting or sleeping. I did not pay too much attention to what they were doing. I simply went to bed.

When I woke up it was light and we were still motionless. That was two hours ago. I joined the others on deck, sheltering in the shade of the little shack. No one spoke. Mamoru sat on the floor, his back leaning against a bench, his head bowed in exhaustion. He did not look at me even when my footsteps passed in front of him. The sun had burned the cloud away; the light spread evenly across the placid sea.

I caught Peter's eye. He shook his head and silently mouthed a few words I could not comprehend. I went back to my cabin and sat before my diary.

Now we are lost, drifting, it seems, to nowhere.

18 October 1941 (Late afternoon)

Still no progress. Peter thinks something is very wrong. He says we are still being blown by the wind. He has been watching the waves all day and believes we are being swept away.

Mamoru still not speaking.

20 October 1941 (Perhaps – I am not certain of the days)
How did we get here? I can scarcely believe it. Nor do I recall exactly what happened. I do not know which came first, or which is stronger: the failure of my memory to record events accurately or the failure of my belief in what is true. All I know is that we are here and we are alive. I know, too, that we have no idea where *here* is.

We drifted all night, rocking gently on the waves that licked against the hull. Johnny lay in bed, sweating under a blanket. I went to him once, but he turned away from me.

I said to Peter, 'Johnny is ill. He has a fever.'

Peter's face was contorted in a deep frown. He had not stopped searching the darkness around us in the hope that some clue, some sliver of light might suddenly appear. He looked at me and said, 'I know.'

Mamoru sat quietly with his maps, examining them and making calculations. He had not cleaned his face nor arms; the light from the lamp danced on his grease-streaked features, illuminating his troubled countenance ('He looks like a civet cat,' Peter said, attempting a joke). He remained this way for hours, isolated from everyone, including me. He looked so alone, so cast adrift and in need of comfort, yet I did not know what I could do. I did not dare approach him.

Honey had, with the help of the rest of the whisky, fallen asleep on deck. His body jerked violently now and then, and he mumbled loudly in a language neither Peter nor I could understand. When Peter laughed at this it felt as though it was the first time anyone had laughed since we got on the boat, and I began to laugh too. We tried to suppress our laughter so as not to disturb Mamoru from what he was doing; the effort of doing this reduced us to tears. It was only when Peter stopped laughing that I realised I was still crying. I could not stop. Peter stood watching me awkwardly; I thought he was startled, even contemptuous of me.

I suddenly felt ashamed and tired and disgusted with myself for this display but still I could not stop. Peter put his hand on my head, attempting to soothe me, but I drew away. I would stop crying and prove that I did not need his help.

'I'm sorry,' I said, but still the hot tears burned my cheeks. I turned to go back to the cabin. 'You just keep watching for lights, Peter.'

'I will,' he said, seeming to smile. 'What I'd give to see a passing ship. Even a pirate boat, for heaven's sake!'

I fell asleep with my eyes and throat feeling sore.

The next morning I found Mamoru in better spirits. I saw him as soon as I climbed up the steps from the cabin. He had washed and changed into a fresh shirt and was standing over the broken machinery looking exactly like a schoolteacher: hands on hip, patient, a quizzical expression on his face. He greeted me with a silent 'good morning' which seemed to serve as an apology for everything that had happened the previous night. It was only then, when I stepped properly on to the deck, that I saw Johnny crouched over, kneeling at the base of the machine. He did not look up as I approached.

'Mamoru,' I whispered, 'do you think this is wise? Johnny is ill, and besides, I have never seen him operate a machine in his life.'

He lifted his eyebrows in an enquiring manner.

'He dislikes all types of machines,' I continued. 'Even the simplest mechanical task has to be delegated to a servant – changing the tyre on a bicycle, for example. He looks away whenever we go past a dredging machine. Honestly, sometimes I think he has a medical aversion to all things mechanical.'

'That is very strange, given his humble background – relatively speaking, of course. You would have thought that machines were essential to village life.'

'Apparently not.'

'Well, it was he who volunteered,' Mamoru explained as we watched Johnny at work. 'I would not have dreamed of disturbing him. He simply came up on deck and said he had an idea; he felt luck was on his side. I was on the verge of despair, so I agreed.'

'Do you think he knows what he's doing?'

'I'd say so, by the looks of things. As I said before, Snow, your husband is a surprising person.'

Johnny did not seem to expend any effort. At first I thought he might be weakened by his fever, but then I saw that he was simply and perfectly at ease where he was, kneeling next to the machine, easing various parts away from it and cradling them in his hands with the gentlest of touches. I noticed that because his hands had never appeared softer or more pliable. Those hands – *those* hands – had never before touched me in that way. Nor did he appear to use the tools that Mamoru had given him. He had no use for them; his fingers were sufficient.

Peter joined us, rubbing his eyes of sleep. He said nothing but merely stood with us, watching Johnny and the machine. The rhythm of his hands on the machine lulled us into silence. We could do nothing but bear witness.

Only once did Johnny look up at us. He caught my eye but quickly returned to the machine. His glance lasted only half a second, but in that look I saw everything I have come to realise. He possesses a world that is locked away from me. That world may, I sense, be rich in secrets, but even if it is not, the fact remains: I simply do not know my husband. The man I married was not the same man who was now saving our lives. Standing on that deck in the clear sunlight, I could not even remember the man I married.

The repair did not take long. Johnny himself went to the helm, and after a shuddering bellow of black smoke and a screeching whine, the boat began to move. Mamoru insisted that we had not drifted far off course, and that the journey would not take long. Peter glanced at me and shook his head, but I did not respond. Now that the boat was moving again and Mamoru was in charge, I knew we would find what we were searching for.

All day we cut across the smooth green sea, steadily following the course Mamoru had set for us. We saw no other boats, no islands, no clouds, nothing; only the sun, white and hazy above us.

'Where are the bloody gulls?' Peter said. 'Where there are gulls there is land. Isn't that right?'

No one answered. The glare hurt my eyes and made my head swirl. I tried to stand next to Mamoru as he steered the boat, but I could not keep my balance. I heard Peter's voice call my name and then Mamoru's arm around my back, supporting me. I blinked and found myself seated on Mamoru's soft travelling bag with a wet cloth draped on my brow.

Hour upon hour passed. We stopped looking at our watches. They seemed silly, useless. I drifted in and out of sleep. The others did too, I think. Only Mamoru remained alert. Every time I opened my eyes I saw him outlined against the painful white light. I should not have allowed myself to believe the journey would be a short one. I should have been like Johnny, who had resolutely and silently returned to the darkened cabin, or like Honey, who sat speaking quietly to himself before falling into alcohol-kissed slumber. I should not have allowed myself to believe the unbelievable, I said, turning to Peter. His eyes were closed in a thin sleep. He nodded, but I think he did not hear or understand what I meant.

And it was this thought that stayed with me as we glided into the still, shallow waters of this island. I would not let myself believe we were saved. We floated closer and closer to the beach until finally we felt the sand on the hull.

The sudden sight of land after days at sea does strange things to men. Honey jumped clean off the boat, mumbling as he did so, and splashed his way to shore. Mamoru dived into the water head first, and when he surfaced he turned his face skyward, eyes closed, mouth open, as if tasting fresh air for the very first time. He declared the water shallow and calm, and stood with his arms aloft, calling for me. I stepped on to the rough wooden steps on the side of the boat, Peter insisting on holding my hand until I was within Mamoru's reach. When I reached the bottom step I simply let my body drop into his; he carried me to shore, lifting me so that only my feet brushed the water.

Peter helped Johnny off the boat, and walked with him until they too reached the beach.

Beyond the wash of the waves the sand was hot and coarse under our toes – too hot to stand on, and we headed quickly into the deep shade cast by a huge sea almond. We lay here while Mamoru swam out to the boat to collect some of our things. He made several trips, and on the final one brought me this diary, still tightly wrapped in its waxcloth.

I cannot say exactly how long we remained there. The hours were meaningless: all night and into the morning, we lay sleeping or merely staring at the rust-coloured leaves of the tree above us. Its boughs pointed like crooked fingers out to sea, curling at the ends as if to indicate the boundary of our makeshift world. Not once did anyone venture beyond its shelter.

We are not dead, and for that I should be thankful. But I do not want to believe that we are properly, completely alive. Not yet.

21 October 1941 (The next day – definitely!)

The coolness of the early evening began to lure us from our refuge. Peter was the first to venture forth, stretching his long limbs uncertainly as he descended the gentle slope of the beach to where the wavelets washed ashore, fading into the sand. He paused before tentatively stepping into the sea, putting one foot slowly in front of the other, as if remembering how to walk. Suddenly, he collapsed, falling into the water in a thrashing, pulsating ball.

'What on earth is he doing?' Honey said. 'Is he having a fit?'

We sat up and watched as Peter's body became still. He crouched in the water with his head bowed. Mamoru stood up and went to help him; then Peter let out a strange squeal, standing up and running towards us as he did so. He was holding something in his hands. 'The bugger's nipped me!' he cried. It was only then that we saw he was holding a large green-black crab.

We cooked it over a slow, glowing fire that Mamoru made from coconut husks and sand. He gathered some glossy leaves from the edge of the scrubby forest behind us and placed the now reddened crab on this plate of foliage. I had not felt hungry before – the sun had dried all thoughts of food from my head – but as Mamoru divided the crab with his knife I felt my insides boil with hunger. He pulled a claw from the carapace and smashed it with the handle of his knife. With his fingertips he pulled away the broken bits of shell and handed me the glistening piece of brown-veined flesh. 'Be careful,' he said as he gave it to me, 'it is still very hot.'

Even though it was a large crab, there was not much meat to go round. When we tasted those little jellies of sweet white meat we all realised we were hungrier than we thought. We took to sucking at the broken pieces of shell, which tasted of firewood and sea salt. Peter declared that he had never eaten anything as delicate and delectable.

'Ortolan pales in comparison,' he said. I was about to ask him what this was when he turned to Johnny and explained that it was a small French bird. 'Like a sparrow,' he said patiently.

Only Johnny did not eat. He seemed too weak to do so. When

I offered him a chunk of meat that Mamoru had prepared for me, he declined. I tried to insist that he ate, but Peter touched my arm and shook his head. He was right: Johnny seemed happier left on his own, resting against the base of the tree, set slightly apart from the rest of us.

When we finished, Honey suggested opening some tins from our rations, which are still plentiful. I looked at Peter. My hunger remained, it was true, but curiously I did not yearn for preserved food. Now that I had eaten that crab, I wanted something similar.

'How could you even think of doing that, Honey?' Peter said. 'It would be akin to raiding your larder for half a cold Scotch egg after dining on *omelette au crabe* at Boulestin. What savagery. I'd sooner starve.'

In the end we did nothing. We simply sat cross-legged around the fire, watching it die down until it was smouldering and hardly smoky. In the blue light I could see Mamoru looking at me. His face was slim and calm.

We retired to the makeshift camp beds Mamoru had prepared. Mine had been specially draped with cotton sheets while the men made do with rough canvas. Mamoru came to me and said, 'Don't worry about Johnny, I will keep an eye on him.'

'Thank you, I said, reaching to touch his shoulder in the dark.

As I fell asleep I could still taste the sweetness of the crab on my tongue. 'Peter,' I called out. 'I nearly forgot: thank you for our dinner.' There was no answer. He must already have fallen asleep.

This morning it felt as though all the things on the boat had happened a very long time ago. We breakfasted on rice (cooked, by Mamoru, in a pot over hot embers) with *ikan bilis* (which Honey declared 'intolerable' before opening himself a tin of beef), jackfruit and coarse coffee. There was much talk about whether this island is one of the Seven Maidens. In the distance, from this isolated beach, we can see two small islands, but there is no way of telling if these too are Maidens without surveying the area around these islands.

'If local *on dit* is true,' said Peter, 'all we'd have to do is wait until sunset to see if they disappear.'

Mamoru and Honey went out to the boat to organise our supplies and consult their maps. They were gone for a considerable length of time, during which I remained here, writing, and Peter coaxed Johnny out on to the beach. They walked along the water's edge, stopping now and then to dig shells and other mysterious things from the sand. They stood next to each other like two toddlers inspecting a toy. Sometimes Peter would run into the sea, throwing himself into the water when it was deep enough to swim; he exhorted Johnny to join him, but Johnny never ventured far, stopping as soon as the water reached his calves. He stood in the shallows, arms folded. Peter frequently broke into song, and every time he did so I found myself perplexed at how his voice transformed itself, suddenly acquiring a rich, silky texture. The sound it made filled the huge silence around us (there are no birds or insects here to make any noise). I began to recognise a few of the tunes he sang; one of them in particular was repeated many times. I am not sure what language it was in, but I found it surprisingly engaging. It was often accompanied by silly theatrical gestures – Peter beckoning to Johnny who, I am sure, did not know what the song meant.

Mamoru joined me when Peter and Johnny were at the far end of the beach. 'Peter and your husband are very good friends,' he said. 'I think they mean a lot to each other.'

I laughed. 'I had not thought of it before. It doesn't seem to me that the two of them are capable of the emotional bonds you speak of.'

'I didn't mean to imply that they have established a spiritual rapport, or that they would remain close friends for ever. I simply meant that they represent something to each other.'

I looked at him. 'What do you mean?'

He laughed. 'I don't know what I mean. I'm not sure. Each seems to symbolise something in the eyes of the other. I have not been able to discern the nature of these symbols. How terrible for an academic to be so vague.'

'Honestly, Mamoru,' I said, smiling at him, 'I didn't think you spent so much time observing people. Your brain must never rest.'

He dropped his head and looked at the sand. (He is so easily embarrassed.) 'I don't spend time watching people,' he said, as if he had made a mistake and was apologising for it. 'I do think about things, of course, but that is after all what my profession demands of me.'

'I was only teasing,' I said. I wanted to touch him, to assure him I meant no offence, but I did not; I was not sure it was the right thing to do. He sat up and looked out at the beach. No one was in sight. He took my hand and placed it against his cheek. 'You are allowed to tease me as much as you like,' he said.

Later in the day we remembered something important. Mamoru noticed the tide coming in and gathered us all together. We gazed out at the islands. The copper-coloured water glowed uncertainly around them. 'They've *got* to be Maidens,' Peter said softly. 'Come on, *disappear*.'

But they did not. The sun had dipped below the horizon but the islands were still there.

'It doesn't mean anything,' Peter said. Mamoru agreed, saying again that we needed to survey the area.

We trudged back to our little camp under the tree and set about preparing supper. I helped Mamoru collect broken coconut husks and small pieces of wood. No one spoke. We settled down with our tins around the hesitant fire. The last of the purple light stained the sky. I allowed myself a final look at the two small islands.

'Look,' I whispered.

In the glowing twilight only one island remained. The other, which previously sat immovably beside it, had vanished into the sea. In its place there was only twilight sky. It was as if it had never existed.

There is only one other thing I need to say (the fire is nearly out): at last I can believe we are truly alive.

22 October 1941

We sailed around the islands in waters smoother than glass. Peter's voice filled the space around us with song. It seemed to echo in the windless sky; each note hung in the air for a very long time, playing in my ears while the next note danced over it. Sometimes (as when Peter sang that song which seems to be his favourite) I could not understand any of the words. The notes seemed to weave in and out of each other, no longer discernible, like a length of shot silk held up close to your eyes. It made me smile. I looked at Mamoru; his hands steered the boat with the lightest of touches, his eyes were clear and very bright.

I sat with Peter and Johnny as we went past each of the islands. Earlier that morning we had made the decision to pack our things and set off exploring the islands. Mamoru was hopeful our reconnaissance would unearth a site suitable for a permanent camp. Although they varied in size – some were little more than large boulders while others seemed to stretch for miles – the coastlines of the islands were similar: rocky barriers punctuated by sandy coves. Behind them, small coconut trees rose from the low, scrubby forests, their trunks dried bone-white by the salty air.

'How will we know which one to stop at?' I said to Peter. 'They all look the same.'

'It'll announce itself to us, my dear, it'll announce itself,' he replied.

By midday, however, we had still only seen six islands, and none of them seemed very special. Not one showed any signs of life. Not a single bird hovered over the trees; the forests looked dry and fruitless. 'Aren't the Seven Maidens renowned for their flora and fauna?' I asked Peter.

'That's what people say, yes.'

'There doesn't appear to be any.'

'How can you tell? That rather unpromising façade may disguise an entire universe of riches.'

'Or it may be even more barren than it appears.'

Mamoru and Honey were deep in discussion, examining one of Mamoru's maps.

'The seventh Maiden isn't where it should be,' I overheard Mamoru say.

'I don't understand,' Honey said, his voice lowered, 'you said these maps were a hundred per cent accurate.'

'They are. Something is not right.'

'Maybe we're not looking in the right place, or we're overlooking something? Perhaps the seventh disappears with the tide too?'

'The seventh is the largest by far. It is low tide for these islands – it shall not be high tide until dark. If it is here, we will find it. Let's retrace our steps.'

The boat began to sweep round in a broad arc until we faced the direction from which we had begun. In truth, we had sailed around these islands for so long now that the sea and the position of those barren outcrops began to appear confusing. Yet we kept up the pretence of being alert, scanning the horizon for some clue we may have missed before.

'Do you know what we're looking for?' I asked Peter.

He had his hand to his brow, shielding his eyes from the sun. 'My dear, I haven't a clue. I've been lost all my life.'

Johnny said, 'There's going to be a storm.'

'You silly monkey,' Peter said, laughing, 'there isn't a cloud in the sky.'

Johnny shrugged his shoulders and said, 'I can smell it.'

Mamoru left Honey to steer and came to consult Johnny. 'Are you certain?' he said, unsure of whether to dismiss Johnny's words as mere speculation.

Again Johnny shrugged. 'I think so. Not a long storm, but a sharp one.'

Mamoru nodded and rejoined Honey at the wheel. They spoke for a while and consulted the map again.

'You're right, Johnny,' said Peter, 'the air does smell different.'

It was then that we noticed it, moving like a shadow over the water in the distance. A single black cloud, heavy with rain, scattering shapes across the surface of the sea. From afar it looked as if the green waters had turned grey under this darkened umbrella. It grew larger as it moved towards us, and soon we could see how quickly it was travelling. 'Christ almighty,' Peter breathed. Underneath the cloud the water was flecked white with the foam of waves; yet just beyond the circle of the cloud's shadow the sea was as calm and green as it was under our boat. It was as if a neat circle had been drawn around those waves, herding them tightly like wild animals.

'Life jackets!' Peter cried.

Johnny remained sitting impassively on a bench, his body slumped against the shack. 'There are none,' he said indifferently.

Mamoru said, 'Hold on tightly to something. Everything will be fine. The storm will pass.' His voice was calm and steady. He came to me and held my hand. We were standing near Johnny. I did not draw away. 'Stay close to me,' he said. 'I will be steering the boat. No harm shall come to you.'

Peter bumped into me as I tried to follow Mamoru. He looked at me with a wild-eyed expression.

The storm hit us before Mamoru was able to return properly

to the helm. I had not even reached the shack. It was as if the storm cloud had sped up, travelling more swiftly than before in order to catch us off guard. As I fell I saw that Mamoru, too, had lost his balance. He was thrown off his feet; his back smashed into the side of the shack as the boat rocked with the force of the first wave. In a second the air passed from being dry and salty to moist with rain; a moment later I felt as if I was breathing water. A wall of rain crashed down upon us as we gasped in vain for air. I tried to keep my eyes open but the force of the rain was so great that I could see only blurred shapes through my half-closed eyes. The boat suddenly felt small and very light. The waves threw it clean into the air and dragged it down again. Where was Mamoru? I thought I saw him haul himself to his feet and stagger to the helm. No other man in the world had the strength to do that.

I had never before known the meaning of the expression 'with all my life', not truly, but in those few moments I did. I clung to the wooden rail on the side of the boat *with all my life*. I wanted to say 'sorry' to Johnny *with all my life*, 'sorry I made you love me'. And with all my life I wanted to see Mamoru again.

I fell into the sea as I knew I would. I had been stupid to believe I could resist its force. Still I kicked against it. The warm foamy wash swept into my mouth, my eyes, my nose and lungs but I kicked some more. I felt my limbs begin to tire from the struggle. Where were the others? I had not seen any of them. I thought of surrendering, but my stiffening legs continued to kick as if obeying a will greater than my own.

Were the waves beginning to calm? Over their crests I thought I saw Johnny's head bobbing lifelessly not five yards from me. I tried to call to him but when I opened my mouth I was dragged underwater. Somehow my body rose to the surface again and that was when I saw Mamoru. He looked straight at my face and called out to me, I know he did. It was him, swimming powerfully towards me. In the distance, another swimmer: Peter? Johnny's head was barely visible now, even though the waves had calmed further. My own body felt heavy and tired, and I realised that both my legs had now seized up. Yet I was not scared. I knew that soon I would be saved. Mamoru was now only twenty yards away and still making progress. I could see the boat now too, far away in the water-washed distance. Someone was standing on the deck, looking out at us. I looked to see where Mamoru was. Why was he swimming away from me? Half choked, I screamed his name and he paused, looking in my direction. But then he put his head in the water again and continued on his course. A few seconds later I saw him pull Johnny to the surface. With his body under Johnny's, he began to swim back to the boat. He cradled Johnny's face between his hands, pointing it to the sky and the open air.

I stopped kicking. A crushing numbness seized my legs and my eyes began to sting. I let myself sink, feeling the sea pull me into its depths.

And then I felt hands; hands on my body, grabbing at my arms, breasts, hair, pulling me to the surface. I coughed, water burning my throat. 'Snow! Snow!' I heard as I felt life return to my lungs. It was Peter.

'Don't struggle, Snow, let yourself go limp,' he said as he pulled my arm over his shoulder. I felt his hard bony back beneath me all the way to the boat. His legs and arms pulled unevenly, jerking rather than propelling us along. His breaths rasped as he swam, and it was some time before I realised he was singing a song. I could scarcely believe it. Over the waves and the dying rain, he was still trying to sing his silly songs.

We watched the storm cloud as it swept away from us. Sunshine and flat green waters returned in an instant. The sodden deck began to dry, steam rising thickly in the heat. Our clothes, too, felt heavy and clammy.

Honey, it seems, had hidden below deck in the cabin. He said it had been a terrifying experience, being tossed about like a cricket ball in that tiny space.

Mamoru came to where I was sitting and asked if I was all right. I did not answer.

'I'm sorry,' he said, 'I did not know where you were. I thought I heard your voice but I saw only Johnny. I knew he couldn't swim. If I did not save him he would have drowned. Peter was there too and I thought – I don't know. I am sorry.' A pained expression settled on his face and I thought he might cry.

'I cannot swim either,' I said, closing my eyes tightly. I did not cry.

He bowed his head and touched my arm. 'I did not know that.' He remained next to me for a while. I felt his slow, warm breath on my arm. When he had gone I saw that he had left something for me. It was the small soft bag that I had been carrying with me, the one in which I kept my diary. I had forgotten all about it during the storm. I undid the straps of the bag and searched its damp contents. It was still there, wrapped tightly in its waxcloth. Mamoru must have rescued it for me. He had saved it from the storm.

Peter approached me but I shut my eyes.

23 October 1941

It was curious, the way the seventh Maiden finally revealed itself to us. Thinking about it now, I still cannot decide if the sudden sight of it was an unexpected shock or something entirely predictable and perfectly natural. We had not spoken much after the storm, and so I do not know what the others felt. I cannot determine the sensations I myself experienced on first seeing it.

We all saw it at the same time. Once the storm had passed, it took us a while to reorient ourselves. We headed back to the first island, all five of us searching the seas around us with added vigilance. We counted the islands and – we thought – anticipated finding six, as we had before. It was only when we passed the fifth, the one closest to our original island, that we saw it. It lay exactly where the first island had been. I could have sworn it did. But where that small island had been there now stood a new one, ten times the size of the previous one and larger by far than any we had seen. It too had a covering of scrubby forest on the edge of its rock-and-sand coast, but behind that rose a dense green jungle, quite unlike anything we had seen since coming to sea. Its rich colouring seemed at odds with the yellowish, sun-bleached foliage of earlier islands. The coconut trees were tall and stood firm and erect, unbowed by the sea breeze. How far it stretched I could not say.

We drifted slowly into its shallows, surrendering to it. The cry of strange animals punctured the air.

'You see?' Peter said quietly to me. '*Life.*'

We set up camp in a shaded clearing on the edge of the jungle, within sight of the beach. Mamoru hacked at some saplings with a parang, felling them with single strokes of the curved blade. The clearing was ideal, Mamoru said. The ground was dry and covered with short grass and sand. Around it stood trees with firm trunks – perfect for hammocks – and thick foliage offering cool respite from the sun; the barrier of scrub at the edge of the beach provided a natural windbreak.

The men left in search of fresh water. Mamoru said that he sensed it close at hand. Once we had a reliable source of water for bathing and drinking, there was little else we needed, he said. He lifted his head as if to smell the air. 'We will not want for much in this place.' They split up, Mamoru pairing with Honey and Peter with Johnny.

'Coming, Snow?' Peter said. I looked at him and Johnny and then turned to catch Mamoru's eye.

'I don't think so,' I said. 'I think I will stay here and get things organised for your return.'

As soon as they left I took out my diary and began to write.

Recording the events of the past few days has not been easy for me. The reliving of certain moments has been more painful than I had anticipated. While writing these last entries, I have found myself pausing in order to contemplate the words, to rethink the sequence of events. I have never done this before. It is as if I am unsure of everything. The world in which I seek refuge – this world, *my* world – is no longer as assuring as it once was. This diary is still my own. I can still be alone within it. But I am not certain now of what it means to be alone.

24 October 1941

Mamoru and Honey returned first. It was as they had expected. A freshwater stream was close by, barely half a mile away. 'Let me show you,' Mamoru said, extending his hand to me.

'Yes, what a good idea,' Honey added. 'I'll leave the two of you to enjoy the walk on your own.' He had a smile on his face yet he looked as if he was frowning with worry. I could not decipher this expression.

We walked through an ancient and silent jungle, the tread of our feet crunching loudly around us. Hazy sunlight filtered through the foliage and conjured shadowy shapes in the air.

'I am sorry about what happened at sea, during the storm,' Mamoru said.

'Please,' I said before he could continue, 'I do not want you to apologise. You did what you believed was right. That is all we can do in our lives. You did not know where I was – how could you have saved me? If you had not acted as you did, Johnny would be dead. I do not want to hear any more on the subject.'

We walked in silence for a while. I reached out and felt for his hand. When I touched it he clasped mine in return.

We reached a clearing by the stream. A grove of wild bananas and elephant grass encircled us.

'Please forgive me,' said Mamoru, unbuttoning his shirt. 'I need desperately to bathe the salt from my body.' He waded into the water, his khaki shorts ballooning as he did so. When he reached the middle of the stream and the water was at waist height, he curled his body and plunged underwater. After a few seconds, he surfaced some distance away, breathing out with a strangled yell of exhilaration. 'The water feels wonderful,' he said, his whole face shining. 'You should come in.'

I stood uncertainly for a second, my toes curling into the mud at the edge of the stream. He turned away from me to swim downriver with the current, and I began to unbutton the blouse of my *samfu*. I was unsure as to what to do with my trousers but finally I undid them too and stepped into the icy water.

Mamoru turned round as I called out with the shock of the cold. He swam towards me but by the time he reached me my skin had acclimatised to the temperature of the water. I experienced the most curious sensation. Whilst my skin tingled with cold, a warmth I had never known grew from the core of my body, spreading inside me, into my chest, stomach, neck, fingers. Where the warmth met the cold a glow covered my body, sheathing me in a new, different skin. My old flesh no longer existed.

'How is it?' he said.

I simply smiled.

He scooped some water in his cupped hands and brought it to his lips. As he drank, a trickle ran down his chin and down his chest. He cupped his hands again and, this time, moved towards me. Without thinking, I opened my mouth and drank. The water tasted of palm syrup and stale rice.

We bathed for a while, paddling silently in the shallow water.

'I promise I shan't look,' he said as I went back to the bank.

I laughed. 'That might be wise,' I said. 'You might be shocked if you do.'

He turned away and swam gracefully, hardly causing a ripple. Against the dark, tree-shaded water, his skin glowed a pure white.

We had only been back at our camp for a short time before Peter and Johnny appeared, breathless from their walk. Johnny was rubbing his shoulder, and Peter's face and arms were flecked with little red cuts.

'I've seen something,' Peter said. 'I've found a ruin.'

25 October 1941

It looked more like an abandoned house than a ruin to me.

'It *is* a ruin,' insisted Peter.

'It has doors and part of a roof,' Honey said.

Peter was not deterred. 'It's not the Parthenon, I grant you, but it's still a proper ruin. Look at it!'

I had never seen anything like it. It was a large building with ornate adornments over its façade – hideous carved animals I did not recognise.

'Interesting,' said Mamoru. 'Some of the decoration looks almost European, neo-Gothic. We know that a few Englishmen built fantastic palaces at the turn of the century – such as Kellie's Castle – which imitated high Victorian architecture, but this is different. It looks like a Mughal dwelling. I cannot place it. There is something in the construction of this place that suggests it is older than the Edwardian castles I have mentioned.'

'Oh, much older. It's clearly ancient,' said Peter.

'There are traces of paint on the doors,' Mamoru said.

'I do not want to go inside,' said Johnny.

But there was no stopping Peter. He had already bounded up

the stone steps and was trying the door. It fell open without resistance.

We hesitated a while. Mamoru was very interested in the exterior of the building. He looked at it so intently it was as if he was taking photographs with his eyes. I knew he was committing to memory the image of that house, down to the tiniest detail.

'I'm not going in,' Johnny said again in a small voice.

'It'll be an utter waste but we might as well,' said Honey as he started towards the house.

By the time we stepped through the broad stone threshold Peter had explored much of the house.

He ran down the wide stone staircase, leaping the final few steps.

'It's magnificent,' he said. 'You'll gasp when you see what I've found.'

I looked around me. The walls were built of a pinkish stone that looked soft in texture. I put my hand on a wall; it was crumbly to the touch. Although the floors were covered in a scattering of dust it did not feel damp and I could not smell any guano. In every way the house seemed remarkably well preserved.

'Who on earth would build a place like this in the middle of the bloody jungle on a godforsaken island?' said Honey.

As we ascended the sweeping staircase and my eyes adjusted to the dim light, I thought I could pick out cobwebs hanging thickly from the ceiling; they appeared to adorn the walls, too, like necklaces. Then, as we stood at the top of the stairs and looked down the long hallway that stretched into darkness, I realised that they were not cobwebs but something firmer, less tentative. Their shapes curved into the darkness, forming an uneven carpet over our heads.

'Can you see?' Peter cried. 'Aren't they wonderful?' He reached into his satchel and found a box of matches. After three or four goes – the box was probably damp – he finally succeeded. He lifted the match above his head. Its flared light danced towards the ceiling.

'Dear God,' Honey breathed.

Every conceivable space on the ceilings and the walls were hung with antlers. There were no stuffed heads or skins, no skulls or skeletons, merely antlers of every shape. They pointed downwards like twisted, ossified fingers reaching out to touch us. I felt Mamoru's arm next to me and was calmed by his closeness.

'Do you think they're from hitherto undiscovered species?' Peter asked. 'They must be. They must be!'

That evening's dinner – tinned rations, much to Honey's delight, with some wild papaya Mamoru had found – was dominated by talk about the house. Who built it? What was it for? When? Peter insisted on calling it a 'ruin', and seemed offended when we did not follow suit.

'To be perfectly honest,' Honey said, 'that derelict house is of no consequence whatsoever.' He had gorged himself on corned beef and seemed very at ease, reclining against a log. He was himself again, speaking as if pronouncing imperial edicts. 'It's an incidental structure, abandoned because it didn't serve any purpose. It isn't very remarkable. I'm not surprised *you* like it, Wormwood.'

Peter smiled. 'You simply can't appreciate beauty.'

'On the contrary,' Honey replied, 'you see beauty even where it doesn't exist.'

We retired to bed and I checked, as I always do, to see if my diary was safe in my belongings. I don't know if it was the result of having spent too much time out at sea, or if I was still suffering from the lingering effects of the storm, but I could not remember the exact position in which I had left the diary. I imagined that the waxcloth had been disturbed. Not much, but enough to make me notice it. I unwrapped the diary and found that all was in order. I tried to put the whole thing out of my mind as I fell asleep.

26 October 1941

I was awakened in the night by a shrill cry, a thin, howling wail that came from the jungle and pierced the night like a dagger. It twisted and danced in the air, breaking now and then into coughing barks. I did not know what creature made that noise; I had never heard it before. From under my mosquito net I looked at Johnny. He was asleep. I could not see Mamoru in the dark – he was too far away. His bed looked peaceful and undisturbed. I listened for stirrings, the ruffling of bedclothes, but heard nothing, and so presumed Peter and Honey were asleep too. Why had no one else been roused by this terrible noise? The sound of it rang in my ears and I did not sleep again until it began to abate, just before dawn.

29 October 1941

I had just come back from a long walk through the jungle with Mamoru. We had made it all the way to the waterfall and back, stopping every so often to fill my bag with fallen fruit. On our return, Mamoru went to the boat with Honey, to discuss rations and other logistical matters, as they always did. I was just settling down to write when I noticed Peter milling around the camp, tightening hammocks and clearing his things into neat little piles.

'Why aren't you with Johnny?' I asked.

'He said he wanted to be left alone,' Peter answered quickly, 'so I thought I'd come back and tidy my things.'

'Why? It's not as if you've ever done it before,' I said, meaning to sound jolly; but my voice sounded oddly flat and humourless.

'I'm just following your example, that's all. I mean, your things are always so neatly arranged. Nothing's ever out of order.' He came and sat with me, and I closed my diary. He picked up a twig and began to draw in the sand, but the twig snapped and he picked at a scab on his leg instead.

'Peter, is something the matter?'

'Not with me, no,' he said. 'Are *you* all right?'

I felt irritation begin to rise within me. 'What are you trying to say?'

'Johnny,' he began, but stopped.

I did not say anything. My throat felt constricted. I opened my diary and flicked through its pages, pretending to read.

'I was just going to say, I think Johnny's feeling better,' Peter said.

I looked up. 'Is he really?'

'Yes, I think so,' Peter said.

I smiled. 'Thank you for looking after him.'

He shrugged and resumed picking his scab. 'What do you think of Kunichika?' he said suddenly. The words tumbled out of his mouth, barely articulated, as if they had been held in for a very long time and suddenly let loose.

'Mamoru?' I said. 'He is a fascinating man.'

'He seems to be extremely knowledgeable on a variety of matters. Things you wouldn't really expect an academic to know.'

'Well, he isn't an ordinary academic. He was made a professor at Kyoto University when he was twenty-five. That's how old I will be in four years' time. It's astonishing.'

'What is he Professor of?'

'Russian literature. He has a natural facility for languages, and speaks at least a dozen fluently. He mentioned yesterday that he learned Italian when he was sixteen.'

'Snow,' Peter said, turning to me and looking me in the eye, 'do you think he's really what he says he is? Haven't you wondered? Look at what's happening around us.'

'Nothing's happening, or haven't you noticed?'

'Everything's happening, Snow. The Japs are in Siam now. Think about China.'

'That is not part of our world. Even Siam has nothing to do with us. Mamoru is not part of this.'

'He's Japanese, Snow. Maybe you didn't realise this.'

I paused. 'Peter,' I said, lowering my voice, 'I am going to tell you something in confidence; something about Mamoru.' I hesitated for a while but allowed myself to continue. 'He was posted to Manchuria at the start of the incident there, as an interpreter. He was a young, prominent academic and the army used his talent for languages. He had no choice, he had to go. Please, Peter, please do not tell anyone. He is terribly ashamed of this and would not want anyone to know. I told you this so that you would understand he is not a demon. He left Manchuria after nine months. He worked in military headquarters – he never went into the field, never held a bayonet – but even that was too much for him. He fell sick; he became half blind with the worry. He hated what he saw. The shame of being there was doubled by the shame of giving up, of being weak. I am the only person he has ever told this to. Please, I beg you, do not speak of this to anyone.'

Peter looked away, peering into the distance at the boat. Mamoru and Honey were beginning to swim ashore.

'As I was saying,' he said brightly as he stood up, 'Johnny's feeling better.'

I watched him walk down the beach. 'Thank you, Peter,' I said.

He stopped and turned round, hands in the pockets of his baggy shorts. He smiled. 'Be careful.'

1 November 1941

Rain, all last night. I fell asleep to the sound of thick raindrops on the tarpaulin Mamoru had stretched over the camp. I was still worried about my diary: twice in the last few days, I imagined that it had been disturbed. Finally, after dinner last night I took it, wrapped in its waxcloth, and buried it in the sand close to my bed, near the base of a tree; then I covered it with twigs and dead leaves.

I was awakened again by that awful wail. Every night since it started, I have been the only one to wake up. I wondered if it was a joke one of the men was playing, but they were all asleep. Nothing stirred in the camp. All the other beds were silent. I got up, pulling a gown over me. The cry screamed in my ears. I had to see where it was coming from. I put on a pair of boots that belonged to Johnny and stepped out from under the mosquito net.

Beyond the tarpaulin the rain dripped steadily through the canopy of trees above. The boots were too large for my feet, and I stumbled slowly into the jungle. The source of that high-pitched call seemed always to lie just ahead of me, a few steps out of reach. Every time I thought I would discover it, its call would echo slightly further away. I kept walking, tripping over small logs and tree roots; the more I walked the less afraid I became. I thought: I want to confront this creature. I did not know if I would destroy it or hold it to my bosom when I found it. I was not frightened of it any more. In the half-light I saw the monolithic silhouette of the house of antlers. The deformed animals, carved in stone, seemed to freeze in mid-leap on the façade. The wailing seemed to come from within those darkened depths. I started up the huge stone steps, my gown falling open as I climbed to the massive door.

Something darted into the darkness. A figure. I could not tell if it was man or beast; it fell from the high wall next to the house and disappeared into the jungle. I stopped and looked around me. The wailing had broken into a coughing bark. More movement, I sensed. Another figure – this one of human definition –

moved swiftly among the trees. I caught a flash of naked skin. It was pale and shining in the broken moonlight, smooth white against the patchy darkness of the jungle.

'Mamoru?' I called.

Again I saw it, gliding silkily, naked, among the trees.

'Mamoru?' I shouted. There was no answer. 'Peter? Frederick?'

I ran to where I had last seen it, but there was nothing there. I searched among the trees for some time, but I was alone. The wailing, too, had stopped. I began to walk home; the rain had made my clothes heavy and cold. I realised that my face was wet not only with raindrops but tears too.

When I arrived back at the camp I picked my way silently past each of the beds. All the men slept soundly. I undressed and went to bed with my skin still damp. I slept badly, even though the wailing had stopped.

This morning, after breakfast, I waited for the men to disperse from camp on their various activities – fishing (Johnny), exploring the house of antlers (Peter), map-making (Mamoru and, I think, Honey) – before I went to collect my diary. The leaves were still piled thickly over the hole I had dug. I felt gently relieved. It was only when I knelt down to dig out the diary that I saw the marks in the sand. Two sets of deep, broad scratches, a foot long, next to the mound which marked where the diary was. They had faded in the rain but I could still see them, clawed heavily into the earth.

3 November 1941

'Tell me about Manchuria,' I said to Mamoru. 'I want to know everything.' It was in the middle of the afternoon and we were alone.

'I've told you everything,' he said. 'I've told you about my shame.'

‘I know. I want to know more. I want to know what you saw.’

‘Terrible things,’ he said, laughing softly. ‘Too terrible for words. Really, I do not wish to speak of those things. They belong to my past.’

He began to look away but I said, ‘Mamoru, please. I want you to share your pain with me.’

‘Why?’

I did not answer.

‘Fine,’ he said, his voice dropping. ‘Let me tell you about some of the things I have seen, some of the things that have happened to me.’ He looked into the distance and when he spoke he sounded as if he was speaking to himself. After a few seconds it felt as if he had forgotten I was there. He seemed to vanish into himself. I no longer knew who was telling the story.

‘One day I was sent out with another officer, a geologist from Osaka. He was a good friend and made my time there easier. Kondo was his name; the finest man I ever met. In the evenings we would talk about art and books. Basho was his favourite. “We have travelled the narrow road to the far north, my friend,” he said when I was returning to Japan. He was the one who was with me on that day. I remember everything clearly, even though I have tried to forget it. We were sent to investigate an incident that had happened near Mudanjiang. A few men had been patrolling an area of rocky, mountainous terrain. They had reported an explosion and a few resulting casualties. Nothing out of the ordinary – this sort of thing happened several times a day. As usual, I was sent to gather information and write reports; Kondo came with me to look at the rock formations. We had to leave our vehicle and walk some distance on foot. We dropped down into a valley and followed an old railway track. This was the most direct route to take. It was difficult ground to cover – loose rocks fell around us all the time. After a while we saw ahead of us a group of soldiers squatting around a campfire. Neither Kondo nor I recognised them. Their uniforms were of the standard variety, but we did not know which regiment they belonged to. As we approached we saw that they were eating a meal; fresh meat was roasting over their fire in large blackened chunks. This was very unusual. Conditions in Manchuria are harsher than you can imagine, and food – particularly meat – is very scarce. These soldiers seemed to be planning something. They spoke quietly to each other, looking at us suspiciously. As we approached, one of them smiled at me. I can still see his yellow teeth set in his cracked brown face. "Brother," he said, "why don't you join us for some food?"

'"That's kind," I said, trying to hide my discomfort. "You are lucky to have meat."

'"Yes, we caught a big snake," he said. "A very big python."

'Next to me I could feel Kondo stiffen. He too knew something was not quite right in the way these soldiers were behaving. The smell of the meat made us even more uncomfortable. It was sweet and inviting, and neither of us had eaten much meat since coming to China.

'"Here, brothers," the soldier said, holding up two pieces of meat. The entire group of them stopped eating and looked at us. It felt as if it was a test. I feared what would happen if we refused, so I accepted the meat. I put it into my mouth slowly, biting into it hesitantly; I could hardly bring myself to do so. The flesh was firm and warm from the fire; once I began eating I could not stop. I finished it quickly and was immediately hungry for more. Kondo had more problems consuming his piece of meat. He gnawed at it weakly and he looked very ill. When I saw this I began to march ahead; I feigned impatience and urged him to hurry.

'"Won't you stay for more?" the soldiers cried, but I said no, we were late in performing our duties and would be punished if we were any later. Kondo was still holding the meat as we walked away. I told him to eat it. If they saw him throw it away I feared we would be shot in the back. He put it in his mouth. When we were certain that we were out of sight we began to run. We ran until Kondo stopped, doubling over and vomiting hard. He was very sick.

'"Did you see?" he gasped.

'"Yes," I said. In the bushes near where the soldiers sat, there was a pile of standard issue uniforms, similar to the ones the soldiers had been wearing, but streaked with bloodstains.

'Kondo and I never spoke of that incident again.'

There was prolonged silence between us. Mamoru remained utterly still.

'There are more things,' he said. 'There were women in the camps. They were brought there for a purpose. For the soldiers –' He stopped. 'No, I cannot even speak of them. To get to my quarters I had to walk past the house in my camp, the one where all the women were kept. It was completely silent. I never heard a single sound from it. The silence was terrible. Every night I fall asleep with that silence screaming in my head.'

I reached across to him and gathered him in my arms. His head lay heavily on me, cradled against my neck.

4 November 1941

It was lunchtime when Peter asked us to accompany him on a walk.

'I'm sorry, I don't think I'm up to it,' I said. I had not slept well – the wailing had disturbed my sleep and I was feeling very tired.

'Come, come,' he said 'a walk will do you a world of good. What about you, Professor? You're game for a stroll through the woods, aren't you? It's not as if there's anything pressing to do.'

Mamoru looked at me and shrugged.

'And why don't you come too, Honey?' Peter continued. 'I know how you don't like being left out of anything.'

'This is ridiculous,' Honey grunted, but stood up nonetheless, tagging reluctantly to the back of our reluctant group.

'Where's Johnny?' I asked as we followed Peter.

'He'll come. He knows where we are.'

I was not surprised to see that Peter was leading us to the house of antlers.

'You're up to something, aren't you, Peter?' I said.

He laughed. 'Of course not.'

He sang all the way there, one tune in particular. He has sung it so many times since we started our trip that I have grown fond of its melody.

We went up the stone steps and into the house. Peter led us through a vast room and out through another doorway to the back of the house. Set in a clearing next to a small muddy brook there lay a table covered with a startlingly white linen tablecloth. Above this floated a canopy of ivory-coloured sheets, fluttering gently in the imperceptible breeze. I looked to see how this umbrella remained suspended in mid-air, but I could see no strings or ropes; it hovered over us of its own accord. The table was laid with the same enamel plates we used at the camp but there were silver knives and forks and glass tumblers. A bottle of wine stood in the middle of the table. On a smaller table nearby there were more bottles and some dishes of food.

Johnny stood up when he saw us and smiled. It was the first time I had seen him smile for some time.

'It's my birthday today,' Peter said, hand in pockets, shifting from one foot to the other. 'My first Oriental birthday.'

'Happy birthday, Peter,' Johnny said.

I turned to Peter and said, 'I didn't realise. Happy birthday.'

'Do you like our tropical *baldacchino*?' Peter asked, noticing me looking upwards. 'Johnny did that.'

I looked at Johnny, not knowing what to say.

'How did you manage it?' Mamoru asked. 'It looks as if it is floating unsupported. Where is your rope system? Did you use pulleys?'

Johnny merely shrugged.

Mamoru smiled and shook his head. 'The power of illusion,' he said.

There was something odd about the clearing we were in. Its edges seemed sharply defined, as if cut out of the jungle. Then I noticed the machete marks on the tree trunks and the pale imprint of dead logs that had been cleared from the ground. Several flowering plants had been allowed to remain, but otherwise the place was stripped of the jungle.

'You've cut down the plants that grew here,' I said to Peter. 'You've made this place yourself.'

'Yes,' he said, looking at his feet. 'It's my little garden. I did it specially.'

Its ordered calm soothed my senses. Amid the tangle of the jungle, this little clearing *did* feel like a garden. 'I like it,' I said. 'I like it very much.'

We sat down at the table. 'Terribly sorry,' Peter said. He reached underneath for a few pieces of broken crockery, which he held aloft. 'The Spode didn't survive the storm. Nor did the wine glasses, so I'm afraid you'll all have to put up with this unspeakable barbarity.'

'Peter,' I said, 'do you mean to tell us that you brought all this with you in your luggage?'

He nodded. 'There was hardly space for my shaving brush.'

Peter poured the wine and passed the food round the table. We began to eat, but were all somewhat subdued. I think we were overcome by the sight of this feast. There was a thick stew of vegetables – tapioca and beans and yam – which tasted of meat, such was its rich taste and chewy texture. There was a bowl of little prawns, their pinkish shells suggesting that they had only just been cooked. Not far from the table, Peter had built a small makeshift grill. Its fruit lay before us: an impressive pile of grilled fish, large *kembong* that Peter said he had netted himself. Their silvery skins bore the hot dark scars of the grill, and they were delicious. Finally, Peter disappeared into the bushes and emerged with a large dish covered with a piece of cloth. With a flourish, he slid the cloth away to reveal a large unidentifiable lump.

'What in God's name is that?' Honey said.

'Bread!' Peter cried. 'Bread which I have baked myself!' He cleared some space on the table and explained how he had built an oven from mud and earth. He had brought a bag of flour with him specifically for this purpose, and was amazed that he had succeeded. He stood over the loaf and gripped it with both hands. He began to pull gently but the bread remained resolute. He set it down on the table and clawed at it awkwardly; his fingers, I noticed, were very slim and fine, his nails long, almost like a woman's. Finally he broke the bread into two uneven pieces. It was soggy and heavy in its texture. 'That can't be eaten,' he said, looking at the pieces of bread in his hands.

'Of course it can,' I said. 'Try it.'

He raised a piece of bread to his mouth and took a bite. He spat it out and shook his head sadly.

'Sit still, everyone,' Honey called out. I turned round and saw that he had taken Peter's camera and was kneeling a few yards from the table.

'Wait,' cried Peter as he came round the table and stood beside my chair; Mamoru took up a position next to Johnny. We sat smiling at the camera. My face felt odd, as if it had forgotten how to smile.

I had never before known the taste of wine. We finished the food and sat under the darkening trees with our tumblers full of that blood-red liquid. I never noticed Peter refilling my glass, yet it was always full, no matter how much I sipped at it. I began to lose track of time. Around me, men's voices and laughter hung in the air like vines, quivering gently with the wind. I tilted my head and looked at the shadows of the leaves swimming across the canopy above us. Peter was singing.

'What is that?' I asked. 'I've been meaning to ask you for ages. It's a beautiful song.'

Peter repeated the tune, louder this time, the rich timbre of his voice vibrating from within his thin chest.

'Is it Italian?' I asked, but he kept singing.

'It is,' said Mamoru. 'It's from the opera *Don Giovanni*.'

'Oh, come on, Peter,' I said, 'do tell me what the words mean.'

'Ask the Professor – he'll tell you,' Peter said, and continued singing.

'What does it mean, Mamoru?' I asked, turning to him and grasping his arm. 'I really want to know.'

He took a sip of wine, his eyes never leaving Peter's happy, singing face. Peter sang seven distinct syllables followed by a tangle of many more (I cannot be sure – the wine in my veins, my lack of comprehension all combined to make the words sound completely mystifying). 'It means, "There we will take hands."'

'Is that all? What about the rest of it?'

Mamoru translated as Peter sang: '*There you will say "yes". Look, it's not far from here. Let's leave this place, my dear.*'

'Oh,' I said. 'It doesn't make much sense to me.'

'It's not very interesting,' he replied. 'Peter, why are you singing Zerlina's part too?'

'Who's Zerlina?' I whispered as Peter kept singing.

'The woman,' Mamoru replied, 'a bride about to be stolen from her husband.'

'I sing all the parts,' Peter said, barely drawing breath before continuing to sing. His voice, though, was tiring. The notes no longer stretched as they did and the words seemed rushed. He seemed out of breath. He stopped singing and looked at Mamoru.

'You sing the next line,' he said.

'What?' Mamoru replied, setting his glass down on the table.

'It's your line next. Actually, the whole thing is yours to sing, isn't it? But you might as well start with the next line.'

'Peter,' I said, 'what on earth are you on about? I think you have had too much wine.' I could not stop laughing even though my head hurt.

'Right,' Peter said. 'I'll sing a line by Zerlina to help prompt you. You then come in with your line, Giovanni. *Molto espressivo*. Do be a sport.'

Peter sang something in a screeching falsetto. 'Come on, you know what to sing, Professor. You know all the bloody words. It's my birthday – sing, damn you!'

Mamoru spoke some words in Italian.

Peter screeched again – different words this time.

I laughed.

Mamoru spoke again.

'And together now,' Peter shouted, standing up and waving his arms. He screamed the tuneless words up into the trees above us, his throat heaving with the effort. He walked away from the table, stumbling towards the house. It was dark now but the moon was very bright. He sat down on some broken stone steps with his head in his arms.

'Leave him,' Mamoru said. I was not sure to whom that command was directed.

We started to walk back to the camp, Mamoru leading the way. My head felt heavy, my vision untrustworthy. I had to stare hard at fallen trees before stepping over them – I could not tell how high they were or what lay on the other side of them. The shadows swam among the trees, chased by the moonlight. I noticed, though, that Johnny had taken the unfinished bottles of wine with him.

I knew that tonight was the perfect time to speak to him, to tell him all that lay in my heart, but I knew, too, that I would not.

I am beginning to doubt if I ever will. In this place, perhaps I will never need to.

5 November 1941

The wailing lasted all night, shriller than ever. I fell into a heavy yet disturbed sleep – I had never experienced anything like it. My body felt shot through with poison; my veins were pregnant with it. My sleep was all-embracing yet unreal. In my sleep, things happened to me – to my body – that I could not discern. I saw everything so clearly, yet I knew they could not have been real. I saw Mamoru with my diary. I saw Johnny with my diary. I saw Mamoru and Johnny together. I saw them speaking, touching each other, their foreheads brought together in intimate conversation. Each of them approached me and spoke in languages I did not understand. The wailing burned through my sleep, never allowing me to escape. Sometimes it sang Peter's song, screeching his words into the depths of the jungle and the fathomless sea.

I awoke when it was light. Mamoru was already up, collecting wood for the fire. I ran as far as I could, towards the sea. I had made it halfway down to the water when I collapsed to my knees and began to vomit. I knelt on the beach, my insides streaming down the sides of my mouth on to the hot sand. I had never felt anything so painful.

As I fell back into bed I noticed that Peter was asleep, as was Johnny. Only Honey was not there.

I woke again – properly – at midday. Mamoru had left some food and water, but I did not feel like eating. Johnny was sitting some way along the beach under a tree; Peter was swimming in the sea. He saw me step gingerly on to the sand and walked towards me.

'What a party,' he said. 'I feel awful. What about you?'

'Worse than death,' I said, and he laughed. When I laughed my whole body hurt.

'Poor thing,' he said. 'First time is always the worst. Trust me, next time you have a glass of wine, you'll *adore* it.'

I smiled. 'Where's Mamoru?'

'Not sure. He said he was off to find Honey. I'm keeping my head firmly below the parapet, though – I'm certainly not his favourite person.'

'Where's Honey?'

'How am I supposed to know?'

'Didn't he come back for you last night? I thought I heard him say he was going back to keep an eye on you.'

'Darling, that was the wine speaking to you. I saw him go back to the camp with you and that was it. I passed out on the steps and didn't wake up until it was nearly dawn. God only knows how I found my way back to the camp.'

'Oh,' I said, 'my head really hurts.'

7 November 1941

Still no sign of Honey. Mamoru is getting very worried.

'I can't understand what the fuss is about,' Peter said when he returned from another fruitless search of the island. 'He'll turn up eventually.'

'He's always running off on his own,' Johnny said.

Mamoru remained silent. He has hardly spoken since Peter's party, not even to me.

8 November 1941

My diary is being disturbed. I know this for certain. I do not know who is reading it, but someone is. This morning I began to write but after a few minutes I felt a stabbing pain in my abdomen. (I have not felt right since the day of Peter's party.) I closed my diary and placed a stone on top of it before walking up the beach to relieve myself. I do not know how long I was away – not more than ten minutes, at most. When I came back the diary was open, its pages fanning gently in the breeze. I must have startled the ghostly reader. Yet I knew for sure that Mamoru, Johnny and Peter had all been engaged in one activity or another. As I stood there I could see, with my own eyes, Peter splashing in the shallows dressed in his shirtsleeves as always. Johnny was building a small house from shells. They had both been doing that when I left. Mamoru was on the other side of the island searching for Honey (who is still missing). Mamoru's expeditions last for hours; often he does not return till dark. I did not know which phantom had been reading my diary.

My hands trembled as I sat down. The nightly wailing may continue but this cannot.

10 November 1941

It was Johnny who woke us up. He took us half a mile up the beach in the pale dawn and showed us what he had found.

There, left stranded on the shore by the retreating tide, lay Honey. The occasional wave licked at his body as it faded into the sand. He was still fully clothed, his wristwatch glinting softly as it caught the light. His neck appeared black, badly bruised, and his shirt was torn in several places. Nothing remained of his face.

'It's been eaten by fish,' Peter said quietly.

Mamoru dug a grave at the top of the beach, under the trees beyond reach of the tide. We buried Honey and Peter said a few words of Christian prayer.

We went back to the camp but none of us was hungry for breakfast.

11 November 1941

Mamoru says Honey must have been so intoxicated with wine that he must have somehow fallen into the sea. We have not spoken about Honey much, though I know that we are all thinking of how Honey could have died. Mamoru's explanation is convincing, but the truth of it is that no one really knows what happened. No one knows anything any more.

15 November 1941

I force myself to record this.

Circumstances left me with no choice. I could not stop myself.

Finally, I accept my fate.

Last night I decided I could no longer bear this emptiness. I saw Mamoru disappear into the darkened woods. He has taken to doing this every evening, after we eat our supper in terrible silence. Each time he leaves I long to follow him yet I have been afraid to incur his wrath. What do I have to lose? I don't know. It feels as if I have lost everything, and yet when I look at Mamoru I still feel the faint pulse of hope, the scent of something new.

In the end I could contain myself no longer. I saw him melt into the trees and I followed him.

I remained twenty yards behind him, treading gently in the dark. It was not a clear night. Clouds drifted thickly over the moon and it was difficult to see where I was going. It was only because of Mamoru's intense whiteness that I was able to keep sight of him. I could not remember if he was wearing white clothes; I was only aware of the purity of his colour, a strange quality that seemed to absorb what little light there was and make it his own. He walked slowly, picking his way smoothly between the trees as if following an ancient, predetermined path. Not once did he pause or turn round.

Several times I stumbled, catching my foot on tree roots and rocks; each time I had to hurry to catch up with him. Invisible branches slashed at my face and neck and arms like whips. I tasted the saltiness of blood on my lips but still I continued, drawn by the glowing white light ahead of me. I do not know how long or in which direction I had been walking, but suddenly I found myself in a clearing by the house of antlers. Mamoru had disappeared.

I walked slowly around the house, pausing now and again to listen for movement: nothing. I came to the back of the house, and there he was, standing in the moonlight on a stone parapet, hands in pockets, silent as the night that had fallen upon us. He looked like a carved figure, part of that dead house. It was only when he moved and his whiteness shifted with him that I knew for certain that it was him. He became human again, walking until he was at the base of the steps, not ten yards from me.

I came out of the dark, into his light. 'Mamoru,' I said.

He turned to face me. 'Snow,' he said simply and without surprise, breathing out as if in relief. He had been waiting for me.

I went to him and touched his hand. We sat down on the steps and I leaned my head on his shoulder. I closed my eyes. His marble-cool body brought relief to my burning head. We did not speak for a very long time.

'I know you are troubled, Mamoru,' I said after a while. 'But Honey's death was not your fault. You cannot be responsible for everything.'

He put his hand on my brow. 'Am I not responsible for the horror of it?'

'What do you mean? You are not responsible for Honey's death, nor the deaths of anyone else. We've talked about this before, Mamoru. I know you carry with you what you saw in China, but that was not your doing.'

'Wasn't it?' he laughed a strange laugh. I could not decipher it.

'No,' I said, sitting up and facing him. 'It wasn't.'

Again he laughed. 'How little you know.' His voice sounded hard and bitter.

'I know what you have told me,' I said. 'I have no need to know anything else.'

I reached for him in the dark and drew him close to me. I held his head in my hands and kissed it. I kissed it and kissed it some more.

He pushed me away. 'Listen,' he said, 'you know nothing. You do not know me.'

'But Mamoru,' I said, brushing his neck slowly with the back of my hand, 'you have told me everything. I have seen your life through your own eyes. I have told no one about it, and nor have you. Only you and I know what has happened in your life.' I tasted blood on my tongue again.

He put his hand on the back of my neck and pulled me to him. He kissed me on my lips, pressing his mouth hard on mine. His coldness stunned my nerves and I could not breathe. I could not even move. He drew away and I gasped for breath.

'Do you really want to see all the things I have seen?' he whispered in my ear.

'Mamoru.'

He gripped my wrists tightly. 'I have seen evil inflicted on men, things that you, Snow, could not possibly imagine. I have seen things happen to women too, things that would make you wish the whole world could be destroyed. How could you possibly want to see those things?'

'Mamoru,' I said, 'you're hurting me.'

He was pressing against me, his hard cold body over me. 'I have been part of those things, Snow. Nothing can save me from that.'

When he forced his lips upon mine I tasted blood again, flooding into my mouth, choking me. I wanted to die.

I do not know how I finally broke free. I struggled like a wild creature, kicking and spitting and clawing and wailing. I cannot recall how it happened, but suddenly Mamoru had disappeared and I began to run. I was running and Peter was there, calling my name, chasing after me in the darkness. I ran from him as hard as I could but I did not get far. My body was bruised and cut, I could feel every mark on my skin. Peter caught up with me and grabbed hold of my waist. I screamed at him, tearing at his shirt, ripping it from his body. Clouds shifted in the sky, and in the new moonlight I saw that my fingernails made harsh red scratches on his milk-white chest. I stopped kicking and held him like a child clings to its mother, tightly, unquestioningly. His skin was wet.

'There now,' he said softly, stroking my hair.

'Oh God, Peter.'

'I thought you didn't believe in God,' he said, chuckling.

We stood in a glade, the space around us cleared of thorny shrubs and dead trees and dark undergrowth. I swallowed and coughed spittle and blood, and in my short breaths I caught the soapy scent of wild frangipani. I gazed upwards and saw a white-filled sky.

'We're in your garden,' I said.

He started to sing his song. I pressed my ear to his chest and heard the song hum softly. It spread itself out to sea, drifting thinly over the waves.

PART THREE

The Garden

This place is the *end*. Twenty-two rooms occupied by twenty-two near-fossils, little more than a halfway house in the short journey to the cemetery down the road. The constant stench of frying shrimp paste – which, after all these years, I still abhor – wafts through the corridors, mingling with the ever-present bouquet of old man's piss. I keep my windows open, even at night. The mosquitoes may suck the life out of me, but when I die I refuse to do so in squalor. The way this place is run, my beautifully dressed corpse would probably remain undiscovered for several days, by which time the aroma of decaying flesh, stale urine and rancid seafood would be somewhat unappealing in an enclosed space. Naturally, having the shutters open does have its drawbacks – chiefly, that I am exposed to the most horrific of all the crimes ever committed in the long and unpleasant history of this house: the garden. I gasp every time I look at this abomination of nature; even thinking about it makes me shudder. It consists solely of a large, uneven lawn – *utterly* jejune – bounded by a wire fence, unadorned except for a single, sorry group of sealing-wax palms whose stems have given up the fight to remain red and instead lapsed into a shade of grey, battered into submission by the relentless briny winds. Why are they there? They serve only to obscure the view of the sea from the veranda.

Every morning I wake up, sunlight pouring in through the floor-length shutters. I look out at this barren waste and I weep.

This is the price I have to pay.

Of course the other old boys think I'm completely eccentric in exposing myself to the elements. Sometimes, even the most senile idiot will try, patronisingly, to convince me that it is better to close the windows as this will keep out the rain and the insects – as if I've lost my marbles (hah!) and don't know what I'm doing. Obviously, I'm not remotely perturbed by this, seeing as I'm already known as the Mad English Devil, an epithet from which I am unlikely to be disassociated even if I do concede the issue of the shutters. As a brief aside, I've never been entirely certain of the accuracy of the translation of my nickname from the Chinese – I suspect that Alvaro politely edited the fruitier connotations from the original phrase when he translated it for me. He has this poorly conceived notion that I am to be pitied, being the lone foreigner in this place. And so he tells me things which I know to be untrue – compliments people supposedly pay me, words of admiration, always in Chinese, or Malay, or Tamil. Of course, one must take everything he says *cum grano salis*.

It's only reasonable to expect, I hear you cry, that I should have some knowledge of Chinese after all these years, but I don't. Not a bit. I have always detested the language; I find it so *trenchant*. And superfluous too, seeing as everyone speaks English – or some form of it – anyway. No, after sixty years of living here, the process of linguistic osmosis hasn't worked in the way you'd assume – in fact, quite the reverse has happened: I have remained wonderfully impervious to Malay and Chinese, but my English, dear God, has been leeched out of me. Some days I can hardly speak. The words don't follow the sentiments, and recently I have developed the habit of stopping in mid-sentence. And as for writing, well – this current project is proving to be a real grind, not at all the thrilling adventure I had envisaged.

Still, I persevere.

I do wonder, though, who will thank me when this is finished. Nobody here, certainly, except possibly Alvaro, whose idea it was in the first place – not the idea that the garden should be rearranged (that was undoubtedly mine), but the idea that we, the residents, should ask the church to make collections in aid of our garden, and that I should be the one to present the new design.

'Oh my dear goodness me,' Alvaro had cried as the idea popped into his thin little head. We had been sitting in the dining room discussing the non-existent view of the sea, of the grounds, of the spire of St Francis Xavier through the casuarinas in the distance. Everything was obscured by something, I said, launching into my usual tirade.

'If it were up to me,' I continued, 'I would tear down the cowshed, reposition the laundry room, remove the wire fence altogether and divide the lawn into sections filled with flowering shrubs – an intricate, exquisite *cloisonné* pillbox of foliage. There would be sun, shade and chairs. Water, fish ponds. You could sit outside in the evenings and play chess with Gecko, next to a fern-shrouded pool, shimmering and damascene, alive with bejewelled Japanese carp.'

For a few moments, he looked pensive, but then suddenly he became frightfully animated.

'But of course but of course but of course. We could do it, man!' he cried.

'What on earth are you talking about, D'Souza?'

'We could rebuild the bloody garden from top to bottom, and there's only one person who could do it. You!'

'Me?' I breathed. '*Surely* not me.'

'Of course. With you at the head of our team, who could refuse us? We would say, "Give us money. We have the kind services of the world-famous aesthete and connoisseur of dwellings, Peter Wormwood." And they will gladly give it to us!'

Alvaro is the best of the bunch. His natural, hot-blooded enthusiasm is still evident. He must have been quite something in his younger days. Last week I watched him as he tried to change a light bulb in his room. He placed one foot on the little wooden chair and spread his spindly arms out for balance before heaving up the rest of his body. He rocked back and forth, arms waving, like a Japanese crane in the final throes of its mating dance. Finally he gave up and hopped off the chair, which toppled behind him. I felt a sudden fluttering sensation in my chest as I watched him and knew instantly what would follow. I tried to suppress the horrible, familiar throb in my head by shutting my eyes tightly and listing the things I had had for breakfast that morning: cheap white bread (toasted), a slice of papaya, some rice porridge. Too late, too late. The memory forced its way back into my head, clear as day, as if it were being played out before me. As always, I felt as if I was watching myself in a Technicolor film. In an instant, I was on top of that hill again – I have forgotten its name, but I remember its shape, broad and irregular like an elephant's head. Johnny is walking ahead of me, so quickly he is almost running. I am struggling to keep up. My shirt is damp with sweat, and beyond the scant shade of my hat the sun is white, mesmerising. By the time I reach the crest of the hill I see Johnny standing on a tree stump ahead of me. He balances on it, swaying gently from side to side, his arms outstretched on either side of him. Against the blue and limitless sky he stands a hundred feet tall. 'Come on!' he yells, and I run towards him, my legs suddenly feeling strong again. When I reach him he lets me stand on the stump, gripping my hand to help my balance. The sight before me stretches wider and further than I ever believed my eyes could encompass. 'This is it,' Johnny says. 'My home, the Valley.'

⋆

Confronted with the monumental task of introducing order into the garden, I decided the best course of action would be to start with my own quarters. If I could decide how I wanted the garden to look from *my* room, all the details would soon fall neatly into place. I tidied the drawers, arranging everything in little piles and throwing out the more unfashionable items of my wardrobe. 'A house is a machine for living in,' Le Corbusier once said, and how right he was. I put my vests in the top drawer so that I can get to them easily before breakfast. And on the bottom shelf I put two shoeboxes filled with an assortment of *objets trouvés* accumulated through the years, including two crucifixes and a Padre-Pio-in-a-snowstorm paperweight given to me by Gecko down the corridor. He's the one who can't stand up straight because his ribcage collapsed last year. I've never been sure what his real name is. I think it's something like Yap Peng Geck – something *very* upcountry at any rate. I've always called him Gecko because he used to scuttle everywhere, just like a little rubbery lizard. His manner of speaking, too, is unfortunate: high-pitched and ejaculatory, entire sentences compressed into single trills. Whenever he sits at my end of the dinner table, the conversation around me suddenly becomes a bizarre symphony, a heavy hum of old men's voices adorned with Gecko *obbligato*. But now, since his chest and spine gave way, it takes him for ever to get anywhere. He shuffles dismally along the corridor, and yesterday I overheard someone saying that he might need his meals brought to him in his room.

In spite of his inability to walk unaided, he went to Italy last year. He bleated about it so much that the house organised a tour for him and a few others. They stayed with some Franciscans in a crumbling monastery on the outskirts of Rome. Two weeks doing the sights, paying homage to our spiritual masters. They even had a private audience with the Big Boss himself. How Gecko managed I'll never know. One rather suspects it was a swan song of epic proportions. He's always been the emotional type and I can just imagine him being melodramatic and tearful at silly things – the first sight of Santa Maria Maggiore or the touch of the Holy Father's hands. When he returned he came to me bearing a small package, neatly wrapped in heavy brown paper. 'A Roman relic!'

I cried as I tore through the wrapping. 'I adore curiosa. What could it be? A miniature sarcophagus? Perhaps a replica of Nero's lamprey?' I opened the box and stared at a glass globe which contained within it a small man wearing brown sackcloth and holding up red hands. Gecko took it from me and shook it so that the sad little snowflakes swirled around the tiny glassed-in landscape. He clasped my hands with his and said, 'We are restless until we find our home.' He said it with a smile, to let me know he was happy.

'Thank you very much for my lovely present,' I said, decidedly *marcato*.

I kept it on my desk for some time, however, unable to consign it to the pile for the church fête. I have no explanation for this uncharacteristic lapse. I've never had a problem getting rid of things. I can leave anything, anyone, at the drop of a hat, so I can't think why I still have that paperweight. But it's been put away now, along with the crucifixes and the sacred heart. Everything has to be neat and tidy when I fade into the ether. Nothing should be left to clutter this room when I leave. Nothing is special. Not even Padre Pio.

I did mention that I'm trying to die, didn't I?

Don't be alarmed, it won't be ghastly or dramatic – I hate the thought of blood. I've been hoarding pills, building my little kaleidoscopic collection in an empty Pond's cold cream jar, waiting for the right time. I have planned it carefully, and it'll be so beautifully choreographed that everyone will applaud when they carry my body out into the courtyard and then into the waiting Bentley. I have left instructions that the hearse should be a Bentley rather than a Rolls – a small concession to modesty – and that the driver should be dressed not in black but in starched white, the stiffer the better. And if the House were able to find someone decorative to wear such a uniform, I wouldn't complain *too* much.

That would be a nice touch, I think.

*

BUT FIRST: I must must must set this all down on paper, as I promised Alvaro and the others, even though their sad shrivelled minds have probably forgotten my brilliant plan to replace the Abomination with something full of grace and love and life.

What spirit shall inspire this new Eden? The answer is obvious. Not the great gardens of England, but the ancient temple gardens of the Orient. Angkor, Sigiriya, Yogyakarta. I read about them before setting out on the journey East, gorging myself on descriptions of these fantastic monuments now reduced to jungle-shrouded ruins. It was a nineteenth-century lithograph of the entrance to a Javanese Water Garden that first fired my imagination. I stumbled across it in my college library, in a book someone had left on his desk. The pages fell open to reveal a perfectly formed arch of volcanic rock, crowned by a carved canopy of scrolling tropical foliage, which led my eye gently to a glass-flat pool of water beyond. On either side of this archway sat mythical beasts, and in the distance, beyond the water, stood a triumvirate of temples, tall and thin with tiered roofs the shape of shallow umbrellas. In the middle of the pond there was a small island which supported two things, a shrine and a single frangipani tree. I learned the name of this place, *Chakranegara*. The very sound of it quickened my pulse and made my eyes swim with visions of hot Eastern lands I never knew existed. I looked around the library and saw no one. I tore out the page and took it back to my room where I pinned it to the wall next to my bed.

Thereafter I burned for such images. Hungrily, I sought books on Angkor Wat and delighted in the sepia tints of the ruined water gardens there. I spent the whole of my last summer in Oxford ensconced in the Bodleian, tucked away in its dustiest recesses. I read about the Summer Palace at Hue, the Fragrant City of central Vietnam, and in my mind's eye rebuilt its gardens, filling them with courtyards of perfect proportions and earthenware pots. That summer was (as old men wistfully and embarrassingly recall) the last of its kind. I wandered in the deer park on my own and lay on the dry, sweet-smelling grass. I felt, in a desperately gauche undergraduate way, life about to change. My skin tingled constantly; I never slept.

One bright autumn afternoon, not long after I moved to London, I was strolling through Grosvenor Square when, through a window, I saw an opulent room decorated with faded panoramic wallpaper depicting temples and elephants and palms under a vast powder-blue sky. I recognised it at once as 'Hindoustan', made by Jean Zuber. I stood on the pavement in the chill of the gathering October wind, gazing into that colourful space. The room seemed to glow with warmth; the turbanned natives in their sampan wore only loincloths as they sweltered in the sun. I drew my coat tightly around me and walked away, through the scattering of dead autumnal leaves. I realised then that no picture could satisfy me. No matter how much I indulged my senses in libraries and museums I would still feel malnourished. I had fasted all my life but now, at last, I was ready to feast. My entire being trembled with hunger, and I decided to leave England for ever.

It is why I came here: this was where I would find my paradise, my tropical Arcadia, my vision of perfection.

I remember stepping off the ship at Singapore harbour, watching the sampans and tugboats bobbing gently in the bay. Smooth-skinned men and women sold fruit the colour of the sun and called to each other in birdlike intonations. The smells, too, were intoxicating. All around me the air had a curious odour of earth and caramel. What was it? *Warmth*. I had never known it to have a smell of its own, but it did. Perhaps I did not know the smell of warmth because I had never truly felt it before.

I did not stay long in Singapore. Everywhere I went, drunken high-spirited troops rampaged through the streets. With their arms draped across each other's shoulders, they sang 'There'll always be an England' depressingly out of tune. I went to the Raffles Hotel a few times, but only because I was told that I might glimpse its Armenian owner waltzing with his guests whilst balancing a whisky and soda on his head. On one of my visits there I was accosted by a plump pink-cheeked man with thinning red hair. He held his tie between his fat fingers and waved it in my face. 'Wormwood! Don't you remember me?' he bellowed, and all heads turned to witness this tender reunion.

'No,' I replied – stiffly, I recall – and turned to converse with the bartender.

'It's me – Lucy!' he cried.

'Lucy?'

'Yes, Bill. *William* Lucy. Parkside – remember? And then Oxford. I was at Brasenose and you were at . . . Magdalen, weren't you? I didn't bump in to you much in Oxford.'

'I was in London most of the time.'

'What the devil brings you here? Last I heard, you'd moved to London to act in musical comedies. You aren't here to entertain the troops, are you?'

I could sense the rest of the room straining to hear my reply: a new arrival in Singapore always aroused interest. I gulped at my gin and tonic. 'No, you must have me confused with someone else,' I said. 'I'm just passing through. Travelling. Thought I'd see the world before I settled down.' I looked him in the eye and smiled.

Thereafter I avoided the Raffles assiduously, and any tenuous associations with my compatriots quickly began to wither. I never saw the waltzing Armenian.

My Singapore was to be found in the alleys of Bugis Street and Chinatown, where shopkeepers recognised me and gave me cups of sweet coffee at three o'clock in the morning. All life – all real life – gathered there after dark, and strangers found solace in each other's company. Merchants, prostitutes and scholars moved as equals in this place. I would sit all night watching the *va-et-vient* of Lascars and madmen; I was alone but never lonely. And it was here, at precisely eleven o'clock one evening, that I met Johnny.

He was sitting on his own in a corner of the coffee shop at the end of Cowan Street, diligently reading a book. It was a rare sight, a Chinese reading an English book in this part of town, so I took a table next to his and decided to engage him in conversation.

'Shelley?' I said with genuine surprise when I saw what he was reading.

He looked up as if confused.

'Have you read a lot of Shelley?' I asked again.

He looked at me blankly. I began to wonder if he understood me. I moved to his table, and as I sat down he lifted the book and placed it on his lap, as if hiding it from me.

I smiled. He was not, as my nanny would have said, an oil painting, but he had the silent, easy grace of a Balinese nobleman of the type depicted in lithographs of sumptuous palaces.

'You must be the only person in Singapore who reads Shelley,' I said.

When he smiled his face transformed into that of a child – radiant, innocent, happy. He said, 'My wife speaks English.'

'You're married. How wonderful.'

'I am improving my English,' he said, looking down at his book, 'so that I can converse freely with her – and her family too.' His smile faded slowly and all of a sudden he looked sad and utterly defeated by the world.

Without thinking I said, 'But English is such a rudimentary language. I will teach you everything you need to know.'

The smile returned and he was a child again.

In a strain of halting English more mellifluous to my ears than Dryden's, he told me about his wife and his home. He told me about his work, and as he did so, opened his satchel to reveal a small piece of silk. It was at once iridescent and delicate, and shone with a colour no Occidental could ever have conceived.

'*Clair-de-lune*,' I breathed, reaching for it across the table.

He seemed perplexed, and watched me as I held it in my hands, allowing it to cascade from my fingers. It was shot through with so many strands of colour that every time it moved its appearance changed: moonlight, emeralds and pearls all passed through my hands. This cold chameleon so transformed itself that I could scarcely believe it was the same piece of cloth.

'Take it,' Johnny said, appearing strangely unconcerned by the imminent loss of this treasure. He put his book in his satchel and finished his tea. He was leaving Singapore the next day; I did not know when I would see him again. I felt a sudden surge of panic. I wanted to hear more. I asked him to tell me about the valley but he looked confused. He shrugged and said, 'What is there to say?'

'Tell me everything,' I said, 'everything.'

My lips trembled as I repeated the names of the towns in the valley. As he spoke, a strange landscape reconstructed itself in my mind's eye: I saw caves disappearing into jagged hills, the land dissolving into the sea; I saw a man swimming in a pool of coloured textiles and a woman, *Snow*, melting into the earth.

'It's nothing special,' he said with a final shrug.

I reached for the piece of cloth and folded it tenderly before placing it in my pocket. I wanted to go to the valley at once.

★

Now, borders. I have sketched out a plan on a large piece of paper showing where they should be. Although they follow a basic east–west scheme to avoid being shredded to ribbons by the prevailing winds, they are cleverly disguised by their languidly snaking shapes and differing masses, and do not therefore appear regimented in any way. One shudders at the thought of the harshness to be found in the great French gardens – in Versailles, for example, the greatest of them all, where rows of trees are lined up like soldiers on parade. In spite of what the French would have us believe, I have always thought their gardens display a certain poverty of imagination, a failure of the romantic impulse.

My designs owe nothing to the tradition of those gardens the French think of as *le jardin anglais*, the grand visions of classical perfection at Stowe or Blenheim, for example. How distasteful that would be in a setting such as this. If anything, this will be a Wild Garden, a creation of seemingly casual beauty, whose charms are quiet, understated. Some of the borders are large and deep, others long and shallow; some are planted with tall shrubs, others with ground cover, many with a mixture of both. Heliconia share their beds with cannas, golden trumpets tumble into masses of wax ginger, bauhinia jostle for space with red hibiscus – *bunga raya*, the national flower. The result is quite breathtaking, a simply presented, richly flavoured taste of something sublime. Is the purpose of a flower bed not similar to that of a poem? Within their artificial boundaries, both contain a tiny world of beauty, a joyous compression of life.

I have put as much detail as possible into the sketch, indicating the approximate sizes of the borders and writing the names of the plants in their respective positions. I have told Alvaro that these details are NON-NEGOTIABLE, and if the church gardeners decide to take liberties with the planting I shall destroy my sketch. 'I am quite capable of it, I warn you,' I said as he pinned the sketch up on the noticeboard outside the dining hall. He did not seem to think this a problem. He merely smiled and shook his head, repeating 'no' gently, over and over again, as if to calm a child. This incensed me and I stormed into my room, slamming the door for good measure. The creation of paradise is not something I take lightly.

At dinner that evening I asked some of the old fools what they thought about my sketch. 'Oh,' one of them said, 'that piece of paper on the noticeboard. Very nice, yes.' I explained again the theories behind my scheme for borders; I talked about Capability Brown and the Georgics, Hinduism versus Buddhism. Of course they did not fully comprehend what I said. Whenever I speak I know it is a case of pearls before swine. They smiled and glanced at each other surreptitiously in an attempt to hide their discomfort and embarrassment at not being able to understand what I was saying. Poor souls.

Whilst the overall inspiration of the garden is, as I must stress, Oriental, I confess that my borders are not entirely devoid of English undertones. Anyone can see that they are a subtle nod of acknowledgement to the humble cottage garden such as that at Hemscott, my childhood home in Gloucestershire whose herbaceous borders were exemplary.

Hemscott's influence on me has been stronger than I imagined. I have only realised this of late. All my life I wanted to escape it but now I find it is still with me, the only thing I have left.

It was not a pretty place. The house itself appeared grey in colour, whatever the weather. Its walls of Cotswold stone – wrongly described by visitors as 'golden' – always seemed cold to me, always silent. My father died when I was four and my mother took a younger man as a lover. They spent all day in her boudoir, festering in each other's company. They surfaced occasionally for meals, and sometimes I was called down from my room to join them at dinner. Mother would look at me with vacant eyes. 'What a funny little face you have,' she would say each time, with the mild surprise of someone discovering a titillating piece of trivia. With her left hand she stroked my hair; with her right she gorged herself (fork only: table manners did not apply to my mother) on scrambled eggs and boiled chicken. Across the table, her dark-eyed lover ate with sickening speed, never seeming to chew on his food. He seemed desperate to return to the languid, lotus-eating surroundings of his fetid *chambre*, to the arms of his intoxicated lover. Not once did he look at me; his lank chestnut hair hung thickly over his brow, hiding his lowered gaze.

Predictably I spent much time on my own. Nanny was around, of course, but she had been my father's nanny before, and was now too infirm to be of use. She sat in her armchair all day, with nothing to keep her company but a tin of shortbread biscuits and letters from a long-dead son, killed on the steep scrubby shores of Gallipolli in the summer of 1915, the year of my birth. When she leaned forward to receive her goodnight kiss from me each evening I could see the sweat stains on the faded chintz behind her. She smelled of damp straw, a perfume I always found repellent.

The potting shed became my place of refuge. I was introduced to its silent, earth-scented charms by Robinson, our one-armed gardener (who was, despite his disability, wholly responsible for the exceptional vigour of the borders in our garden). He regarded my solitudinous boyhood with pity, I think, and one day invited me to share in his tasks. I stood beside him on a low wooden stool, learning to prick out seedlings and plant them in little pots, ready to be moved to the cold frames. Robinson took his glove off and held my fingers with his one hand, guiding them as he showed me how to squeeze the compost gently around the base of the trembling plant. I began to go to the shed when no one else was there. Light struggled to filter through the murky windows; its dimness comforted me, for in the shadows that Funny Little Face of mine became invisible. Sitting on the dusty, soil-scattered floor, my mean bloodless lips and mink-like snout seemed not to matter; no one could see me there. The tender plants, too, became mine. I didn't know, nor care, what I was potting up: every time I saw a tray of seedlings I would seize upon them, desperate to move them on so that, before long, they could be planted in the ground.

One day I found a shovel and took it to a spot far away from the confines of the house and its walled garden. I chose a long-abandoned border as the site for my first planting, and began to prepare the ground for the imminent arrival of some lupins. I began to dig. The shovel came to my armpits and was difficult to manœuvre; the earth was as hard as bedrock but still I persevered, holding the handle against my chest and pushing down at an angle. I dug until the skin on my palms became thin and raw; a splinter pierced my thumb, embedding itself just beneath the fingernail. I knelt down, exhausted. It began to snow. It was nearly April – Passiontide, I recall; my young ears were rich with the strains of *Erbame Dich, Mein Gott*. I looked at where I had dug and saw that I had only succeeded in scraping away a thin layer of soil. Snowflakes alighted on the sorry, shallow patch I had created, their frail crystals resting gently for a moment before dissolving into the black earth.

I remained like this, crouching and defeated, until Robinson found me and led me back to the dark solace of the potting shed. Poor Robinson. He alone brought colour to the gardens and kept Hemscott alive for me, until one summer I returned from school to find that my mother had dispensed with his services. Well, she said, he was getting too old for the job. The truth was that there was no money to pay him. There had been none for a very long time. In spite of my best efforts, the plants soon went to seed and the garden finally – fittingly, one might say – became a dilapidated mess.

And yet, curiously, whenever images of Hemscott invade my sleep now, it is not this sorry tangle that I see. What appears before me is the late-winter view from my bedroom as I stand at the dormer looking at the neat rows of box hedge against a snow-softened landscape, the topiary animals poised under a chalky sky. Although the hard bare beds sparkle with frost, I know that soon it will be spring, and life will return to the garden once more.

*

After my first meeting with Johnny, I returned to the coffee shop every night, hoping to see him again. I sat on my own, testing my bladder with cup after cup of milky tea. Carefree matelots and pouting cocottes called to me as they went past, but I would not be seduced from my solitude. I asked the wizened old woman who ran the coffee shop about the valley, but she seemed incapable of comprehending my need to go there.

'Are you a tin miner?' she kept asking, as if that were the only reason anyone would wish to visit the valley.

One evening I took my place as usual, surveying every passing face, carefully looking out for Johnny's. After some time a very young woman, little more than a girl, approached my table and sat down in the manner of a familiar old friend. She lit a clove cigarette and looked out at the street with me.

'Waiting for your girlfriend?' she said. I knew immediately she was a prostitute.

'No,' I replied, somewhat curtly. I did not appreciate this disruption of my vigil. 'I'm waiting for a friend.'

'OK,' she said, exhaling a plume of pungent smoke. Her crude *maquillage* of thickly rouged cheeks and bright lipstick emphasised rather than disguised her youth.

'Actually,' I added, 'I'm waiting to join my friend. He is going to take me somewhere rather wonderful.' I do not know why I felt the need to elaborate.

She lifted an eyebrow as if to say, 'Where?'

'The Kinta Valley,' I said.

She opened her mouth and threw back her head in an ugly laugh. Her cackle revealed a set of perfectly brown teeth which stood out starkly against her powdered skin. The chrysanthemum she wore in her hair suddenly seemed ludicrous and inappropriate. 'That place,' she said, 'what a shit pile that is.'

'No it isn't.'

'It's full of nothing,' she said.

'I'm sure you're mistaken.'

She turned to the shopkeeper. 'This idiot wants to go to the valley, can you believe it?' Their rough laughter tore into my head.

'Please, go away.'

'Hey, I'm telling you the truth.' She leaned across the table. Her voice was hard, stabbing.

'How would you know?'

'It's my home, mister. My home.'

I got up and left the table, managing to raise a weak smile as I did so. Their laughter rang loudly as I stepped out into the street. I blinked back the first prick of hot tears in my eyes. I ran back to my lodgings and began to pack. I left for the valley at dawn the next day, after a breakfast of sweet coffee and glutinous rice.

I found a lorry driver who offered to take me to the valley in return for the brogues I was wearing (which I gladly surrendered – they were a battered old pair from Ducker's on Turl Street). He did not enquire as to the purpose of my journey nor question the wisdom of it, and for that I was glad. He seemed content to sit in silence with my shoes now adorning his feet. Every so often he would raise one foot on to his seat to admire his trophy. I did not fear for our safety as much as I admired his dexterity. My limbs and joints suddenly felt ridiculously stiff and superfluous; my blood, after a month in the Orient, still felt cold and viscous.

We drove past tranquil villages where sleepy-eyed children with distended stomachs played among rainbow-plumed fowl. Their tiny wooden houses looked fragile, perched as they were on delicate stilts. They seemed so vulnerable to the forces of nature, to the sun and rain and the very trees that surrounded them; they were transient, almost nomadic, I thought. In the shade, indolent as Bruegel swineherds, young men watched me with reddened eyes without ever rousing themselves from their tropical languor. I thought, naturally, of Gauguin, and realised how wrong he was in his quiet romanticism. The beauty of these hot lands is not feminine nor lyrical, I thought; it is dusty and muscular.

'How wonderful to live like this,' I said to the driver, hoping to encourage conversation, but he merely looked at me with an uncomprehending expression.

I began to feel the heat and the dust gather on my face, yet I refused to yield to their force. Like my silent companion, I sat staring at the red road before me as if I had travelled it many times before. On either side the jungle seemed ancient and impenetrable. Every so often its murky darkness would suddenly vanish, giving way to a plantation of rubber or oil palm whose trees were arranged like columns in a vast cathedral. I closed my eyes and felt the base of my neck throb with the heat. I knew I was not far from the valley now.

When I stirred from this gorgeous stupor I found my driver shouting aggressively. Cyclists swarmed around the lorry, impeding our progress and inducing bursts of swearing from my hitherto taciturn companion. The houses looked different here. Rough timber dwellings gave way to larger, sturdier-looking brick-and-mortar buildings. Shops advertised their wares by displaying them prominently in their doorways: sacks of dried fish, peeled open to reveal their contents; large pyramids of rice; strange, dried, mud-coloured leaves; combs of tiny golden bananas. My driver stopped abruptly and, without looking at me, said, 'Kampar.' He reached for his shoes and laced them up tightly. He walked down the street with his back held straight, lifting his feet so that his new leather heels clicked loudly against the gravelled road.

I found a guest house at the far end of town. The room was exactly as I imagined it would be, invaded at every moment by the sounds and smells of life around me. The kitchen lay at the other end of the small courtyard, and its aromas seemed to have embedded themselves in the upper-floor rooms. Roasting coffee produced a perfume that was unpleasant but not unbearable; it paled, however, beside the smell of shrimp paste. The cooks pounded the dried shrimp in a mortar and pestle together with an assortment of other noxious ingredients before moulding it into a damp mass and leaving it to ferment in the courtyard right below my room. I arrived to find a huge basin of it sweltering in the late-afternoon heat, filling the air with its fumes. The emaciated man who showed me to my room pointed excitedly at this glorious creation and intimated that it would play a starring role in my dinner that evening.

I bathed – as everyone else did – by dousing myself in spring water from a vast earthenware tub. I scooped the water with a wooden pail and poured it over my head, delighting in the shock of the cold on my travel-weary senses. Afterwards, as the tropical night fell swiftly around me, I moved my bed next to the large windows. I left the shutters open and lay shirtless as I listened to the feasting downstairs. I was not hungry. The heat and the sharp smell of the shrimp paste had drained me of all desire. Nonetheless, curiosity got the better of me and I stood at the top of the darkened stairs and spied on the convivial gathering below. On the table lay a single oval dish bearing a mass of dark green vegetables which, I presumed, were cooked with the shrimp paste. All eight people hungrily attacked this offering; there was nothing else on the table. I crept back to my room, careful not to make a noise.

Much later, I woke in darkness and silence. I thought I had heard a knock at the door, but when I opened it no one was there. A plate of food had been left for me, protected by a piece of muslin and a fly net. I felt a dull throb of hunger in my belly, but when I unwrapped my promising little picnic I found that it contained nothing but some rice and those vegetables, desecrated by shrimp paste. I lifted a spoonful of rice to my mouth, carefully leaving aside the more offensive items on the plate; but I found that the rice had become infected by the sour, rancid smell. I simply could not eat it.

Rain began to fall, heavy drops thudding one by one on the tiled roofs before gathering into a steady, hypnotic drumming. I had not expected rain: it was, after all, at the very height of the dry season. The noise outside – a strange and intense hushing as the rain rustled the leaves on the trees – soothed my ears. I lay on the side of the bed next to the open window so that my skin would catch the odd droplet of moisture, blown astray by the swelling breeze. Lightning illuminated the distant skies, and I fell asleep to the comfortable rumble of thunder. It was my first true equatorial downpour.

That night I knew my life was about to change. For many years afterwards I relived the quivering, insistent sensations of that particular storm-washed evening, and wondered if I had merely imagined it all. But now, at the end of my days, I see that it was true. Although the passing of time has tried to muddy it, the clarity of that night remains with me. Even in my sleep I sensed that I was poised on the brink of something epochal. It was not – I am utterly clear about this – my Road to Damascus, but rather a gradual, gentle realisation that by the morning, the course of my life would be altered irrevocably.

When, therefore, I was awakened by a thundering that shook the timbers of the guest house, I knew at once it was not the storm: it was the start of the rest of my life. I lay in bed with my eyes open for a few seconds, listening to the cries of the people running into the street. As I sat up there was another explosion. I felt it trembling in my ribcage. Out on the street, a small child lay crouching in a doorway with her hands on her ears. The rain was falling hard; shimmering pools had formed in the muddied road. In the distance, about half a mile away, a spire of black smoke rose into the sky. I dressed hurriedly and joined the throng of people hurrying in the direction of the smoke. No one spoke; we merely splashed our way through the rain and the red mud, guided by the charcoal cloud that hung in the air. At last I saw the inferno: a giant mass of flame engulfing a building that was collapsing, timber by timber, as I approached it. A large crowd had gathered on a grassy bank nearby, and as I pushed through I became aware that they too were not speaking. Nothing was audible but the sound of the same rain which had washed through my sleep. At last I found what lay at the heart of this silent congregation: a pair of bodies, one shielding the other. I moved closer and saw that they were two men. The younger man, naked to the waist, lowered his face slowly towards the elder's; he hesitated for a moment before pressing his lips firmly on to the old man's weakly gasping mouth. I held my breath as I watched this young hero breathe life into the pale and lifeless body. It was some time before the old man, motionless on the wet grass, began to cough, wheezing as he heaved air into his lungs. He opened his eyes and stared at the sky. The younger man withdrew, exhausted from his exertions. He lifted his head to look at the crowd around him. Even before I saw his face I knew, with absolute certainty, that it was Johnny.

*

The brown shrike, *Lanius cristatus*, is a noisy and quarrelsome bird. It spends its summers feasting on insects in Siberia and Manchuria before journeying south to spend its winters infesting the countryside around this house. From morning till dusk, they squeal, chatter and fight in the garden, flitting across my field of vision so as to make it impossible for me to concentrate for any length of time. Now that the other residents have realised the seriousness of my undertaking, they pester me constantly with requests to devise a planting scheme that will encourage these violent hordes of irritating little birds to remain longer in the environs of the house. Unlike me, they seem actually to enjoy the sight of these winged pests.

'What about a bird bath?' Gecko trilled. 'Right outside the

dining-hall window, so we can watch them whilst we breakfast. Or a table with rice and breadcrumbs and groundnuts on it.'

'No,' I said. 'How common.'

'What beautiful red heads they have,' Alvaro said, lowering his binoculars. 'I hope you are going to have lots of tall grasses, and maybe put in some big rocks too. They seem to like perching on the stones and reeds by the paddy field down the road.'

'Do you want me to recreate the Steppes just for these little buggers?'

'It's not only for them,' Gecko chirped, 'there are lots of other birds too.'

'Look here,' I said, 'this is a garden, not a bloody bird sanctuary. Its primary purpose is to provide pleasure to humans. It isn't a playground for truculent birds.'

'You told me that this garden – any garden – is a re-creation of the Garden of Eden,' said Alvaro. 'It is the recapturing of our Paradise Lost, you said. Those were your exact words.'

'My dear boy,' I replied, 'I think I may have been misinterpreted.'

'No, those were the words you used,' he repeated, shaking his head like a stubborn child.

'Well then, you've been too literal in your understanding of what I was trying to express.'

He looked puzzled. 'Explain it to me again, please.'

'No,' I said, gathering my sketches and notebooks. 'If you haven't already understood my philosophy, a lengthy exegesis is unlikely to provide further illumination. The bottom line is: no bird bath.'

I retired to my room where I paused briefly to reflect on – and, I must admit, admire – the strength of my resolve. I felt absolutely justified in standing firm on the matter. Although harmony with nature is of considerable importance in planning a garden, it must never be allowed to obscure what lies at the heart of the design: the salvation of the human spirit. In creating a garden, we acquire, by force, a patch of land from the jungle; we mould it so that it becomes an oasis amid the wilderness. It is an endless struggle. Turn our backs for a moment and the darkness of the forest begins its insidious invasion of our tiny haven. The plants that we insert – artificially, it must be noted, for no garden is a work of Mother Nature – must not only provide shelter for the soul, they must be able to absorb and then disperse the creeping darkness of the jungle around us. The decorations do not merely adorn, they protect. They create a place where, at the end of our lives, we may find peace.

And no peace will ever be found amid those infuriating little birds.

Those who truly know the jungle do not invite it into their homes. They fight to keep it from their dwelling places, fiercely patrolling the boundaries; they understand that the threat from the denizens of the tangled forest is constant. The jungle is alive and it is dangerous. This was one of the very first things I learned when I came to the valley, when Johnny took me on a walk across the Cameron Highlands. Since our reacquaintance in Kampar, he seemed exceedingly keen to show me the valley, and we had been on several long walks already. Each time the drill would be the same: Johnny would appear at my guest house, where he would be greeted by the *towkay* with considerable enthusiasm (from my room, I could hear Johnny's polite, protracted refusals to join the family for tea); he would then appear at my door, wearing a smile of undimmed delight. Always, he held a book, and although the choice of reading material sometimes changed, he clearly had his favourites. Shelley, as I have explained, was one – 'Shows impeccable taste,' I told him – and Dornford Yates another. Our conversation on those first walks was always the same. He asked the questions, I answered them.

'What is the meaning of "expostulation"?' 'Who was Ozymandias, actually?' 'Was Hamlet really crazy?' 'What is the difference between "toilet" and "lavatory"?'

He drank my answers as if quenching an ancient thirst. They were all that he needed to sustain himself on these walks, it seemed. He never drank from the flask of boiled water we carried with us; all he wanted to do was ask and listen. He was inexhaustible.

This particular walk in the high, cool hills above Tanah Rata was the longest yet: seventeen miles, Johnny said, all the way through the Camerons, up to the peak of Beremban, taking in Robinson Falls. The prospect of an entire day treading through the prehistoric jungles of the valley filled me with such naked joy that, for the first few miles, I easily kept up with Johnny. We walked along undulating paths that ran along the bottom of steep slopes clad with tea hedges. The bright green of these bushes blanketed the valleys so thickly that I almost believed I could plunge into it and not be hurt. Beyond these low-lying slopes rose the spine of the hills, huge and silent, covered in ancient rainforest. The morning sun fell on every undulation: a softly bronzed valley painted with zebra-striped shadows.

The nature of our conversation up to that point was entirely predictable.

'Why do people in England have to change into special clothes for dinner?' Johnny asked.

'What do you mean?'

'Well, you wear "a black tie",' he said. 'What is that?' I noticed that in the jungle he spoke freely, and without the hesitation that made his English seem stilted and primitive in Kampar.

'My dear boy,' I replied, 'I fear you have been paying too much attention to Dornford Yates.'

'So you don't wear a black tie, then?' he said. A look of mild disappointment settled on his face.

'Of course I do,' I said quickly. I cannot fully explain the fabrication that followed. I can only say that I wanted desperately for the smile to return to Johnny's face, for him to be thrilled and mystified once more. And so I continued: 'I am famous for my sartorial sensibilities. I have even been known to dress for dinner when I am at home on my own! Did you know, a great ballet dancer once said that he wished his shirts were as elegant as mine. He saw me in a restaurant and crossed the room to pay me that compliment. The next day I selected a few of my less favoured shirts – made by Charvet in Paris – and had them sent round to his dressing room. I dare say he was mightily pleased with them.'

He smiled broadly and turned to look at me with his all-absorbing eyes.

'Really?' he breathed. 'What was this person's name?'

'Nijinsky,' I said without hesitation, knowing he would not know any better.

He continued picking his way through the trees, negotiating tree roots and fallen logs as easily as I might have strolled through St James's Park on a summer's day.

'In fact,' I continued, 'I have not one but two dinner jackets with me back at the guest house. It's one of my rules of travel: never be underdressed. I was thinking, though, that perhaps you should have one of them. A man should always be appropriately attired, after all.'

He looked shocked at first, uncomprehending. I made my offer again, and he accepted it with a silent smile. Thereafter he began to fire questions rapidly, speaking with a looseness I had never before seen in an adult. This had a curious effect on me. My answers became more and more elaborate, happily gilded with stories from a glittering past I never knew I had. He seemed to draw energy from these tales, laughing loudly whilst striding powerfully ahead of me. I tried hard to keep up, but the effort of explaining, *inter alia*, Jacob's Ladder and the devotion of Mary Magdalene was too much for me, and my breath became truncated and painful. We stopped in a glade by a shallow valley filled with rhododendrons. My vision swam with multicoloured shapes.

'Rest a whilst,' Johnny said. He poured some water on to a small piece of cloth and offered it to me. I placed it on my neck and caught my breath. The landscape around us seemed bizarre in its variety. Part tropical, part temperate, wholly perplexing. All manner of epiphytes clung to the trees: bird's-nest ferns, many-headed orchids, twisting vines with flowers the colour of hot coals. We were in the heart of the forest now, tiny creatures dwarfed by the towering columns around us.

'What's that tree called?' I asked, pointing.

He shrugged.

'That one?' I asked again.

'I don't know.'

'That one's teak,' I said.

'We call it *jati*,' he said.

I walked to the edge of the clearing, listening to the cries of hawks.

'*Jati* is what we use to build houses,' he said.

'Isn't your house made from teak?'

He laughed. 'That is my father-in-law's house – but yes, it is teak. Some day I too will own a house made from teak.'

'Was your shop made from teak?' I said, continuing to gaze at the thick canopy of leaves above me.

He laughed suddenly, a different laugh this time. It sounded cold and sad. 'My shop was destroyed. By fire.'

I had just begun to turn to look at Johnny when I felt something on my shoulder. Just for an instant: a blunt thud accompanied by a sharp, pricking pain in my neck. Johnny's eyes widened and he ran towards some bushes, picking up a long stick as he did so. In a single fluid movement he brought the stick down hard into the earth; he lifted his arm again and repeated this several times until finally I saw that he had killed a snake. A small one, dull green in colour. Its bloodied body hung limply over the stick. My neck began to throb gently. Johnny came to me and said, 'I thought it was a viper, but it's not. This snake is only slightly poisonous.'

'*Slightly* poisonous?' I said, my voice constricting into a whisper. 'What do you mean?'

'Don't worry,' he said, 'you'll be fine. It didn't bite you properly.' He came very close to me and held my neck. I could not see what he was doing. I could barely feel the flick of his knife on my skin as he made a tiny incision. He squeezed the cut so gently I could not feel anything apart from a spreading warmth on my neck; and then he wet a thin towel with some water from the flask and pressed it to my numbed skin.

'We should go,' he said.

We walked slowly, descending once more into the foothills. The early sunlight had given way to mist which settled thickly in the tea valleys. The air I breathed was so densely humid that I felt I was drinking it. The path disappeared under my feet. I could hardly see where I was stepping. Only a blind trust in Johnny's judgement kept me going, and I stumbled along in his wake, desperately following the blurred outline of his body ahead of me. 'Look,' Johnny said, pointing to the sky. A hawk wheeled over the valley, vanishing into the mist. Several times it did this, falling from the cloud in a slow, tilting arc above our heads before disappearing once more into the ether. I could not keep track of its movements; I did not know if I could trust my eyes.

It was not an ideal introduction to Johnny's home. Many times before, I had imagined myself arriving dressed in perfectly pressed clothes and a fetchingly elegant cravat: witty, engaging and adored. Instead, I found myself staggering up the stairs to the verandah at the front of the house, holding a blood-streaked cloth to my neck. My legs began to buckle and I felt a burning sensation at the back of my throat.

'Water,' I heard Johnny call.

All this time, I was acutely aware of how ridiculous I must have looked. I saw various people pass before me, and I wanted to explain to them that this was a ghastly aberration. My behaviour is entirely inexplicable, I wanted to say; and as for attire, well – I had been caught unawares; no one had told me I would be invited here. And yet, curiously, I could not speak. My throat had seized up and I found it difficult to articulate even the simplest words.

'Calm, calm,' Johnny repeated.

I'm not certain how long my embarrassing little turn lasted, but slowly I began to regain my composure. My breathing became more even, and when I coughed I felt my voice vibrate once more at the back of my throat.

'I'm awfully sorry,' I said, looking around, 'you must think I'm terribly vulgar.' I stood up and offered my hand in greeting to the people now assembled: a frail, frightening old man, whom I recognised instantly as the one saved by Johnny from the fire; an equally stern-faced woman with grey-black hair piled in a thick bun; and finally a timid girl, a maid of some sort, who stood tentatively behind an enormous rosewood armchair.

'You have been bitten by a snake, I hear,' the old man said, without offering a handshake. I didn't know what to do with my still-outstretched hand.

'This is not surprising,' his wife said. 'Ever since Johnny came here we have seen many snakes. Cobras. Even in the house.' When she said 'Johnny' she seemed to spit the word, as if getting rid of an unpleasant and unexpected piece of food from her mouth.

Johnny stood in silence, his head hung as though in shame.

'What do you mean?' I said. 'Johnny had nothing to do with it.'

The woman laughed, looking at me as if I were a recalcitrant child. 'This man comes from out there,' she said, waving her hand. She spoke in the tones of a tired schoolteacher. 'The jungle is part of him. It follows him everywhere.'

'It *is* everywhere,' I said.

'Not in our house.'

Johnny spoke quietly. 'It's the hot season. The snakes are following food and water. There is plenty of that here.'

'No, they are following *you,*' the woman said, casting a sideways look at Johnny.

'Mother, you exaggerate,' a voice called, 'there have only been two snakes in the house all year, and one of them was a mere baby.' I looked up and saw a woman walking towards us, emerging from the shadows of the house.

After all these years I can still see her walking barefoot on the polished hardwood floors. Time has fixed her image in my head, and now, half a century hence, I tell myself, with great certainty and little embarrassment, that my pulse quickened rapidly on first seeing her. But is this really true? If I stop for a moment and close my eyes – as I sometimes do, just before drifting slowly into my geriatric's nap at two o'clock every afternoon – I am able to transport myself back to that precise moment in time. Not for long, though: the sensation is fleeting, and I cannot hold on to it. I am in the cavernous sitting room at the house of TK and Patti Soong, on the outskirts of Kampar, at half past five in the afternoon on 31 August 1941. When this woman – this person – walks into the room, am I certain it *is* a woman? The truth is that I am not. At this moment, I am somewhat light-headed but otherwise perfectly *compos mentis*. I see everything with utter lucidity, but somehow, there is a disconnection between my brain and my eyes: I behold what stands before me but I cannot compute what I see. I know she is a woman, but her body has the straight lines of an adolescent boy, flat-chested and slim. She is taller than any woman I have seen in the Orient; her face is almost level with my collarbone. When, some months after this first moment, I hold her to me I find I can rest my chin on the top of her head, and I will remark that nothing has ever felt so comfortable, so right. But that comes later, after I knew that I *loved* her – yes, that too is a word I can now utter with alacrity. At that first meeting, however, I feel nothing but a spreading numbness. The delicacy of her complexion is cut, savagely, by the lines of her cheekbones. Her eyes are dark as agate. Still I cannot respond. The room feels airless around me. The gorgeous breathlessness and thrilling pulse – those are sensations that the years have layered on top of the initial emptiness, like sheet after sheet of silk covering a bare table. More than fifty years later I can only sec the cloth; the table has been obscured.

Nightly, I pray for that blankness, that fragile tabula rasa, to return. I try to hold on to that moment when I had not yet loved her, when I stood before her a clean, innocent man. There I go again. Innocent? I was never innocent, nor even clean. Traces of poison ran through my blood that afternoon, as they have from the day I was born. I should have known that soon my bitterness would seep into her world and rot it slowly to the core.

'You're hurt,' she says. Her first words to me. She walks towards me, and it feels as if hers is the only movement in the room. The others are perfectly still; it is only Snow who moves amid this curious *tableau vivant*. She leads me by the hand across the floor, and I become aware of the darkness of the rafters above us. At both sides of the house there are tall shuttered windows that allow a breath of wind to stir the air in the house. Mother-of-pearl shines luminescent from the chairs and tables as I go past them into the kitchen. Snow – I know it is she, despite the fact that we have not been introduced – pours hot water from a flask into a large porcelain cup. She brings this to me; I see tea leaves unfurling, slowly sinking to the bottom of the crackled base of the cup. She puts one hand on my forehead, and then pulls at the skin below my eyes – what she is searching for I do not know.

'Did Johnny see the snake?' she says.

I nod.

'Then you should recover in a short whilst. It doesn't look serious.' She smiles and leaves me with my cup of tea. I drink the tea, finding it pleasantly hot at the back of my throat. When I finish, I press the bulbous curves of the empty cup to my swollen neck, feeling its warmth creep over my skin.

Of course the poison soon wore off, and my limbs regained sufficient strength for me to cycle back to my lodgings. Johnny accompanied me, cycling beside me in the murky darkness.

'I hate them,' he said quietly.

'I know,' I said.

'All of them.'

'They're not the easiest people to be with, I must say.' I raised my voice into a laugh, but it elicited no response.

'If I can just be alone with my wife, everything will be fine.'

I could think of no reply to this – nothing that would not sound false.

As we approached the guest house Johnny stopped cycling. 'Peter,' he said, looking at me; he wore a crumpled-up expression of such seriousness that I began to laugh. 'I have a secret to tell you.'

*

When I was in my teens, I was once taken on holiday to France by the sympathetic family of a school friend. One day we walked from Compiègne to Pierrefonds, *sans parents*, strolling blithely through the Royal Forest. It was May, but the infant summer was already ferocious in its aridity, and the fallen branches snapped easily when we stepped on them. I was in one of my Italian phases, I recall, having recently been introduced to Mozart's glorious Da Ponte operas by a pederastic housemaster who was, the other boys tittered, 'sweet on me' (*nota bene*: that is another story, to be ignored for the present). I began to devise a kind of pidgin Franco-Italian throughout this walk, delighting in my friend's growing irritation as we tramped merrily along *sous des alberi*.

'It's a bloody desecration,' he said. Pritchard was his name; he was an earnest boy. 'The purpose of a holiday in France is to imbibe its culture and its language,' he continued. 'You don't take anything seriously, Wormwood.'

I was humming the tune to 'Voi che sapete', squeezing my larynx to make as high-pitched a squeal as possible.

'That's horrible,' Pritchard said, 'stop it.'

'*Tremo senza le vouloir,*' I replied, falsetto.

We argued briefly about our route. He wanted to make a detour to the village of Rethondes, to visit the place where the terms of the armistice were presented to the 'defeated Hun' in 1918. I, on the other hand, wanted to press on towards the wonderful fairy-tale chateau in Pierrefonds. In the end, after half-hearted demurrals, I conceded and allowed him to lead me to the Clairière de l'Armistice. I was about to continue with my singing when I saw, dead ahead of me, a vast carpet of lily of the valley spread out on the forest floor, sprinkled with faint pearls of dappled light filtering through the trees. In this hot dry weather, it was the only plant that had survived in the dense shade. I stood perfectly still, drinking of this magnificent sight. It made me think of the woods near Hemscott, my poor dilapidated home. It was enough to make my lip tremble, I am ashamed to admit. I stood gazing at this shaded field of lily of the valley, unable to move, whilst Pritchard marched blindly into them, trampling the tiny plants underfoot. He continued his quiet diatribe against frivolity, accusing me of not having properly appreciated the lessons and sacrifices of the Great War; I did not understand what dangerous times we lived in, he said. Silently, I wiped the moistness from my eyes and followed him quietly, tracing his path through the crushed foliage.

I remember this moment because I have been toying with the idea of planting lily of the valley in this new garden. I think they might just thrive here. That summer in France was exceptionally hot, yet those delicate-looking perennials seemed undimmed in their vigour. In transplanting a foreign plant to these tropical climes, I shall also be following the footsteps of those intrepid Victorian gardeners who brought exoticism to English gardens and made it part of the landscape there. Of course, I shall be recreating this process in reverse, but if I succeed, my deeds may have far-reaching consequences. Just think: fifty years from now, if lily of the valley does become naturalised in this country, a quintessential English flower will become a tropical plant. Will it then, sometime in the very distant future, be exported back to England? I wonder. Who will consider it exotic where? I tremble at the possibilities.

And not just lily of the valley, but ox-eye daisy, foxglove, cranes-bill, snake's head fritillary: I will plant them all in this hot earth. I want woodruff, too, so that I can dry its tiny star-shaped leaves and use them to infuse my linen with the scent of new-mown hay. And lavender – I must have lavender. There is a perfect spot for a long, slim bed of lavender, just outside my window, as it happens. Its perfume shall greet me when I wake and mollify me as I fall asleep. No longer will I have to wait for summer to enjoy its scent, for here it is summer all year long. Therein lies the genius of my garden. It captures the happiest months of the year, containing them in perpetual fecundity within its boundaries.

My garden will not stop there. It will travel to China and Japan and other temperate Eastern climes, proudly displaying cloud-pruned Japanese holly, Chinese peonies, pink cherry blossom, bitter orange, tiny gnarled bonsai. Thus I will emulate not only Victorian gardeners but Oriental emperors too, the very ones who created the gardens that first inspired this endeavour. Like the Emperor Chenghua, I will create a microcosm of all that is beautiful here.

Of course I have not told anyone about this idea. It would be entirely wasted on them, and I fear their lack of enthusiasm might escalate slowly into scepticism and eventually into a full-blown revolt. The locals are, I find, very sensitive nowadays to any perceived slight to their national pride. I made the mistake of intimating to Alvaro the nature of my planting scheme, and he looked instantly displeased. That same morning, he approached me after having consulted the sorry collection of books that form the house's 'library'. He said, 'Your idea cannot work. It is unscientific.'

'The Victorians achieved more implausible things,' I replied calmly.

'Those plants cannot survive. Maybe you should have a look at the books downstairs.'

'I will do no such thing. *The Reader's Digest Gardening Weekly* didn't create Sissinghurst,' I said, turning away. I did not want to become embroiled in a protracted discussion with a simple ignoramus.

He sighed. Before leaving my room he said, 'Will you really not use any local plants?'

I didn't answer. I merely smiled, as if to say, 'Perhaps I will, perhaps I won't.'

'Crazy,' I heard him say as he closed the door.

I shrugged, my eyes and face feeling hot with anger. He would never have understood. Images of the Forest of Compiègne fluttered in my head once more, the scent of lily of the valley filling my nostrils. I knew that even Alvaro was not truly a friend. Like Pritchard all those years before, he would never be close to me. I was never meant to have 'friends'. What happened to Pritchard? He went up to Cambridge and then ventured to the Sudan with the Shell Exploration Company; he married a nice girl, I heard, and settled in Rye. He never spoke to me again after our holiday in France.

No, I was destined never to have friends.

*

When, on one of our walks, Johnny divulged his great secret to me I was not in the least bit perturbed. 'A communist?' I shrieked, feigning horror. I had, in truth, expected something far more shocking.

'Quiet, please,' he urged, looking over his shoulder for phantom enemies. He began to tell me everything about himself – the meetings he organised deep in the jungle; the leaflets he wrote and distributed to rural communities; the funds he raised for the party. He also told me of the so-called army. I thought they sounded nothing more than a band of rogue bandits who roamed the valley with tinpot ammunition and canvas shoes coming apart at the seams.

'I presume your capitalist father-in-law knows nothing about this,' I said.

He shook his head.

'And Snow?'

With his machete, he slashed at the foliage that fell across our path, but did not answer.

'I see,' I said.

We were climbing a small hill; the trees gave way to a stretch of long, prickly grass, and I believed we had reached the summit. It turned out to be a false peak, and we paused to catch our breath. Johnny had not spoken for a whilst.

'If anyone finds out about me I would be finished,' he said eventually. I knew, from the flatness in his voice, that this was no exaggeration. 'I would lose everything. My business, my wife . . .' His voice trailed off.

'Is it worth the risk?' I asked.

He looked at me and smiled. 'The Japanese will soon invade Malaya, you know. Look at what is happening in China. None of your countrymen seem to think this will happen. But it will. And when it does I may lose everything anyway. So I think it is worth the risk, don't you?'

'Isn't it difficult to live like this, though?' I pressed. The thought of this poor innocent child embroiled in a brutal war was beginning to induce a sense of panic in me. 'I mean, constantly living in fear of betrayal.'

He smiled, a picture of calm. 'That is a danger we face all the time, every day of our lives, in one way or another. I myself do not fear it – if it happens, so be it. I would rather *be* betrayed than betray someone else. Wouldn't you?'

'But what about Snow? It must be torture, not being able to speak about it to her.'

'No,' he said, with a hardened edge to his voice. 'I don't want her to know that about me.'

'Why not?'

He shrugged. 'I just don't want her to know about me.'

'It's nothing to be ashamed of. You never know, she might – well, admire you more for it.'

He laughed a hard quiet laugh. 'There are some things I would prefer to keep hidden from my wife. Besides, there are worse things than not having anyone to talk to.'

'Are there?'

He didn't answer. I continued: 'What do you think will happen if, as you say, the Japs invade? I don't get the impression they're terribly keen on communists, do you? You have an awful lot to lose.'

'No more than anyone else.'

'Now you're just being stupid. What about Snow?'

'Am I stupid?' he said, sounding remarkably sanguine given the obvious perils of his situation. 'And what will *you* do when the Imperial Army invades?'

'Oh, I'll be long gone. I'll have taken the high road to the bonny banks of Loch bloody Lomond. Evacuated on some special ship with a lot of other ruddy-faced Englishmen and all the gin I can drink.'

He did not respond for some time. After a whilst he said, looking away, 'All my life I thought I would be alone, but now that is no longer true. I have Snow. As long as she is with me, there is little I fear.'

I sipped some water before resuming the climb. 'How lucky for you.'

'Peter,' Johnny called after me, 'I have never told anyone about this part of my life, no one except you.' The tawny, waist-high grass shimmered silkily in the breeze. In the golden sunlight he looked as if he was being washed by the waves of a fawn-coloured sea. 'What I said earlier was wrong. I do have someone to talk to now.' His face was suffused with an unspoilt innocence that I had never seen in all my Occidental years. It was an expression I knew to be impossible to describe to those who had never travelled in these tropical climes; it spoke of instinctive trust, communicated by an intimacy that we in the cold West lost many years ago. I found myself curiously unable to respond. I began to say something, but stopped; my voice sounded stiff, cold and mannered compared to his. The sun bore strongly on my forearms and knees. Beyond the shade of my panama the landscape seemed tenuous, trembling in the afternoon heat.

Many times I have analysed that strange moment, carefully unweaving the richly twisted strands of emotion that ran through my nerves as I stood watching Johnny, poor wonderful Johnny, standing on the slope of that hill. As the fabric of that memory comes apart in my hands, I see that the answer is really very simple. For those few brief seconds, I found myself looking into the face of a *friend*, the first and only one I would ever have, the only one I would ever love. For it is true, isn't it: greater love hath no man than this, that a man lay down his life for his friends. That is what I was taught at school. I always laughed at what seemed to me a perverse linking of love, friendship and sacrifice – never would it apply to me, I thought. And yet it did, for a few fleeting moments, at least. Looking at Johnny then, I truly believed I would die for him. Now, in the cold light of old age I can see I was merely fooling myself: I was never as noble as that.

*

There is a painting entitled *Francesca da Rimini*, which depicts the final moments of the eponymous heroine's life as she lies dying in the arms of her lover Paolo. Like so many French paintings of the nineteenth century, it is voluptuous and exciting – the tragedy of the lovers' story is somewhat lost in the sinuous display of brightly lit flesh against a darkened background. But make no mistake: Francesca's is a sorry tale indeed. She was forced to marry the hideous Gianciotto Malatesta, but fell in love with his beautiful younger brother Paolo. One day, as the lovers lay together covertly reading *Sir Lancelot and Queen Guinevere*, they were discovered by Gianciotto, who exacted terrible revenge by stabbing them both to death. Their wounds are clearly seen in the painting, thin dark cuts on otherwise unblemished alabaster skin. They are both naked, entwined in a white sheet; she clings weakly to him, her cheek pressed tenderly to his smooth flat chest. After death they were condemned to wander the stormy darkness of Hell's Second Circle together with all the other souls of the lustful. How wretched and unfair it is that the price of love is eternal damnation.

This is what I found myself saying to an assembled audience at Johnny's house the first time I was properly invited there. The occasion was the Autumn Festival, and TK Soong had thrown an 'open house', which in theory meant that anyone in the valley could turn up unannounced – although the guests seemed too well mannered and nicely spoken to qualify as true valley plebeians. Everything I said seemed to be greeted with smiling Oriental inscrutability, and my stories became increasingly desperate as I scratched around for conversation. To compound my discomfort, there were three other English people in attendance. One of them was a weak-chinned, pink-cheeked schoolmaster type with slowly thickening jowls, who might as a child have been considered cherubic. His name was Frederick Honey.

'What a silly story,' he said prissily, 'I don't believe any of it.'

'It isn't a question of believing,' I said. 'Why can't you just accept it as a beautiful, tragic story of an ill-fated love affair?'

'Well, what's the moral of the story? Every story has to have a moral,' he said, as if irritated by my lack of logic.

I remained civil, albeit with great difficulty. 'I don't know. What's the moral of *Romeo and Juliet*?'

'That's Shakespeare,' he said, rolling his eyes and sighing heavily, letting his shoulders fall in a gesture that was meant to be disdainful; he had obviously affected it in imitation of some over-bearing housemaster from his youth. 'As I see it,' he said, swelling with self-importance with every passing second, 'you're trying to confuse the moral of the story by bringing in love and tragedy and all that romantic nonsense. The point is clear. She was married, he was her husband's brother, they knew they were in the wrong. They got what they deserved.'

'QED,' I said. 'Very good.'

'I agree with Frederick,' one of his cohorts said. She was a young plumpish woman named Una Madoc who spoke briskly in a businesslike manner, and with the faintest of Scottish accents. Of the tropics she had declared the heat unbearable and the sausages 'strange, not at all like the ones back home'.

'It isn't that simple, darling,' her husband said. He was a quiet man with a full-prawn moustache that smothered his words. 'What we know of Francesca comes from Dante, and he was plainly seduced by her. He was completely taken in by her story. We don't actually know the whole truth about this woman.'

'But weren't you moved by her words?' I said. 'Like Dante, I felt faint with pity when I read her story.'

Honey grunted in derision.

'Yes, it's undeniably sad,' Gerald Madoc said, 'but how do you know you can trust her? Is she above twisting the facts to her advantage, to gain your sympathy?'

'I must say,' I said with some indignation, 'that seems very cynical.'

'Always remember what the monstrous Minos says to Dante: be careful how you enter and who you trust. Did Paolo really seduce her, or was it the other way round? It isn't so simple, that's all I'm trying to say.' He beckoned to an ancient Chinese servant bearing some drinks and called, 'Boy.' There was no response.

'You still haven't got the measure of it,' Honey said. He turned to face the room and bellowed '*Boy!*' which promptly secured him the attention of several servants. 'Another *stengah*?' he said smugly. He and the Madocs proceeded to converse in a language I could barely comprehend. One half of their vocabulary consisted of abbreviations, the other of pidgin Malay. Madoc, for example, was APC. I took this to mean his employers, rather than his status. There were, I deduced, people who were employed by Guthries or Sime Darby. Una had lunched with Mrs ADO in that ghastly PWD house. The *makan* was awful, and there was a scene because the *syce* hadn't been given his *gaji*. Nowadays, it seemed, the *chop* of Socfin didn't count for anything, not among the Malays at least, and if they weren't careful Bousteads would soon follow suit.

'You must all come round for *pahits*,' said Una Madoc. 'Our boy mixes a very passable gin *pahit*.'

'Cocktails,' Madoc said, noticing my frown. '*Pahit* actually means "bitter", but that's what Europeans call cocktails here in the FMS.'

'Frederick says you're an actor,' Una said to me, looking me up and down. 'It'll be marvellous to have one of those around.'

I began to feel hot and very uncomfortable. My collar cut into my neck and I felt somewhat constricted. 'I'm afraid Mr Honey has been misinformed, but thank you anyway,' I said. I strode across the room, cape flowing magnificently in my wake, on to the verandah. I fumbled in my pocket for a cigarette, which I lit inexpertly on the third attempt. Then, as now, I abhorred nicotine, but I thought that a cigarette or two, properly mounted on an ebony holder, would suit the rest of my attire nicely. Let me explain. On hearing that I had been invited to the Soongs' famous house, I decided that I should atone for the shabbiness of my appearance on my first visit, that unfortunate afternoon when I had limped, snake-bitten and distinctly *brutta figura*, into their sitting room. I wanted to make up for my slurred speech and lack of conversation, so I resolved to dress as smartly as I could. When Johnny told me that this was one of the most important festivals after the Chinese New Year, and that he would be wearing his finest clothes, I instantly thought that it would be appropriate for me to wear something more extravagant than I might normally. After all, it was not a mere tropical *fête champêtre* that I was attending, but a rather more sumptuous affair altogether; I therefore thought that something spectacular was called for to mark this event. Johnny would be there, and so too would Snow. I had further understood from Johnny that this was very much a Chinese event, and I should expect to be the only Westerner present. This distinction in mind, I eventually settled upon my *déguisement* for the evening: a salmon-pink cape worn over a dinner jacket, with a cigarette holder I had found in the general store in Kampar. My 'cape' was not a proper one, but simply a length of satin Johnny had given me for this purpose. I thought it would suffice – after all, who in this part of the world, at a Chinese gathering, would be in a position to quibble over sartorial detail? My dismay at discovering not one but three other English people was, you can imagine, considerable.

I stood on the verandah puffing at the noxious cigarette. The drone of men's voices hung heavily in the air, punctuated by the staccato clinking of glasses and china. Someone was playing the piano – a pleasant, if somewhat heavy-handed, rendition of a Chopin nocturne. Its rich melody competed awkwardly with the song from the gramophone; I recognised the hard-edged voice and atrocious French accent as that of Josephine Baker, shrilly declaiming 'Si j'étais blanche'. All around the house, paper lanterns in the shape of fantastic animals hung from hooks, lit by candles inside their hollow bellies. There were dragons in various shapes – some chased after paper pearls, others stared wide-eyed at me as I passed, their concertina bodies quivering in the gentle night-time breeze. There were rabbits and dogs and butterflies, all painted a riot of colours, all bizarre and deformed. Outside, beyond the pale sphere of light, men stood chatting in the shadows. Escaped from their wives, they muttered conspiratorially about things I could not discern; I merely watched the firefly glow of their cigarettes in the dark. Johnny approached me as I was undoing my tie. 'Black tie,' I said, holding it before him like a dead animal. 'You can have it.'

'Why are you taking it off?' he said. 'Everyone is impressed by your attire. Everyone here is thrilled by the way you look.'

'No, Johnny – *you* are thrilled by my attire. No one else cares, no one has even noticed, for goodness' sake. Even Snow hasn't mentioned anything.' It was true. All evening, not a single person had complimented or even passed comment on my meticulously assembled costume. It was wasted on this lot. Perhaps satin capes and dinner jackets were commonplace in Chinese culture. In any event, I made a mental note never to rely on the good citizens of the valley as barometers of taste.

'But you are the – what's the word you used earlier?'

'Epitome.'

'Yes, the epitome of an Englishman.'

'No – Frederick Honey's the type of Englishman you're after. He's your *epitome*.'

Johnny looked puzzled. He shook his head, frowning. 'Frederick Honey is nothing.' He was not going to be convinced otherwise.

We went back into the house, walking on the wide veranda that ran along all four sides of the house. I made for the piano, where a slender young woman was brusquely bashing out a rendition of the *rondo alla Turco*.

'Shall we try something for four hands?' I said, easing myself on to the edge of the stool. She flashed a coquette's smile at me and moved aside, swatting absently at the folds of my cape as if it were an insect that had landed too close to her. We found some sheet music for Schubert's famous *Fantasy* and managed to blunder our way through the opening lines. 'You're too fast for me,' she complained, even though I thought I had slowed down.

'I'm sorry,' I said, frightened that I had committed another faux pas by offending a fellow guest. A small crowd had gathered to listen now, including, I noticed, my host and hostess themselves.

'No, that was very impressive,' TK Soong said. 'Why don't you play something else, Peter? On your own, perhaps.' I felt like a terrified schoolboy being set a test. I nodded and placed my fingers on the keys. In the polished façade of the upright I saw Honey's white jacket as he joined the small audience. I began to play some Bach – a partita I had always been fond of; but not long after I started I realised that I would not be able to finish it: I had forgotten how it ended. Ignoring the panic now swelling within me, I closed my eyes and allowed my fingers to be guided by instinct. Cunningly, I repeated bars here and there, until finally I could keep up the pretence no longer. I allowed the piece to end, *pianissimo*, hoping that no one would notice, although to my ears it sounded horribly brutal.

'Interesting interpretation,' Mr Soong said. 'I like Bach very much. Play more.'

I smiled, and played a little Scarlatti sonata, something less clever than the Bach, but which I was certain I knew. I went on to Liszt's cheerful transcription of *Die Forelle*, which was greeted with scattered applause. When I turned round I found Mr Soong seated at the edge of his voluminous rosewood chair; he was smiling and slowly clapping his hands. I glanced at Honey, whose face was set in studied indifference; my eye caught his and he smiled, his thin lips seeming to twist into a cruel little sneer. All this time, Johnny had been perched on the edge of the upright, watching my fingers on the keys; occasionally he would look at the people behind me and smile tentatively – at Snow, perhaps? I wasn't sure – and then glance at me with a look of untainted optimism. He was thrilled simply to be there, and that, in turn, made me feel the same.

'Shall I sing?' I asked Mr Soong, knowing he would agree. I had the wind in my sails now and nothing was going to stop me. I began with a bit of *Dichterliebe*, which I thought I did remarkably well, given that I was accompanying myself. And then I went on to some folk songs – French and English, bright wholesome tunes, full of fun. 'Thank you,' Mr Soong said, smiling, as he stood up. And then, as he walked away laughing, 'How young people are nowadays.' I regaled the remaining audience with some recent songs by Cole Porter and Ivor Novello, and was pleasantly surprised to find that some knew the words and sang along. The whisky had gone to my head too, I'm sure. I was singing an old English folk song, 'I know Where I'm Going', when I realised that there were only two people left listening to me – Johnny and Snow. All evening I had been looking out for her – partly to thank her for her kindness to me on the day I had been bitten by the snake, and partly because I could scarcely remember her face. I wanted to assure myself that really, she wasn't as extraordinary as I remembered her to be; that it was the poison in my blood that had played tricks with my vision. But throughout the party she had been surrounded by other guests, many of whom appeared to be admirers. I could not get close enough to her to examine her face, yet now she was right in front of me, watching me intently as I played the piano. I became conscious of my voice, of its ridiculous Englishness and incongruous baritone amid the softness of Oriental tones.

'That was very pretty,' she said. 'My father approves of – indeed admires – your musical abilities, as we all do.' She spoke in a very direct manner, open and forthright, unlike the charmingly veiled way in which the other young women in the room spoke. It was impossible to tell how old she was. Her face was distinctly pubescent, yet there was something in her features that made her seem harder than a mere teenager – a quality of manliness, I thought. The way she carried herself, too, lent her an air of maturity. I bowed my head to hide the flush that had inflamed my cheeks. 'Thank you,' I said. 'Do you play the piano? Yours seems an unusually musical family.'

She laughed. 'Considering we are Chinese, you mean.'

'No,' I protested, 'that's not what I meant at all.' I felt at once tainted with the same horrible brush as had smeared Frederick Honey. I rose from the stool, the tide of anxiety rising ever higher inside me; my cape was caught under the legs of the stool, and I struggled to free myself. 'I merely meant that you seem exceptionally appreciative of good music, and that's very rare.'

She smiled, looking unconvinced. 'Of course,' she said as she sat down. 'We are unusual, you're right. People in the valley generally can't afford the luxury of music.' When she brought her fingers to the keyboard I saw they were long and slightly stiff, but perfectly formed. She played slowly, a rustic, even crude melody that sounded entirely foreign to my ears. It was the loveliest thing I had ever heard.

'It's a Malay folk song,' she said, 'a love song. Not very smoothly transcribed, I'm afraid.' She said it unapologetically, smiling peacefully.

'It's beautiful,' I said. She rose from the seat and walked slowly to the kitchen, her dress – a shapeless silky smock hanging loosely over equally voluminous trousers – obscuring the outlines of her figure. I began to follow her, but found Frederick Honey in my path instead. He held a drink in each hand and offered one to me. 'Enjoying the party?' he said.

'I loathe spirits,' I said, looking at the tumblers of whisky.

'I was never overly fond of Scotch myself,' he said, continuing to hold the drink before me, 'until I came out to the tropics. Away from home – many thousands of miles away – my tastes have changed. I rather enjoy my whisky now; I drink it all the time. It's much better for you than the filthy water here.'

'How Byronic of you, existing on alcohol and nothing else. Was that a tip you picked up at the School of Oriental Studies? Any other helpful hints you'd like to pass on?'

His face contorted slowly into a smile: mirth did not come easily to him. He leaned in close and pressed the drink into my unwilling hand. 'Everything's different here. Forget home; the same rules don't apply. Just bear that in mind.' The smile faded and he left to regale Una Madoc with an inebriated, out-of-tune serenade, which she greeted with exaggerated hilarity. They linked arms and did an awkward little jig as if they had been transported back to the Scottish Highlands; they looked like conjoined Siamese twins suddenly separated, constantly falling away from each other but somehow unable to let go. The other guests looked upon this spectacle with bemusement; they remained resolute in their reticence, chatting quietly as they did before. Some hardly seemed to notice the commotion. Dancing, it occurred to me, was not a very Chinese activity. I looked around for Snow but she was nowhere to be seen.

Afterwards, Johnny accompanied me as I cycled back to the rest house. I gave him my miserable cape and he wrapped it around himself, letting it trail behind him in the dark. His words were still rushed from the excitement of the evening. 'Snow's father cannot believe how a person like me can be friends with someone as cultured as you are.'

'Johnny, please,' I started to say, but I knew that nothing I could say would change his mind. I was feeling strangely exhausted, and wanted to be on my own.

'In his eyes I am an uncivilised animal and whatnot, you see. How can a sophisticated Englishman be my friend? With his daughter, yes, because she is educated and so on and so forth. Snow's father thinks it is impossible for me to communicate with you, I know that for certain.'

'Does it matter what he thinks?'

'When he looked at me this evening I could see in his eyes, for the first time ever, that he was impressed et cetera. He regards me differently because of you, I think.'

'He can think what he likes, it makes no difference to anything.'

We rode on in silence for a whilst. My head began to throb; even at this time of the night the heat had not abated.

'Peter,' Johnny said. I did not even realised that he had stopped bicycling. His voice, quieter now, emerged from the dark some distance behind me. 'Can I ask you something?'

I didn't answer.

'If anything bad happens with the Japanese,' he said, 'you'd help me, wouldn't you? Me and Snow. I don't care about the others. Just me and Snow.'

'We don't know yet that anything is going to happen at all,' I said.

'But if something does happen.'

In the dark, I remembered the picture of his innocent, trusting face squinting into the sun as we stood on that hill. St John. Friendship. Love. Sacrifice. The first time I had ever known the truth of those words.

'Yes,' I said, 'I promise.'

*

This afternoon we were taken on a shopping expedition to Malacca Town. Half a dozen of us squeezed into the rickety minivan, a clatter of walking sticks and obdurate wheelchairs refusing to fold. Merely getting into the vehicle was a military campaign, I thought, as I sat serenely in the front passenger seat, disassociating myself from the unearthly clamour behind me. It is a wonder that these trips do not more often result in someone leaving behind a prosthetic limb. 'Taking a group of eighty-year-olds anywhere is an act of mercy,' Alvaro said as he took his seat.

'Not an act of mercy,' I said, peering at him from behind my sunglasses, 'an act of foolishness.'

The purpose of our trip was to buy presents and a few sad little decorations for Christmas, still two months away – plenty of time for the boxes of chocolate to be forgotten (or eaten) and the baubles lost amid the general confusion that holds reign over our house. As usual, the instigator of this idea that we, the residents, should participate in Christmas festivities was Alvaro. 'We can't let the house organise everything,' he said when we learned that a special collection had been made at Sunday Mass for us that week. 'We are not a bunch of invalids!' he cried. 'Aren't we?' I said, looking around the room, but there was no stopping him. He is, I suspect, excited now that there is every possibility of our garden being transformed. I suppose it is only natural that he expects the interior of the house to match its eventual exterior. Some hope.

We were dropped off by the Stadhuys, the journey having lasted a mere quarter of an hour (though, as always, it felt much longer, what with the constant grizzling from the back of the van). Our minders – three earnest volunteers, sixth-form boys from the church school – greeted us and quickly took charge of those unfortunates in wheelchairs. There followed the usual cacophony: who wanted to do what where when, etc. I stood apart from this unsightly mêlée, taking stock of the 'Red' Square.

I never thought of the square as being particularly red when I first saw it more than fifty years ago. The colour of the Stadhuys was, I think, truer to its original then – a weather-worn terra-cotta, red only in the sense that an Etruscan urn is red. Now, meticulously repainted by the town council, it looks too shiny and too orange. Given the nationalistic evangelism of the town council, I doubt very much that this colouring was a subtle *hommage* to its Dutch heritage. Christ Church is, of course, properly red, built as it is of laterite. When I first saw it, I was struck by the richness of its colour, which spoke of all the warmth of these new tropical lands. I discovered only recently that the red stone is only a façade; a pretty cladding over the church's true fabric of bricks imported from Holland. Suddenly it appeared colder, more foreign; a fake. Not that it makes much difference anyway, seeing as we are actively discouraged from visiting this great bastion of Dutch Protestantism. As if to spite me, *our* church is, in contrast, a dull nineteenth-century monstrosity – built, naturally, by a Frenchman.

I followed the others acquiescingly into the new shopping precinct, a frightful collection of fluorescent-lit shops selling an array of plasticky objects of virtu. I endured, as usual, the tediously unimaginative taunts of 'Mat Saleh', spat at me by bored adolescents. It has always baffled me how the name of a minor Malay nationalist who fought against the British came to be a term of cheerful abuse, hurled with alacrity at any passing Caucasian. If memory serves me correctly, Mat Saleh died in vain, shot by the British Army. Independence didn't come to this country for another sixty years after his death; he was hardly a hero. These vulgarities never used to happen to me – not even after independence, when so many people were fiercely proud of their new country. I cannot recall when the insults first began – in the seventies, I suppose. So inured am I by twenty years of these moronic taunts that I scarcely notice them nowadays. I did, however, notice what the other old men were buying: Christmas tree angels dressed in the costume of Straits Chinese; boxes of vile-smelling durian cake, tied with bows; *dodol*, that gum-rotting confection of condensed palm sugar; lengths of violently red-coloured paper – 'for cutting into animal shapes,' Gecko told me. He also bought a CD of Christmas music which had, on its cover, a group of smiling, vacuous American teenagers whose gleaming teeth betrayed a startling over-consumption of calcium. It included such songs as 'I Saw Mommie Kissing Santa Claus', and 'Mamasita, Donde Esta Santa Claus?'

'What on earth are you going to play this on?' Alvaro demanded of Gecko.

'My radio,' he said with utter certainty before wheeling himself away in his shiny new wheelchair.

I drifted to the back of the group and waited until our teenage minders were distracted by a poster of a young woman, tartily dressed and inappropriately named 'Madonna'. Then, when I was sure no one was looking, I slipped quietly away, escaping via a nearby fire exit. Out in the open, I retraced my steps, heading down to the water's edge. At Porta de Santiago I paused to buy myself a bottle of purple Fanta, for which I have an abnormal weakness. The athletic young woman who ran the stall smiled at me sweetly, and I felt obliged to buy a bag of pickled mango too; I discarded it in some bushes as soon as I was out of sight. On the esplanade that runs along the sea wall, I strolled under acacia trees whose tiny leaves lay scattered like confetti across the ground. In the deep shadows of the undergrowth young men and women canoodled, too drenched in young love to notice my hobbling presence. I stopped at a dirty wooden bench, looking out at the mud-grey sea. A raft of flotsam, ensnared by a fisherman's net, drifted placidly on the scum-topped waves. I did not have to wait long before I heard a tuneless whistle and a soft coo-cooing from the bushes behind me. 'Hello-o, mister,' a voice called. I turned round and saw a young woman leaning against a tree, her powdered face accentuated by scarlet lips. She sashayed towards me, eyes hidden behind huge mirrored sunglasses. I knew at once that she was a transvestite, and a prostitute too. Slowly, I began to relax, washed by the waves of familiar excitement as she sat with me and struck up the usual anodyne patter: what's my name, where do I come from, what nice thick hair I have. The girls may come and go but their talk remains the same. Always, I invent the answers. It's easier for both of us. How could I respond truthfully and fully to the question 'Where is your home?' I couldn't possibly begin. My only dwelling place is now no longer on this earth – I destroyed it many years ago. And so, over the years, I have sought occasional refuge in the fleeting company of these glossy-haired girls. Their hands are always quick and smooth, their lips cool and efficient. I do not seek these girls to relive the fervid longings of younger days. Memories are things to be buried. They die, just as people do, and with their passing, all traces of the life they once touched are erased, for ever and completely. Some years may pass until another encounter with such a girl, but I know the next one will be just as this one was. She will finish with me, smiling kindly at my flaccid failure and earnest pleadings; she will take her small fee and deposit it swiftly in her handbag; and then she will walk away, leaving me whimpering quietly to myself, all alone before the silent, muddy sea.

*

The first time I saw Kunichika he was standing under a tree looking through a pair of binoculars. I was returning from an outing with Johnny and chose to walk along the ridge of hills that ran above the rest house. I walked down the path that led to the rest house, singing 'La donna è mobile' with much *brio*, when I suddenly noticed a tiny mirrored glint, a pinprick flash of light from the escarpment above me. It took me a whilst to locate him standing in the shade of a small tree whose tiny, twisted trunk seemed all the more tiny and twisted next to his easy, erect figure. Never one to leave the itch of curiosity unscratched, I scrambled up the rocky path, through a tangle of trees, to where he was standing. He did not drop the binoculars when I approached; for a second I thought he had not noticed me.

'Don't move,' he said, binoculars still held to his eyes. He spoke softly in an even voice that compelled me strangely to obey without the faintest demurral. 'Over there, in those trees,' he continued quietly in his tempered bass-baritone, 'do you see?'

'What?' I whispered.

'A golden oriole. What a beautiful bird.'

I peered hard at the canopy of leaves ahead of us, expecting the flash of unmistakable yellow-and-black plumage, but I could see nothing in the shadowy recesses. 'Where?' I asked.

'It's gone now,' he said, lowering his binoculars and offering me his hand with an easy smile. 'Mamoru Kunichika. Pleased to meet you.' I learned that he had arrived in the valley only that day; that he was staying at the rest house; that he was an academic with a position at Kyoto University.

'How wonderful,' I said. 'What is your field of study?'

'Anthropology,' he said without a moment's hesitation. 'And linguistics,' he added, as if it were an afterthought.

I studied him closely. Pressed white shirt, maroon-and-red tie, nicely fitting trousers. He was, I had to admit, an impressive-looking man. 'I suppose the two go hand in hand,' I said, noticing that he was almost exactly my height. His hair, too, was combed in much the same way as mine, parted to the right – though his looked somewhat neater. His shoulders were much broader than mine and his frame suggested that the rest of his body bore similar musculature under his immaculate clothing. Nothing was out of place with him – everything in appallingly perfect proportion. Next to him, I suddenly felt very skinny and malnourished.

Though our rooms were at opposite ends of the rest house, I expected that our paths would cross – over breakfast, say, or when taking tea on the veranda. Two educated gentlemen, each with a background that might interest the other. I certainly wasn't inclined to avoid him the way I might have had he been European. But I rarely saw him. Often he remained in his room for long periods; other times he would slip away noiselessly, and it became impossible for me to tell if he was in or out. When I was certain that he was in his room, I would listen at my door for some clue as to the activities behind his firmly closed door. Nothing – not even the scrape of a chair on the floor or the closing of a cupboard door. We were the only two people at the rest house and yet we remained solidly encased in our separate cells.

One morning I left my lodgings to join Johnny on his continuing quest for a marital home. I had bicycled some distance before I realised that I had forgotten my camera, a handsome Leica (stolen, no doubt, from some unsuspecting foreigner) I had bought 'second-hand' for a few dollars from a rickshaw-puller in Singapore. As I approached the rest house I heard music. It was so perfect and so strange in this setting that it took me several moments to realise that it was really playing, that my imagination wasn't running wild in this tropical heat. It was music I knew well and held very dear to me – I had in fact been humming the tune some days before – 'Porgi amor', from *Le Nozze di Figaro*. I knew, as I entered the house, that it was coming from Kunichika's room. I felt compelled to share my enthusiasm for this music with him, and so I went to his room and knocked on his door. The music stopped immediately, and after a few moments Kunichika opened the door, looking perfectly *soigné* and unruffled.

'What marvellous music,' I said, 'and how lovely to hear it played here. I haven't heard that in a long whilst – except in my own head, of course, where it replays endlessly.'

He stood squarely in the barely open doorway; behind him I could only see a low, empty set of bookshelves. 'Thank you,' he said simply.

'How wonderful to have a gramophone? You must have taken some trouble to bring it here.'

'Yes, it was slightly cumbersome.'

'All the way from Japan?' I continued, feeling myself wilt slowly under the steadiness of his gaze. 'I wouldn't have associated the Japanese with opera – well, apart from *Madam Butterfly* of course, and oh, *Turandot* – no, that's China, isn't it? I take it you listen to a lot of opera?'

'Only a little. I studied in Europe for a time.' His manner of speech was *legato* as *legato* can be, flowing effortlessly from the depth of his chest to his throat to his perfectly drawn lips. He lifted a hand to smooth his already smoothed hair, and I noticed the quiet gleam of his signet ring. Instinctively, I reached to feel my own ring; I could have sworn that his was, in shape, weight and colour, identical to mine.

'Well,' I said, shifting on my feet, 'perhaps we might exchange views on Mozart some time.'

'Yes, perhaps,' he said, closing the door.

I left the rest house and found Johnny waiting for me by the river bank a few miles to the south. He was impatient to see a house we had glimpsed several days earlier; his eyes were narrowed in a frown and he did not seem to want to hear about my strange new neighbour. When we found the house it was smaller than I had remembered it: a compact whitewashed cube, its only ornamentation a pair of pilasters on its façade. It appeared abandoned, and we did not have any trouble pushing the heavy wooden doors open. The space inside seemed far too large for the shell that contained it; it swelled up above us in the one enormous room that made up the front portion of the house. It contained no upper floors: when I lifted my head to look at the ceiling I could barely make out the rafters in the inky darkness above me. Beyond that initial cavern a door led into a small courtyard overlooked on all sides by a further building concealed behind the unprepossessing exterior we had frowned at from the street. Instantly I imagined that courtyard filled with heavy earthenware pots containing ferns and goldfish; I saw the shutters painted eau-de-Nil green; I heard the haphazard clanging of saucepans and smelled the aroma of pungent curries. We clambered up the steep narrow stairs and ran through each of the empty rooms, flinging open the shutters to let in the light. One of the smaller rooms reminded me of my bedroom at Hemscott, its low ceiling instantly recalling the lonely sanctuary of my childhood. I looked out of the window. The great silty river meandered gently by, so slowly it barely appeared to move at all. An ancient tree, its massive trunk enrobed in a tangle of epiphytic roots, hung thickly over the water beside a frail pontoon that protruded into the river. Small cherubic children swung naked from the thick hanging vines and splashed into the water below; their laughter filled the still morning and made me inexplicably sad. When Johnny came into the room he found me standing at the window, blinking into the distance. He asked if I was all right.

I nodded and said, 'This is it. This is home for you.'

*

Artemisia absinthium, commonly known as wormwood, is a hardy perennial with feathery silver-green leaves. It thrives in a variety of garden conditions, its fine foliage providing useful contrast to broader, darker leaves in mixed borders such as those we had at Hemscott. Even after the garden began its descent into dilapidation, the *Artemisia* remained vigorous, its pale green glowing amid the creeping, darkened tangle around it. It is also reputed to have hallucinogenic properties, and is a principal ingredient in the making of absinthe. One of its qualities stands out over the others: its bitterness. Simply crush a leaf and place it on your tongue and its acridity will be evident. The ill effects of wormwood have assumed legendary status, enshrined in no less a work than the Bible: the end of the world will, according to the simply divine St John, be announced by seven angels. For those of you lucky enough to have escaped a religious education, you need only know that the third of these angels causes a great star to fall from heaven, burning as it were a lamp, and it fell upon the third part of the rivers and upon the fountains of waters; and the name of the star is called Wormwood, and the third part of the waters became wormwood and many men died of the waters because they were bitter.

There. Repeated verbatim, after nearly seventy years. Brother Anthony was right: I would remember it for the rest of my life. I was nine when I first encountered that passage. I had allowed myself to become embroiled in an unseemly spat with a foul-mouthed boy who had scrawled 'CUNT' on my tuck box, and before long our feud developed into a pathetic little fist fight – more shoving and kicking than actual grown-up punching, if truth be told. I was brought before the gigantic Brother Anthony, my housemaster, who, before he administered what was to be the first of the many thrashings I suffered at his hands, sneered at me and called me the work of the Devil. 'Wormwood,' he said, as if tasting something odious on his brutish palate, 'that says it all.' He opened his drawer and produced two things: a short cane and a Bible, bound in cheap black leather. He bent me over the edge of his desk and set the Bible in front of my face; with a thick nicotine-stained finger he tapped at a spot on the page and said, 'Read that aloud.' I began to read the verse. He struck the first blow and I cried out. 'I didn't tell you to stop, you dirty troublemaker,' he said. I continued to read through choking breaths; my eyes clouded with hot tears. The name of the star is called Wormwood and many men died because the waters were bitter. 'You'll remember that for the rest of your life, Wormwood.' Every time I was punished I was made to read that passage, as if repeating it would rid me of the bitterness of my name, my self. After a only a short whilst I could recite it by heart without recourse to the Bible, and the beatings, too, became bearable. I stopped hating the good Brother Anthony, but when I meet him in purgatory I will have to tell him that it didn't work: I remember the words, but all my bitterness is still there. But for a few brief days in 1941, I have carried it inside me all my life.

When did the tide of wormwood begin to rise within me after I got to the valley? I thought I had rid myself of it. On all my walks with Johnny I felt nothing but uninterrupted happiness. Even when I searched for some lingering trace of malevolence within myself I found none. And then one evening I experienced the prick of discontent, a sickly tingle at the back of my throat that I had not felt since coming to the valley. I had been invited by the Soongs to join them at the *wayang kulit*, or shadow theatre, which I understood was a kind of Oriental *Punch and Judy* accompanied by wind instruments with trenchant chords similar to those of a bagpipe's. I dressed appropriately for a tropical evening – open-necked cream silk shirt and flannels – and dabbed some Essence of West Indian Limes on my jowls. I arrived at the Soong house feeling fresh and very lively. I was looking forward to seeing Snow again.

She was not among the people gathered in the sitting room pleasantly sipping drinks. Someone else was there, though – my elusive neighbour, Kunichika.

'What a surprise to see you here,' he said brightly, hiding what I took to be a mixture of displeasure and shock behind a charming smile and a little bow. For a few minutes he behaved with exuberant fake bonhomie, joking about various things – the diabolical food at the rest house, the envy with which he regarded my camera, the troop of monkeys that gathered in the trees every evening, begging for food from the kitchen. 'Goodness knows how Mr Wormwood gets any peace with all their chattering!' he said to TK Soong.

I smiled politely and said, 'I manage.'

Snow did finally emerge, wearing a brocade blouse over loose-fitting, dark-coloured trousers. She looked very refined, just like an imperial Manchu consort.

'You are staring at something, Peter,' she said wearily. 'Is something the matter with my dress?'

'No, of course not – nothing at all. It's marvellous,' I said, feeling myself blush.

She greeted Kunichika with more warmth and familiarity – rather *too* much warmth and familiarity, I thought. He bowed low and she offered him her hand, which he accepted with one hand and clasped with the other. She smiled timidly, dangerously, and held his gaze. I looked at her parents, expecting their disapproving countenances, but I found none. They merely smiled vapidly, as they always did. Mrs Soong turned to me and said, 'Professor Kunichika is a *marquis*, you know.'

I paid little attention to the show. Our seats were a row of tiny wooden chairs arranged in the middle of the clearing in front of the screen. All around us the rest of the audience sat cross-legged, or else squatted in that loose-limbed oriental fashion, almost resting on their haunches. I felt very disconcerted; I could barely stretch my legs for fear of kicking some poor urchin in the back. I found myself seated next to Snow, who remained utterly still throughout. My eye was constantly drawn towards her pale, luminescent blouse which matched the intensity of her skin. It was impossible to concentrate on the show; I could not understand the constant lunging of the bizarre spectral shapes. I leaned across to ask Snow to explain what was going on. She spoke somewhat curtly, as if displeased at being disturbed during the performance. Yet a few moments later I noticed, out of the corner of my eye, that she was exchanging whispers with Kunichika. Quickly, I leaned over towards her again. 'Who's that character? There, that one,' I said, pointing. Kunichika answered for her, providing me with rather more information than I needed – I paid little attention to his tutorial on the philosophy of Eastern theatre. I was not effusive in my thanks, and spent the rest of the show trying to anticipate the next exchange between Snow and Kunichika. Every time I sensed she might be about to speak to him I quickly presented her with some spurious question about the characters, the story, the music, etc. I could not stop myself from doing this. I knew, of course, that there was a risk that my behaviour would be interpreted by Snow as being juvenile in the extreme, but the risk of not behaving thus felt even greater. Whenever Kunichika bent his nobly sculpted neck to whisper in Snow's ear, the sense of panic that welled inside me was violent and painful. I had to do everything I could to stop it.

As the performance ended I noticed Johnny looking at me with an expression of some concern. We had been separated throughout by Snow's parents, who sat between us, unmoving and silent as boulders. 'Is everything all right?' Johnny asked me later.

'Oh yes,' I said, 'I was on the edge of my seat. Utterly gripping.'

Back at the Soong house Snow took her leave and retired to bed. She offered her hand once more to Kunichika, who did, this time, kiss it briefly as he bowed. To me she said, 'Goodnight, Peter,' and then disappeared down the long dim corridor to her bedroom.

The bitter seed had been sown inside me. I tasted it at the back of my mouth and felt its dark, dirty tentacles creeping slowly inside my body, probing for where I was weakest. Johnny walked me home, chattering constantly about some poems – Shelley or some other nonsense – he had just read; about plans for his new house; about one day travelling to Europe. 'Will you teach me to play the piano?' he said brightly.

I grunted.

'Is something wrong, Peter? Are you unwell?'

'I'm tired,' I said. I left him standing at the steps to the rest house with a vague promise of meeting the next day. I went to the bathroom and retched with dry, painful heaves. I fell asleep after drinking half a bottle of neat gin I found in the communal drinks cabinet. My dreams were filled with a single repeating image, that of Kunichika violently ravishing Snow. Their bodies twisted and glistened and pursued me wherever I went. In my bedroom at Hemscott they copulated in a frenzy by the window, silhouetted against the winter sky; in the Bodleian they thrashed among the dusty bookshelves; here, in the rest house, they formed a single pure-white creature, thrusting and jerking and swooning before my eyes. I could not escape this monster. I ran into the jungle but they were above me in the trees, shrieking, wailing, crying. They pointed at my limp penis, for I was naked. It hung miserably like a rag, turning a bilious green in colour as I tried furiously to resurrect it, pumping it with both fists. All this time that howling two-headed white animal laughed at me from the forest above. I could not escape it.

Not once did I think of Johnny, my only friend in this world.

*

A Chinese sparrowhawk has begun visiting the woods behind the house. No one has seen it but me. It comes at the quietest times of the day, when I am the only person about. Just after dawn, when the last wisps of sea mist have faded away, it hovers against a pearl-grey sky, shivering tentatively in the chilled breeze. In the afternoons, when everyone else is ensconced in their geriatric siesta, I watch it dart between the trees, wheeling furiously between the casuarinas, or flashing its wainscot-coloured wings as it speeds across the paddy fields. Sometimes I spot it perched silently on a bough, deep in the foliage, staring at me with huge yellow irises. I smile at it and nod a greeting. It knows I am an ally, and so it reveals itself only to me. For only I know that it is responsible for the recent and oh-so-terrible decimation of the local brown shrike population.

'Do you think it could be a mongoose?' Gecko trilled anxiously. Speculation had been rife in the days following the initial discovery of a few brick-red shrike feathers lying on the patio where those annoying creatures feed on morsels of food left for them by Gecko and the others. A list of suspects was drawn up: civet cats, snakes, flying foxes, dogs, rats – even the cook's cat, which was finally exonerated on the grounds that its age and girth prevented it from venturing past the kitchen doors.

'Ah bollocks,' said Brother Rodney, a burly Australian who likes to think of himself as rather more worldly-wise than he is. 'It's a bloody shitehawk,' he said.

'How charming,' I said. 'What exactly is a "shite" hawk?'

'One that shits all over the place,' he said, as if it were perfectly obvious. 'You get great big colonies of them this time of the year, out in those islands across the straits. Yep, thousands of them, shitting all over the place. Bloody awful. I've seen it with my own eyes. Some islands get turned into a huge shite pile, nothing but shite as far as the eye can see.'

I stood watching flocks of birds winging their way wearily across the straits. This is where they complete their long, lonely journey, all the way from Manchuria and Siberia. Some of them travel the extra distance across to Sumatra (where they will certainly not be bothered by the likes of Gecko), others remain here. Why? I don't suppose anyone will ever know the mysteries of migration. I have always loved the idea of being a migrating bird, a hawk or some other raptor, riding the warm thermals across the vastness of continents, all of Asia under my wings. I would follow my prey south, ready, like my little shitehawk, to swoop at any moment. There would be no plan for my journey, no map, no coordinates. And yet I would find my way, guided by forces too powerful and ancient for me to discern; I would simply follow my destiny.

Alvaro set up a rota to keep watch over the bird feed. The idea was firstly to identify the culprit and secondly to prevent the repetition of such terrible crimes that we all hate, you know.

'I'm not volunteering,' I said, 'I have other – better – things to do. The garden, in case you've all forgotten, is still in the making. There's plenty of work for me. Why don't you people just accept the workings of nature? Some things die, other things live. Predators and prey – it's a long-standing arrangement. Man needs to establish a rapprochement with Mother Nature.' The plan, of course, did not work. No one could stay awake for the duration of their watch, and nothing was seen. Once, Gecko *thought* he saw a python at the end of the garden. But the monsoons are upon us now and the rain, when it comes, falls in sheets, blurring the vision and turning every shape into a ghostly spectre. He could not be sure.

Erring on the side of caution, I crept into the kitchen and stole little pieces of raw chicken from the refrigerator. I took these to the woods and laid them out on the highest bough I could reach. I wanted to make sure that the sparrowhawk did not go away.

*

Johnny was ill-tempered and sullen right from the very start of the journey. He would not be cheered up, not even by me. By the time we reached the Formosa Hotel he was entombed in his own silence.

'Is he ill?' Snow asked me after he had gone ahead to their

room. For a brief moment, I found myself alone with her in the gloomy foyer. We stood apart from each other like two chess pieces marooned on their own tiny square of the chequerboard floor. 'I don't know,' I said, lowering my voice to match her hushed tones. The whispering hid the slight tremor that had crept into my voice. Perhaps she trusted me at last. She looked at me with a faint smile of conspiratorial concern. Before I could prolong this moment of intimacy, however, Kunichika appeared. 'May I take your things upstairs?' he asked her, lifting her case before she had time to acquiesce.

I went up to my room and had a long soak in the cavernous roll-top bath. One of its claw-and-ball feet was missing, replaced by a sturdy block of wood. As I reclined in the lukewarm water I looked at the flakes of peeling paint on the ceiling and the glossy green-black moss forming on the cornices. The rugs on the floor were threadbare, patched and tufted like mange on a feral Malayan dog. Nonetheless, my bath seemed transcendentally luxurious after an arduous day on the road; it brought relief to my aching limbs and washed away the red dust that had formed a film on my skin. I made a quick mental note: not even Rolls-Royces are immune to the forces of nature.

At the bottom of the sweeping, dimly lit stairs, I paused to straighten my tie. I wanted to make sure that Snow saw me in the best possible light: freshly scrubbed and shaved, immaculately dressed, fully revived and bursting with *joie de vivre*. The voices from the dining room drifted into the foyer, muffled and inarticulate but audible nonetheless. I listened for Snow's voice but heard only those of Kunichika and Honey. They spoke softly but firmly, forming each word carefully and with great deliberation. One or two words were emphasised heavily, but their voices were never raised.

'Ah, Wormwood,' Honey said breezily when I walked into the room. 'What will you have – whisky? Always take it neat in the tropics. Kills the germs, you see.'

'I know, you've already told me that. How kind,' I said, accepting the cigarette he offered me. I looked at Johnny. He wore an ivory-coloured shirt of mine which I had given to him some days earlier. I had noticed him looking at it longingly, and told him it had been made for me in Paris (I had in fact bought it in Tunbridge Wells). When I gave it to him he said, 'That is the kind of thing I want to sell in my new shop.' This evening he was wearing it for the first time, and he looked awful. The yoke was too tight across his shoulders, the sleeves too long and the colour too pale for his complexion. His face looked flushed and damp with perspiration, and he stared resolutely at the melting cubes of ice in his drink. With his forefinger he drew shapes in the moisture on the glass, his eyes hollow and unblinking.

For the rest of dinner, Honey held court like a schoolmaster lecturing a group of fifth-form boys. His stories of petty tin-mining heroics failed to impress anyone. He filled his chair magisterially, speaking with an air of studied superiority, frequently exhaling plumes of cigarette smoke. In every respect he resembled a young child imitating the mannerisms of an adult. He looked at Johnny as he spoke – singling out the easiest target, as it were: no one else seemed interested.

'Nonsense,' I said, challenging every assertion he made. I spoke with as much sang-froid as possible. Snow had now joined us, and it was important to pitch my voice in exactly the right manner: clever but not cynical, involved but not aggressive. I cast a quick glance at her. I was not surprised to see she was looking at Kunichika, and he at her.

'I don't believe a word of it,' I said at the end of Honey's long and implausible story about the killing of an English tin miner by a Chinaman coolie. Whatever control I had over my voice seemed suddenly to have vanished, and I was aware of the sharpness of my words: waspish, acidic, adolescent. It was too late now, and I lashed out at the inconsistencies of his story. To my surprise, this unseemly little rant raised a smile from Snow – though I could not decide whether the subject of her mirth was me or Honey.

We had an execrable meal of *réchauffé* leftovers – bacterial soup of an unidentifiable variety (though mutton was clearly an important component), bland chicken and lumpy rice pudding. 'I think this presages the end of the Empire, don't you?' I said. A string quartet sat under the dry drooping leaves of an enormous potted palm. Like the plant, the members of the quartet seemed near death. They moved their bows feebly and played out of tune, turning every piece into a sad funereal farewell. Even the most recent songs were somehow transformed into antique death marches – 'J'attendrais', for example, a blithe and simplistic song (learned, no doubt, from an itinerant French planter), was executed with moaning top notes which begged to be accompanied by the tolling of an Orthodox funeral bell. Over this horrific continuo, Honey sounded off on every conceivable topic. He was a *soi-disant* expert on everything relating to the tropics, from fungal infections to the politics of the Malay sultanate. The cacophony was so distracting that I barely noticed Snow slip away from the table. I waited a minute before following her, making the appropriate excuses as I left. I thought I might catch her before she got to her room – I would use Johnny's 'illness' as an excuse to engage her in conversation. I hurried up the stairs but saw no sign of her. I ran along the darkened hallways, pausing every so often to listen for her footsteps: nothing. With an air of mild deflation I made my way back to the foyer quietly humming the insidious, sickly-sweet tune to 'J'attendrais'. It was then that I saw her, slipping quietly into the shadows out on the balustraded veranda. I walked on tiptoe to stop my shoes clicking loudly on the floor, and made my way towards her. I hid behind a screen and then shielded myself with a pillar, waiting for the right moment to approach her. In half-profile her features seemed finer than before, yet touched by a gentle muscularity. Her short hair revealed the smoothness of her neck; every time she turned her head the skin stretched to reveal a flash of white amid the dark. She moved with slow, certain movements, utterly in control of every part of her body. Crouched in the shadows, I felt clumsy and foolish. I straightened my posture and began to walk towards her, lifting my feet so that they did not crash awkwardly on the cold tiled floor. I had barely progressed beyond the pillar when she turned round and stared at me with hot dark eyes.

'Hello,' I said gently, assuming as quiet and masculine a demeanour as possible. 'What are you doing out here?'

'Looking at the garden,' she said.

My ears pricked. 'Garden?' I said. 'Where?' What luck. I was in my element now. I could engage her in conversation all night on the subject of gardens. Fate had presented me with a perfect entrée into her world. All her likes and dislikes, her sense of aesthetics, her memories of childhood – everything was there for me to discover now. I peered into the darkness beyond the faint circle of light cast from the hotel, but I could see nothing except the amorphous shapes of the jungle that surrounded us. The sharp angles of a ruined structure protruded from this shapeless mass, silhouetted against the night sky, but otherwise there was nothing – nothing I could identify as a *garden*. My hopes of finding my Eden were dashed.

'Aren't there any beds or borders?' I said. 'There is at least an ornamental pond somewhere, surely?'

'Perhaps,' she said. 'This was once the most famous garden in the Federated Malay States. It had a European-style garden, whatever that means. It's all still there – though now it's part of the jungle, I suppose.' She stood with her hands resting on the balustrade. Her face was clear and untroubled.

'What a shame,' I said, leaping up to sit on the wide stone ledge. I had not even settled properly when she bade me an abrupt 'goodnight', leaving me stranded on the balustrade. I sat there for a long whilst, listening to the call of cicadas. The nebulous remains of that once-fabulous garden lay before me, but still I could see nothing.

The dining room was empty by the time I made my way back to my room. The quartet had disbanded and the tables had been stripped of their linen. The lights, too, had been turned off, and the shadows of the palm leaves cast tiger-stripes across the floor. I had just begun to walk up the stairs when I realised there was someone standing on the landing, leaning against the wall with a drink in his hand. I knew, of course, it was Honey.

'You went missing for some time, Wormwood,' he said.

'Yes, I thought I'd lurk in the shadows for a whilst, rather like you're doing now.' I continued walking without looking at him.

'Here's some advice,' he said as I went past him. 'Watch your step. You think you can just breeze into the valley to the sound of trumpets? Think again. No one appreciates your behaviour. There are things an Englishman can do and things he can't do – that's just the way it is. I told you before. The same rules don't apply out here. We have to behave in a certain way, otherwise everything falls apart. You think you're special? You're not. No one is. Let me tell you one thing: nobody likes you. Take this as a gentle warning from someone who knows.'

'Thank you – sahib is most kind,' I said and continued on my way. My face felt hot with anger and shame. I kept on walking, closing my eyes to the harsh prick of tears. I took a deep breath, then another, then another, until finally I reached the top of the stairs. 'That tin miner of yours, the one who was murdered,' I said, turning around. 'He got what he deserved. He had it coming.'

I proceeded slowly to my room. In the end, we all get what we deserve, I thought.

The rain lasted all day and into the night. It washed mud down from the hills on to the flagstones beneath my window and turned the open drains into angry red rivers. Here in the tropics the rain dominates the landscape, turning everything into strange images of itself. Its pale haziness becomes opaque, even mirrored, and blurs every shape that falls within its shroud so that you can never be certain where something begins and ends. If you stare hard enough at it you might even see a reflection of yourself a mere ten paces away. These tropical storms do not leave room for indifference; they wring apathy from your body, electrifying your thoughts. It is often said that the sun makes the White Man go mad, but I do not agree. It is the rain that does it. It turns you into a different person.

Solitude, I decided, was the most fitting state for me, and by the time we reached the rest house I had resolved to isolate myself in dignified silence. I barricaded myself in my room, or else strolled through the expansive, attractive grounds of the house, singing to myself in perfect pitch. '*Ich habe genug*,' I sang *con molto espressivo*, surprising myself with a sustained low B: I did not think my voice was still capable of such things. Encouraged by this unexpected treat, I moved on to some Mozart arias, and found that the words came back to me easily. I thought I lost them when I travelled the seas to these hot lands; where I kept them all this time I do not know, but they must have found a hiding place inside me, for I had never made any attempt to keep them safe. Alone under the damp whispering trees, my voice did not sound at all foreign; it reached out and danced amid the foliage, as much a part of the jungle as the vines that reached down and brushed my face with faint caresses. My natural singing voice was, of course, a baritone – everyone used to tell me so at Oxford. But why stick with what's natural, I thought? I always wanted to be a counter-tenor. I wanted to be able to sing all the roles – Julius Caesar, Tamberlaine, Orfeo; I wanted to be the Countess as well as the Count, to be Cherubino, that amorphous, ardent little creature. I wanted to sing all things to all men – and all women too. I was about to lift my voice in a violently sentimental rendition of 'Porgi amor' when I saw a figure disappear into a thicket of trees some distance away. I dropped my body and crept slowly into the bushes, smelling the pungent odour of wet mud under my feet. The person – it was a man, that much I could tell – moved stealthily and with the litheness of a young animal, appearing and disappearing among the trees, touching them gently as if he knew each one by name. He kept to the shadows, never venturing into the pools of dappled light that filtered through the foliage on to the forest floor. Out of the corner of my eye I spied another two figures walking slowly across open ground, heading towards a small cream-coloured gazebo that stood on the shoulder of a hill. It was Snow and Kunichika. I looked for the creeping figure in the adjacent woods – nothing. I moved slightly to gain a better view of Snow and Kunichika. He was quite the model of unhurried elegance, leaning against the poles of the gazebo with his hands resting on the frail little banister that encircled them, utterly relaxed in his expensively tailored clothes. He chatted softly, his head dropping and rising in a display of empathy and understanding, his entire body looking soft and accommodating – not at all the man I knew from our humble Kampar rest house. Throughout this time Snow sat facing him; I could not see her face. The strains of my Handelian heroes and Mozartian heroines filled my head in a riotous polyphony, and I became aware of the quickening of my breath. The morning sun was gaining in intensity, and I began to feels dizzy. I leaned back against a tree stump to catch my breath. I pressed my palms to my eyes, and saw, imprinted in phosphorescent hues, the image of Snow and Kunichika laughing in the gazebo. When I opened my eyes they had left and were walking briskly back to the house.

I ran into Johnny as we were preparing to leave the rest house. 'Hello, stranger, where have you been?' I said.

'Out walking,' he said, taking his things to the car. His movements were leaden and wrung of enthusiasm, and when he looked at me he did not do so with his usual fondness.

'Is something the matter, Johnny?' I said, grabbing him by the elbow as he shuffled across the porch.

'Of course not,' he said, shrugging. Although he had put on a new shirt, he still looked shabby and tired.

'What's wrong with you?' I said. 'Just look at the state you're in. You've got mud all over your shoes.'

He briefly caught my eye as he squinted into the light. 'So have you,' he said.

*

When, some years ago, I began to feel the ravages of middle age, I roused myself from the stupor that had settled over me and began to travel. I gathered my slowly ossifying limbs for one final, tentative peek at the country I had made my home. My spirit of adventure had petrified in the years since the war, and the thought of boarding a bus or a train with a horde of jostling bodies frightened me. Instead, I acquired a car and drove around the country. In the deep north I saw the jewel-green expanses of paddy fields in Kedah and the husks of abandoned villages, emptied by a gathering exodus to the great, growing cities of the newly independent nation. I drove across the mountainous spine that splits the peninsula in two and stayed for some time in Kota Baru, in a motel called the New Tokyo Inn. I wandered through the teeming market, looking at the silversmiths at work with their primitive, intricate tools. The shiny silver boxes they produced were laid out on straw mats on the dirt floor. Massed together in the sunlight, they glinted like beds of crushed glass. I went to the *padang* where the men threw their giant spinning tops, releasing them violently from coiled ropes as thick as pythons. The tops spun for hours, their painted surfaces a blur of colour on the dry, mouse-brown soil. As I stood watching the local kite-flying competition, I was befriended by an aged Englishman who was older then than I am now, but alarmingly full of panache. The huge kites trembled in the air; they were tethered to the earth by ropes decorated with small pieces of cloth that fluttered in the wind. Galsworth (that was his name, I think) could tell which kite would win the contest. He pointed it out with a wizened forefinger as it swooned gently in a shallow arc over our heads, the two sickle-moons of its body outlined proudly against the ultramarine sky. It came to a rest directly above us, hovering untroubled by the breeze. I had never seen such a thing before.

Afterwards, Galsworth invited me back to his house for a drink. We were attended by houseboys and girls, all dressed in the gold-woven *songket* of the north. They waited tremulously as we reclined with our drinks; their smiling presence made me uncomfortable. I asked Galsworth how he came to live there. 'I was the Sultan's personal adviser,' he replied simply, smoothing the gilded uniform of one of his androgynous youths with a reptilian hand. He showed me his house, every room sparsely decorated with beautiful things: a bedroom with nothing in it but a mattress on a carved divan and a leopard-pelt rug on the floor; a long shadowed corridor with a single Buddha head in an alcove. Through a window I glimpsed his garden, planted with a single rose bush. It bore no flowers, its branches were spindly, its leaves sparse. It had not taken to the hot winds of the seaside; I knew it would never survive this climate. Galsworth mumbled something about 'memory' and 'England', and hurried me along. I smiled as I was meant to, complimented him on his house and praised his servants. He said, 'How nice it is to have one's things appreciated by someone civilised.' When he smiled his teeth revealed themselves: sharp and small, whittled away by age and discoloured by cigarettes.

I made my excuses and left as quickly as I could. I walked alone on the Beach of Passionate Love, watching the swell of the waves unfurling as they reached the shore. The sand was grey, not white; the tinge of amber was fading now in the darkening sky.

As I drove back south I knew that trip would be my last. I was ready to surrender to death, and hoped the end would be swift. How could I have known that thirty years later, I would still be here, still waiting? It is a futile exercise, this contemplation of the end. My lungs still heave and my automaton limbs carry me downstairs to breakfast every morning, but the truth is that I died many years ago, suffocated by my own hands.

*

The boat was called the *Puteri Bersiram*, the name painted in small calligraphic letters barely visible on the rotting woodwork of the bow. As a means of initiating conversation with Johnny, I asked him what it meant. 'The Bathing Princess,' he said brusquely and disappeared below deck. He had been sullen throughout the day; no amount of cajoling could coax him from his obdurate silence. During the drive, Snow had leaned over to me and asked again if I knew what was wrong with Johnny. She whispered close to me and I felt her cool breath on my neck. Trembling, I lowered my head to her ear, and said, 'Don't worry, I'll get to the bottom of things.' She smiled and placed her hand briefly on my forearm. When I looked up at Johnny, I found him staring at me with a dark-eyed glare. He had the look of a man succumbing to an unnamed sickness. *Malaise en Malaisie*.

'Come on, Johnny,' I called down the hatch after him, 'some sea air will do you a world of good.'

No answer.

'Please,' I said, 'I don't know what I've done wrong, but whatever it is, I'm sorry, all right? If you come up on deck with the rest of us I'll do something to make it up to you.'

No answer for some time, and then a tentative frown took shape, the corners of his mouth curled in a half-smile.

'We'll recite some Shelley together, how about that?' I said. 'Come on, it's the start of our adventure!'

As we sliced effortlessly through glass-green waters, I watched Snow and Kunichika standing side by side at the helm, their sleeves touching and fluttering in the wind. They were like figures in a bas-relief, hewn on to the side of an ancient monument, perfectly postured and inscrutably countenanced. Johnny and I sat down on the deck watching the deepening sun. We rested our heads on the splintered boards of the shack that housed the helm. I was heartened to see that a little colour had returned to Johnny's cheeks, but his eyes remained hollow and distant as we sat gazing into the sun. I touched his arm to enquire as to his condition, but he withdrew from me and smiled weakly. The long painful strains of Kunichika's 'Porgi amor' began to play in my head, and there was nothing I could do to make them disappear. The boat emerged from the sheltered inlets and suddenly we were in open waters, the sea supine before us.

Johnny said, 'And many there were hurt by that strong boy. His name, they said, was Pleasure.' He mumbled rather than articulated the words, but they were clear enough to me.

'Is that Shelley?' I said. 'How clever of you to remember it. What's it from?'

'I don't know,' he shrugged, 'I just saw it in the book.' He avoided my gaze, staring at the setting sun with indolent eyes. The wind disturbed his hair, ruffling the short, fine strands into a jagged mass that sat up on his head like a crown. Some of them fell down over his forehead; I reached across to brush them from his eyes, but he pushed my hand away with a small slap – I could not tell if the force of this blow was intentional. For a brief moment, my fingertips had touched his brow – it was hot and clammy.

'I see. *Noli me tangere*,' I said. 'I suppose you're waiting to ascend to a higher plane? Tell me what's wrong, for God's sake.'

He laughed a quick, snorting laugh, quite unlike him, and continued looking sleepily into the distance.

I sneaked a glance at Snow and Kunichika, that perfect lascivious pair, and saw them still entranced with each other. 'Listen, Johnny,' I whispered. 'I know what's the matter. It's Kunichika, isn't it?'

He turned to me at once, regarding me with a frown of genuine surprise. His eyes were bloodshot and glassy.

'It isn't right,' I continued. 'I know it isn't right, and it must be uncomfortable for you, but it'll pass, I'm sure. It's the novelty of him – I mean, the novelty of someone new appearing all of a sudden. We're all like that, after all. People who enter our worlds from the outside are always more fascinating than the ones close to us, but in the end we always see sense. There's no need to worry, you know.'

He looked confused.

'Snow,' I said, lowering my voice even further. 'She isn't behaving, well, quite herself, is she?'

His face twisted in an ugly smile. He said, 'How would you know what her *self* is?' And with that he returned to his barricaded silence, locking me out of his world. The unfathomable, inscrutable East, I thought. I was cut adrift from the shores of understanding. The sea spread itself before me, leading to a blank, blank horizon. There was nothing I could do but sing. I opened my voice to the marbled sky. The songs I sang were the ones I thought I had forgotten: *Drink to me only with thine eyes*, I intoned in the last light of the tropical afternoon. They were the songs of my boyhood, and I had scarcely sung them in the years since. Still I carried them with me, alone here on these hot seas.

It did not surprise me when the boat broke down. It began with a grinding roar, the motor complaining of its age and disrepair with the most awful rattle. And then it gave way abruptly to a thin protesting whine before quietening completely. I welcomed it with glee.

Before this fortuitous intervention, I had gathered myself for sleep, nestling against some boxes and pulling a thin blanket around me. I kept to the shadows, shying from the moonlight that drenched the boat with thrilling whiteness. So bright was the moon that it painted out the stars with its silver-hued wash; I could not bear to look at the sky. I rested my head on the deck, allowing the rumble of the machinery to lull me to sleep. The intricacy of this mechanised heartbeat surprised me. It pulsed steadily, rising and falling with all the rhythms of a sentient existence; it spoke with a voice, mumbling now, singing then. Its vocabulary was primitive but articulate nonetheless. With my ear pressed to the cracked boards I could hear everything – Honey's clumping footsteps settling down at last; Kunichika's measured movements at the helm; and, directly beneath me, the uncomfortable creaking of Snow's wooden bed. Only Johnny was not in communion with this silent congregation. The noises abated after a whilst, but I knew the silence would not last. It was uneasy and tremulous, and when it was broken I was not surprised. I heard footsteps move slowly from below deck, emerging not far from where I lay. I knew they belonged to Snow, of course, and I knew they would carry her to the helm. I feigned sleep until she had passed, and then dragged myself very slowly across the deck until I had a view of the helm. The shuffling and scraping of my clothes on the rough wood rang terribly in my ears. I stopped and lay utterly still for a moment, waiting for the fragile silence to settle over the boat once more. I lifted my head and saw Snow standing very close to Kunichika; though their bodies did not touch, there existed an ugly complicity between them. I wanted to rush at them, screaming, and tear them apart. And then, in a single movement so fluid my eyes could barely discern what had happened, they were standing as one, pressed tightly together. His arm held her tightly around her waist, drawing her close to his side. I closed my eyes and waited for that dreadful sight to pass. When I opened my eyes again, I thought, they would surely be apart – but every time I did so I saw them clinging to each other like survivors on a raft, detached from the rest of humankind. I let my head fall to the deck, pressing my ear to the comforting, rudimentary throb of the motor. I could hear the waves washing against the side of the boat; the fathomless depth of the sea suggested a noise of its own: a howl wrung dry of sound so that only its resonance remained.

Not long after Snow's footsteps padded softly past my prone, shivering body, I sensed the first tremors in the motor. A faint ticking which erupted into a ferocious roar, calming to a shuddering halt. Silence, everywhere. Honey was instantly roused from his sleep; he spoke to Kunichika in hushed, angry tones. When I approached them Kunichika was standing at the side of the boat, peering into the inky depths of the water.

'Don't worry,' he said, beginning to unbutton his shirt as he prepared to dive overboard. 'It's only a small thing, I'm sure.'

We drifted placidly on the windless sea, so slowly I could barely discern the boat's gentle pirouettes. The flat and unbroken surface of the water spread silently around us; the empty horizon offered us no hope. The absence of gulls was strange, Kunichika said, we couldn't have been far from land. The truth was that we might have been two miles or two thousand miles from our destination and we would not have known.

Night brought relief from the scorching intensity of the sun. 'It also brings out the beast that lurks within every man,' I said to Snow. 'Witness.' I motioned at Kunichika, who was attempting to repair the boat. He tore at the machinery as if butchering a carcass. Sometimes he used tools, often he used his bare hands. When finally he gave up and sat down with his maps, the light from his lamp lit his grease-streaked face. 'He looks like an animal, one of those fox things – the ones people say are incarnations of ghosts.' I said.

'You mean a civet cat,' she replied.

'That's the one.' I searched the darkness for signs of light.

'Peter,' Snow said, lowering her voice. She placed her hand on my forearm. 'I'm worried. About Johnny.'

My arm tensed sharply at her unexpected touch, and I pulled away involuntarily for a brief moment before allowing her hand to settle once more. 'Really?' I said, continuing to peer into the dark. 'It's only seasickness, I expect.'

'Come on, Peter,' she said, her fingers gripping my arm. 'You know as well as I do that his fever has nothing to do with his body.'

'Hasn't it? I honestly can't see what else it might be if it isn't seasickness. Perhaps homesickness?'

She turned to look at me, but still I looked into the infinite night. 'He hasn't got a home – how can he be homesick? You know him better than anyone, I think, even better than I do. You're very fond of him, aren't you?'

'We've become good friends, I suppose.'

'You mean a lot to him, you know.'

'Do I? Can't think why.'

'If anything happens –' She stopped and laughed a gentle, snorting laugh. 'If anything happens to me, to us, you'd look out for Johnny, wouldn't you?'

It was a murky night, the moon a dab of white on the black paper sky. I said, 'Yes, of course.'

She fell silent.

'Of course I would,' I said, in a light-hearted voice, '*if* anything happened. I mean, we're a long way from the war, and who knows – it might never get to the valley. In any case, I doubt very much I'll be in a better position than you if we *are* invaded.'

'I don't just mean the war,' she said quietly.

'What then?'

'I don't know – everything. I wish I could tell you about Johnny. I wish you could know everything, Peter.' She drew her hand away, and instantly I wished she would touch me again.

'Tell me,' I said. 'Please.'

'Just promise you'll help. Do it blindly, don't ask why or when or anything else. Just think of Johnny, and promise.'

And so I did. I promised.

Honey's whisky-saturated body lay nearby. He had been snoring fitfully and now he began to mumble incoherently in the surly tones of a schoolboy. His legs kicked out and his fists jerked violently; his voice became compressed, pre-pubescent, demanding. I felt laughter well from within me, dancing from my stomach to my throat and I could not stop. Snow began to laugh too, her shoulders shaking. It was only when I had stopped to draw breath that I realised she was no longer laughing, but crying. I did not know what to do – my hands reached out to touch her, but I drew back. I wanted to gather her in my arms, to tell her that everything would be fine, that we'd soon be home, and don't be surprised if we end up having a wonderful holiday and come back with some bloody good stories to boot, now wouldn't that be fun? Instead, I put one hand timidly on her hair, afraid of frightening her from me. She wept without covering her face. She held her head high and looked me in the eye, strong and proud and beautiful. And I – I only watched her, tentatively pawing at her hair until she got up and left me alone on the tar-black sea.

I promise I promise I promise. It came *de profundis* and instinctively, just as she said, and with all the certainty in the world.

But I was not thinking of Johnny.

*

Gautama Buddha is said to have attained Enlightenment whilst sitting under the distinctive heart-shaped leaves of the bodhi tree, *Ficus religiosa*, whose gently spreading boughs and short, gnarled trunk makes for an especially attractive garden specimen. Nearly every Buddhist temple has *F. religiosa* planted somewhere in its grounds; one in Amarapura in Ceylon is said be two thousand years old. During my travels in Siam in the fifties I made a point of sitting under every such tree I happened upon. I would make offerings of prayer in the temples I visited; I would then search out the *Ficus* and settle in its shade, forcing my limbs into a cross-legged sitting position (the true 'lotus' was, I'm afraid, quite beyond the capabilities of my overly long occidental limbs). A period of meditation would follow, my mind emptying itself of its accumulated corruption in the serenity of the temple grounds. Mind and spirit cleansed, I would venture out into the streets to pollute myself again, knowing that another temple and its bodhi tree would not be far away. There is certainly something in the properties of that particular type of fig tree that lends itself to quiet contemplation. I have tried sitting under various trees of that genus – the banyan tree, *F. benghalensis*, for example, a spectacular colossus that dominates roadsides and river banks alike here in South-East Asia. Its aerial roots droop from its branches, sturdy as rope and strong enough for a small child to swing on. I once watched children in a village along the River Perak play all afternoon in precisely this manner, swinging from banyan vines that hung over the water and splashing into the treacly river. Though I sat cross-legged under the tree I could not settle: it did not cast its spell over me. The massive trunk is said to be the dwelling place of spirits, and I have often seen propitiatory offerings of fruit and flowers placed near it by pantheistic (well, superstitious) villagers, and yet it does not engender the calm that Buddha's fig tree does. It is too big and impersonal, a child's playground rather than an altar to the human spirit. No, the Buddha chose wisely.

He knew his trees, and I shall follow suit. I have marked out a spot for a bodhi tree in the far corner of the garden, away from all other plants and structures. I have sketched it into my plan, and I must say it looks rather splendid.

For scent, I will have another of my sentimental favourites: frangipani, or what the locals call *chempaka*. Nothing rivals the fragrance of the tropical garden. The smells of an English garden after a light June rain shower seem tragically reticent compared to the seductive perfumes of a single tropical flower such as the frangipani. Many times in the past I have found myself strolling in the evening and catching the first scents of this flower, released by the onset of darkness, when its odour is most compelling. I have marked it on my plan, dotted around the garden in sites where I think its balletic shape will be admired as much as its scent – next to the veranda where we sometimes take high tea, for example (imagine the smell of frangipani mingling with that of buttered toast and dry beef curry! O the champak odours, sweet thoughts in dreams!), or next to the proposed fish pond. I knew, of course, that having frangipani in the garden would not be popular with the other residents. '*Chempaka*?' Alvaro said, a frown of deep anxiety disturbing his normally placid sandstone features. 'We really can't have that here.'

'Why on earth not?' I said, knowing what the answer would be.

'It's the tree of death,' he said. 'Muslims plant it in their cemeteries.'

'Superstitious claptrap,' I said. 'This country is riddled with it. I'm surprised *you* of all people indulge in it, D'Souza.'

'It's not superstition,' he said earnestly, 'it's just – well, no one will like it. For whatever reason, they won't like it.'

'Rubbish. The Siamese at least have a decent excuse for not wanting it in their back gardens. Their word for *chempaka* is virtually the same as that for "sadness". But that doesn't stop them from planting it in monastery and temple gardens. The monks are above superstition. If it's good enough for devout Buddhists, then it's good enough for a bunch of ageing papists like us.'

'This is a Muslim country. If Muslims wouldn't do it then I don't think we should either.'

'Am I going mad? May I remind you that you're Roman Catholic – you aren't supposed to believe in this nonsense.'

'As I said, it's cultural.'

I knew it was hopeless arguing with him. Moreover, he is the most reasonable character in the house, and the others will be much more violent and nonsensical in their arguments; and so, with much reluctance, I have pencilled 'PROVISIONAL' in brackets next to the sites marked X: FRANGPN. I fully intend to erase these unsightly parentheses once the fuss has died down and the Tree of Death has been engulfed by the senile forgetfulness of this place. Stealth is the only way to survive here, and I must have my frangipani.

In Penang, shortly after the war, I once stood on the windswept shores near the Snake Temple, looking out at the choppy waters. It was early in the evening but there was still a faint glow of light from the sea. I wandered down some broken stone steps that led from the winding hilltop road to the beach, picking my way through a thicket of trees. I stumbled and fell and lost my way. When, finally, I emerged in a clearing I saw around me the slim, sinuous trunks of old frangipani trees. I looked around and realised that I had wandered into the ruins of a Muslim cemetery. I sat on the cracked, crumbling ramparts that encircled this burial ground and looked out to sea. The wind gusted gently and carried with it the thick scent of frangipani – sweet, heady, sad. I wept silently in the dark, letting the hot tears run down my face. I was not thinking of the war. I did not think of the three years I spent in prison in Changi – I had forgotten the beatings and the meals of watery rice porridge and the cigarettes made from rolled-up Japanese newspaper. I could barely recall the staring eyes and hollow cheeks of the men who died from dysentery and gangrene and sheer exhaustion. What were their names – Chapman? Le Fanu? Shepherd? I doubt I ever knew. I worked from sunrise to sundown and endured the torture as everyone else did, but that was not the end of it. I volunteered for extra work, taking the place of weakened compatriots. I surrendered my meagre rations to those dying of starvation. I did so willingly and refused to accept thanks. I spoke to no one; my suffering had already begun, and it was worse than anything the camp could inflict. The war was insufficient punishment for the things I had done; prison alone was not enough to expunge my sins. I barely felt the passing of those three years.

That was why I cried, sitting alone at the edge of the cemetery, infused with the scent of frangipani. I had not suffered enough; I had not atoned. Nothing could ever be enough.

*

I was seized by despair when I saw Johnny at work repairing the broken-down motor. There was something in the way his hands moved over each rusty bit of metal – cradling, cajoling, caressing – that suggested that salvation was imminent. We would soon be on our way, and the strange fleeting intimacy I shared with Snow the previous night would be lost for ever.

'Are you sure you know what you're doing, Johnny?' I said when I found us alone for a moment. 'It looks a frightfully complicated machine. You're not just guessing, are you? We don't want to land ourselves in more trouble.'

The pallor had lifted from his face and he seemed well again. His right shoulder lifted in a half-shrug and he returned to his work without speaking to me.

'I see, still in a mood. Fine. To be perfectly honest, I don't care to know what's wrong with you. I've stopped being concerned about your well-being. But I am concerned about *my* well-being and that of the others on this boat. All I ask of you is that you stop messing about with that machine and let Kunichika deal with it instead.'

He looked up, smirking with an ugly curled lip. I said, 'That doesn't become you.'

'I know.'

'Then don't do it.'

'I know,' he repeated, 'that you're still concerned about the well-being of the *others* on this boat.' His voice was mocking and hard.

'Look here, I've had enough of your nonsense,' I said, my face flushing with anger. 'You're a pathetic little child. Something troubles you – God only knows what, because you won't talk about it – and you deal with it by being thoroughly uncommunicative for days on end, surfacing only to pour vitriol on the ones closest to you. Let me tell you this. If I don't look out for you, who will? I know what Kunichika is up to – of course I do. I see it too.'

Again, that hard laugh. 'You see nothing,' he said, and returned to his work.

I left him and found a small triangle of shade cast by a stack of boxes. After a few minutes Kunichika sat down beside me. 'Strange thing, the sea,' he said, sighing as if with exhaustion. He seemed friendly and gently comic, resigned to a long wait.

'Is it?'

'Yes, it has a peculiar effect on the minds of men. It affects their thinking.'

'Really – how interesting. And women? Does the sea do funny things to them too?'

'I would think so, but sadly I have not had the opportunity to observe many women at sea.'

'Well, here's your chance to observe one at close quarters. A fine specimen, too, I'm sure you'll agree. Not that there's anything I could tell you about your new subject. Your students at the university will read your paper with the utmost interest, I'm sure.'

'What was all that about just now?' he said, his voice changing suddenly, becoming sharp and incisive.

'What?'

'You seemed to have had a very long discussion with Johnny.'

'Wasn't much of a discussion, I assure you.'

'An argument, then.'

'I'm afraid to disappoint, but it wasn't that either.'

'What did he tell you?'

'Ask him.'

He relaxed against the boxes once more, his body resuming its casual, weary posture. 'Sorry,' he said, 'I didn't mean to pry, I was just being inquisitive.'

'The strange effects of the sea, I expect.'

He smiled. 'You're good friends, aren't you? I think you mean a lot to Johnny.'

'Good friends? Not particularly. Have you got a cigarette?'

'I'm afraid not,' he said. 'Why do friends argue?'

'The strange effects of the sea,' I repeated.

'Perhaps. We're all very tired, I think.'

'Are we really going to find the Seven Maidens – or is this all going to end in disaster?'

'If we can get the boat moving, we'll find them.'

'You seem very certain of that.'

'You seem unusually pessimistic, Peter.'

'Those maps of yours – I had a look at them. They're very detailed, aren't they? I didn't think there were such maps of the straits.'

'Those maps are all we have,' he said, rising to his feet. He stood over me, blotting out the sun. 'Please don't interfere with my things.'

⋆

He was wrong. We did not find the Seven Maidens, they found us. We sailed into their shallow crystal waters as if we were lured there, guided by the wind and the invisible current into those sheltered shores, whose calm façade disguised Pandemonium, the place of demons. The serpentine curves of the talcum-white beaches, the coyly swaying palms and the soft deep cladding of forest – how were we to know that these were the high capital of Satan and his peers? We had been succoured, it seemed. We ate, we slept, we washed the fiery brine from our souls. We set off again, hope and vigour renewed. We did not know that we were sailing on a burning lake; we thought that we had found paradise but in truth we had already lost it.

It was the storm, I suppose, that first made me believe I had been thrown headlong into a tropical Eden. It appeared in the distance, heavenly and portentous, sweeping majestically towards us. 'Christ in Heaven,' I breathed, standing in awe before the advancing storm: lightning, racing in fissures across the sky; the exuberant *feu de joie* of thunder all around us. A frenzy of activity as we searched for life jackets; but we knew that there would be none. I stood with my face lifted to the sky, waiting for the waters from above to cleanse me. Snow ran across the deck, pushing past me. She paused for a half-second and looked at me with shining eyes. She too knew that our moment was at hand. I did not shy from my destiny but faced it squarely, surrendering myself to it. I opened my lungs to the drowning rain and began to sing.

'Bloody madman!' I heard Honey scream. I remained where I was and did not seek shelter. A moment before the storm hit the boat, I felt myself pulled to the deck, the aria from *Don Giovanni* stifled in my throat. It was Johnny, holding me powerfully by the waist as he tried to drag us both towards the hatch that led down below deck, down to safety. He was too late.

I once saw a picture by Jacob Epstein, a delicate pen and

watercolour study called *We Two Boys Together Clinging*. In it, two slender figures sway reed-like in the wind, their slim sexless bodies melding together to form a single arcing sinew set against the blue wash of the sky. The first time I saw it I stared so long, so intensely at it that the sky turned to a pool of water. The figures began to swim before me, inviting me to join them; the water seemed so close, so real that I could smell its cool moisture. I clung to Johnny and he to me as we fell into the boiling sea. We did not struggle to keep afloat; we merely held tightly to each other. The thunder and crash of the storm dulled to a mere drone as we were engulfed by a wave and dragged into the warm depths of the water. Over and over we spun. The sky and the bottom of the ocean no longer seemed at odds; I could not tell where I was. I clung to Johnny and tried, O God I tried, to hold him close to me, my only friend and anchor in this world, but then he too was lost. I let myself be taken by the sea, but it did not want me. I was rejected, pushed to the surface, gasping as I blinked into the dazzling sky. My chest burned as I coughed brine from my lungs. The storm was passing, but the waves were still tall and angry. I kicked hard and felt the strength in my arms. I searched for Johnny but could not see him. I called and called and called but there was nothing. Over the swell of a wave I glimpsed Kunichika, swimming powerfully with his head above the water. I shouted for him but he did not pause. I struck out to find him and then, in a valley of waves, I saw Snow, her head struggling to break the surface of the water. I screamed her name, my voice ringing more loudly and clearly than I had ever known it. The sea bore me to her, each wave carrying me on its crest until I reached her. I swam easily; my chest expanded in song as I lifted her and eased her on to my back. 'Don't leave me,' she called out weakly. She put her arms around my neck and held tightly as I swam back to the boat; her face was pressed to my neck, and in my ear I heard her gasping whisper: 'Why?'

I did not reply. How could I explain the strange workings of fate? I was meant to save her, to bear her over the waves on my own body. All the time I sang to her, my voice carrying over the flattening waves. *Vieni, mio bel diletto*. There was no reason, my treasure. This was simply the way we were meant to be.

*

A heated little debate took place over dinner this evening. I unveiled the latest plan of the garden, complete with sketches of the various plants I intend to use. There was the usual bewildered lack of interest at first, but then Brother Rodney happened to walk past my table. 'What funny-looking things you have there,' he said en passant, raising his voice and enunciating his words as if speaking to a deaf imbecile. 'I don't recognise any of them.'

I did not dignify this with a reply. After he had gone Alvaro said, 'I agree, Peter. Most of the plants aren't familiar to us – perhaps you could use more ordinary things?'

Gecko and the others nodded in ignorant acquiescence. I struggled to contain my anger. For some weeks now, this endeavour has consumed every waking moment, and quite possibly every sleeping one too. 'I do not believe,' I began calmly, 'that you appreciate quite how much effort has gone into this garden. The reconstruction of a paradisaical place requires imagination far beyond that which you lot could muster. It requires belief and passion and intellect – none of which you seem to possess.'

'Oh no, of course we appreciate your work,' Alvaro said, using his best placatory voice. 'We were just thinking about the practicality of this arrangement. These plants all seem quite exotic to me – where are we going to get them from? Wouldn't it be simpler to use ordinary *native* plants?'

I drew a deep breath and sat erect in my chair. 'Native?' I said, my voice authoritative but kind. 'Let me explain to you what "native" means. A great many of the plants that we commonly take to be native to the Malay archipelago were in fact brought here by early colonisers,' I explained, trying to remain calm. Christopher Columbus was given a bristly cone-shaped fruit by the people of Guadaloupe when he visited them in the fifteenth century; it reminded the Spanish of pine cones, so they called it *piña*, yes, the pineapple, which now fills acre after shabby acre in the flatlands all around us. (Gasps of surprise and exclamations of 'Are you sure? Did it really come from – what's that place called again?') More recently, in the late nineteenth century, *Hevea brasiliensis*, the rubber tree, came from Brazil via Kew and changed the fortunes of this tinpot little country. (Cries of 'That's not fair – we had other things besides rubber, you know, damn you Britishers.') Oil palm from Africa, chillies from Mexico – what would our lives be without these *exotics*? Personally, I would be very glad never to eat another mouth-burning bird's-eye chilli for the rest of my life, which incidentally, I hope will not be very long; but I dare say that much of this country's cuisine would become extinct if chilli was eradicated from the menu. (Much head-shaking and general grumbling.) And as for flowers, well, where do we begin?

'Bougainvillea,' someone said, 'that's a nice flower – and definitely native. Why can't we just have that on the verandah, instead of this – what is this thing?' he pulled my sketch towards him. '*Pa-ssi-flo-ra*.'

'Bougainvillea,' I said, stressing the French vowels. 'Does it sound like a Malay name to you? Brought here from Brazil by Louis Antoine de Bougainville. So sorry to disappoint. Why should we have passion flower? Because it's perfectly suited to this climate. It's bolder than bougainvillea and doesn't shed its petals like cheap confetti. And since we are, after all, living in a house run by the church, I thought it fitting that we should have a flower that reminds us of the crown of thorns. Every time we take tea we shall look at it and think of Christ's suffering.'

Quiet, uncertain glances.

'*Bunga raya*,' Gecko said. 'That's our national flower, so you can't goddam tell us that's not native.'

'Most botanists think that particular strain of hibiscus originated from China, hence its common name, Chinese rose. No one knows for sure, though, but who cares? It looks like some strange half-evaginated hermaphrodite genitalia, gloriously labial with a thin stamen that droops like a failed phallus – the whole thing desperately vulgar.'

Uproar.

'OK, OK, OK,' Alvaro said, emollient as ever, 'I'm sure Peter's only joking. Aren't you, Peter?'

'Of course,' I said. 'I was only trying to illustrate a point.'

'And what was your point?'

I sighed. 'That things thought of as native aren't always what they seem, and that we shouldn't be constrained by ideas of what belongs where. Some might say, for example, that since this is where I have lived for almost three-quarters of my life, *I* may be considered native.'

A deep silence fell over the table. I thought that perhaps finally I had won my battle. But then a chair scraped against the floor and an obese old troll stood up. Errol was his name; I had barely spoken to him in the past. 'You are not native,' he said, his fat voice suffused with grease. 'You just go *fuck off* back home.'

As I left the room I heard Alvaro playing umpire amid the mêlée. 'OK, OK, calm down,' he said as I walked along the darkened corridor back to my room, where I sat alone before the open shutters. The sea breeze had calmed and the air in the room was still. I lit a mosquito coil and placed it by my bed to keep the tiny winged vampires away. In the dark I could not see the flotsam that lay scattered on the grey, muddy sea. At night only the light of fishing boats is visible on the purple-black waters, and the sea almost looks beautiful. I lay down on my bed, watching the jewelled specks of light on the faint horizon. I did not fall asleep for quite some time.

*

There was nothing this island could not offer us. The forest was rich with wild mango, custard apple, breadfruit and coconut. Huge shoals of tiny silvery fish shimmered in the shallows; they did not swim away when we cast our net over them, but swum lazily in different directions, flashing iridescent in the sun.

'This placc is very strange,' Johnny said. 'It's an island, but somehow doesn't feel like an island.' We were out walking together, exploring the low shoulder of hills that rose above the sheltered bay in which we had camped.

'What on earth do you mean?' I laughed.

'I don't know,' he shrugged. 'The trees, the streams – everything seems perfect but wrong. It feels as if we could live here for ever and yet . . . oh, I don't know.'

'I expect you're still exhausted after the storm – and everything else,' I said. He looked better now, and his humour had improved immeasurably. He looked fit again, walking ahead of me on the cool damp forest trails. His eyes were shadowed by dark circles of fatigue, it was true, but his limbs had recovered their litheness, and his stride was calm and steady.

'I don't like the sea,' he said, 'I can't swim.'

'I can certainly testify to that.'

'Last thing I remembered,' he said, turning to look at me with a faint smile, 'you weren't doing so well yourself.'

'Oh the cheek of it!' I cried as we negotiated a slippery uphill path. 'The cheek of it, the cheek of it. I was enjoying standing on the deck. Don't you know the laws of physics don't apply to me? I would have withstood anything that storm could have thrown at me. Like Idomeneo, I would have survived even if we had been shipwrecked. My catlike reflexes would have seen me through – but no, you came hurtling towards me, determined to spoil the moment.'

'Sorry,' he laughed, 'you were whimpering like a madman. What was I supposed to think?'

'I wasn't whimpering, my dear boy, I was *singing*.'

'Sounded like whimpering to me.' As he turned to look at me he stumbled on a small rock; his foot scraped a long angry scar on the mud as he slipped and fell, landing heavily on his right elbow.

'Good God, are you all right?' I said, crouching by him. 'You haven't twisted your ankle, have you?'

'No, it's my shoulder that hurts,' he said, breathing heavily. He cradled his arm to his body as if it were a dying animal. 'Funny – I must have landed awkwardly.'

'Look at you: how are the mighty fallen. This wouldn't have happened if you'd had my mountain goat's agility,' I said. 'Come on, we'd better head back to the camp.'

'No, I'm all right. We must try and find a good supply of fresh water. It's important.'

'You don't look in any state to continue,' I said firmly. He was still sitting on the muddy path, shaken and weak once more.

'I'll manage,' he said, raising a smile. 'Besides, Kunichika and Honey are out on a search too, and we don't want them to beat us to it.'

I laughed. 'That's a good point, but not good enough for you to go charging off. You should be back in camp nursing a stiff drink.'

'I'm fine,' he insisted. 'I want to continue.' The familiar flash of stubbornness returned to his eyes, but his arm was still held awkwardly, as if any movement of it might cause pain.

'How about this for a compromise?' I said. 'I'll go on a quick reconnaissance, just till the brow of that next hill. If I do see something I'll come back for you, otherwise we shall head straight back to camp.'

He looked dubious, but nodded solemnly. 'Look carefully, Peter,' he said as I set off. 'There's water nearby, I can sense it.'

'Yes, yes,' I called as I strode away. Of course I had every intention of dashing quickly to the top of the hill and then returning with the disappointing news that no stream had crossed my path. The terrain proved to be more difficult than I expected, however. The trail soon disappeared in a tangle of roots and foliage, and though I managed to regain it, some time later it vanished again, washed away by recent rains. The trees closed in around me, the broken cover of leaves becoming a thick canopy. I did not panic, but kept moving in a straight line. I had fixed the position of the next hill in my mind's eye, and trusted my instincts to find my way there; not once did I feel that I was cut off from Johnny. The calm of the jungle impressed itself upon me, and I resolved to forget all that had happened before our arrival on this island – the storm, the rescue, everything. The sea *did* encourage madness among men, and women too. We all said things we did not mean; we were not ourselves when we spoke. Now, with solid ground under my feet, I knew better. Where was Snow, and what was she doing at that precise moment? I didn't know: I hadn't thought of her for a moment since arriving here. Such was the lucidity with which I was thinking that when I saw the first of the stones emerge from the forest before me, I merely paused to examine them. They were ancient and monumental, that much was clear, but still I did not rush to conclude what they might once have been. I was measured and calm throughout, testing the accuracy of my senses by touching every stone I saw. I followed the broken trail of stones until finally I saw it: a perfect tropical ruin, rising proudly from the jungle as if emerging from the pages of a dusty antiquarian lithograph. I walked around the ravaged, crumbling wall that guarded the perimeter of the tenebrous building. *Che veduta*: Piranesi could have spent a lifetime sketching this place. The ruinous state of the structure rendered it unidentifiable. A temple or a dwelling place? The creeping vines had long since claimed it as their own; epiphytic plants, some bearing grotesquely shaped flowers, sprouted from every crack in the once-magnificent masonry. Wasn't it Aldous Huxley who likened tropical botany to late and decadent Gothic architecture? I had never truly believed him until now. Roots and stems and arching leaves so shrouded the stone structure that they ceased to become mere ornamentation; without them the building would surely collapse.

Remembering Johnny, I resisted the urge to venture inside the building, and began to make my way back. Retracing my steps proved impossible. Nothing seemed familiar; all landmarks had vanished into the jungle. The blackened stump of a tree felled by lightning was nowhere to be seen, the egg-shaped boulder had camouflaged itself amid the undergrowth. I sought higher ground, thinking that this would at least afford me a view of how hopelessly lost I was. I pushed my way through the unyielding trees, my arms becoming lacerated by invisible razor-thin whips. My progress was not encouraging: the topography of the land suddenly conspired to be flat and densely forested. Finally, however, a gentle incline offered itself to me, and I began to see the clear glint of sunlight at the top of a hillock. When I reached its summit I found myself surveying a shallow valley. A stream ran through this clearing, its banks lined thickly with gentle spikes of elephant grass and umbrellas of wild banana. And in the water there were two naked figures, Snow and Kunichika. I crouched low and watched them paddle in the water. He cut through it like a straight sharp knife whilst she splashed tentatively, occasionally arching her neck backwards to feel the cool of the water on her hair. She let the stream carry her to where it was deepest and darkest, allowing herself to be borne gently away before splashing back; he never seemed to venture far from the shallows, where the current was at its gentlest. Against the black water their skins glowed with an eerie luminescence. Pure white? No, it was beyond colour. They approached each other and he lifted his hands to her face. I turned away, my face hot, temples pulsing. I ran down the hill, letting instinct guide me through the trees. I had to get back to Johnny.

He was sitting on a tree stump watching me as I ran back up the path. 'You took a very long time,' he said. 'I was worried. I nearly went out searching for you.'

'Sorry,' I coughed, 'I got slightly lost on the way back. I'll exchange my agility for your sense of direction, I think.'

'Did you see anything?'

'No,' I said. 'No water. I searched, though – that was why I was so long, I remembered what you said. But no, I didn't find water.'

'That's strange,' he said, as we began to head back to our tiny spartan camp. 'I can feel it close by. Just instinct, that's all.'

'Yes, well, I looked. But I did find a ruin. I think it may be a temple.'

He raised an eyebrow, a trait of mine he had begun to imitate. 'A ruin?'

'You shall see for yourself soon enough.'

We wandered slowly through the trees, pointing out birds – little black-and-white hornbills and iridescent flycatchers – and chatting about books he wanted to read. 'I wish I could read Dickens,' he said, 'as Snow does.'

'Why can't you?'

'I tried, it's too difficult.'

'Some day soon I'm sure you'll learn to appreciate it.'

He smiled and shook his head. He was looking very tired again. 'I am resigned to certain things.'

As we approached the camp I reached to touch him on his shoulder. 'I meant to thank you. The storm. I mean, I was foolish, I know. So. Thank you for . . .'

He shrugged. 'For what? Look how we ended up.' His attempt at a smile was not convincing.

'We're here, aren't we? And alive, too, I should add.'

'I suppose,' he said, as we walked into the camp. The broken shade of the casuarinas and sea almonds cast snakeskin patterns on his face; his voice had become papery and dry, like the dead leaves that lay scattered on the sandy soil.

This island of abundance would erase the events of the past days, and we would start anew. That is what I believed, and for a whilst I was proved right.

'Isn't it strange,' I said to Snow, 'how one can forget something as awful as that storm we encountered? It's only been a few days and already the memory of it is devoid of terror. I can recall the events, of course, but I can't feel anything. Funny, isn't it, how the human mind works?'

'We humans have a remarkable capacity to disguise emotions,' she replied, drawing lazily in her notebook. 'We suppress feelings, we force ourselves to forget things until, finally, we truly believe those things never existed.' We were sitting in the confines of our camp after breakfast, sheltering from the sun. I reclined on the sand, propping myself up on my elbows as I chatted to her.

'Such cynicism in one so pure,' I said. 'Do you really think so?'

'Of course. It's how we survive, isn't it?'

'You're right, of course. I mean, let's take the storm as an example. I remember being washed overboard; I can remember, clearly, being battered by the waves, swallowing gallons of water – I can still taste the salt at the back of my throat, but can I recall the terror? No, not really. Similarly, I can remember surfacing once the squall had passed, and I can remember seeing you, but as for how I felt: nothing! The elation of being alive, intense as it was then, no longer exists. I've simply forgotten. Of course I remember carrying you back to the boat, but I'm afraid I draw a blank as far as emotions are concerned.'

She closed her book and said, 'I've forgotten too.'

'Quite.'

'What about death?' she said.

'You mean: would I forget a person once he's passed on?'

'Exactly. Their face – their image – would stay with you, of course. You'd remember how they looked. The details may become vague, but you'd still remember. Just like a photograph. In your mind's eye, you'd be able to recreate all their habits – the way they slept, how they ate: everything. But would you remember how you felt about them? And how they felt about you?'

I returned her gaze and tried not to blink. 'No. I don't think so.'

'Nor would I,' she said. 'Death, I believe, erases everything. It erases all traces of the life that once existed, completely and for ever. Of course we help it in its task – we're the ones who do the forgetting.'

'I couldn't argue with you.'

Her notebook rested on her knee. She tapped it with her pen as she gazed into the distance.

'You write every day, don't you?' I said. 'You're religious about it.'

'Just aimless scribbles, nothing much. A woman's frivolity,' she laughed. Although she sat casually on the sand, her head and neck were held with such poise that I felt round-shouldered and shabby, a dirty schoolboy dressed for games. 'Besides,' she added, 'it passes the time.' With that, she picked up her pen and opened her book.

I was almost out of earshot when I heard her call my name. 'I meant to ask: how's Johnny?'

'Fine,' I said. 'He's fine.'

I walked the length of the beach, heading towards a rocky headland in the distance. By the time I sat down on the barnacle-clad rocks I already knew that I would steal her diary.

*

On the way back from my wondrous ruin I ran into Johnny and Honey. 'Hello,' said Johnny, 'I've been looking for you. Where have you been?' His voice was flat and bare of inflection, and his question hardly sounded like one.

'I've been at the ruin,' I said. 'You?'

'Just chatting,' said Honey. 'We were both out searching for some food for dinner this evening – I'm tired of tinned stew – and we literally bumped into each other. All the paths in this place seem to intersect a dozen times. I was just saying to Johnny that I'm sure they all lead to the same place. You agreed, didn't you, Johnny?'

'Yes.'

'I'd never have thought of you as a hunter-gatherer, Honey,' I said. 'What have you found?'

'Nothing yet, but I'm sure something will turn up. Johnny was going to teach me how to set snares for birds.'

'You seem very bloodthirsty, Honey,' I said. 'Won't fish do for dinner?'

'Fish and rice may do nicely for those of you who *go native*,' he said, 'but I have a craving for a decent cut of meat. Anyway, I must be off. Hunting and gathering, you know.' He crashed through the narrow path heading back to the camp.

'Come on,' I said to Johnny, 'I want to show you something. At the ruin.'

'Some other time, maybe,' he said. 'I'm a bit tired.'

'You weren't too tired to go off a-hunting with Frederick Honey.'

He remained silent; he blinked several times but his eyes stared vacantly as if incapable of focusing.

'Come on,' I urged, taking him by his arm, 'a gentle walk will do you no harm. There's something I'd like you to see. No one else knows about it yet – I want to keep it a secret, but I want *you* to see it.'

He nodded and tried to smile, but it seemed as if the faint frown that had settled on his face held his features in too tight a grip; his brow remained locked, his eyes were dead and dark, his mouth drawn thinly as if smirking. No laugh could break through that cladding; fatigue had imprinted itself on his face. He trailed after me without saying a word until we reached the ruin.

'I don't see what's so interesting about this place,' he said.

'I seem to be the only one on this island to appreciate the beauty of abandoned buildings. A ruin resonates with the lives of the people who once lived there. Just shut up and follow me, will you?'

'But it's just a pile of rocks. Why do you spend so much time here?' he said as I scrambled down a bank to a clearing on the edge of the forest behind the ruin. He remained standing above me, hands obstinately on hips.

Containing my impatience, I said, 'Being an aesthete, I am always hungry for beauty. You wouldn't understand this.'

'I've noticed this hunger.'

'So has everyone. I don't hide it.'

'But maybe there's something else they haven't seen about you?'

'*Something else*? What – like that something you were sharing with Honey just now?'

He made his way down the sloping bank and fell in step with me as I headed for the trees; we did not speak until we were in the broken shade. 'This is it,' I said. My earlier enthusiasm had dissolved into the afternoon heat. We stood in the middle of the irregular-shaped clearing I had made – created – over the past few afternoons. I had brought down saplings with a machete, slashed away the shrubby undergrowth and broken off the lower branches, cutting a view towards the ruin and the dirty brook that ran beside it. I worked vigorously, singing as I heaved and perspired in the jungle's hot hammam, but now it seemed that love's labour was lost. The clearing no longer seemed as clean and virginal as it had when I left it: its boundaries were obscure, encroached by plants that seemed to have crept into its confines overnight. Outlines of dead logs I hauled away remained impressed on the damp earth, scarring the ground with their funereal shapes. Broken branches littered the place I had worked so hard to cleanse, and above us the canopy of leaves suddenly seemed more opaque than ever.

'What's that?' Johnny said, pointing at a shady corner.

'A few things I brought with me,' I said, shuffling over to the small parcel I had left under a bush. 'Some wine, knives and forks, one or two dishes. Most of them were broken in the storm.'

'Peter,' he said, fixing me with a squinting look of incomprehension. 'Why did you bring this here? And your luggage – you must have had no room for your clothes. What's this, you brought *wine*?'

I shrugged and surveyed the sorry assembly of dull silver and cracked china. Against the dark foliage and muddy soil they looked silly, a still life long abandoned by its painter.

Johnny said, 'Peter, this is wonderful.'

'It seems a waste of effort, doesn't it?'

'No, it's magnificent,' he said, placing great stress on the second syllable. When he did so I recognised that it was the way I pronounced the word. 'Why did you do it?'

'I really don't know. It seemed a good idea at the time. I had visions of a rather romantic holiday – a backdrop of steaming tropical forest, beautiful servants waiting at the table, crystal glasses, laughter and merriment, music. I wanted a celebration. Instead, we have this,' I said, looking around me, 'this abject failure. Rather fitting, I think. You see, it's my birthday tomorrow. Or the day after – I've lost count. It doesn't seem to matter now.'

We remained silent for some time, fatigued, I think, by the

intense afternoon heat. Then Johnnny said, 'I want to tell you something. I don't care if you repeat it or not – as you say, nothing seems to matter now. But all the same I want you to know it. It's about Kunichika. He has given me a choice. He knows, Peter, he knows. He knows everything about me – what I do away from the shop. He knows about the people I meet, the places I go to, the things I say. He knows what I believe in.'

'How?' I said weakly.

'I don't know. Someone must have told him. I have been betrayed. You were right, Peter – I will never know who my friends are in this valley. It must have been someone who wants something from Kunichika. Who? I don't know. Could be anyone. Kunichika can give anyone anything they want. To me, he has given a simple choice. It is more than anyone else will ever get from him. If I choose correctly, if I help the Japanese, I will have everything I desire. They will protect me. I will be richer than TK Soong, richer than anyone in the valley, more powerful. If. But if not, then I lose everything I have. My shop, certainly, but also my wife.'

'And you already know what you are going to do.'

He sat down on the ground, resting his back against a tree stump. 'There is no way ahead for me.' He smiled.

I said, 'Principles are one thing, survival is another.'

'Survival,' he said, chuckling as if chancing upon a novel idea. 'Do you know what will happen to me if I collaborate with the Japanese?'

'No one need ever know.'

'I will always know, Peter,' he said, a thin smile settling on his features. 'And you will always know.'

I looked at him and tried to recall the face I had first seen in Singapore. It was still there, obscured by the lines of doubt and fear, but there nonetheless. 'Listen,' I said. 'When we get back to the valley we shall sit tight and let Kunichika make the first move.

If it looks as if the Japanese will invade, you shall come with me to Singapore. There we shall ensconce ourselves in the disgusting opulence of the Raffles Hotel, where we shall sit listening to the firing of British guns whilst sipping pink gins.'

He laughed and shook his head. 'That may work for you but not for me.'

'Why on earth not – don't you like pink gin?'

'I've never had one. Is it nice?' he said, his face breaking into a broad smile. 'Do you think Chinese people are allowed to drink it too?'

'You were made for pink gin. I've never been so certain of anything in my whole life.'

'It'll be your fault if I don't like it.'

'Don't worry, you'll adore it.'

'Thanks.'

'I'm serious, Johnny. I shall take you with me, wherever I go. You'll be safe with me. God knows there are some privileges of being British.'

He laughed and shook his head.

'You poor bastard,' I said. 'You really have been sick, haven't you?'

He didn't reply, but leaned forward and rested his forehead on his arm. I could not see his face.

'Don't think about it, Johnny. Kunichika's nothing.'

He was breathing very heavily, and when he spoke his voice was quiet. 'I'm not afraid of that. It's Snow I'm worried about.'

'What?'

'I'm resigned to losing her.'

'You silly creature,' I said, 'I told you to forget about Kunichika – he'll move on. You won't lose her to him.'

'Not him,' he said, *diminuendo*. 'You.'

I did not answer. I sat on the moist soil next to him, legs crossed uncomfortably.

'At first I was angry,' he said, without bitterness. 'I saw you talking to her. You spoke so freely, and she to you. I knew I would never be able to speak to her like that. But now I think – perhaps it's better for her. Who wants to be the wife of a communist? When the Japanese invade it'll be the end for me, however I choose. If she is not with me, at least with you she will be safe.'

'Please don't speak like this.'

'Just promise me, Peter. Whatever I choose to do, you know that I am finished. Please look after her.'

'You aren't finished. Nothing will happen to either of you. You will both be with me in Singapore.'

'Look after her. Promise. Swear it to me.'

I did. We sat staring up at the impenetrable forest.

After a whilst he said, 'This is a nice spot for a party.'

'You don't think it's too small, do you?'

'No, but it could do with a tidy-up.'

'That's easy enough.'

'I don't mind that you love her,' he said calmly.

I paused and looked him in the eye. 'Johnny, Johnny,' I said. 'I'm very fond of Snow but I don't love her.' I don't know why I lied.

He put his hands over his face and began to cry. There was nothing I could do to console him. I put my arm around his shuddering shoulders but he would not stop. He cried in a thin wail that cut my insides to shreds; it ran through the trees, filling the jungle with its noise. To this day I can hear its shrill soliloquy, reciting in my head. It comes to me at night, when all is quiet and I can feel nothing but pain.

*

'The best thing about the tropics,' I said as I watered the orchids, 'is that the seasons never change. There are the monsoons, of course, but there's never a time when the garden becomes a frozen graveyard. We don't have to worry about dead leaves littering our perfect lawns or the ornamental ponds freezing over.'

'I think autumn in England is very beautiful,' said Gecko without looking up from his newspaper, 'I've seen pictures of it, the mountains all covered in red leaves. Very nice.'

'I think you mean *New* England,' I said, knowing that the latest issue of the *National Geographic* contained a photographic feature on the people of Vermont and their ghastly *faux-naïf* clapboard houses. 'That's in America.'

Alvaro put down his paper and took off his glasses to look at me. I was hanging the last of the orchids on the ceiling of the verandah. I had bought them from the market early that morning – ten little clay pots, each bearing a different specimen. Hanging from the low eaves, they formed a half-curtain that ameliorated the view of the as yet barren lawn. 'I must confess,' he said, with none of the contrition of a confessional, 'that I have always wanted to go to England in the winter. There's something about the cold weather that's always fascinated me. Frosty air seems so mysterious. Sometimes it gets too hot here, you know, just too damn bloody hot and I wish I could just fly away to somewhere cold. People are nicer in cold countries, aren't they? More civilised.'

'I shan't disabuse you of that notion,' I said. 'If you're ever unlucky enough to find yourself in an English winter you will quickly learn the truth for yourself.'

'Oh look,' Gecko trilled, straightening his newspaper for emphasis. 'That man has died, the one everyone said was a gangster. Johnny Lim – look, there's an obituary and a little article too.'

'Don't slander him – he was a war hero, you know. Where's the article?' Alvaro said, flicking through the pages of his own paper. 'Ah, here. "The famous business tycoon and community figure Johnny Lim passed away yesterday aged 77. Mr Lim was a highly respected member of the community in Ipoh and the

Kinta Valley. His trading company the Harmony Silk Factory became well known throughout the country, but although its interests became diversified, it remained faithful to its roots. In the fifty years that Mr Lim ran the company, it never left its original site on the banks of the River Perak, where it was once the centre of commercial activity in the Kinta Valley. Mr Lim set up the Harmony Silk Factory towards the end of the Second World War, defying the Japanese authorities, and established what would quickly become the most prominent privately owned business concern in the valley. No other company flourished as the Harmony Silk Factory did under the Japanese. Most observers attribute its success to Mr Lim's bravery in facing the Japanese, particularly the chief administrator of the Kempeitai, or secret police, Kunichika Mamoru, the so-called 'Demon of Kampar'. The two men had numerous meetings during which it is believed Kunichika attempted to coerce the respected community leader to aid in Japanese military efforts. These meetings were fruitless, and the two men established an uncomfortable respect for each other, one that saved the Harmony Silk Factory and its workers from the fate that befell many other Chinese businesses during the war. Rumours of Mr Lim's collaboration with the Kempeitai were rife but never substantiated.

'"Mr Lim was the son-in-law of the scholar and industrialist TK Soong, who died during internment by the Japanese during the war. Many believe he was a victim of summary executions ordered by Kunichika. Mr Lim married Snow, the only daughter of TK and Patti Soong. She died in childbirth in 1942; they had one son, Jasper, who survives Mr Lim. The funeral will be held at the Harmony Silk Factory on Monday 17th."'

Gecko said, 'That doesn't tell you anything about the man. It doesn't say he was a communist, for example.'

'Nor does it give you details about his heroism in the war,' said Alvaro.

'Or that he was a goddam collaborator. I don't suppose it matters now,' said Gecko, 'it was so long ago.'

'Peter, did you ever come across Johnny Lim?' Alvaro said. 'You spent a lot of time in Perak just before the war, didn't you? I remember you saying that you knew the Kinta Valley quite well.'

'He's an Englishman,' Gecko said. 'Englishmen didn't mix with local people back then.'

I poured water on to a flame-coloured orchid, watching beads of moisture collect on its sinuous leaves. 'No,' I said, 'I never knew him.' I put the watering can on the table and went back to my room.

*

I was determined that my birthday party would be a riotous success. Johnny and I spent many hours clearing the chosen site of debris. With a shovel and a pickaxe we flattened the smallest undulations on the surface of the soil; we filled in depressions and poured sand on to the boggiest patches of earth. Straggly shrubs were cut down and all offending weeds hacked to the ground with Johnny's parang. We assembled a camp table which we brought from the boat, placing it so that each diner would have a view of the ruin. With surprising ease, Johnny built a rudimentary but perfectly sturdy bench with some logs he found. We talked about the kinds of food the jungle could offer us – some root vegetables, possibly an edible flower or two, fish from the sea in abundance. Other animals, we decided, would not be on the menu. Birds were too difficult to snare, Johnny said, and the only mammal we had seen was an anaemic macaque sitting dejectedly in a seaside tree. Johnny was certain, however, that snakes and lizards could be easily caught. He drew pictures in the sand of the simple traps he would use, and assured me of the delicacy of such prey; but my stomach instantly felt uncomfortable at the thought of a reptilian dinner (*mon dieu: civet de vipère!*) and I convinced him that we did not need such exotic meat. I showed him the bag of flour that I had found among our rations.

'What are you going to do with that?' he asked.

'I shall make bread,' I announced.

'How?'

'I honestly don't know,' I replied, watching him convulse with laughter.

All this time no more was said about Kunichika.

The day before the party I left Johnny at the site. I said, 'I've left something back at the camp, something I need – a damask tablecloth I've brought with me in my luggage. Do you mind terribly if I retrieve it? I shan't be gone long.'

'You go ahead, there's something I need to do here anyway,' he said, somewhat hesitantly. For a moment I wondered if I should abandon my plan, but I held my nerve. *Courage, mon brave*. 'See you later,' I said.

I ran back to the camp, gambling that Snow would not be there. It was a foolhardy thing to do, but I had to have her diary. I had seen her embark on a walk with Kunichika earlier, and since their strolls tended to be long and leisurely, there was every chance that they would not have returned. I slowed to walking pace as I approached the camp, shortening my stride to appear as casual as possible. Who knows – Honey may have been lurking. I paused, listening for sounds of movement, but there was nothing. I sauntered into the camp, hearing the soft slush of my feet on the sand.

'Peter,' a voice called. It was Kunichika, kneeling beside Snow's camp bed. His knees were buried in the soft sand but he held his torso erect, hands on hips. He spoke in a bright and over-friendly voice. 'I thought you were off somewhere with Johnny.'

'I forgot something. What are you doing over there?'

'I forgot something too. It seems to have gone missing, and I'm searching for it.'

'Where's Snow?'

'She's bathing – on her own.'

'I thought you two went for a walk.'

'We did. How did you know – have you been spying?'

'I might ask you the same question.'

He stood up, and I noticed again that we were well matched in height. I said, 'I know what you're up to.'

He laughed, crumpling his face into his chest as if defeated by exhaustion. 'You're a real joker,' he said. 'I've never met anyone as amusing as you.'

'I'm watching you. I know.'

He looked me straight in the face with cold eyes, black beads set in white stone. 'What has Johnny told you? That man's a liar, you know. His own people don't trust him.'

'If you must know, Johnny has hardly said a word to me since we came on this trip. But you've got me interested now – is there something he ought to be telling me?'

'No. I should just warn you that he is not what he appears to be.'

I moved half a step closer to him. 'Who is?' I said, before walking away with my cheeks hot and my eyes swimming with brightly coloured shapes.

When I arrived back at the little clearing by the ruin I stopped and stared above me. 'Good God,' I breathed. Fluttering overhead was a white sheet, suspended in mid-flight as a mystical rug in some strange oriental myth. It captured the thin streams of light that broke through the foliage, intensifying them in the small area above the table.

'Do you like it?' he asked. A half-smile illuminated his face. Behind him, the murky backdrop of foliage framed him as if including him in a narcotic, half-dream landscape, a Giorgione canvas.

'The word "paradise",' I said, 'comes from the ancient Persian word for "garden". Did you know that?'

He shook his head. 'It's easy to see why we used their word,' he said.

'Really? I've never seen any similarity between backyard allotments and the Garden of Eden. I've never been fully convinced.'

'Oh.'

'But this is different. This truly is a garden.' I looked up above me once more. I wanted to say, 'Thank you, Johnny,' but I didn't; there was no need for it.

The wine was too much for me. It colluded with the heat and worked its insidious way into my blood. There it became infused with the poison that ran thickly throughout my body; my limbs became leaden, my head light as yarn on a weaver's spindle. My vision dazzled with the colours of richly shot silk; above me the sky was a tentative white canopy. Every time I looked at Kunichika he was leaning over to Snow, hissing sweet nothings in her ear, looking at me with a slow, sly, sideways leer. The execrable remnants of our meal lay on the table, filling the air with its fetid odour. The two halves of the hunk of bread I had baked (in my 'Mongolian oven', a small mud kiln Johnny had built) lay at the heart of this devastation. Its damp lumpen texture began to harden in the hot air, crusting scab-like on the surface.

'That was delicious,' Snow said.

'No, it was truly awful,' I said quickly before Honey had a chance to do so. Humiliation is always more bearable if inflicted by oneself. 'Tasted of vinegar and hyssop.'

'Not at all, it was a lovely surprise,' Kunichika said, a smile tearing his face slowly in two. I lowered my face and rubbed my aching temples with my fingers. Under my breath I could hear my incoherent, mumbling voice. What was I trying to say? There was nothing to do, I thought, but sing.

Là ci darem la mano,
là mi dirai di sì.
Vedi, non è lontano;
partiam, ben mio, da qui.

Yes, my dear, come with me, let's leave this place. I looked up and saw Snow's flushed face smiling intensely; her wine-glazed eyes were moist and reddened, her face damp with perspiration. Kunichika continued to speak to her, the low rumble of his voice playing *sostenuto* in my ears. I continued to sing: *I fear I will be deceived.*

'Why are you singing Zerlina's part, Peter?' Kunichika said politely. 'Why are you playing the woman's role?'

'So that you can sing your part – your true part. Come on, sing; you know the words.'

Snow laughed. Kunichika spoke his words slowly in unaccented but articulate Italian. '*Io cangierò tua sorte*,' he said. 'I will change your fate.'

I sang again, falsetto, my voice cracking and ugly. *I can resist no longer.*

He spoke again, entreating us all into his lair.

I stood up and walked away from the table, stumbling towards the ruin. *Misera me, misera me.*

I sat down on the broken stone steps and began to weep. I closed my eyes, a sea of silk shimmering before me. I stepped on to the water and began to sink into its voluptuousness. I was weak and there was nothing I could do.

When I awoke it was dark and I could taste the bitter furriness of food and wine in my mouth. My shoulder was stiff and aching where I had fallen asleep; I could still feel the poison of the alcohol in my blood and I sank to the ground again.

A voice said, 'Feeling sick? So you should. That was a nasty little performance you gave just now.' It was Honey, sitting on the step above me, smoking a cigarette.

'Go away.'

'No, I rather like being out here,' he said. 'You see all manner of things in the jungle at night.'

'Just bugger off.'

'Language,' he said, lighting a cigarette. 'I'm only now discovering just how vicious you can be. You're a right little vixen, aren't you? How pathetic. An attention-seeking, misguided child, that's what you are.'

I heaved myself into a sitting position. My head convulsed with pain.

'What do you think she thinks of you? Do you think she even notices you leering at her?'

'I haven't a clue what you mean. Please leave me alone. I don't feel well.'

'She loathes you. She finds you faintly amusing – a ridiculous freak in a travelling circus. She wants a man. A real man, not some confused schoolboy like you. She told me herself.'

'You're a liar,' I said, louder than I expected. My throat felt hot and inflamed. 'You make things up as you go along, just like the rest of your type.'

'My *type*?' he said, moving down to sit next to me. 'My type is *your* type, I'm afraid to say. And that type is not *her* type. You poor stupid fool. Can't you see that these people loathe us? They'll always keep to their own colour, even if it means lowering themselves for some peasant like Johnny. Do you think they want to get involved with an Englishman like you, only to produce half-caste babies who'll be shunned by their friends? You haven't a chance. Kunichika's the one she wants. Even you must see that.'

I didn't answer. I could feel the heat of his cigarette.

'And not just her. Her parents do too. That's why they sent her on this bloody holiday.'

'No, she's here because she never had a honeymoon with Johnny,' I said.

'She's here as bait for the Professor, who may or may not rise to accept this tasty morsel. He's only interested in Johnny, that filthy commie guerrilla. The whole trip's been arranged so that Kunichika can become best chums with his soon-to-be chief informer.' He leaned in very close to me, inclining his head towards mine. He had rolled up the sleeves of his shirt, and over the brilliant pain of my headache I could almost feel the clamminess of his skin. 'And the girl, well, she's just a plump little carrot dangled oh-so temptingly.'

'I'm not listening to your revolting lies.'

He laughed amid a plume of purple smoke. 'Listen. I'm only telling you this because you're one of us, and it's my job to look after our kind, even if they're as foolish as you. And you really are very stupid, I must say – you still haven't worked things out for yourself. That's what love – or lust – does to you, I suppose. Her father's a clever man, isn't he? He knows the Japs are coming. I do too. And when they come, he wants to be in their good books, he wants all the favours he can get. What can he give them to make sure he gets this? Mining concessions, certainly. Information on his dirty Bolshie son-in-law, gladly. And of course, there's his daughter too, oh yes. No, it's not nasty, it's a question of survival. Everyone's just doing their bit.'

'And what about you – what's your bit?'

'Keeping the peace. Making sure everyone's able to do their bit. Saving what I can for our lot.'

'Aren't you afraid things might backfire?'

He laughed. 'No fear of that. That's why I've been sent along, to make sure business happens as usual. As long as I'm here nothing will rock the boat.'

'So you're here as a chaperone, I take it.'

'I suppose so,' he said, moving closer to me. I felt the hot smoke of his cigarette on my neck. 'But I told you – I'm also looking after our kind,' he said.

'You're lying about all of this,' I said.

'Am I?' he said, flicking the stub of his cigarette into a tangle of bushes. 'Put the woman out of your mind. You'll walk away from her and in a few months' time you'll forget she ever existed.' He reached across and put his hand on my thigh, his fleshy fingers gripping hard. I pushed him away, feeling a sudden rush of strength in my arms. He fell against a stone step, looking at me quizzically.

'I shan't forget her.'

He smiled, his body supine, relaxed. 'Come, come, dear,' he sneered, his teeth showing in the hazy darkness. 'You're being silly. She loathes you; you're a freak. Johnny hates you too. Everyone does except me. Come here.'

And then I was upon him, hitting and scratching and kicking. His neck was soft as mud as I forced my hands around it, pushing and pushing and pushing until he struggled no more. A sneer remained etched on his face as I dragged him out into the sea, letting the waves take his body. It was nearly morning and I felt very strong.

*

I never swore not to see Johnny again. There was never any need for such dramatic oath-making. I simply knew our paths would never cross.

After the war I drifted slowly from Singapore to Kuala Lumpur and then embarked on aimless wanderings around the country, never staying in one place for very long. I walked in the thickly forested hills that ran down the spine of the peninsula, but the jungle induced panic within me and I had to leave. I went to Port Dickson and watched young families at play on the beach; the swell of the waves made me anxious and I moved on again, heading inland away from the coast. All over the country I saw things that unsettled me – a young woman scribbling in a notebook in Kuantan, a smiling square-shouldered youth cycling under an indigo sky on a sultry afternoon in Terengganu. I did not know if I was escaping or searching: it felt as if I was doing both, and neither. Then one day I came face to face with it, that which I was escaping or searching for, that remained nameless to me. I took the train to Kuala Lumpur with the vague intention of travelling back to Singapore. In truth I hardly cared where I went. I was content to go wherever my failed instincts led me, and on this day they led me to that platform at the station in KL. I stepped off the train and paused to buy a bottle of warm orangeade. I lifted the bottle to my lips and there, sitting calmly on a bench before me, was Johnny. He sat with his back to me, the familiar broad shoulders hunched forward as if holding something to his chest. Through the dust-heavy air sunlight fell in broken streams on his back; the shapes on his batik shirt curled wavelike on a deep blue background. I hid behind a pillar and watched him from a distance. Every few moments he would lower his head to his chest, as if falling asleep. It was only when I moved round to another hiding place that I saw he was cradling a sleeping child, keeping it close to his chest. He bent his neck and kissed the top of the child's head, and then he shifted his right arm, freeing his hand to stroke the infant's glossy hair, soothing its sleep. The child was no more than two or three years old, a boy of clear, pinkish complexion. He clung to Johnny's shirt, his tiny fists gripping the colourful cloth as he slept. His legs kicked out now and then in spasms of sleep; every time he did so Johnny would kiss his head and blow gently on his face, chasing the heat away. I watched the child wake, sleepy-eyed and uncertain, surveying the platform – the hawkers touting their wares, the chickens in cages, the rickshaw-pullers and porters. He stood on the bench next to Johnny, never taking his hands off his shoulders. I saw his eyes – bright and deep and soft. He looked around, his delicate brow curving into a frown I knew so well. I moved away from the pillar, hoping that he would look in my direction, but he did not. As I retreated into the shadows once more he returned to the safety of Johnny's embrace, resting his head in the hollow of Johnny's neck. And there the two remained, clinging to each other in the hot dusty afternoon until their train arrived to bear them away from me. I caught a glimpse – only a glimpse – of Johnny's eyes as the train drew out of the station. He sat at the window, passing so close to where I was standing that I feared he had seen me. But his eyes were dark and hollow, and he saw nothing.

Long after the train had gone I found myself sitting on the platform, alone amid the chaos. I reached into my satchel and took out a photograph, something I carried with me everywhere I went. Without hesitating I tore it in two, separating myself from Snow and Johnny. Before my nerve failed me, I walked to the post office and put husband and wife in an envelope. And then I sent them away and waited for my memories of them to fade, completely and for ever. As they dropped out of my life and into the postbox I saw the words I had scribbled: *The Harmony Silk Factory, Kampar.* I couldn't remember the rest of the address, but it hardly seemed to matter.

*

'Isn't it funny,' I said, 'how your wonderful Marquis-Professor has stopped speaking altogether.'

'He's troubled by Honey's death,' she replied.

'He's even stopped speaking to you, it seems. How odd that a man who's been through as much as he has, who's been part of that vicious butchery in Manchuria, should be so upset by an accidental drowning.' We were sitting in the meagre glow of the after-supper embers, she with her notebook balanced tentatively on her knees.

'I told you never to mention what I've said about Mamoru. You aren't even supposed to know.'

'Only you and I have speaking roles now,' I continued. 'Kunichika and Johnny hover silently on the edge of the spotlight; Honey lies inert in the dressing room.'

'I'm not sorry,' she said, 'about Honey. I never liked him.'

'Nor I.' In the hesitant light she looked tired and worn and I wanted to sink my head to her bosom. I said, 'You do know he isn't in love with you.' No answer. 'Johnny, I mean.'

She said, 'How do you know he doesn't love me?'

'I didn't say he didn't love you. I said he wasn't *in* love with you.'

'That is not the same thing. You're right.'

I did not answer.

'And what about you, Peter?' she said. 'Are you capable of love?'

'Of course I am.'

'Are you? Name someone you have loved.'

I paused for a moment. A sudden rush of blood inflamed my face and my throat felt dry, unresponsive. I was glad it was dark: surely she could not have seen my strangled expression. 'Not merely one person,' I managed to say after a whilst. 'I am in love with all of this. The Orient and all its peoples.'

She laughed a rich deep laugh. 'That is definitely not love.'

'Yes it is.'

'How so?' she demanded.

'Because,' I said, 'the desire and pursuit of the whole is called Love.'

'I never know who you are quoting when you speak, Peter,' she said.

'It's not important.'

I got up and brushed the sand off my legs. 'Tread carefully with Kunichika,' I said.

'I've told you before, Peter, there's nothing to fear,' she replied, her voice falling. She did not wish to discuss the matter, that much was clear.

'You can't be sure of that,' I said.

There was no answer. I walked away, treading the line where the trees met the sand; the forest hushed and the sea burned into the shore. My hands throbbed; I looked at them and remembered my fingers tightening around Honey's fleshy neck. I had no choice. I knew what I had to do.

I have something to tell you, I said to Kunichika, a secret, something you would kill to know. Meet me at the ruin, I said, and I will reveal something that will change your life. It will change all our lives and lead us to our true destinies. He laughed and said, anything to make you happy. Please, this is not a joke, I said, I'm deadly serious. I am Johnny's best friend, if you see what I mean; I know things about him. I understand, he said, I'll be there. Of course I was there before him, hiding in the undergrowth, lying in wait. Johnny's white baldachin cloth lay fallen, hanging from a broken branch. Its pale beauty captured the moonlight as it shivered gently in the night; but I did not reach for it because I was safe in the shadows and did not wish to venture into the light. And yet soon I would have to. I felt for the knife in my pocket – it seemed strangely superfluous, as useless to me at that moment as a Fabergé egg or a box of chocolates. I did not know why I had bothered to take it with me: my hands were all that I would need; they alone would carve my destiny. Who said that the jungle is silent and mysterious? It isn't. It spoke to me in all its voices, screaming its tale in the sentient darkness. I did not understand the language of this violent polyphony; I was its mere dumb audience, waiting for the story to suggest itself to me. And then it began: the first player strolling on to the stage, skirting the ramparts of the gorgeous painted set (a ruin! the audience gasps, stifling involuntary applause). He is contemplative, hands in pockets, wistful in the way all lovers are, and we the hitherto uncomprehending audience sense at once that this will soon end in tragedy. But wait: what's this? Another player – but it is not the dashing lover's bitter enemy, the evil murderous villain of the piece whom we are expecting. It is a woman; her appearance is unscripted. The slenderness of her figure and the strength of her purposeful stride lend her the appearance of a youth: a castrato, perhaps, or an Elizabethan heroine? Ah, the audience understands: it is the lover's lover, she whose star crosses his, utterly and irreversibly (the orchestra strikes a shivering convulsing tune, the chorus shrieks discordantly). But what is going to happen? The lovers talk, clasp hands, smooth each other's gorgeous coltish hair. Our hero is reluctant, troubled, distant. He cannot respond to the pleadings of his *bella donna*. He draws away in anguish, for he knows they will never live happily ever after. Montagues and Capulets they are; the divide will never be bridged. She is distraught: Why, why, why? she wonders. What have I done, what has come between us? O cruel and vengeful gods, why have you taken my love away from me? (The chorus is silent and only the strings remain in the orchestra, *dolcissimo*, as our hearts sink. Tears in the audience, for she does not know what we silent voyeurs do: that he hides something from her.) She brings her lips to his once more, but is repulsed by our tortured hero. And then he is upon her, forcing his hard lips on her face and neck, pinning her body to the beautiful cold stone as he manœuvres himself on to her. Shock. What is happening? He tears at her clothes, exposing her limpid skin to the strained light from above. She is silent, bewildered as we are. He pushes her legs apart, her sinuous androgyne's thighs flashing in the dark. And the audience is stunned, for now we understand that this is the awful denouement: the hero is not the hero, but the villain. O Melpomene, Muse of tragedy, how cruel art thou! Our anti-hero now fumbles with his trousers. He cannot undo them, for he is breathless and shaking with impatience. The audience screams silently, but our heroine does not call out. Resist, resist, we implore – but we are powerless. But wait: if the hero is revealed as the villain, then he whom we have thus far known as the villain must be the true hero! O joy, O rapture – but where is he? Will he be too late to save the day? There is no sign of him, he is still hidden in the forest. This tale is destined to end in despair. A scream. Our heroine realises that she has been deceived. *Scellerato!* Monster! She struggles against the weight of this evil duplicitous scoundrel. He pins her to the ground with the weight of his beautiful hard body, but still he cannot free himself from the constraints of his clothing. She kicks and screams and scratches, but is powerless against her assailant. But then another man arrives, bellowing in rage: at last, he is here, our newly uncloaked hero. He has emerged from the trees to save the day. The noise he makes distracts the villain for the briefest of moments, but it is enough for our heroine. She breaks free from the grip of her tormentor and runs, runs from the scene of this betrayal. (*Exit* the true villain, slipping away into the shadows: the audience does not care for him any longer.) Our distraught heroine is in tears, and our new hero pursues her, seeking to give her succour. Come to your true love, we exhort! At last he catches her, pulling her close to him. We thought he was weak before but now we know he is not. With the heroine in his arms he seems stronger than ever; we understand, at last, that he needs her truly to become himself. It is only when he is with her that we can see him for the good and loving man that he is, and that all his life he has needed someone to love and now he has found her. No longer do we recognise the pathetic figure of a man, alone and drifting, stripped of all dignity. This heroine is the one who transforms the lives of the men she touches. Funny, isn't it, the way one man can be so utterly different, as if containing two separate lives within him. Music: *smorzando*, fading away until only the hero's voice can be heard, singing calmly, *molto, molto tranquillo*, to his beloved. The painted backdrop is different now; the ruin has faded into the distance and we find ourselves in a clearing in the forest, a strange garden of restrained beauty, adorned by a single frangipani tree. Only the two true lovers remain. They sink to the ground in desperate embrace. He kisses her brow. Only now do they both realise that they have found someone who cares for them. It is the only moment of truth they will ever experience in their whole lives. The spotlight expires and the lovers dissolve into the deep dark night.

I watched her bathe in the cold dawn stream. Mist drifted down from the hills and clung to the trees around us. The cobalt waters seemed scarcely to ripple as she waded slowly into its depths. I sat naked on the grassy bank, my wet skin prickling in the dewy air. I could not look at her face, her silent eyes. She rose from the stream, picking her way slowly through the muddy shallows. Beads of water clung to her skin, adorning her body with a thousand tiny jewels. Even then I knew, of course, that we would never be together again. We would return to the forlorn remains of our camp, where Johnny would be waiting with wordless inscrutability, and Kunichika would be calm and charming once more; we would not speak about this night again; we would scarcely even touch, other than the accidental brushing of hands as we passed food or water to each other in some prosaic domestic routine. Only we would know what had passed between us. I wanted to believe that this secret acorn would flourish in its hiding place and one day grow into a stately invisible oak; but even as we walked back through the lightening dawn I knew it would not happen. Our secret was always destined to fester, growing more unhappy with each passing day, for such is the bitterness of Wormwood: it poisons everything.

I fell heavily into a dreamless sleep, and when I awoke there was no one around. The tarpaulins had been dismantled and packed bags lay piled on top of each other like the bodies of small dead animals. I walked calmly over to Snow's things and searched for her journal. I found it – a simple cloth-bound notebook filled with neat handwriting on unlined paper. I took it and placed it in my satchel.

The tide was at its lowest when we carried our things through the trees across the wide flat beach. The sea had retreated a long way into the distance, leaving the boat marooned on an expanse of grey sand. We splashed through the shallow streaks of warm brine as we ferried the remnants of our camp to the boat, and then we sat on the deck waiting for the tide to come in and bear us away. The sky was deepening with rain clouds and the air was very still.

I fell ill almost as soon as I arrived back in Kampar. I collapsed on my bed and locked the door, leaving strict instructions not to be disturbed. My room smelled of mothballs and catpiss; I sank heavily into a fever, my bedclothes damp and peeling from my bare skin like old bandages every time I moved. And then came the shivers, the awful gripping shivers that made me whimper silently into the wet sheets. I could not escape this punishment, so I closed my eyes and surrendered to it. I let my insides be burned by the fever and cut by the cold until I began to find relief in this cycle. Fever sweats shivers fever sweats shivers. Several times Johnny came to the door, imploring me to emerge. His frenzied voice cajoled and begged and raged, but I remained in my fetid den. I was safer there; torture had become my companion and I did not wish for anything more. When, several days (weeks? Who knows) later, my condition 'improved', and the tremors no longer racked my body, I sat on my bed and found myself alone in a bare, airless room. The thin hiss of the wireless was the only noise I heard. The *Prince of Wales*, it announced, had been sunk. Together with its mighty companion the *Repulse*, the HMS Unsinkable had been destroyed by Japanese kamikaze planes in the South China Sea off the coast of Kuantan. Pearl Harbor, I learned, had already been attacked. Hong Kong and the islands of the Philippines had fallen; Siam would soon follow. Landings had been made in the north of the country, in Kota Baru, and soon they would be upon us in the valley. I rose unsteadily to my feet and made for the door.

The journey to the Soong house was an arduous one. The glare of the sunlight was too much for my etiolated constitution and instantly my head began to swim. My legs felt shaky, and I stumbled repeatedly on the smallest pebbles. I marched on, my shirtsleeves hanging dismally from my torso; in the warm valley afternoon I became aware that my body had become reed-thin and worn. My shoes chafed at my toes and I felt blisters begin to form. I walked through the plantation and into the yard of the Soong house. A group of men, neatly dressed in clean, smart clothes, stood leaning against a car smoking cigarettes. All shared Kunichika's sharp hawkish features, his muscular stance. I passed without addressing them and proceeded up the stairs, heading straight for the front door. When I reached the verandah at the top of the steps Kunichika emerged from the house, his brow knotted tightly in a frown. He paused when he saw me, his face relaxing into a smile. He looked at me with languidly narrowed eyes, and then, wordlessly, descended the stairs and joined his cigarette-smoking coterie.

The house was dark and cool as I stepped inside. I passed through the ante-room into the large sitting room. TK Soong sat at the piano, his fingers moving lithely over the keyboard. He played a Chopin nocturne, gently and easily, without any hesitation or restraint.

'I thought you didn't play the piano,' I said.

He did not turn round. 'A little. We all have our secrets.'

I stood motionless listening to him play. He remained looking into the shiny black face of the upright.

'Your daughter,' I said. 'May I see her?'

'Snow,' he said, over the sad playful notes, 'is not here.'

I stayed for a whilst, listening to him finish the nocturne and proceed seamlessly into the next one. And then I left the house. I walked down the steps and crossed the dusty yard into the plantation. The rubber trees on either side of the path stood unmoving in the windless afternoon. I passed into their shade and looked up; not a single leaf quivered. Where there was a gap in the trees sunlight fell in deep bright pools, bathing me luminous white. I walked like this, through shadows and light, until I reached the main road back to the rest house.

'There you are!' a voice called as a car juddered to a halt next to me. It was Gerald and Una Madoc, the couple I had met at the party. 'We heard you were back, but no one knew where you were,' he said, out of breath as if recently returned from a long walk.

'I've been – I haven't been well, you see.'

'Well, you could have told one of us, what with all this going on.'

'I'm sorry,' I said, 'I didn't know there was such a fuss about things.'

'Such a fuss?' he said. 'Good God, man, haven't you heard what's happening?'

'Yes,' I said, 'yes, I have.'

'Come on,' Una cried, her face flushed and agitated by the heat, 'just get in the car. We have to be quick.'

'Good boy,' Madoc said as I climbed in. 'We're rounding up the stragglers and taking everyone down to Kuala Lumpur. The plan's to get to Singapore. There'll be boats back to Blighty. We'll stop to get your things. Don't take everything – just the essentials. Be quick.'

I knew exactly what to take, and soon we were speeding away from the rest house. In town the shops were closed, their painted concertina doors drawn firmly shut. A few people walked briskly in the street, and a lorry was being loaded with sacks of rice, but otherwise the main street was quiet. On the outskirts we found ourselves caught behind a herd of cattle. They milled indolently in the road, ignoring the harsh barks of the cowherd. We fell into a slow crawl behind them, Madoc furiously gesticulating at the skinny half-naked boy who flailed pathetically at the cows with his rattan whip.

'I couldn't believe it,' Una said quietly, 'I just couldn't believe it. The *Prince of Wales*, my God. Could you?'

'No,' I said, clutching my satchel to my belly.

The road began to widen, curving towards the river, and the cattle broke into a lazy trot.

'A lot of us were hit hard when we heard the news,' Madoc said. 'We couldn't believe the Japs could do that to us. One of the chaps was at the naval base in Singapore when the *Prince of Wales* docked, and he said it *was* unsinkable.'

A small row of whitewashed houses appeared before us, sheltered by a colossal banyan tree; I remembered that I had been here before, with Johnny. I remembered that we sat on the river bank and talked about how he would make this his new home. He talked about where he would position his bed – facing the window, looking out on to the wide sweep of the river, so that Snow would be able to rise to this view every morning. His eyes shone when I suggested filling the courtyard with earthenware pots decorated with dragons, with lilies and goldfish. He laughed when I asked him about children. 'When I have a son,' he said, 'he will inherit this place. He will inherit the home that I built. No, that *you* built.' And then he threw back his head and chirruped with laughter.

Johnny was standing in front of this house as the car crept

past. The sight of him did not surprise me, for in truth I was expecting him. Boxes were piled high at the entrance, and all the doors and windows lay open. Johnny stood shirtless in conversation with a few labourers. He shielded his eyes from the sun as he spoke.

'Bloody animals,' Madoc cursed through his moustache, the car slowing to a halt.

Johnny was pointing to a spot on the façade, making wide circling sweeps with his arms, and the workers were nodding acquiescently. He turned round and looked at the car, and for one dreadful second caught my eye. His open-mouthed face fell silent, the light in his widened eyes dying even as it flickered to life. I allowed my eyes to glaze over, fixing my gaze at some point in the distance, as if I had not seen him. And then I bowed my head and turned away.

'At last,' said Una. The cattle began to scatter across the widening road, and the car picked up speed.

I wanted to look back but didn't. Cows cantered clumsily alongside the car until the herd parted and the open road lay before us. It began to drizzle, a light flurry of brilliant watery jewels glinting in the sunlit sky. I lifted my face to the open window, feeling the gathering breeze on my skin as the car sped through the glittering afternoon.

'When the ships sailed into Singapore there were so many people there to greet them,' Una was saying. 'It was just like Portsmouth, wasn't it, Gerald, Portsmouth in Navy Week. And now it's all gone.'

*

My taxi is late and I am impatient. '*Hujan*,' rain, the porter-cleaner-cook said, shrugging, when I went to complain a few minutes ago. It explains everything, the rain. Power cuts? *Hujan*. No post? *Hujan*. What, no vegetables at dinner? *Hujan*. Why are you looking so sad today? *Hujan*. It drips steadily from the eaves outside my window, forming trembling pools on the flagstones below. Out over the silent sea the rain falls in fluttering pulses, like great lengths of translucent cloth caught by the wind. The shapes float across the broad and empty sky, chasing after each other until finally they fade, sinking into the sea.

I sit at my desk and survey my room. Nothing is out of place. The bed is neatly made and not a single *objet* appears on the surface of the tables. Inside the cupboards and drawers only a few items of clothing and two pairs of shoes remain. I am certain that these will soon find new owners among the impoverished, eagle-eyed staff here (who, mercifully, appear untroubled by sartorial trends). When *I* am removed no one will be able to tell that anyone lived here. All that will remain is a large room of spartan furnishing. The new occupant will move in and fill the place with his own dismal ephemera, and all traces of me will soon be erased.

I am taking nothing with me to Kampar. Only a small box, carefully wrapped in a piece of moonlight-blue cloth. Before I secured the parcel with string I paused and looked at its contents one more time. My drawings for the garden, folded and laid flat at the bottom of the box. On top of that a notebook whose crinkled, yellowed pages I have read a thousand times before, the words repeating nightly in my head. I opened it one last time and looked at the even, rounded handwriting. And then I returned it to the box, along with the final item – a torn fragment of a photograph. In it I am standing alone. My right hand is missing from the picture; the jagged tear runs through my forearm, leaving me marooned and disabled in the jungle. I fill in the image of Snow, composing her from nothingness as I have done countless times before, and the picture becomes whole again. I can see her sitting next to me. My hand rests on her shoulder; she does not shrink from me, but moves her neck to receive my tentative touch. It is my birthday. Though we do not yet realise it, we are already somewhat in love. I am frowning but impossibly youthful; she is placid and half smiling, her cheeks blushed, hot. In the distance a ravaged building rises from the trees. My gorgeous ruin, fading, as I am, on the sepia-tinted paper.

I hesitated for a moment after I wrapped the box in its silken cloak. I wanted to fling it from my window, out on to the soggy lawn, and myself with it. But I breathed deeply, and the murmur of doubt soon passed. And I am resolute: I shall take these things with me to Kampar and present them at the funeral to the son whom the newspapers say survives his father; they say his name is Jasper. I have no other gift for him, only this little box. So many lives have I changed, destroyed. It makes little difference now, Wormwood.

Forty years have passed since I last saw Jasper. My body has begun to dissolve into the dank air of forty long monsoons and the desiccating heat of forty dry seasons, and yet, strangely, I know I will recognise him. How little he will have changed since the last time, when I stumbled across a group of children at play by a river bank. He will be older now, his hair will be streaked with grey and his face scarred by the passage of time, but he will be as blithe and carefree as the day he spoke to me, the day when my meanderings led me innocently to the object of all my loathing, my love.

Correction: I was never innocent. Even that day, when I had resolved to spend some time in meditative, monastic isolation in the cleansing air of Fraser's Hill, the purity of my intentions was quickly sullied by the primeval bitterness that resides deep within me; and soon I found I was driving towards the low heart of the valley, where the flatlands are cleft in two by the great river. I was drawn by the languid flow of the muddy water; the river would run along the road for a time, appearing between gaps in the trees before curving out of view again. I followed it unthinkingly, until finally I came to the outskirts of a small town where the view of the river broadened and bade the weary traveller stay for a moment or two. I knew this place. Did I know that my journey would lead me here? I think, perhaps, I did. I left the car and walked to the river bank. I could hear the carefree calls of children at play, the splashing of water over the stillness of the afternoon. I sat in the shade of an immense banyan tree, watching the children swing from its thick hanging vines, arcing ever higher into the air, again and again, as if hoping to break free from the constraints of gravity and propel themselves for ever into the heavens. They fell silent, unsettled by my presence, and huddled together in the shallows. I shifted uncomfortably, preparing to move away, when one of them swam from his shoal and walked up the slippery bank towards me. He was a boy of ten, perhaps, his slender nakedness unwearied and unencumbered yet by the awfulness of life. The boldness of his loose-limbed stride made me shrink away; I could not bear to look him in the face. I knew – immediately and absolutely – who he was. I heard the wet slap of mud under his feet as he ran the last few steps towards me, slowing to a halt. I felt the weight of his stare but still I continued to look into the distance, pretending not to notice him. Out of the corner of my eye I could see him examining every line, every tiny imperfection on my face, and I felt my skin grow hot. How easy it would be to turn my head now, I thought, and smile. How easy. But I did not. I looked away instead, at the unmoving clumps of elephant grass on the other side of the river, the white spears of their cotton-tipped flowers rising proud above the dull green carpet. At last he walked to the base of the tree and began to climb its lower branches; and then he paused and turned towards me one last time. 'You look just like my father,' he said, his voice playful, teasing. 'So sad.' And with a laugh he was away again, shimmying and scrambling until he was halfway out on a broad bough. He reached for a vine and, in one fluid motion, launched himself into the air. He went so high I thought the vine might break, but it did not. At the zenith of his untrammelled flight he tilted his head, lifting his chin to face the sun. For a moment – a moment that is embalmed in my mind's eye – he remained utterly motionless, fixed against the cloudless sky, his arms flung deliriously behind him, face thrust forward to confront the world. Jasper. Clear as crystal, the foundation of a new Jerusalem. Only I was marooned outside the city walls. And then he fell headlong into the river beneath, sinking into its depths. I gathered myself and ran to my car, breathing hard in the damp afternoon. For a second I thought that tears had begun to form in my eyes but I blinked once, twice, and realised that it was just the dust; and soon I was on the road once more, heading away from the valley. I think I was humming, though I cannot remember the tune.

So. Here I sit. Old Mat Saleh, waiting to be taken away, singing in his broken voice. *Dove sono i bei momenti?* The mosquito net shivers in the wind. Outside, the rain. *Hujan, hujan.* Nothing more to do. *Consummatum est.*

P.S.

Ideas, interviews & features . . .

About the author

About the book

Read on

Unravelling the Story

Louise Tucker talks to Tash Aw

You were born in Taiwan but brought up in Malaysia then England: where is home and why?
I've always thought of Malaysia as 'home' because that's where my family still live. Having been born in Taiwan does make me feel as if I have different insights into Malaysian life, but I've never considered myself anything but Malaysian. But I've now spent nearly half my life in England, so London (where I now live) is, if anywhere, 'home'. My flat, my friends – nearly everything I have is here.

What did you want to be when you grew up? Have you always wanted to be a writer?
Yes, I've always wanted to be a writer – but only in the way I wanted to be a swimming instructor or a fireman. No one ever encourages you to aspire to such jobs.

How did you start writing?
By writing short stories.

What inspired you to write this book?
The fact that there isn't much interesting or challenging fiction set in Malaysia. Apart from a few notable exceptions (Burgess, for example), you have to go back to Conrad to find innovative writing set in South-East Asia.

The novel crosses many landscapes: how and where did you do your research and how long did it take?
I researched the Second World War in the British Library. I was working at different jobs during this time, so my research took nearly

two years. Everything else in the novel came from the vast store of trivia I have in my head – I'm always hoovering up bits of useless information!

You write from the perspective of three narrators, all different ages, backgrounds and nationalities: what made you decide to do this and how did you approach it?
I began experimenting with this structure as a way of keeping myself interested in the writing process – I wanted to challenge myself to create a complex storyline that would take as much time to unravel as it would to create. I've always been drawn to novels with complicated structures, richly textured stories that don't reveal everything at first glance. It took a long time to get the narrative arrangement right – I had to figure out what the end of the novel would be before I could even begin to write the first line.

> 'I was inspired to write this book by the fact that there isn't much interesting or challenging fiction set in Malaysia.'

Which of the three narrators was the most difficult to create?
Jasper, because he wasn't involved in the events that shape the book. His voice had to be determined by how much he knew or didn't know. And that in turn could only be decided once I knew how the whole story would be played out. ►

Unravelling the Story *(continued)*

◄ Jasper, Snow and Peter all fail to see beyond their own viewpoint, thus never really knowing Johnny or the others. Was this a comment on the nature of relationships, the nature of countries at war, or neither?
Both, but particularly the nature of relationships. I wanted to show how all three of them project their own insecurities and aspirations on Johnny without ever really making an effort to become close to him. That's why we never know him – he's just a construct of various neuroses.

‘I've always been drawn to novels with complicated structures, richly textured stories that don't reveal everything at first glance.’

What did it feel like to finish and sell your first novel?
An incredible relief.

What motivates you to write?
The fear of having too much time on my hands.

Who are your influences as a writer?
Flaubert, Faulkner, Nabokov.

Are there any books that you wish you had written?
Of course – far too many to list here.

What do you do when you're not writing?
Swimming, shopping, music, cinema, ironing, paying the bills – much the same as everyone else.

What's your next book?
A novel set in Indonesia and Malaysia in the 1960s. ■

Top Ten Books

1. **The Sound and the Fury**
   William Faulkner

2. **Moby Dick**
   Herman Melville

3. **Earthly Powers**
   Anthony Burgess

4. **Haunts of the Black Masseur: The Swimmer as Hero**
   Charles Sprawson

5. **East of Eden**
   John Steinbeck

6. **Anna Karenina**
   Leo Tolstoy

7. **Lord Jim**
   Joseph Conrad

8. **In Patagonia**
   Bruce Chatwin

9. **Trois Contes**
   Gustave Flaubert

10. **Lolita**
    Vladimir Nabokov

LIFE AT A GLANCE

Author photograph © Andrew Whittuck

Tash Aw was born in Taiwan to Malaysian parents. He moved to England in 1990 and now lives in London.

A Writing Life

When do you write?
I have one long session in the morning and a shorter one in the afternoon.

Where do you write?
On a round table in a small book-lined room.

Why do you write?
Because I enjoy it, and because I need to pay the rent.

Pen or computer?
First draft in pen, thereafter on the computer.

Silence or music?
Both.

What started you writing?
Having no friends.

How do you start a book?
By spending months researching.

And finish?
With a full stop, normally.

Do you have any writing rituals or superstitions?
No.

Which living writer do you most admire?
Can't say.

What or who inspires you?
Food.

What's your guilty reading pleasure or favourite trashy read?
Those expensive Hip Hotels books – incredibly superficial but incredibly seductive. I don't read them, I just look at the pictures. ■

Shortbread in Malaysia

By Tash Aw

One of the questions I'm most often asked nowadays is 'How much of the novel is autobiographical?' and whether I see myself in any of the characters, particularly Jasper. I'm always quick to say 'No'. For a start, I've never been good at using autobiographical material in fiction – I find it too personal, too difficult to handle, too restrictive: I don't enjoy having to be faithful to real-life events. I also love the process of creating something fictitious, the excitement of building something from very little. For me, *The Harmony Silk Factory* has always been a construct of pure imagination – not at all about me or my family.

But in the last few days I've realized something strange. The hardback has just been launched and I have been preparing to do some readings of the novel. Going through the book, I have been drawn again and again to the same passages – utterly unsuitable for readings but oddly comforting nonetheless. In one of these scenes, Peter, now a very old man, recalls his miserable childhood in a cold Gloucestershire house. All his life he has fled the loneliness of England and, for the most part, he thinks he has succeeded. Yet at the very end of his life he finds that these early images are startlingly vivid; they are all he has. It dawned on me that, whilst I haven't sought to flee my past the way Peter has, memories of my childhood are still incredibly clear. Things I thought I had left behind are still with me, imprinted in my mind's eye with crystal clarity. Although I have lived in England for fifteen years, my most powerful recollections are of silly incidents and relatively nondescript things from the Malaysian countryside. Unwittingly, I had channelled some of these sentiments into Peter, who, like me (I now see), lives in a kind of strange voluntary exile. Each of the characters in the novel is in some way adrift, dislocated from their surroundings, so in that way I suppose there *is* a part of me in each of them. I function, as they do, perfectly happily on a day-to-day basis – I even have a few more friends than they seem to – and yet, occasionally, images from my youth in Malaysia insist themselves upon my consciousness with such force that I feel part of *that* world and not of this, my London life.

Another example. I have a tiny garden, little more than four square feet of soil, into which I have crammed all manner of exotic sub-tropical plants. All winter I battle, ridiculously, to keep them alive, brushing snow off their leaves and wrapping them in swathes of fleece. Why don't I just plant a holly and be happy? Or something equally doughty and robust and boring – some kind of conifer, perhaps? Why is Peter Wormwood obsessed with temperate European plants? Clever psychology students would probably point this out as a symptom of a confusion over where to 'put down roots', of some deep disorder of always wanting to be somewhere else. I'd disagree. For me, my garden simply provides the perverse pleasure of making something survive when it shouldn't. I find it thrilling to see dark-green broad-leafed tropical foliage nodding proudly in clear ▶

'I find autobiographical material too personal, too difficult to handle, too restrictive: I don't enjoy having to be faithful to real life events. For me, *The Harmony Silk Factory* has always been a construct of pure imagination – not at all about me or my family.'

Shortbread in Malaysia *(continued)*

◀ winter sunshine. Even when the plants are being lashed by hailstorms I find it more exciting than alarming to see them clinging desperately to life. I've always loved things that are out of context: a contemporary painting in a maiden aunt's sitting room, a tin of shortbread biscuits in a Malaysian kitchen – little things that become more noticeable, less taken for granted, when moved out of their 'natural' environment. That's why I wrote *The Harmony Silk Factory* as I did, wilfully (and somewhat haphazardly) throwing together stories, characters and little digressions that have entirely different origins. I wanted, for example, to place Western art images in a South-East Asian setting, just to see what that tiny collision would produce. But most of the time there was no logic or planning to my mixing of these elements. I just put them in the soil (so to speak), and tried desperately to keep them alive over the winter. So in that rather circuitous way there is quite a lot of me in the novel – though the reader will have to look quite hard, and in all the wrong places, to find me. ■

' I've always loved things that are out of context. That's why I wrote *The Harmony Silk Factory* as I did, wilfully (and somewhat haphazardly) throwing together stories, characters and little digressions that have entirely different origins. '

If You Loved This, You Might Like . . .

In Another Light
Andrew Greig
After a serious illness, forty-something Edward Mackay decides to find out more about his father's colonial past, when he worked in a maternity hospital in 1930s Penang. Switching between modern-day Orkney and pre World War II colonial Malaysia, the narrative uncovers Dr Alexander Mackay's mysterious past and the path to Edward's recovery.

Long Day Wanes: A Malayan Trilogy
Anthony Burgess
Burgess's trilogy, which includes *Time for a Tiger*, *The Enemy in the Blanket* and *Beds in the East*, describes the chaos of post-war independence in Malaya as many cultures mix and clash.

Lord Jim
Joseph Conrad
Narrated, like *The Heart of Darkness*, by Marlow, this is the story of Jim, a sailor who, after a disastrous shipwreck in which the crew abandons ship without helping the Malay passengers, is the only one to turn himself in to the maritime authorities. Unable to sail, he moves from job to job, moving on when he is recognized and finally ending up in a Malaysian trading post. However, when a group of thieves arrives, the memory of his earlier disgrace returns and the reverence he receives from the local people is threatened. ▶

Read On *(continued)*

◀ ***The Casuarina Tree***
Somerset Maugham
Maugham's stories recreate the atmosphere of remote posts of the British Empire in 1920s colonial Malaysia, detailing the lives both of the expatriates and of the Malaysians.

The God of Small Things
Arundhati Roy
Roy's Booker Prize-winning novel tells the tale of twins Rahel and Estha, who must come to terms with the past, the loss of their cousin and their mother's transgression. Set in Kerala, the story is lyrical, the language poetic and the history tragic.

The Jewel in the Crown
Paul Scott
In the first book of the Raj Quartet, set in India in 1942, supporters of Indian self-rule are starting to gain ground and relations between the colonial British and the Indians are changing dramatically. When Daphne Manners is raped in the Bibighat Gardens, her young Indian lover is subjected to the same brutality and hatred as his country and the deterioration of Anglo-Indian relations around the incident reflect the developing split between the two powers.

The Singapore Grip
J G Farrell
The final part of Farrell's Empire trilogy, this novel charts Singapore's fall to the Japanese and the end of British rule in the colony.

The Sound and the Fury
William Faulkner
Three different narrators, all from the Compson family, describe the collapse of that family from their own very different perspectives.

Out in the Midday Sun: The British in Malaya 1880–1960
Margaret Shennan
Shennan, who was born in Malaysia, tells the story of the British colonial occupation from the arrival of the Victorians to independence.

Murder on the Verandah: Love and Betrayal in British Malaya
Eric Lawlor
Described as a Malayan *White Mischief*, this is the story of Ethel Proudlock, who was found guilty of murdering her lover one Sunday after Mass in 1911, sentenced to death, then released by the Sultan of Selangor. In this social history, Lawlor examines the trial, the Empire, and the hypocritical world of the colonial expatriates. ■

Find Out More

WATCH . . .

In the Mood for Love

2046

Wong Kar-Kei's films depict an Asia that is resolutely beautiful and emotionally stultifying. *In the Mood for Love*, set in 1960s Hong Kong, is the story of a couple who move in next door to each other and, left alone by their respective spouses' business trips, become friends. When they discover that their spouses are having an affair, they resolve not to follow in their footsteps but are then tormented by this decision. In *2046* some of the same characters recur, including Tony Leung (who starred opposite Maggie Cheung in *In the Mood for Love*) who writes about the future but longs for the past, some of which is reprised from *Mood*.

Indochine

Catherine Deneuve stars as Eliane, the owner of a rubber plantation in 1930s colonial Vietnam. When her adopted daughter Camille falls in love with Jean Baptiste, the lover that Eliane has spurned, Eliane determines to get him posted far away from the girl.

SURF . . .

www.geographia.com/Malaysia

A brilliantly detailed and presented site: plenty of the usual tourist stuff but a lot more interesting information about history, people, and places to visit. This is actually the Official Homepage of the Malaysia Tourism Promotion Board, New York, but it is better than www.tourism.gov.my, another official MTPB site. ■